T0277090

one small favor

one small favor
judith arnold

THE
ST●RY
PLANT

The Story Plant
Studio Digital CT, LLC
PO Box 4331
Stamford, CT 06907

Story Plant hardcover ISBN-13: 978-1-61188-341-1
Fiction Studio Books E-book ISBN-13: 978-1-945839-68-9

Visit our website at www.TheStoryPlant.com

For information, address The Story Plant.

First Story Plant printing: October 2022
Printed in the United States of America

Like Sarah in *One Small Favor*, my sister was brilliant, beautiful, and ladylike, and she died much too young. Unlike Sarah, my sister was my champion, my confidante, and my most enthusiastic cheerleader. She taught me how to read, how to write, and how to live. We bickered, as sisters do, but if either of us was under attack the other was her staunchest ally. Our parents dubbed us "Sisters United," and that was always how we thought of ourselves.

Carolyn, this book is for you.

chapter one

"**D**ON'T FEEL SORRY FOR ME," Sarah said. "You could get hit by a car and killed tomorrow."

Annie clutched her phone so tightly her fingers began to grow numb. Wasn't that how you were supposed to feel when you got bad news? Numb?

Except that only her fingers felt numb. Her legs, tucked beneath her desk, felt fine. Her heart continued to beat at its usual steady pace. Her brain sharpened, as if her gray matter had been compressed into a dense mass somewhere in the vicinity of her ear, where Sarah's voice was emerging from Annie's phone and penetrating her mind.

"I don't feel sorry for you," Annie said, although she wasn't quite sure that was the truth. "Tell me everything the doctor said."

"Everything?" Sarah sighed. "She used a lot of big words. Technical terminology. But she said that judging from the lymph node involvement, I'm stage three and that isn't good. The chemo will make me lose my hair—including my eyebrows. Remember those cheap Mr. Potato Head rip-offs we had when we were kids, and the eyeballs looked like fried eggs? I'm figuring that's what I'll look like."

"How much lymph node involvement?" Annie asked.

"A lot." Sarah sighed again. "I'm probably in the forty-percent survival range."

"It could be worse," Annie said. "You could be in the twenty-percent survival range. There's absolutely no reason you shouldn't be among the forty percent who survive."

"Well, that's a five-year survival rate. Dr. Glassman didn't say anything about a ten-year survival rate."

Annie did a quick mental calculation. Sarah would need to survive at least ten years if she hoped to see both her children graduate from high school.

I'm not going to cry. Her eyes weren't among her numb body parts, but they remained dry. Sarah had said not to feel sorry for her. Annie focused on the odds that she herself would get hit by a car tomorrow. Lower than forty percent, probably.

And really, this was her sister. When had she ever cried over Sarah's pain and suffering?

A moot question. Sarah never suffered. She never experienced pain. She was Miss Perfect, living the ideal life. Everything about her was flawless, until now.

"So what happens next?" Annie asked, pleased that she sounded normal.

"I start treatment as soon as possible. First surgery, then chemo. I have to have a hysterectomy. I'm going to go through menopause. Ugh. I'll be all wrinkly."

And lacking eyebrows, Annie thought, although she didn't say it. Her gorgeous sister was going to look ravaged, not ravishing. Sarah's thick, wavy hair was going to fall out, her eyes were going to look like fried eggs, and she was going to get wrinkles. The notion boggled Annie's mind. At one time, when they were teenagers, Sarah had had boys chasing after her like hungry dogs after a T-bone steak, while the only attention Annie had received from boys was their utter astonishment when they found out that she—an awkward, disheveled twerp—had actually emerged from the same gene pool as spectacular Sarah Baskin.

But Annie had outgrown her jealousy long ago. Sort of, maybe. All right, even if she hadn't outgrown it, she would never wish baldness and wrinkles on her sister. "One of my life goals is to live long enough to have wrinkles," she said. "Getting wrinkles is a good thing."

"Not when you're thirty-nine." Sarah paused, then said, in a bright voice, "So that's my news. What's up with you?"

"Seriously, Sarah—I'm kind of in shock."

"A little numb?"

"Actually, yes." Annie exerted herself to relax her hand around her phone, in the hope that sensation would return to her fingers. "Anything you want me to do—anything at all—just ask."

"Could you do one small favor for me?"

"Absolutely. Anything."

"Could you tell our parents?"

Hell, no. That was one thing Annie did *not* want to do. Her father would collapse. He would implode. He would bypass numb and dissolve in a puddle of tears and depression. He would fade into a ghost of himself, bemoaning fate, wailing at God.

Her mother...well, she would be herself. Which was not a good thing.

Still, Sarah had just received catastrophic news. She had learned that those stomachaches and back pains and irregular periods she had been experiencing since last spring were not in her head. They were in her ovaries and her uterus, and they were real, and she had only a forty-percent chance of surviving five more years. If anyone deserved not to have to deal with their mother, Sarah did.

"Okay," Annie said. Then, more enthusiastically, "Sure."

After saying goodbye to her sister, she gazed around her tiny office. It looked the way it always did—cozy and pleasantly messy. The shelving on the wall opposite her desk was lined with books, but they were in no particular order. Some lay on their sides, binders, hardcovers, catalogs, and paperbacks cluttering every surface. A feeble geranium shedding its pink petals sat in a ceramic pot on the narrow windowsill to her right. Directly in front of her, her computer hummed, reminding her of the applications awaiting assessment. Many of them had already been vetted by one of the other counselors on the staff of Cabot College's admissions office; all applications were reviewed at least twice in the preliminary round. Annie was supposed to score each application with an "accept," a "reject," or a "defer." Two "rejects" from two different admissions counselors, and an application went into the digital trash bin. Any application that got at least one "accept" or "defer" would remain active for discussion.

The applications awaiting Annie's attention right now were the earliest of the early decision submissions. She was always inclined to give them all "accepts" for no other reason than that they'd arrived so far ahead of the deadline. The more applications she could review in October, the fewer she would have to plow through in November. But the office had strict standards. No one was granted bonus points for sending in an application earlier than necessary.

The thought of assessing applications right now nauseated Annie. Her sister had just been given a death sentence. Almost.

Sarah had always been the more optimistic of the Baskin sisters, Annie the more realistic, probably because Sarah's life had always been easier than Annie's. Sarah was the first-born. The graceful, gorgeous Baskin girl. The one who preceded Annie into the world, embodying a standard compared to which Annie was invariably found wanting. Annie had learned to be realistic because, when you had drab brown hair and a nose that was more moguls than ski-jump, and you didn't know how to flirt, and you never quite knew what was expected of you and therefore often failed to fulfill those expectations, and you lived in the shadow of a magnificent, accomplished, radiant older sister, being realistic—about yourself in particular and life in general—made sense.

If ever there was a time to stop being realistic, however, it was now. Because being realistic meant acknowledging that Sarah was going to die.

Annie forced her gaze back to her computer monitor. She had been reading the essay submitted by an earnest young lady named Miranda Griffith when Sarah had phoned. The admissions counselors were not supposed to know the financial status of applicants—Cabot College claimed to be a needs-blind school, although Annie suspected that the barrier between the admissions and the financial aid offices was fairly porous—but Miranda Griffith was likely not to apply for a scholarship. Her home address was a ritzy Connecticut suburb, and she was currently a boarding senior at Phillips Exeter. In her essay, she described the *awesome*—her word—summer she'd spent building a Habitat for Humanity house in Guatemala. "It was so rewarding to know I was helping these people, who so desperately needed my help," she wrote. "I am so grateful to my parents for giving me this opportunity to contribute to the betterment of these people in dire need of housing, and I felt it was a privilege for me to be able to do this for them. I really appreciated contributing in this way. They were grateful to me and I was grateful to them because they allowed me to do this for them, and that's so awesome."

Bless her noble little heart. Miranda Griffith had sacrificed a summer by taking a trip to Central America, paid for by her parents, to rescue the benighted natives, and now she believed herself deserving of the ultimate reward: an early-decision acceptance to Cabot College. Her transcript placed her in the college's average range: she had a 3.4 GPA, she'd taken several Advanced Placement classes, she was a singer in one of Exeter's choirs as well as an a cappella group, and she was "a student leader in every way," according to the letter of recommendation her chemistry teacher had supplied. Annie was hard-pressed to imagine how a high school kid could be a student leader in every way in a chemistry class.

In any case, Miranda met the basic qualifications for admission to Cabot College. Her application would be judged on what Annie thought of as "atmospherics": whether either of her parents was a Cabot College alum, whether she dazzled Annie with an in-person interview, whether one of Cabot's a cappella groups was in desperate need of a soprano. Whether her essay blew Annie's mind.

"I can't do this," Annie said aloud, swiveling away from her computer. Miranda Griffith might be a charming girl, smart and creative and eager to contribute to the betterment of humankind. That her parents had financed her do-gooder junket in Guatemala to improve her chances of getting into a selective college didn't justify Annie's cynicism.

But she was mentally far away from Cabot. Far away from Guatemala too. She was floating toward an unfamiliar world, one that didn't have Sarah in it. And that scared the hell out of her.

Sarah hadn't sounded terribly upset when she'd called. True, she'd had time to digest the news about her biopsy. She'd had time to discuss the situation with her gynecologist, with her brand-new oncologist, and with her husband. Maybe with her kids, too, although they were eight and ten, too young to grasp the implications of her diagnosis and how their lives would change once Sarah started treatment.

Now she had discussed it with Annie. The only important people she hadn't discussed it with were their parents. Annie had to admit that she was almost as upset about having to break the news to Leo and Gilda Baskin as she was about the news itself.

"I can't do this," she said again, her voice echoing in her ears even though she'd uttered them in a near whisper. She wasn't sure if she was referring to the applications awaiting her attention or the task of informing her parents of Sarah's illness. She reached for her phone, then shook her head. She couldn't tell them over the phone. Sure, Sarah could tell Annie over the phone. But Annie was sane. Her parents...

They were neurotic. Both of them wore their emotions like a thin gray veil—visible, darkening their behavior the way a veil would darken their skin.

Still, Annie had promised her sister this one favor. She had made the offer. And given Sarah's catastrophically compromised health, it was quite possible that informing their parents herself might just kill her.

On the other hand, Annie might die before she had to tell them. She might get hit by a car. Anything was possible.

○ ○ ○

Cabot College's admissions office boasted a small staff—Dean Parisi, a stern but cordial woman who had graduated from Cabot thirty years ago and believed she understood the college better, even, than the school's president; Annie and three other counselors who reported directly to Dean Parisi; and Brittany, the perky secretary who kept everyone on task, compiled the acceptance and rejection mailings, and greeted the high-schoolers and their parents who arrived in a constant stream, eager for campus tours and interviews. Brittany was young and cute and had a smile as refreshing as seltzer infused with lime. Annie was in awe of Brittany, even though as an admissions counselor—and a Cabot alum, like all the admissions counselors—Annie perched on a higher rung than Brittany in the office's hierarchy.

"I need to leave early," she told Brittany now, her voice sounding scratchy and uncertain. "I'm sorry."

Brittany favored her with one of her sunshine-fresh smiles. "Anything wrong?"

"Yes, kind of." *My sister's dying and I have to tell my parents.* "Family emergency."

"Well, you just go and take care of that emergency," Brittany said, her voice so warm and reassuring, Annie almost believed herself capable of doing that. "I'll let Wanda know."

Annie still thought of her boss as Dean Parisi, but Brittany called the dean by her first name. That was the kind of person Brittany was—relaxed and confident, as if the world was a well-upholstered easy chair molded exactly to the shape of her butt. Every now and then, talking to Brittany made Annie want to apply to Cabot College. She had to remind herself she had graduated from the school fourteen years ago, and had been working in this office—currently as Brittany's superior—for the past five years.

She mumbled her thanks and managed a feeble smile. Then she exited the admissions office, which occupied a small, gabled building at one end of the quadrangle that formed the heart of the campus.

Late-afternoon sunshine glazed the quad, which was arrayed in full autumn color. Cabot's campus could have been the set of a clichéd Hollywood movie about a small New England liberal arts college. Aesthetically weathered brick buildings, some cloaked in ivy, stood shoulder to shoulder with clapboard buildings and brownstone buildings around the quad. Paved walkways cut through the grass, flanked by shade trees, the leaves of which flamed with autumn color, and lush evergreens. Students ambled along the walkways or lounged on the grass. The air was as crisp and dry as a saltine, the sky a blue so vivid it seemed to glow. Annie halted halfway across the quad, took a deep breath, and gazed around her.

Was the campus always this beautiful? Yes. Even on rainy days, when the sky was a blur of clouds. In the winter, when the maples and oaks were mere skeletons and snow buried the lawns. In the spring, when the snow receded, leaving swaths of mud that gradually produced sprouts of new grass, and the maples and oaks revived, their branches dappled with buds. In the summer, when the grass fried beneath the relentless sun and the number of students on campus doing research or working in the library or augmenting the maintenance crews was sparse. Cabot College was always beautiful.

But most of the time, Annie was oblivious to Cabot's beauty. She had been wowed by the campus when she'd first visited, as a junior in high school. She had been greeted by someone who wasn't Brittany—she had no memory of the receptionist who'd sat at Brittany's desk back then. She recalled touring the campus with her mother, who had monopolized the student guide's attention with irrelevant questions that segued into speeches about her own college days and comments about how proud she was of her older daughter, who was attending Brown University—an Ivy League school, unlike Cabot College, which wasn't to say that Cabot wasn't a perfectly good school, too, although it wasn't Ivy League.

But Annie had been working here so long—first as a clerk in the registrar's office, then as a supplementary interviewer, then moving up into admissions full-time—that she no longer saw the place. She no longer looked.

She was looking now. At the walkways, the yellow and orange leaves, the lush lawns, the charming buildings, the blue, blue sky. She didn't want to move. She didn't want to go home to her boring condo. She definitely didn't want to go to her parents' house. She just wanted to stand here forever, surrounded by all this beauty. She wanted time to stop.

Better yet, she wanted time to go backwards. She wanted to retreat to the minute before her cell phone rang and the screen read "Sarah Adler." Back to a time when she was who she'd always thought she was. An admissions counselor. A woman who had no fashion sense but could throw together a decent meal with whatever ingredients she had handy. A daughter semi-adept at avoiding her parents. A younger sister who knew she would never measure up to her older sister, and who resented her older sister for it.

She couldn't resent Sarah now. How could you resent someone who had a sixty-percent chance of dying within five years?

But she could stare at the colorful foliage, and the sky above it, and the world around her. She could take a moment to realize how magnificent that world was.

chapter two

EMMETT WAS SEATED ON THE FRONT STEPS OF ANNIE'S BUILDING, a ninety-year-old three-decker with a cracked front walk, a few valiant rhododendrons flanking the front porch steps, and faded gray shingled siding in desperate need of fresh paint. Annie—or, technically, a mortgage company—owned the second floor of the building, each floor containing a single unit. The ground floor unit had access to the minuscule backyard. The top floor unit had access to the roof. The second-floor unit—Annie's unit—had access to nothing but the stairwell leading up and down, and it had the added disadvantage of noise. Annie's upstairs neighbor wore heavy-soled shoes, and she could hear his footsteps so distinctly as he clomped around his condo, she knew when he was eating, when he was sleeping, when he was peeing. Meanwhile, in an effort to be a good neighbor, and not particularly wanting the first-floor residents to know when she was peeing, Annie made a habit of tiptoeing around her home most of the time.

Her consolation was that her unit cost significantly less than the other two units. Cabot College might charge its students an obscene amount of money to earn a degree, but little of those gargantuan tuition payments found their way into the bank accounts of the admissions office staff.

Annie earned enough to avoid destitution. In fact, she earned enough to have qualified for a mortgage to buy her condo. Because she was single and childless, she didn't have to spend a lot on food, clothing, and toys for her offspring—let alone set aside money to save for the staggering tuition payments she would have to fork over if they wound up attending private colleges like Cabot. But because she was single and childless, she, unlike Sarah, provided her mother with nothing to brag about. "Sarah is married to a lawyer," her mother liked to tell people. "A partner in a major law firm downtown. You should see their house. It's a mansion! And their children are spectacular. Good-looking and smart, like their parents. Like their grandparents, I should add. My other daughter, well, she's not married—but she does work at a college."

Annie might not be married, but she had Emmett. As she emerged from the narrow driveway that led to the tiny off-street parking area behind the building, she spotted him sitting on the building's front steps, watching for her. She didn't think they had planned to see each other this evening, but after learning her sister's news, she couldn't trust her memory. Her brain was as tangled as the computer cables under her desk at work.

Even if they had made a plan, why would Emmett be here now? Annie had left work early because she had a family emergency to deal with. Why had Emmett left work before quitting time?

He gave her one of his adorable lopsided smiles as she approached the front steps. "Hey," he greeted her. "You're home early."

"You're done with work early too," she said, eyeing him up and down, trying to figure out what was going on. Had he gotten fired? Simply walked off the job because it bored him? That was the kind of thing Emmett might do.

"You busy this evening?" he asked. "I got kicked out for the night. Frank has a lady over and he asked me to make myself scarce."

When Emmett and Annie spent the night together, they invariably did so at her condo, not his apartment. He shared a cramped one-bedroom place with his buddy Frank. Even though they were in their mid-thirties like Annie, they still lived like teenagers. Their refrigerator was stocked with cans of beer and open boxes of Cap'n Crunch, but not much else. And when Annie asked Emmett why he and Frank stored their Cap'n Crunch in the refrigerator, he'd replied, "We like it cold," as if that explained anything. Their living room was furnished with mismatched pieces from Goodwill, their walls decorated with superhero movie posters. Their bookshelf held every video game ever created, but no books. And their bedroom contained twin beds. Which was fine when it was just the two of them but not when one of them wanted to entertain a woman for the night.

Emmett was an acceptable boyfriend, even if he had stopped maturing when he'd hit late adolescence. He was chronically broke and utterly lacking in ambition, as might be indicated by his having quit work early to come to her condo. He was also the hottest guy Annie had ever been involved with. He was absurdly handsome, with wavy dark hair, mesmerizing blue eyes, a tantalizingly scruffy beard, and a lean, hard body. He was a carpenter—the sexiest profession a man could hold. He knew his tools.

But today had turned into a very bad day. "Actually, I am busy this evening," she said. "I have to go see my parents."

"Oh." Emmett looked sheepish, his mouth curved in another heart-melting smile. "Can I hang out here while you visit them?"

"You could come with me," she said, certain he would reject that idea. Her parents didn't think much of him, and he knew they didn't.

Yet she was tempted to bring him with her. As tall and strong as he was, he could catch her father in mid-collapse. He could give her parents someone to focus on so they wouldn't fixate on Sarah's bad news. He could give Annie a good excuse to leave if things got ugly.

But it would probably be best if he didn't accompany her to her parents' house. She didn't want him to have to witness Baskin family bullshit, any more than she wanted her downstairs neighbors to hear her when she was peeing. "You can stay here," she told him, unlocking the front door and leading him into the building. "I'm in a terrible mood, though."

In fact, her mood was too weird to qualify as terrible. She felt a little dreamy, a little delirious and disoriented. As if she'd slipped through a portal into a new reality, one where the world was too beautiful for pain, where the air was sharp with the scent of apples and pine and no one ever got struck by cars.

Ten minutes with her mother would likely turn her mood toxic, however.

"So, what's up?" Emmett asked as they climbed the stairs together.

"My sister just found out she's got ovarian cancer," Annie said.

Emmett mulled that over as they reached the second floor. "Does she have a bad case of it?"

"It's not like the measles," Annie said, reaching her unit's door ahead of him and unlocking it. "You don't get a case of it."

He followed her inside. Like at Emmett's place, her furniture was old, but hers came from Sarah, not Goodwill. Sarah and Gordon had redecorated their house a few years ago, relying on the expensive services of an interior designer whose projects frequently got written up in the *Boston Globe*, and they'd offered Annie some of their discards. The peach-hued upholstery of the sofa, the ornately curved legs of the occasional tables, and the florid pattern of the area rug that covered most of the living room floor reflected Sarah's taste, not Annie's.

But then, Sarah *had* taste. Annie didn't.

She had tried to develop taste over the years. But it was just one more area where she fell short. As children, once they'd grown old enough to choose their own outfits, Sarah had always worn ensembles that matched, and Annie rarely had. She didn't understand complementary colors or coordinated patterns. She didn't notice stains or sagging hemlines; she didn't realize that fashions that flattered Sarah's curvy figure looked frumpy on Annie's fireplug physique. When they were teenagers, Sarah often criticized Annie for wearing scuffed shoes or the wrong T-shirts. Being able to tell the difference between wrong T-shirts and right T-shirts was a skill Annie lacked. All she had known was that unlike Sarah, who had always looked well put together, Annie had always looked like someone who had recently climbed out of a dumpster.

She wouldn't call Sarah's house a mansion, although it was larger than any ordinary family of four required: ten rooms, each one precisely arranged, every detail creating an ambience or making a statement or leaving an impression. In the kitchen, matching copper-bottom pans hung from the ceiling, so shiny they could serve as mirrors, and a bowl of real fresh fruit created a mouth-watering centerpiece on the granite-topped center island, across from the six-burner gas range. In the living room, elegant floor-length drapes were tied back with swags the same burgundy fabric as the sofa. In the family room, built-in teak storage units held Trevor's and Becky's toys and games. Sarah's children were trained to put their things away so they wouldn't lay scattered across the beige Berber carpeting, which somehow never got dirty.

Sarah had a magic touch. Everything she did was magnificent, from dressing herself to decorating her home to raising her children. The only not-magnificent thing she'd ever done in her life was to get cancer.

Which was why Annie felt disoriented. It just didn't seem as if Sarah could have done something so careless, so wrong-headed. Sarah didn't make mistakes. She didn't botch things. How could she possibly be sick?

If it was true, if Sarah really did have this awful disease, if she truly had stage-three, forty-percent-survival-rate ovarian cancer, she would find a way to endure it tastefully. If her hair fell out, as her doctor had predicted, she would probably turn out to have a gracefully shaped skull and a gorgeous scalp. She would look like a Nubian goddess, only pale.

And she would be among the forty percent who survived. Because she was Sarah.

"So, this cancer—is your sister going to be all right?"

"I don't know." Annie dropped her purse on the counter of her compact kitchen—which did not have a six-burner gas range, granite counters, shiny copper pans, or a picturesque bowl of fresh fruit. It did have a pile of mail from yesterday on the table, a threadbare dish towel draped over the oven handle, an empty yogurt cup in the sink, and a smattering of charred rice kernels in the vicinity of the microwave. She spun around to face Emmett, who loomed over her, at least half a foot taller, smiling hesitantly as he studied her. "I'm a terrible person," she said. "My sister is very sick, she might die, and I'm thinking negative thoughts about her."

"What negative thoughts?"

"That she's always so fucking perfect."

He laughed. "Oh, yeah. That sounds really negative." Stepping closer, he gave her a sweet hug that would have comforted her if she were at all receptive to being comforted. "So...what? You're going to your parents' house to plan her treatment?"

"My parents don't know. I'm going there to tell them."

"They don't know she has cancer?"

"She just found out yesterday. She told me today and she asked me to tell our parents. She doesn't want to deal with them."

"You don't want to deal with them either," he observed. For someone with a late-adolescence mentality, he could occasionally surprise her with his perceptiveness.

"I don't have cancer," she explained. "I told Sarah I'd do this for her."

"You're a good sister."

No, I'm not. Annie broke free from him and glanced at the digital clock in her microwave. Four thirty. As an accountant, her father worked insanely long hours from January to June, but autumn was his off-season and he would probably get home from work by five. If she left her condo now, she could arrive at her parents' house around the same time as he did. She could talk to them before they'd started their evening ritual, which generally entailed a cocktail, a bowl of salted peanuts, and a half-hour of local news on the television so they could find out what the following day's weather would be—and if the forecast was ominous, so they could drown their sorrows with their cocktails.

They might wish to drown their sorrows over Sarah with their cocktails too. If Annie timed her visit right, she'd catch them while her mother was stirring their martinis in the martini pitcher she'd bought at Home Goods and considered quite classy, even if it wasn't actually crystal.

"I should probably head over to their place now," she said. "I want to get this over with."

"Should I order a pizza or something?"

"If you want." Emmett would probably devour most of it while she was out. He would thoughtfully leave one last cold, limp, rubbery slice for her. But she had no appetite at the moment, and she doubted she'd have one after spending time discussing Sarah's ghastly diagnosis with her parents.

She rummaged in her everything drawer—the kitchen drawer that held any item that didn't seem to belong anywhere else. The everything drawer contained pens, scissors, some sticky-note pads, a magnifying glass, a deck of cards, masking tape, the rubber bands the cashier at her local grocery store snapped around egg cartons to make sure they didn't open and spill their contents in transit, a ruler, an empty business card holder her father had given her in case she ever stumbled into the sort of career that required business cards, and her spare key—fastened to a key ring attached to a plastic charm in the shape of a palm tree, a souvenir Sarah had brought her from her Hawaiian honeymoon with Gordon. Annie hadn't expected her sister to give her a souvenir, but Sarah had explained that, because Annie had been her maid of honor, she deserved a little something from the honeymoon.

The key ring was a very little something, but as trivial as it was, Annie hadn't deserved it. She had been a lousy maid of honor. The raspberry-pink bridesmaid gown had looked wretched on her, the color emphasizing her olive complexion in an unfortunate way despite the ministrations of the cosmetologist Sarah had hired to polish the faces of her bridal party before the big event. And Annie had spilled some red wine on the dress at the reception. The garish pink satin should have camouflaged the stain, but it hadn't. She'd hosted Sarah's bridal shower in a restaurant that offered only one vegan entrée on its catered-events menu—some sort of eggplant thing that Sarah's vegan friends whined about. She'd also organized a spa day for the bridesmaids, but the spa she had chosen wasn't as high-end as what Sarah and her friends were used to, and they'd muttered about the limited nail enamel colors they'd had to choose from for their manicures.

They had all known one another, whether from college or from high school. Annie hadn't known any of them, although the two who'd been Sarah's friends in high school had squealed, "Oh, we remember you, Annie! You were Sarah's funny little sister!"

Annie was still Sarah's funny little sister, and for doing her best as Sarah's maid of honor—which had failed to measure up to Sarah's standards—she had been rewarded with a funny little palm-tree-shaped key ring, which Sarah had undoubtedly purchased in the airport's gift shop at the last minute. It was cheap. It was tacky. But right now, it seemed immeasurably precious. Sarah had given it to her, and Sarah had cancer.

Annie handed the key to Emmett. The last time he had ordered pizza at her condo while she'd been out running an errand, he had locked himself out when he'd gone downstairs to pick up his order from the delivery person. She had found him sitting on the porch steps, munching his third slice, when she'd gotten home. "I'm dying of thirst," he had said. "I left my beer inside."

"Don't lock yourself out," she reminded him this time before gathering her purse and heading for the door.

chapter three

ANNIE'S PARENTS STILL LIVED IN THE HOUSE WHERE SHE AND SARAH HAD GROWN UP, a vinyl-sided raised ranch on a winding suburban block with the cloying name of Red Robin Drive. Classic, boring suburbia, Annie had always thought of it while she'd been living there. After residing in her condo for a couple of years, and before that a dreary basement apartment which would have offered a fine view of the commuter rail tracks if the windows hadn't been so close to the ceiling, she realized that her childhood home hadn't been that bad, after all, even if her mother had installed orange carpeting in Annie's bedroom and foil wallpaper in the bathroom Annie had shared with Sarah. Seeing herself in the mirror above the sink had been bad enough. She hadn't needed to view her blah visage and stumpy figure reflected back at her from the shiny walls.

She should have been grateful to have her own bedroom growing up. She had heard countless hard-luck stories about her father's childhood, when he'd had to share a bedroom with his two brothers. But she had resented being relegated to the smallest bedroom in the house simply because of the arbitrariness of birth order. Her parents had naturally taken the master bedroom for themselves, and they'd assigned the larger of the two remaining bedrooms to Sarah because she was older. Sometimes Annie wondered whether Sarah got the better bedroom, which occupied a corner of the house and boasted two exposures, because their parents knew Annie was disorganized, and in a smaller room there would be fewer places to lose important items—her homework assignments, her earrings, her wallet.

But no, Sarah got the bigger bedroom for no other reason than that she was older. Sarah was assigned fewer chores because she was older. "She has more homework," their mother had explained when Sarah was in sixth grade and Annie was in third. "You have more time to do chores." When Annie reached sixth grade and had the same amount of homework Sarah had had when she'd been in that grade, however, Sarah was in ninth grade and had more homework again, so Annie continued to get stuck with more chores.

Sarah got a bigger allowance, because she was older. Gilda spent more money on toiletries for Sarah because she was older. Sarah got the filigreed pocket watch their great-grandfather had smuggled out of Romania because it always went to the first-born child in each generation. Not that Annie particularly wanted a pocket watch—what would she have done with it? Not worn it. Not used it.

But still.

It didn't matter anymore. Sarah had a bigger house now, not because she was older but just because. Annie wouldn't begrudge her that enormous house. She had cancer.

When Annie rang the bell, Gilda answered the door. She wore a pretty sweater and tailored slacks, and her frosted ash-blond hair was arranged in a sassy bob. She looked surprised to see Annie, but she often looked surprised, thanks to the eye lift she had undergone last year.

"Annie! Hi, sweetheart. What are you doing here?"

"Can I come in?" Annie stepped across the threshold, not waiting for an invitation. "I need to talk to you and Dad. Is he home from work yet?"

Was her mother's sigh of resignation a reaction to Annie or to her father? "He's in the garage, putting windshield washer fluid in his car. He said the warning light went on while he was driving home." She led Annie up the short flight of stairs from the entry landing into the kitchen, where her martini pitcher sat on the counter, filled with a clear liquid. "What's going on?"

"I'll wait until Dad comes in," Annie said. "I don't want to have to say everything twice."

Her mother belatedly gave her a half-hearted hug. "You look grim. Have you lost your job?"

"No."

"You aren't planning to stay for dinner, are you? I only defrosted two chicken breasts."

"No. Emmett is waiting for me back at my place. I'll be having dinner with him." *If I have an appetite and he leaves me a slice of pizza.*

"Emmett." Her mother's eyes narrowed on her. "You aren't pregnant, are you?" Before Annie could answer, her mother added, "At your age, maybe it's for the best. If you don't have a baby soon, it'll be too late."

"I'm not—"

"Emmett isn't exactly a world-beater," her mother continued, turning to give her martinis a stir with the tapered glass swizzle stick inside the pitcher. "But he's good-looking. If he's the father, you might make a gorgeous baby."

Annie didn't bother to point out the insult implied by her mother's comment—that she needed Emmett's genes to produce a baby who didn't look like a gargoyle. "I'm not pregnant," she said, then felt her spine slump with relief as she heard her father's footsteps on the stairs. Her mother was easier to take when her father was present to dilute the atmospheric tension.

Her relief didn't last long. Once her father entered the kitchen, she would have to tell her parents Sarah's bad news. As soon as she'd accomplished her mission, though, she could leave. Something to live for.

Shit. Would Sarah ever again think, *something to live for*? Or did you have to come up with a new cliché when you had only a forty-percent chance to live?

"Annie!" Sweeping into the room, her father seemed delighted to see her. "What a nice surprise! Are you staying for dinner?"

"She can't," her mother answered for her. "I only defrosted two chicken breasts."

"We have a microwave," he said. "We can defrost another one."

"No," Annie said, accepting a hug from her father. "I'm not staying for dinner."

"She has something important to tell us," her mother said.

Her father leaned back, his hands planted on Annie's shoulders as he appraised her. He had on his work clothes—a suit, a dress shirt, his necktie loosened—and his thin graying hair swirled in lint-like tufts across his scalp. "Something important? What, are you pregnant?"

"No."

"I like that boy, Emmett," her father continued, releasing her so he could pull two cocktail glasses down from a cabinet. "You want a drink?" he asked, then closed the cabinet door when she shook her head. "A nice Jewish boy. He'd make a good father."

"He's not Jewish, Dad."

"I thought his last name was Levy."

"Dunleavy," Annie said. "He's Irish." She'd had the same conversation with her father several times. For some reason, Emmett's ethnicity never registered on him.

"Oh well, Irish. He doesn't drink too much, does he?"

"Shut up, Leo," her mother said. "She has something important to tell us." Her gaze narrowed on Annie. "Are you getting married?"

"Mom—"

"Because he's Irish, not Jewish. And he isn't exactly a world-beater. He's in construction, right? He's always wearing those clunky work boots."

"Shit-kickers, we used to call those shoes," Annie's father added helpfully.

"Maybe you should sit down." Annie gestured toward the table by the window. Four chairs were set around it—the same table she and Sarah had eaten at, from their high-chair days until they'd reached adulthood and moved out.

Her mother filled the two cocktail glasses and carried them to the table. She and Annie's father obediently sat. Her father looked curious and hopeful, her mother impatient. Annie was stealing time her parents allotted to drinking cocktails, nibbling on peanuts, and watching the weather forecast on the local news, after all.

She took her place across the table from them—the same chair that had been hers as a child. The salt and pepper shakers—the same ones, shaped like two porcelain chickens, a hen for the salt and a rooster for the pepper—stood to her left, and the window on her right let in the early evening light, the sky a delicate lavender so lovely Annie wanted to cry. How many more sunsets would Sarah get to enjoy? How many more sunrises?

She forced her gaze from the window and blurted out the words: "Sarah has cancer. She asked me to tell you."

"What do you mean, she has cancer?" Her father's smile hadn't quite faded. It hung on like an afterthought. "She's a healthy girl. She can't have cancer."

"She does."

"Why didn't she tell us herself?" her mother demanded to know.

Annie opted for tact rather than honesty. "She's tired. It's been a rough day. She asked me to tell you."

"She told you but she didn't tell us?" Her mother appeared deeply offended. "She couldn't tell her own parents?"

"She's resting." Annie had no idea if Sarah was, in fact resting, or if she was tired. She was pretty sure Sarah had had a rough day, however. She hoped Sarah was seated outdoors on her spacious slate patio right now—or in the hot tub built into one corner of the patio, steamy water swirling in soothing bubbles around her ailing body. The sunset was lovely. Sarah should be enjoying it.

"I can't believe this," her father said. "What kind of cancer?"

"Ovarian. It's a bad kind," Annie said.

"But it can be cured, right?" he asked.

"She's got good doctors," Annie said, hoping that was true. "They'll do everything they can for her."

Her father began to deflate like a balloon with a slow leak. He lost height. His face lost color. His eyes grew dull. "But it's a bad kind?" he pressed her.

"I don't believe this," Annie's mother wailed. "She got this disease, and she didn't tell us herself. How could she not tell us?" She glared at Annie, as if it was her fault that Sarah didn't want to deal with her parents.

"*I'm* telling you," Annie said. "She asked me to tell you. Okay?"

"I'm her mother."

Annie was tired too. She was having a rough day. She wanted to rest. If she had access to a hot tub, she would want to be in it.

Instead, she retorted, "Why does everything have to be about you? Sarah is sick. She's upset. And all you care about was that she asked me to tell you. Right now, she needs our support. Not some bullshit about who she told first."

"This is not bullshit," Annie's mother shot back. "I'm her mother. I have a gravely ill child. Oh, my God—ovarian cancer."

"She's got good doctors," her father said, evidently trying to convince himself that Sarah would be fine. "They're doing everything. Annie said."

"*Sarah* should have said," her mother muttered. "I shouldn't be hearing this from Annie." She pushed away from the table and crossed to the built-in desk attached to the counter, where her computer tablet was plugged in and recharging. "I assume there are support groups."

"If Sarah needs one, I'm sure her doctors will steer her in their direction."

"I wasn't talking about her. I was talking about me. Support groups for mothers of cancer patients."

Suppressing a groan, Annie met her father's gaze. His eyes were moist. "She's going to be okay, right?" he asked plaintively, his voice crumbling like a soggy cookie.

"I hope so." She wasn't going to lie. She also wasn't going to volunteer that Sarah's cancer was stage three. Eventually, Sarah would talk to their parents. Annie would let her fill them in on her prognosis, on how she was going to lose her eyebrows and look like a cheap version of Mr. Potato Head. She would let them know whether she would still be able to view a sunset five years from now.

"I was right," her mother broke in, tapping her tablet screen with a stylus. "There are support groups for mothers of cancer patients."

Annie pushed away from the table and stood. "I should be going. Emmett is waiting for me back at my place."

"Emmett," her father mumbled, shaking his head and sniffling. "Irish. Who knew?"

"I'm sure Sarah will call you soon," Annie added, not wanting to leave when her mother was fuming and her father was broken, but not wanting to stay.

"Tell her I'm her mother. Tell her she should have told us herself. And no, I'm not making this about *me*." Her mother glowered at her. "I gave birth to her. I raised her. She should have told us herself, that's all."

Of course. Annie's mother gave birth to Sarah and therefore should have been the very first person to receive Sarah's ghastly news. Annie would let Sarah know. They would have a good laugh about it.

○ ○ ○

As expected, Emmett had left her one slice of pizza. It sat forlornly in an oily white delivery box on the kitchen table, cold and limp, its cheese congealing. Annie could reheat it in the microwave, or she could throw it away. She threw it away.

She swung open the refrigerator door and spotted an open bottle of Chardonnay in the door shelf. Tonight she would drink dinner.

Carrying a glass of wine into the living room, she found Emmett lounging on Sarah's hand-me-down sofa, his legs propped up on Sarah's hand-me-down coffee table and a bottle of beer in his hand. Across the room, the TV was turned on to a Bruins game. He smiled up at her as she settled into the plush peach-hued upholstery next to him. "How'd it go?" he asked.

"It went as expected," she told him. "My mother did her narcissist thing. My dad fell apart. He thinks you're Jewish, by the way."

Emmett laughed. "I'm circumcised. Does that count?"

"I didn't mention that to my dad."

He arched his arm around her shoulders, urging her against him. "I left you some pizza."

"I'm not hungry." She took a sip of wine. She wasn't really thirsty, either, but the wine was medicinal.

On the television screen, hockey players skated back and forth, their movements so fast and slick Annie could scarcely register them. If there was a puck somewhere on the ice, she couldn't see it.

After one small mouthful of wine, she wasn't drunk. She was fatigued, though. Distracted. Wondering what it would feel like to know that within five years, you would no longer be able to drink wine because you were dead. How did a person cope with that understanding?

Stop being morbid, she scolded herself. Sarah would be in the lucky forty percent. She would be fine; she always was fine. Their mother would develop all sorts of insights from her support group, and finally come to realize that the universe didn't revolve around her. Their father would remain sweet and sympathetic, but he wouldn't fall apart so often because he wouldn't have reason to, because Sarah would beat her disease and her hair would grow back thicker than before. Annie would get a raise, and Emmett would finally decide to go into business for himself, which would force him to grow up and develop a sense of responsibility, and she would accept that he was the man she wanted to spend the rest of her life with. Ten years from now, she and Emmett—and maybe their offspring, who would be beautiful because of Emmett's genes—would attend a festive graduation party for Becky, hosted by Sarah. Trevor would come home from college for the event, and the wine would be of a much higher quality.

No. None of the above. Optimism was Sarah's forte. Realism was Annie's.

On the television, several hockey players began to brawl. What was their problem? Why couldn't they be happy just to have their health, to be paid exorbitant amounts of money to play a game? Why did they have to punch each other?

Annoyed by the mindless violence in the hockey game, Annie pulled away from Emmett and stood. "I'm going to call my sister."

"Why?"

"Because she's my sister."

He peered up at her, appearing genuinely baffled. "You always told me you hated your sister."

"I never said I hated her."

"You said you didn't like her."

"That's totally different." Annie slugged a little wine. "I don't always like her, but I love her. I want to talk to her."

"Can we screw around afterwards?"

"My sister has cancer, and you want to screw around?"

He mulled over her question, temporarily stumped. Then he shrugged. "Well, yeah."

"You're an asshole," she said, which didn't seem to faze him. He shrugged again. She couldn't say why she felt the compulsion to explain herself to him, but she needed to explain herself to *someone*, and he was the only person present. "My entire life, my sister never needed me. She had everything going for her. I was at best someone who did her share of the chores, and at worst an embarrassment, this awkward little creep she had to babysit for while our mother was out of the house. Sarah was everything I wasn't. She was beautiful and smart and cool.

And now, for the first time in our lives, she needs me. Okay? I'm going to call her."

She pivoted and stalked back to the kitchen to get her phone. Emmett called after her, "You're smart." Which, being a realist, she took to mean that she wasn't beautiful or cool.

But she was needed. By Sarah. That alone was a miracle.

chapter four

EMMETT WAS A SOUND SLEEPER. Maybe all that manly physical labor he did, framing new buildings, installing cabinets in renovated kitchens, replacing doorsills that had disintegrated with dry rot, and moving walls—a task that sounded herculean to Annie but was something Emmett seemed to do fairly often for clients who wanted to reconfigure the rooms in their houses—tired him out so much that he could sleep through anything. Or maybe it was sex with Annie that tired him out.

He was good in bed. Better than good. The truth was, he was the first lover Annie had ever had who could make her come during intercourse. The men she'd been with before him... The nicer ones had bestirred themselves after flat-lining from their own lovely orgasms and diddled her with their fingers until she experienced something that clearly could not compare to their own ecstatic release but was better than nothing. The not-so-nice ones didn't even bother.

But Emmett knew what he was doing with his circumcised penis. Bless him for that.

Unfortunately, sex didn't interest her lately. She had actually faked her orgasms with him the last few nights so he wouldn't feel obligated to satisfy her with a postcoital diddle. Instead, they'd snuggled until he'd fallen asleep, and she'd remained awake beside him, wide-eyed in the dark, trying to figure out what was wrong with her.

It didn't require much analysis. What was wrong was that she was associating sex these days with ovaries. With illness. With lousy survival rates.

Why should she feel so attuned to Sarah? Annie was in fine health. She didn't have cancer. She wasn't facing that god-awful survival rate.

She had been spending too much time online recently researching the symptoms of ovarian cancer, and she'd recognized a few that Sarah had mentioned over the past year: the irregular periods, the backaches, the bloating, the unexplained weight loss—actually, Sarah had bragged about that, and Annie had suffered a twinge of envy. The only way she ever lost weight was when she swapped out food that tasted good for celery sticks, unadorned Brussels sprouts, and bluish skim milk.

According to her research, another symptom of ovarian cancer, which Sarah hadn't spoken about, was pain during sex. Annie didn't have pain with Emmett, but ever since she'd learned about Sarah's illness, she'd been associating sex with pain. It wasn't Emmett's fault. It wasn't even her fault. It just was.

At least one of them had had a grand time in her bed last night.

Emmett had spent the past four nights with her. His roommate, Frank, was apparently enjoying quite a torrid fling in their tiny apartment, and Emmett was in no rush to suggest that Frank and the new woman get a hotel room for a night so Emmett could sleep in his own bed. He liked Annie's bed just fine.

She wouldn't have minded, except for all that research and the welter of emotions Sarah's illness stirred inside her—fear, panic, resentment, self-loathing because she had no right to feel resentment, and more resentment because simply by handling her diagnosis far better than Annie ever would, Sarah had once again managed to make Annie loathe herself.

When her cell phone launched into its cheery jingle, announcing a call early Friday morning, the sound didn't rouse Emmett. His respiration remained slow and steady, his ridiculously thick-lashed eyes firmly shut. Annie reached for her phone on the night table beside the bed and checked the screen: Sarah Adler.

She should come up with a new ring tone for Sarah. Not the funeral dirge she'd programmed to signal phone calls from her mother, but something a little less chipper. Something that sounded like a ringing phone, perhaps. Or a siren. A whoop-whoop alarm. Incoming! Duck and cover!

She swiped the phone, whispered "Hello?" and swung out of the bed. Emmett rolled over and released a faint snore.

"Annie? Are you okay?"

Annie tiptoed out of the bedroom, closed the door, and settled on Sarah's former couch in the living room. "I'm fine," she said in a louder voice. "I just didn't want to wake Emmett."

"I thought you would be up already, having breakfast. Don't you have to go to work?"

Annie pulled her phone away from her ear so she could read the time on the screen. Seven forty-five. Sarah had probably been awake for an hour already, doing yoga or whipping cream and slicing up fresh fruits to throw together a breakfast trifle for Trevor and Becky. Annie didn't have to prepare a fancy breakfast for anyone. She could stumble into and out of a shower in five minutes, throw on some clothes, fill her travel mug with coffee, grab a bagel for the road, and be out the door in under a half hour.

As for Emmett, he woke whenever he felt like it and generally stopped at Dunkin for coffee and a couple of doughnuts on his way to a job site. He arrived at work according to his own schedule, once he was well rested and fueled with caffeine and sugar. He liked his boss well enough, but he refused to let the guy tell him what to do. He'd confessed to Annie that this pissed his boss off, but the clients—especially the female ones—all loved Emmett so much, his boss didn't dare to fire him.

"How are you feeling?" Annie asked Sarah, remembering that she was the one who was supposed to be worrying about her sister.

"How should I feel?" Sarah's voice contained a shrug. "My surgery is scheduled for Monday."

"You'll sail through it," Annie assured her. "Hysterectomies are routine." They weren't routine when cancer was involved, but reminding Sarah of that wouldn't be helpful.

"I was wondering if I could ask a small favor of you," Sarah said.

Annie hesitated before reflexively replying, "Of course." The last time she had agreed to do her sister a favor, she'd had to deal with their parents. "What's the favor?" she asked cautiously.

"I have to be at the hospital early Monday morning. Gordon's taking me, obviously. I was wondering if you could maybe be here to get Trevor and Becky off to school, and be at the house to let them in when they come home. The school bus usually drops them off at the corner around three fifteen. So you could put in a few hours at work if you need to. You could go to your office after the kids have boarded the bus and then return here before they get off the bus. Or you could work the whole day from my house. The kids won't bother you. I just don't want them coming home to an empty house. They're a little too young for that."

This favor didn't seem onerous. But it wasn't exactly easy either. "You didn't want Mom to stay with them?"

"She was going to, but then she changed her mind. She wants to be at the hospital with Gordon. That's why I'm calling you so last-minute about this."

Friday to Monday wasn't last-minute to Annie. For her, last-minute meant phoning someone and saying, "Can you get here ten minutes ago?"

"Poor Gordo," she said. "I bet he's really going to enjoy spending the day at the hospital with Mom."

Sarah laughed. "She'll be awful. But she insisted."

"Well...okay." Annie could help out with her niece and nephew. They were much easier to deal with than her mother. "How early do you need me at your house Monday morning?"

"What I was thinking was, you could come Sunday and spend the night. We'll get some takeout for dinner, or maybe throw something on the grill. I won't be eating anything. I'm only allowed clear liquids before the surgery. You and Gordon and the kids can have whatever you'd like."

"Sure." Compared to conveying Sarah's bad news to their parents, spending a night in the Adlers' spectacular house and eating something more substantial than Emmett's leftover pizza sounded like paradise to Annie. And Trevor and Becky were always well behaved. They had to be. Sarah wouldn't have it any other way.

"I'll have to let them know at work," she told Sarah. "Dean Parisi's been scheduling a lot of meetings to discuss the early-decision candidates, but I could join the meeting remotely if that's okay with her." Annie's mind sped ahead as she considered attending the meeting via Zoom or FaceTime. "You'll have to give me your Wi-Fi password."

"No problem."

"And a list of anything I need to know about the kids. After-school snacks, dinner if Gordo stays at the hospital into the evening..."

"I'll write everything out for you. And you can always phone Gordon if you have any questions. I really appreciate this, Annie."

Of course she appreciated it. She was perfect. "How are you, seriously?" Annie asked.

A pause, and then Sarah said, "I'm looking forward to getting this disease out of my body. I'm not looking forward to the wrinkles."

"You won't get wrinkles." Annie had no way of knowing that, but she said it anyway.

"And post-op pain. They're going to give me good drugs. My oncologist promised me."

"Good drugs." Annie forced enthusiasm into her tone. "Sounds like fun."

"I just want it over with." Sarah sighed. "I want this shit cut out of me. I want to wake up and hear them say they got it all and I'm going to be fine. And then give me some good drugs."

That did not sound like the sort of thing Sarah would say. In fact, it sounded more like the sort of thing Annie would say. "You're going to be fine," she said—which, in fact, sounded more like something Sarah would say. Sarah was so self-assured; she always came up with the ideal words to comfort someone, the right words to cheer someone up. To be sure, Sarah never needed cheering up. Her life was one big cheer.

Only now it wasn't. And Annie felt obligated to cheer and comfort her. "I'll work things out at the office," she said. "Don't worry about anything. I'll be at your house Sunday afternoon."

"Bring a swimsuit if you want to use the hot tub," Sarah said before ending the call.

◦ ◦ ◦

Annie raised the subject at the admissions counselors' meeting on Friday. Now that the early-decision applications had increased from a trickle to a vigorous stream, the counselors met at least three times a week to discuss them.

Dean Parisi clearly had a special fondness for meetings. When she had her staff arrayed around the conference room table—a baroque construction of thick, weathered oak that looked as if it should be laden with legs of mutton and silver goblets of mead and surrounded by rowdy knights and royal wenches—she beamed. She always sat at the head of the table, where the king would sit if a medieval feast was being enjoyed there, and gazed happily at her minions. It was one of the only times her smile appeared genuine.

Perhaps she was pleased because the admissions counselors represented a diversity expert's wet dream. There was Annie, the ethnically Jewish white girl; Jamal Brockett, a Black man a couple of years older than Annie, who dressed much more stylishly than Annie and was blessed with a sharp, sardonic wit; Evelyn Lau, a prickly, sometimes pugnacious forty-something woman whose parents were Chinese immigrants; and Harold Stickney, the token old white dude. Harold had to be well into his fifties, probably older even than Dean Parisi. That she, and not he, was the dean of admissions vexed him relentlessly. He often stroked his silver goatee and issued pronouncements in the plummy tones of an exalted professor, which, of course, he wasn't. In his mind, however, he was the voice of wisdom and experience, habitually condescending to Jamal, Evelyn, and Annie, explaining how *things* were *done*.

Dean Parisi, in addition to overseeing the admissions department, also served as the LGBTQ representative on the team. At least Annie was pretty sure she did. She actually came across as kind of sexless, which might make her a Q, but she lived with a woman who taught in Cabot College's biology department and did research on the reproductive organs of amphibians, which seemed rather lesbian-ish to Annie. Dean Parisi always referred to Professor Thurston as her "friend," and they could often be seen walking side by side to the staff parking lot at the end of the day, their shoulders bumping and their heads bowed together as they conversed. The only time Dean Parisi's smile looked genuine, other than when she was presiding over a meeting in her Tudor-vibe conference room, was when she was with Professor Thurston.

And really, for the admissions staff to be properly representative, they did need an LGBTQ person on it. They also needed someone of Hispanic heritage on their team, and Annie sometimes wondered whether, if Dean Parisi hired one, Annie would be laid off to free up an office for the new arrival. As the last person to join the admissions staff, she would be the first one fired if a layoff was necessary.

The chair at the foot of the table remained empty when Brittany wasn't present. She came and went, fulfilling her multiple roles as secretary, data resource, receptionist, and gofer, and proving to be the hardest-working member of the team. Unlike Dean Parisi, Brittany's smile matched her face. It looked as if it belonged there.

That Friday, Annie found herself seated next to Jamal and across from Evelyn, nearest the chair Brittany would occupy if she were participating in the meeting. Annie's laptop was open in front of her, a queue of early-decision applications glowing on her screen. She had already read and rated them—all the counselors had—but now they had to evaluate them together. The room was redolent with the scent of French roast coffee, the only kind Dean Parisi would serve at these meetings. Annie thought it tasted burnt, but she didn't dare complain. She wanted Dean Parisi's smile to remain in place.

"Before we begin," Annie said, nodding her thanks as Brittany filled her mug with the harsh black coffee, "I need to let you know that I won't be in on Monday. I can join in the meeting remotely, but I have to be at my sister's house."

Dean Parisi favored her with a chilly stare. Her smile turned as brittle as an egg shell. "And why is that?"

"My sister is having surgery. She needs me at her house to take care of her kids."

"I believe the school's policy calls for *parental* leave, not *aunt* leave," Harold reminded her, pronouncing the word "ahnt." He sat next to Evelyn, literally Dean Parisi's right-hand man.

"It's *family* leave," Jamal corrected him. "Annie's sister and her kids are family." Annie sent him a grateful smile.

Brittany topped off Harold's mug. "I can set up a Zoom link for Annie," she said cheerfully, earning her own grateful smile from Annie. Brittany peered diagonally across the table at her. "Does this have something to do with your family emergency, when you left early the other day?"

"I'm afraid so," Annie said, drowning out Harold's outraged cry about her having dared to leave work before five o'clock. "My sister has ovarian cancer," she explained to the others. "She's pretty sick. Her husband and our mother will be at the hospital with her. That leaves me to take care of her kids. I'm sorry."

"Don't apologize," Jamal said. "Your sister is sick."

Annie nodded her appreciation. She couldn't exactly say "Thank you" for his observation that her sister was sick. That wasn't something you thanked people for.

Dean Parisi hadn't said anything yet, but her expression softened slightly. "Well, if it can't be avoided, it can't be avoided. Brittany can make the technical arrangements." She paused, then added, "I hope we won't have obstreperous children popping in and out of the screen."

"You won't," Annie promised. "My sister's children are perfect."

chapter five

ANNIE PACKED A SWIMSUIT.
Emmett lounged atop her bed, a pillow turned vertical against the wall so he could lean back comfortably and extend his legs toward the foot of the mattress. His tall, sprawling body took up so much space that Annie had only one small corner of the bed on which to prop her duffel bag. She owned a nearly new suitcase with wheels and a telescoping handle, designed to fit into the overhead compartment on airplanes, but the last time she'd flown anywhere was three years ago, when she'd traveled to Denver for the wedding of her college roommate. Sarah took all sorts of exotic vacation trips—the Azores, Banff, a Rhone River cruise—but Annie couldn't afford such excursions. The most expensive trip she'd taken since Jenna's Denver wedding was a four-day weekend on Martha's Vineyard with Emmett in September. They'd split most of the costs—the inn, the restaurants, the official Martha's Vineyard Black Dog tee shirts—but she'd had to pay the entire ferry charge for her car herself, since—as Emmett had reasoned—it was her car.

She didn't need to pack a suitcase just to spend the night at Sarah's house. Her duffel bag would do. She had sewn it herself, in her middle school consumer science class. Every student who took the class had to sew a duffel bag; they came in kits, with pre-cut fabric, matching thread, zippers, and straps. Sarah had sewn her duffel bag when she'd taken the class three years before Annie, and her duffel bag had been beautiful, the zipper lying flat, the seams smooth. Annie's duffel bag didn't come out nearly as well, but it remained functional all these years later.

"Why are you packing a bathing suit?" Emmett asked, his gaze locked on the demure black tankini sitting on the bed beside the duffel bag. "I thought you were going to be babysitting."

"I am. They have a hot tub." She tossed the swimsuit into the duffel bag. "I probably won't use my swimsuit, but Sarah told me to bring one, just in case."

"Well, if Sarah said to bring a bathing suit, you've got to bring a bathing suit." His tone was rich with snark.

Annie shot him a hard look. "She invited me to use her hot tub. What's wrong with that?"

Even pouting, Emmett looked gorgeous. "If she's got a hot tub, why can't I come with you?"

"Because I'm babysitting." He had asked her that morning over breakfast if he could join her for the night at her sister's, and she had said no. Now he was asking again, and she was saying no again. "My nephew and niece are ten and eight. They're young and innocent. I'm not going to explain to them why you're in my bed when we aren't married."

"I don't have to sleep with you. I could stay in the guest room," he suggested.

"*I'm* staying in the guest room. How many guest rooms do you think they've got?"

"You said it's a big house." He ruminated on that and added, "Big enough to have a hot tub."

"Number one, the hot tub is outside. Number two, no, you can't come."

"Why can't I stay here, then?"

"Because I won't be here. I don't want you spending the night at my place when I'm not here."

He looked forlorn. "Where am I supposed to stay?"

"In your own damned apartment." She didn't mean to snap at him, but honestly. "Tell Frank and his new best friend that if they can't keep their hands off each other for one freaking night, they can use the living room couch so you can sleep in your own bed. Or let them have sex in the same room with you. I don't care."

"You want me to be a...what's the word? A voyeur?"

"I want you to tell your roommate that you pay half the rent and that means you get to sleep in your own bed. Tell Frank that if he wants to have sex with this lady, they should go somewhere else." *Grow a pair,* she almost said, but she knew, after having spent the past several nights with Emmett, that he already had a pair. He just needed to apply his pair to a different task than banging her.

"I don't understand why I can't stay here," he said. "Your place is much nicer than mine."

Then make some more money and get a nicer place, she wanted to shout. *Be a world-beater.*

She would never tell Emmett to be something he wasn't. After all, she wasn't the most ambitious person in the world either. She liked her job, and occasionally loved it. She liked owning a condo, even if it was the middle unit with no yard or roof access, and she could tell exactly where her upstairs neighbor was by following the thump of his footsteps—he'd just this moment walked from his bedroom to his living room. She liked not having to think too hard about whether to buy the tuna steaks rather than the cod fillets, which cost half as much at the fish market. She liked tuna better, and she could splurge a little. Maybe she couldn't afford a cruise on the Rhone, but she could enjoy a sushi-grade tuna steak now and then.

If Emmett wanted to live in a condo like hers, he could save some money. He could ask his boss for a raise—although that would necessitate his showing up at his worksites on time and putting in a full day of labor. Or he could start his own business, an idea he occasionally mentioned but never acted on. If he started his own renovation business, it would cost him money at first but would pay off down the road—if he put some effort into it. If he showed up on time. If he decided to beat the world.

But then he wouldn't be Emmett. He wouldn't be the mellow, lackadaisical guy who grew a beard because shaving every morning required too much exertion, and it turned out the beard looked wildly handsome on him. He wouldn't be the man who poured all his energy into being charming and easy to be around.

She tossed some underwear into the duffel bag, and spent several minutes attempting to fold one of her more presentable sweaters neatly so it wouldn't get wrinkled in the bag. She could wear jeans to the admissions counselors' meeting tomorrow, because she would be attending via computer link and her colleagues would see her only from the waist up on their monitors. But she needed a professional-looking top. The sweater she'd chosen apparently didn't want to be folded, however, and after several attempts she gave up, rolled it into a ball, and threw it into the duffel bag. Then she went into the bathroom to pack up her toiletries.

When she returned to the bedroom—her toiletries bag bulging with deodorant, moisturizer, hairbrush, toothbrush, a travel-size bottle of mouthwash and tube of lipstick, in case she looked washed out on the computer screen—Emmett was still sulking. "I'll miss you," he said.

They spent as many nights apart as together—especially when Frank wasn't having a week-long orgy in his and Emmett's bedroom—but coming from Emmett, that statement was pretty romantic. "Absence makes the heart grow fonder," she responded with a smile, wondering if she'd feel more fondly toward him after a night at her sister's house.

○ ○ ○

Sarah looked awful. "You look wonderful," Annie told her.

"I look like shit," Sarah responded, welcoming Annie into her house with a hug.

Annie returned her embrace, then stepped back so she could appraise her sister. Sarah did look like shit. Her hair lacked its usual gloss and bounce. Perhaps, in anticipation of going bald from her chemo treatments, she had stopped visiting the salon to get it trimmed and enhanced with highlights and lowlights. Her skin was pale, although at this time of year, when the days grew cooler and shorter, Annie's summer tan had also faded. The weight Sarah had lost, maybe ten pounds, showed on her, because she'd had a perfect figure before she'd gotten sick. On Annie, a ten-pound loss would probably be an improvement. On Sarah, it made her collarbones protrude and her jeans droop on her slender hips.

"The hell with how you look," Annie said, following Sarah across the marble-floored foyer to the stairs. "How do you feel?"

"Like shit," Sarah said. "Let's get you settled, and then I'll fix you a drink."

"Are you allowed to drink anything worthwhile?"

"Just clear fluids," Sarah said, leading Annie up the curving stairway. Sarah had once told Annie that the term for such a structure was a bridal staircase. Evidently, when Becky was ready to tie the knot, she could descend this dramatic stairway in her wedding gown. Annie had no idea who would be waiting for Becky at the bottom of the stairs, but surely they would gasp at the vision of beauty she presented, all in white, like an angel descending from heaven.

"You said clear fluids. That would include vodka, right?"

"No alcohol," Sarah said sadly. "I've been drinking lots of water. And peeing a lot."

Her kidneys were working. That had to be a good sign. "Where are the kids?" Annie asked as she and Sarah reached the top of the stairs.

"Gordon took them to the roller rink. We're trying to make these days as happy as possible for them."

Annie wasn't sure how to take that. Were Sarah and Gordon making these days happy for their children to compensate for the sad days to come? Did they believe Trevor and Becky could stockpile happiness like a bank account, so that when their mood wallets emptied out they could withdraw happiness from an emotional ATM?

Sarah led her into the guest bedroom. "Why don't you unpack," she said, gesturing toward the closet door. "There are hangers in the closet if you want to hang anything up. I'll be downstairs."

Annie nodded and watched her sister leave the room. Was Sarah moving more slowly, or was Annie viewing her through a sad-days-to-come lens?

Maybe her slower steps had nothing to do with her illness. Maybe she wasn't moving at her usual brisk pace because she wasn't taking care of the kids at that moment, or the house. Or her various other commitments: class mother, parent-teacher organization fundraiser, board of directors for her town library, aerobics dance class, the Spanish lessons she was taking in preparation for a family trip to Barcelona during Trevor and Becky's spring break from school.

Would she be well enough to go to Barcelona?

Right now, she had nowhere to go and nothing to do, other than to anticipate her surgery and drink clear fluids. If that was the sum of Annie's existence, she wouldn't be moving so fast either.

She didn't have much to unpack—just the sweater, which she hoped wasn't too wrinkled. She pulled it from the duffel bag, shook it out, and carried it to the closet, which was empty of clothes but filled with an elaborate construction of shelves, drawers, and hanger rods, with a few empty hangers awaiting her apparel. If Annie's bedroom closet had modules like this in it, would it be any neater?

Probably not. In her closet, she had long-sleeved shirts and short-sleeved shirts crammed together, interspersed with her few skirts and dresses. The floor below was a jumble of shoes, the shelf above a jumble of belts and purses. It would take a lot more than a professionally de-signed closet to organize Annie's wardrobe. She would need a personality transplant, or at least some gene-splicing. Sarah had inherited all of their generation's Baskin family neatness genes.

Annie hung up her sweater. It looked lonely all by itself in such a fancy closet, but she wasn't going to hang up her underwear and swim-suit just to keep the sweater company.

The guest room had its own private bathroom, which was twice the size of the bathroom in Annie's condo. She set her toiletries bag on the polished marble counter beside the sink. No hairs in the sink, no dried globules of toothpaste. The mirror above the oversized vanity had no spatters on its surface. All Annie saw in the glass was herself.

She might not be facing cancer and major surgery, but she looked like shit too. Her hair lacked highlights and lowlights. Her cheeks were wan. Her collarbones didn't jut out above the neckline of her shirt, but she would probably look marginally better if they did.

Sighing, she returned to the bedroom. Its gentle blue walls failed to soothe her. The puffy white duvet and the avalanche of pillows cover-ing the queen-sized bed looked more off-putting than inviting. All that fluffiness would swallow her if she lay on it.

Crossing to the window, she gazed out at the backyard with its elegant landscaping—birch trees, sycamores, and maples fiery with autumn color, holly and rhododendrons still bright green, neatly edged lawns accented by patches of dark mulch, and the expansive patio with its inlaid mosaic of brick and slate, wrought-iron furniture, gas grill, and hot tub. The view beckoned her. Or maybe it was the idea of escaping from this neat, beautiful house that tempted her to stuff her sweater and toiletries back into her duffel bag and climb out the window.

Or maybe it was just that Sarah's backyard was so beautiful. Why hadn't Annie ever noticed that before? She had always thought of it as just a backyard. A huge one, for sure, and the patio was a bit overstated. But the trees had always looked like nothing more than trees to her, the lawn like a lawn. Why did it all seem so vivid now, so alive even as autumn was in the process of shutting down all that life?

An eruption of voices downstairs signaled that Gordon and the children had arrived home. Reluctantly, Annie turned from the window, pulled her laptop from its carrying case, set it on the dresser, and plugged it in to charge it. Then she left the guest room and descended the bridal staircase. She didn't feel like an angel, let alone a bride. She felt like someone with too much worry burdening her: worry about Sarah's health, worry about whether her niece and nephew would behave well for her, worry about where Emmett was going to spend the night. That was his problem, she told herself, but he was her boyfriend. Had refusing to let him stay at her condo been bitchy? Selfish? Uncalled for? Evidence of how imperfect she was?

The curving stairs made her a little dizzy. She was relieved when she reached the foyer. Following the clamor of the children's voices, she strode down the hall to the kitchen. Trevor and Becky both seemed to have grown an inch in height since Annie last saw them, less than two months ago at Sarah's annual Labor Day barbecue on the patio. Her parents had been there, her mother orchestrating the party as if she were the hostess even though she remained enthroned on one of the lounge chairs, ordering everyone else around. "Annie, help your sister with the salads," she'd commanded. "Becky, get your grandmother one of those drinks from the pitcher—not the lemonade, the other pitcher, with the grown-up drinks in it. Leo, go see if Gordon needs help with the grill. Annie, why didn't you bring Emmett? If you're going to be dating him, you may as well include him in these get-togethers."

Emmett had spent the Labor Day weekend with Frank and a couple of other friends at a cabin in Maine, ostensibly fishing but most likely drinking vast quantities of beer, playing video games, and acting like idiots. Annie half-suspected that he'd come up with the idea of renting that cabin a hundred and fifty miles away simply so he would have a valid excuse not to attend Annie's family gathering. He had met her parents enough times to know they didn't think highly of him, and he had considered Sarah and Gordon snobbish and condescending the one time the four of them had gone out to dinner together. Sarah and Gordon could definitely be those things, and in fact Sarah had made it clear she didn't think much of any of the men Annie dated. "He's good-looking," she'd appraised Emmett when she and Annie had ducked into the restaurant's powder room for a quick confab, "but looks aren't everything."

Gordon was good-looking, too, if you liked clean-cut, clean-shaven guys with tall, well-toned bodies. Gordon was buff thanks to his membership in an expensive fitness club, as well as a plethora of exercise gear in the house's finished basement. But that wasn't the same as being buff because you spent your days moving walls.

As Sarah would say, looks weren't everything. Gordon was also a power player in Boston's legal universe. He spent his days at a major downtown law firm facilitating deals, acquisitions, and capitulations among behemoth-sized corporations, for which he was paid staggering sums of money. Enough money to buy an oversized house for his family. Enough to tell Sarah that unless she wanted a career of her own, they could live extravagantly on his income alone, so she should feel free to do all that volunteer work and take those Spanish-language classes. Unlike looks, *that*—the wealth, the power, the indulgence—was everything. Gordon's symmetrical features and sculpted muscles were simply a bonus.

Then again, Annie suspected he would look a lot better if he grew his hair in a little longer. And maybe added a beard.

"Aunt Annie!" Becky raced into Annie's arms for a hug. "We went roller-skating! Daddy made me rent the regular skates. He says I'm too young for in-line skates. Trevor got those, though."

"Yeah." Emilie's older brother—whose head now came up to Annie's shoulder, which disconcerted her—gave her a toothy smile, then turned to his mother. "Can I get a pair of Rollerblades so we don't have to rent them anymore? I could rollerblade right here in the street."

Sarah glanced at her son, then sharpened her gaze on Becky, even though her words were addressed to him. "Your feet grow a size bigger every week. It would be silly to buy you a pair of skates you'd outgrow in an instant. And no, you can't skate in the street. It's too dangerous."

"Why don't we wait until the spring?" Gordon suggested. "You can't skate outside in the winter, anyway. Hi, Annie," he remembered to add, sending her a bland smile. "Thanks for helping out."

"You're the best babysitter ever," Becky announced. She was clearly angling for an extra few cookies in her lunch bag tomorrow.

"What is that on your shirt?" Sarah asked, squinting at Becky's top, a pink long-sleeved tee with the words "Princess Power" emblazoned across the front in glittery silver script.

Becky tucked in her chin and tried to view the front of her shirt. "I don't see anything."

"Right there." Sarah pointed to a spot of brown to the right of the second silver R, no bigger than a poppy seed. "What is that?"

"It must be ice cream," Becky said. "Daddy bought us ice cream cones."

Sarah sent Gordon a disapproving look. "Ice cream?"

Gordon shrugged, looking only mildly repentant. "They deserved a treat."

"If you were going to buy something that unhealthy, you could have bought them ice cream in a dish. Cones are so messy."

"They wanted cones," he said.

Trevor smirked. Evidently, he had avoided dripping ice cream on his shirt. Either that, or any drips blended into the fabric's busy pattern.

"Go put on another shirt," Sarah ordered Becky. "I need to work on that with some spot remover before it stains."

"But this is my favorite shirt!" Becky moaned. "I want to wear it for Aunt Annie."

"If it's your favorite shirt, you don't want it permanently stained. Go change into a different shirt." With a gentle nudge, she steered Becky toward the back stairs that led to the second floor from the kitchen. Why the house needed two flights of stairs, Annie couldn't say. But no blushing bride dressed in well-fashioned white silk would make a grand entrance descending the back stairs, which were straight and covered in an industrial-strength brown carpet.

Becky made a grand exit, stomping as loudly as she could with her small, sneakered feet. Annie was tempted to argue that chocolate ice cream didn't stain, that a little water would wash it out. She ought to know, having dripped chocolate ice cream onto her own shirts on multiple occasions.

But she held her words. Sarah had always pointed out Annie's spots and stains. Now she was pointing out Becky's. Becky probably couldn't help but drip food on her clothing sometimes. It was what younger sisters did.

Sarah had embarrassed Becky, though. Annie knew from painful experience that it was humiliating to have someone publicly calling out your imperfections. Becky wanted to be a powerful princess in her hot-pink shirt. But Sarah had cut her off at the knees. Powerful princesses didn't drip chocolate ice cream on their shirts.

"I'm going to go help her pick out a top," Annie said, following Becky up the back stairs.

chapter six

BECKY'S BEDROOM WAS LARGER THAN THE GUEST ROOM. One wall was decorated with a mural of *Winnie-the-Pooh* characters as interpreted by Disney. Becky's bed, like the one in the guest room, was queen-sized, covered with a puffy down comforter and buried beneath a mountain of pillows, augmented by a few stuffed animals. The carpet was white, which seemed like a poor choice for the bedroom of someone prone to dripping ice cream, but Annie saw no stains or grime marring it.

Becky's eyes glistened with tears as she yanked open various drawers in her white French-Provincial dresser. Annie moved behind her, her footsteps muffled by the plush carpeting, and gave her a hug. "I always spill food on myself too," she said. "It's okay."

"I'm so messy," Becky whispered, her voice clogged with a sob. "I always make messes."

"You didn't make a mess. You just got a little drip on your shirt. No big deal. But your mother is kind of nervous about her surgery tomorrow, so we should humor her."

"What does that mean, humor her?"

"Indulge her. Let her wash your shirt. It will make her happy." Saying this made Annie realized its truth. It wasn't compulsion that drove Sarah to keep things neat and clean. It was pleasure.

Becky gave Annie a watery smile. "Okay." She tugged the shirt over her head, her tawny waves of hair crackling with static electricity, and handed it to Annie. Annie studied it for several long seconds before spotting the drip of ice cream. How had Sarah even noticed such a microscopic dot? Apparently her eyes, along with her kidneys, were still working fine.

"Do you really spill food on yourself?" Becky asked as she pulled a paler pink long-sleeved tee from a drawer. "You're a grown-up."

"I'm still a little sloppy." A lot sloppy, actually. "I think it's just a part of being a younger sister."

Becky donned the new shirt, which featured a silkscreen of a prowling tiger and the words "Cat Power" across the front. Becky clearly favored power shirts. "Trevor never spills anything on himself, and he's a boy."

"I'm sure he gets dirty sometimes."

Becky shook her head gravely. "No. He never does anything wrong."

Annie doubted that, but she didn't want to argue with Becky. The girl might no longer be crying, but one wrong word could set her off again. "I bet the ice cream tasted great, though, didn't it?" she asked. "And that's the whole point about ice cream cones. They're *supposed* to drip. If Trevor didn't get any drips on himself, he must have been eating his cone all wrong."

Becky peered up at her. Maybe Annie was over-interpreting, but she saw gratitude and admiration in Becky's expression. A little auntie wisdom could win her a lot of respect.

They returned to the kitchen, Annie carrying the "Princess Power" shirt, which she handed to Sarah. Sarah looked almost gleeful as she vanished into the laundry room to attend to the ice cream calamity. Trevor and Gordon stood at the center island, hunched over an array of take-out menus. "Pizza or Chinese?" Trevor asked.

"If it's my call, Chinese," Annie said. With Emmett moping around her condo for the past several days, she'd consumed more than enough pizza lately.

○ ○ ○

After a dinner of spring rolls, lo mein, chicken with cashew nuts, and for Sarah a glass of filtered apple juice, the children went upstairs to bathe and get ready for bed. Sarah headed up the stairs after them. "Do you want some help?" Annie offered.

"No. I want this time with them," Sarah said wistfully as she reached the second-floor hallway.

Annie cleared the table while Gordon vanished into his study. Rinsing the dishes and then stacking them in the dishwasher, she wondered whether Sarah believed she wasn't going to survive her surgery. That didn't make sense; hysterectomies were pretty standard procedures. But there was something dark and foreboding in Sarah's voice, in her eyes, as if she believed this might be the last time she would oversee her daughter's bath. Maybe she'd thought it was the last time she would clean her daughter's shirt too. Maybe she was becoming fatalistic.

That was wrong. Annie was the fatalistic sister. Sarah was supposed to be the optimist. Things always turned out well for her, without any effort on her part.

When the kitchen was clean enough to meet Sarah's standards, Annie went upstairs to the guest bedroom and pulled her phone from her purse. She wanted to talk to someone—someone who wasn't Emmett. If she talked to him, he would remind her that Sarah drove her crazy a lot of the time and she shouldn't be so solicitous of her, and by the way, he had to sleep on the sofa in his apartment tonight because he had been unable to dislodge Frank and his lady friend from the bedroom and it was all Annie's fault.

Instead she sent her friend Chloe a text: *Can you talk?*

Chloe texted back: *Dealing w/my senile grandpa. Tomorrow would be better.*

Annie phoned Jenna in Denver, but Jenna was trying to calm down her colicky new baby—Annie could hear the infant's shrieks and howls in the background—and couldn't talk either.

Before she resigned herself to phoning Emmett, Sarah appeared in her doorway. "Gordon is taking a soak in the hot tub," she announced. "Why don't you join him?"

"Will you be in the hot tub too?"

Sarah shook her head. "I'm beat, and we've got to get up early tomorrow. And hot tubs can elevate your blood pressure, which wouldn't be an issue except that I've got surgery tomorrow. I'm going to take a bath and go to bed."

"Okay." Annie heaved herself off the plush bed and gave Sarah a hug, which Sarah tolerated rather than returned. "Everything is going to be fine," she said.

Ignoring Annie's encouraging words, Sarah pulled a sheet of paper from her pocket, unfolded it, and handed it to Annie. "Here's some information you might need tomorrow. Gordon's cell phone number. I wasn't sure if you had it on your phone. And our Wi-Fi password. Also, this—" she pointed to items on the list "—is what goes into Trevor's lunch bag, and what goes into Becky's, and the time they have to get on the bus, and the time they'll get off it in the afternoon. Here's the name of my surgeon, although I don't know why you'd need that. And the hospital contact information. And a list of foods you can prepare for the kids' supper if things run late and Gordon can't get home in time, although I guess you could heat up the Chinese leftovers for them too. Just don't touch the turkey. That's for Thanksgiving."

"You already bought your Thanksgiving turkey? Thanksgiving's a month away." Not that Annie would have made the turkey for the children's dinner. Unlike Sarah, Annie considered cleaning, stuffing, and roasting a turkey a major ordeal, not something you'd throw together last-minute for the kids.

"I had to drive up to the turkey farm in New Hampshire where I buy our turkeys. I wanted to take care of that before my surgery. I won't be allowed to drive for a while afterward."

"You bought your turkey from a farm in New Hampshire?" That seemed so arduous. So unnecessary. So utterly Sarah.

"I bought a turkey from a farm here in Massachusetts a couple of years back and it was kind of chewy and tough. I think that turkey was older than the sales clerk said. Anyway, I've never had any problems with this turkey farm in New Hampshire. It's worth the drive."

"Well...okay. I won't make Trevor and Becky a turkey dinner tomorrow." Annie studied the list, then folded the paper back along its creases and left it on the dresser next to her laptop. Turning, she scrutinized her sister's weary face. "You sure you don't want to spend some time with your husband in the hot tub? It might relax you."

Sarah shook her head. "I'm tired. I just want to go to sleep and wake up tomorrow evening, and this will all be over." She forced a feeble smile and headed for the door. "If I don't see you in the morning, make sure you get the kids to the bus stop on time."

"You'll see me." Annie would wake up early enough to wave Sarah and Gordon off. "I don't know about the hot tub. I should review my notes for work. We have a meeting tomorrow."

"Don't be a grind," Sarah said. "Go cheer Gordon up. He's a wreck."

Annie recalled that at dinner, he had seemed…not exactly a wreck, but definitely subdued. Trevor and Becky had dominated the conversation, Trevor filling Annie in on his soccer team's stellar record, Becky asking questions about how long Sarah would be in the hospital and whether the doctors and nurses were nice, and did they give lollipops afterwards. It dawned on Annie that, as difficult as Sarah's situation was for Sarah, it had to be nearly as difficult for Gordon. He was so reserved, though. So restrained. So lawyerly. He probably never dripped ice cream on his clothing. He sure as hell wouldn't tell Annie he was a wreck.

"Do you really think he wants my company?" she asked, crossing to the window and gazing out. One story below, the patio was mostly dark. A couple of outdoor pole lamps glowed near the hot tub, and lights from somewhere deep in the hot tub illuminated the stone-lined circle of blue. She could see Gordon seated in that circle, leaning back, his arms extended along the lip of the tub. His body was nearly invisible beneath the churning surface of the water.

"He'd never admit it," Sarah said, "but yes. He withdraws. He holds everything inside and pushes people away. He needs to reach out. You'd be doing me a favor if you sat in the hot tub with him."

Well, what was Annie's purpose in life these days, if not to do favors for Sarah?

That sarcastic thought was chased away by a surge of guilt. Her sister would be going under the knife tomorrow—or having organs yanked out through her vagina, or having them sucked through tiny laparoscopic tubes inserted into her abdomen. Annie didn't know what Sarah's surgery would entail, but the details didn't matter. What mattered was that Sarah was facing a sixty-percent death sentence, and even if the surgery proved to be a huge success and she emerged from it cancer-free and robustly healthy, she was going to get premature wrinkles. She was going to experience pain. She was going to be missing some significant chunks of her anatomy. How could Annie possibly resent her for requesting favors?

"Hey, twist my arm," she said, forcing a grin. "If you really want me to, I'll go sit in the hot tub. It's a tough job but someone's got to do it."

Sarah's smile looked as artificial as Annie's felt. Her eyes didn't smile at all, but they remained dry and steady. She gave Annie a nod and then left the guest room, off to take her bath, to withdraw into herself and push people away, just as she'd accused her husband of doing.

And Annie would don her tankini, even though it was mid-October, and do her best to be sociable to Sarah's withdrawn, pushing-people-away husband.

chapter seven

SHE FOUND A TERRY-CLOTH ROBE HANGING FROM A HOOK ON THE BACK OF THE GUEST BATHROOM DOOR. A closer survey of the modules in the closet revealed a pair of flip-flops in one of the cubbies. Even so, Annie scurried from the sliding glass door off the family room across the patio to the hot tub, aware of the autumn chill in the evening air. It was much too cold for someone to be wandering around outdoors in a swimsuit and sandals.

Steam rose off the frothing water, advertising its warmth. Gordon gave Annie a passing glance as she untied the robe and eased herself into the tub, as far from him as she could sit. The water scalded her. "I feel like a lobster," she said, trying not to wince at the stinging heat. "I'll turn red and someone will dip me in melted butter."

"You'll get used to it," he said. Then he closed his eyes. As she'd been warned—withdrawn and pushing her away.

She tried to recall the last time she had been alone with Gordon, without Sarah present to moderate, and realized that time was never. Annie had always related to him through Sarah. She'd managed to exchange pleasantries with him at family get-togethers. But everything she knew about him she knew by way of Sarah. He worked hard. He grew up near Chicago. He belonged to that fancy fitness center. He had no hobbies. He liked to read non-fiction histories and biographies about former presidents and the Founding Fathers. Annie had learned all of that from Sarah, and it represented pretty much the sum total of her knowledge of her brother-in-law.

Was she supposed to make conversation with him now? Was that part of the favor Sarah had requested?

She tried to think of what to say. That he looked good in a swimsuit? Hard to tell; all she could see of him was his head and the tops of his shoulders—which weren't lobster red, so unlike her, he wasn't going to wind up on a plate in front of someone wearing a plastic bib. His hair glistened with droplets of water. His face wore a sheen of either perspiration or condensation from the steam. The rest of his body was submerged, ripply and indistinct. His swim trunks were a dark color; she could see that much. His legs extended across the bottom of the tub, but didn't quite reach her side. She hoped she didn't accidentally bump his feet with hers.

She closed her eyes as well, listening to the *glub-glub-glub* of the motor agitating the water, feeling the hair at the nape of her neck grow damp. She'd pulled it into a haphazard pony tail, but it was going to wind up soaked. If she knew Sarah, there would be a hair dryer in one of the drawers in the guest bathroom's vanity. And given how hot the water was, the moisture at the base of her skull felt kind of refreshing.

Gradually her body adjusted to the water's temperature. She stopped feeling like a lobster. She opened her eyes and found Gordon watching her, his lids at half-mast. He looked pretty calm. The hot tub must be working its magic on him.

"So, Gordo," she said, figuring they couldn't just sit in silence forever. "Sarah gave me your cell phone number in case I have to reach you tomorrow."

"She printed up those instructions earlier today," he said. His gaze narrowed. "Why do you call me Gordo? It sounds like a Spanish pumpkin."

She'd never before seen evidence that he had a sense of humor. Maybe he didn't. He wasn't smiling. He might be serious.

"Gordie sounds too juvenile," she explained. "Gord sounds like an American pumpkin."

"What's wrong with calling me Gordon?" he asked.

"Too formal. It makes you sound like a lawyer."

At last, a faint smile. At least she thought he was smiling. With the plumes of steam and the atmospheric lighting, she couldn't be sure.

"It's too bad Sarah isn't here," she said. "She said she was going to take a bath and go to bed. This is much more relaxing, once you get used to the heat."

"She won't be allowed to take baths for a month after surgery," Gordon said. "Tonight is her farewell bath."

Annie nodded. The water bubbling around her was soothing, massaging her, almost hypnotizing her. She willed herself not to relax so much she slipped beneath the surface and drowned. "If the kids ask me questions tomorrow, what should I tell them?"

Gordon sat up straighter. This was a serious question, and he had to adopt a serious posture to answer it. "They know she's having surgery. They know she hasn't been feeling well. We told them the surgery is going to help."

"They don't know she has cancer?"

"Not yet." He rolled his head back and gazed up at the sky. The moon was half full, radiating enough light to make the stars hard to see. "They'll know soon enough, once she starts chemo. For now, they know that when she comes home, she'll be weak for a while. No heavy lifting. No driving." He steered his gaze back to Sarah. "I don't suppose you'd be available to drive sometimes?"

"I have a job," she reminded him, hoping she didn't sound too testy. Favors were fine, but she wasn't about to resign from Cabot College and become Sarah's chauffeur. "Maybe on weekends I can help out a little. My mother's probably available during the week, though."

"Your mother." Gordon didn't exactly spit out the words, but his distaste came through. "I can't believe I'm going to be stuck with her at the hospital tomorrow."

"Seriously, you should let her drive the kids to their soccer practices and stuff," Annie said. "It'll make her feel important, like she's at the center of the action. She loves that."

"But then she'll be around all the time," he said.

"You'll be at your office. You won't have to deal with her."

"Hmm." He closed his eyes and settled back into the water. "I guess so. I can hide at the office until she leaves, and Sarah can call and tell me that the coast is clear."

"There you go."

"There's also Uber," he said.

Annie smiled. This time, she was certain Gordon was smiling back at her.

○ ○ ○

She set her phone to wake her up at six o'clock. The world beyond her window was more dark than light, the faintest hint of dawn just beginning to seep into the sky. To her surprise, she felt fairly well rested. A night without Emmett snoring gently beside her had enabled her to sleep soundly. And much as she hated to admit it, the fluffy duvet and all those pillows were pretty damned comfortable.

The robe she'd worn to and from the hot tub had dried overnight, and she tied it on around the oversized tee shirt she'd slept in and padded down the stairs in time to find Gordon and Sarah in the kitchen, reviewing the contents of a tote bag. Sarah wore a soft green warm-up suit that looked a little looser on her than it ought to. Gordon was dressed in a crisp shirt and blue jeans. Both garments appeared to have been ironed, possibly even starched. Or else it was Gordon's personal starchiness filtering through the fabric.

"Phone," Sarah said, ticking items off on a sheet of paper while Gordon confirmed that each item was in the tote bag. "Charger. Hair brush. Toothbrush."

"They'll give you a toothbrush at the hospital," he told her. "You're going to be there only a couple of nights."

"I'm bringing my own toothbrush," she insisted. "It's got the special layered bristles. And my toothpaste. They probably have some no-name toothpaste there. Did I pack sanitary pads? I'll need those. I'm going to be bleeding afterwards."

"They'll give you pads," Gordon said. "You're going to a hospital in Boston, not an ice floe in the Arctic. They'll have everything you need."

"They won't have my phone and charger."

"If you leave anything behind, I'll get it for you. Or—" he acknowledged Annie with a nod "—I'll phone Annie and have her bring it."

Annie stopped herself before reminding him that she would be attending a work meeting remotely for most of the day. She couldn't just check out of the meeting and drive to the city with a tube of Sarah's preferred toothpaste.

But she didn't argue. Let Gordon and Sarah believe she would drop everything and race into the city with Sarah's toothpaste. By the time

Sarah was wheeled out of the operating room, toothpaste would probably be the furthest thing from her mind.

Sarah acknowledged Annie's presence with a barely perceptible
nod, then turned back to her checklist. "Is my e-reader in there?" she
asked.

"You can read on your phone."

"The screen is too small."

"And you're not going to be reading, anyway. You're going to be
tripping on painkillers and then you're going to be sleeping."

"I want my e-reader," she insisted. Gordon let out a weary breath,
then walked out of the kitchen. "And the charger," Sarah called after him.

"Try to relax," Annie said. "This surgery is going to be a piece of
cake."

Sarah rolled her eyes. "I'm going to wake up and find out they ar-
rested Gordon for murdering Mom."

"He's a lawyer. He'll get off," Annie assured Sarah.

Gordon returned to the kitchen with Sarah's e-reader and a charging
cord neatly wrapped into a figure-eight shape and held together with a
rubber band. He placed the items in the tote. "Are you going to bring a
snack for yourself?" Sarah asked him.

"Sarah. It's a hospital. They'll have a cafeteria."

"All right, all right. I'm being stupid," Sarah said.

That didn't sound like her. Sarah had been a straight-A student
throughout her school years. She'd made Phi Beta Kappa in college. She
could have gone to law school herself, or medical school, or any other
kind of graduate school. But she'd been engaged to Gordon by then. All
she'd wanted to be was his wife.

That didn't mean she was stupid. It just meant she wasn't a
world-beater. But she didn't have to be. She had Gordon to beat the
world for her.

With a hug and another prediction of how magnificently Sarah
would weather her surgery, Annie ushered her and Gordon to the garage door and waved them off. Then she returned to the kitchen and
brewed a pot of coffee. If today were a regular workday for her, she
would still be in bed—unless Sarah phoned and woke her. Rising so
early this morning, she had time to kill.

Not too much time, though. Trevor and Becky were awake by seven, dressed and in the kitchen, clamoring for breakfast. "What do you usually have for breakfast?" Annie asked them.

"Organic cereal," Trevor told her. "It has no sugar in it."

"Sometimes we have toast," Becky added. "But we're not supposed to put jelly on it because there's too much sugar in it. Mommy doesn't like us eating sugar in the morning."

"Or ever," Trevor added.

"You had ice cream yesterday," Annie reminded them.

"That was Daddy, not Mommy," Becky explained.

Annie nodded. "Would you like cinnamon toast?" she asked.

Becky and Trevor exchanged a glance. "What's cinnamon toast?"

"It's got sugar in it," Annie warned, rummaging through the cabinets until she found a lidded sugar bowl. The cinnamon was in a narrow drawer that held nothing but spices, all in matching jars, lined along its built-in racks in alphabetical order. She poured the white and tan granules into a bowl, mixed them, added butter, mixed them some more, and smeared them onto slices of bread. Whole wheat, at least; that would provide some nutritional value.

Trevor had to locate the toaster-oven, which was hidden behind a sliding panel on the counter, along with a blender and a mix-master. "It's called an appliance garage," he informed Annie.

Of course. If you were going to live in a house this big—with a garage huge enough for three cars—you might as well have a garage for your kitchen gadgets too.

Not surprisingly, the kids loved the cinnamon toast. If they told Sarah their Aunt Annie had made it for them, Sarah might think twice about asking Annie for any more favors. And if they didn't tell her, she'd never have to know her children went off to school with sweetness in their tummies. Either outcome worked.

The house seemed cavernous once the kids were gone. How could Sarah stand being alone in such a huge house every day? Well, she didn't spend her days here; she was too busy doing her volunteer work or meeting friends for lunch or wine or whatever. What did women who didn't work *do*? According to Annie's friend Jenna, who was on maternity leave, being home all day was ghastly. Then again, she was home all day with a colicky baby.

But at least her house wasn't so quiet. Better to be surrounded by the screeches of an irritable infant than by all this echoing silence.

The admissions team meeting was scheduled to start at ten o'clock. Annie returned to the guest room, showered, dressed—her sweater still had a few wrinkles in it, but she wasn't going to iron it—and carried her laptop downstairs to the kitchen. She poured herself a cup of coffee and reread a few of the applications her colleagues had already evaluated. She wanted to be able to cast a fair vote—admit, reject, or defer—on those candidates, but she had barely skimmed them last week. She'd been distracted.

At 9:00 a.m., she phoned Brittany and said she was available if anyone in the office needed to contact her before the meeting. At nine fifteen, her phone rang. According to the screen, the caller wasn't anyone from the admissions office. It was Gilda Baskin.

She inserted her ear bud and tapped the phone screen. "Hello, Mom," she said warily. Why would her mother be phoning her already? Could Sarah's surgery possibly be already done? Or had it been postponed? Was Sarah's blood pressure too high, despite her having avoided the hot tub last night?

"Annie, I am beside myself," her mother said. "We've been here for two hours and they've only just finished the paperwork and all this prep stuff. They'll be taking Sarah into the operating room soon."

"Good," Annie said. "That's why she's there."

"I'm going out of my mind with worry," her mother said. "I'm here in this tiny little lounge. There's a TV and I don't know how to change the channels, and there's a sign that says, 'Please don't use your cell phone.' Well, excuse me. What am I going to do?"

"You could stop using your cell phone," Annie suggested.

"That's ridiculous. They can't expect people to stop using their cell phones just because they're in this lounge. If I couldn't use my cell phone, I wouldn't have been able to call you."

Which wouldn't have been such a bad thing. "Where's Gordon?" Annie asked.

"He went off to the cafeteria to get some breakfast. What is wrong with that man?"

"Maybe he's hungry," Annie said.

"His wife is about to have surgery. And he's off eating. Has he no heart?"

"He has a heart," Annie said. "But he's also got a stomach. He didn't eat any breakfast before he and Sarah left the house this morning." Annie would have made him some cinnamon toast, but that might have upset Sarah, and then Sarah's blood pressure would have soared, and if she was going to have high blood pressure anyway, she could have enjoyed the hot tub last night.

"Eating breakfast," Gilda huffed. "It's like I'm the only one here who takes this seriously."

"I'm sure her doctors take it seriously," Annie said. "And Gordon takes it seriously too. That doesn't mean he can't eat breakfast. There's nothing for him to do once they start prepping Sarah."

"They won't even tell me what they're doing to her. I asked three nurses and a doctor, and they all told me they were taking care of her and I had to wait here in this horrible lounge with a very boring talk show on the TV, some woman in a skin-tight dress babbling about dog-grooming products. Why should I give a good goddamn about how curly your poodle's hair is? I'm Sarah's *mother*. My daughter has cancer."

"Maybe you should go and get some breakfast too," Annie suggested.

"I ate at home. And now I have heartburn. I'm just so worried, Annie—I can't think straight."

When could she ever think straight? Annie sighed. In a mere five minutes, Gilda had managed to exhaust her. "Mom. Try not to worry so much."

"She's my *daughter*. My baby. You can't begin to know what it's like to have someone tell you your daughter is this sick."

"You're right. I don't have a daughter and I don't know. I have a sister, though. She's going to have her surgery, and the doctors will do their best to make her well."

"What if they don't? What if they can't?" Annie could hear the anguish in her mother's voice, an undertone of keening.

"You've got to trust the doctors to do what they have to do. Sarah and Gordon trust them. You need to trust them too. They'll let you and Gordon know how the surgery went once it's done."

"They should let me know now." Hearing what she'd said, Gilda laughed forlornly. "I can't help going a little bit crazy. I'm her mother."

She was going more than a little bit crazy, but Annie didn't point that out. "I'm sure everyone at the hospital is aware that you're Sarah's mother," she said. "I can't tie up the phone right now, okay? I'm working remotely, and the office has to be able to reach me." She didn't admit that her laptop was open and humming, and Brittany, Dean Parisi, or any of the other admissions counselors could easily email her if they tried her phone and couldn't get through. She hadn't heard the beep that indicated another call was coming in, but her mother didn't have to know that either. "Just try to stay calm," she said. "That's the most helpful thing you could do."

"Don't tell me to be calm," Gilda argued. "This is not the time to stay calm." She paused, then added, "I went to a support group meeting for parents of cancer patients yesterday afternoon, and they said being upset was normal. I'm actually being very normal."

"Maybe it's normal," Annie conceded, "but Sarah needs you to be calm right now. I've got to get to work. Why don't you call me after Sarah is out of surgery and you know how she's doing?"

"Fine. I'll let you know. Are you going to eat breakfast too?"

"No," Annie told her. "Like I said, I'm working. You should have something to eat, though. It might make you feel better."

"I'm not going to eat until Sarah is out of surgery," her mother declared. "I don't care if I starve."

Annie groaned. Skipping breakfast was not the same thing as starving. If her mother wasn't hungry, she wouldn't eat. If she *was* hungry, she'd surely make her way to the hospital's cafeteria, sooner or later. Or a vending machine. Hospitals had vending machines, didn't they?

Annie hadn't eaten any breakfast, but she wasn't hungry. She was too worried about her sister, although she would never admit that to her mother. She would pretend she was as calm as she wanted Gilda to be.

She might not want anything to eat, but she wouldn't mind something to drink, something a bit stronger than plain coffee. Of course, it was too early to add anything alcoholic to her coffee—and she wasn't sure where Sarah and Gordon stashed their booze. Besides, she had to work. As if her mother hadn't scrambled her thoughts beyond the ability to concentrate on the queue of applications awaiting her.

As if, no matter how calm she pretended to be, she wasn't freaking out about her sister.

chapter eight

HER PHONE RANG AGAIN AT TEN FIFTEEN. She glanced discreetly at the screen: Gilda Baskin.

The meeting had already started. Annie had wandered from room to room in her sister's house, wondering where she should set up her laptop and log in. Her concern was what would show in the background once she turned her computer camera on and her colleagues could view her. The kitchen looked too informal, the living room too formal. She had peeked into Gordon's study, which contained a stately mahogany desk, two leather arm chairs, wall shelves filled with important-looking books, and a fireplace. She would feel like a trespasser entering the room, let alone remotely attending the meeting from that location.

The rec room in the finished basement looked like a rec room. The exercise room, with its glaring lighting, its glistening chrome stationary bike and treadmill, and the array of graduated weights on a rack, looked like the sort of venue in which a person would work hard and sweat a lot. Annie wanted her co-workers to believe she worked hard, but not that she sweated.

She'd finally settled at the dining room table, choosing a seat in front of the elegantly draped windows instead of the china-filled breakfront. Maybe the folks in the office would think she was sitting at a desk rather than at a banquet-sized table, its surface polished to a high gloss that would reflect the chandelier above it if Annie turned on that light. She didn't, instead lighting a floor lamp near the doorway into the butler's pantry—a freaking *butler's pantry*, which unfortunately didn't come furnished with a butler. She could see herself in one of the Zoom tiles on her computer, and the setting looked sedate but not too domestic. Her sweater didn't look too wrinkled either.

The group was discussing Miranda Griffith's early-decision application when Annie's mother called. Annie saw the entire team on her laptop monitor, each occupying a tile like hers. She knew they all had their laptops open in front of them so they could view all the applications they were considering, but she appreciated that they also had their cameras turned on so she could see them.

Dean Parisi was grilling Annie as to why she'd rated Miranda's application as "deferred." "Her grades and scores are solid," Dean Parisi pointed out.

"And she's at Exeter," Harold Stickney argued. "So we know those grades are authentic."

Annie wasn't convinced that grades from a pricy prep school were more authentic than grades from a public school. But they probably weren't less authentic either. "She's not an awful candidate," Annie admitted. "But her essay..."

"Adequate," Evelyn said, her tone clipped and dry. "Not overwhelming. She favors run-on sentences."

"It was more the subject matter than the grammar," Annie clarified. "Her parents paid for her to do a good deed so she could brag about it in her essay. I would be more impressed with her generosity if she'd raised the money for her Guatemala trip herself. Her parents wrote a check so she could earn her gold star."

"Her parents will be able to write a check for her to attend Cabot too," Harold said.

"We don't consider the applicant's financial need," Dean Parisi said, her tone chiding but also warm with amusement. They all knew they weren't supposed to consider the applicant's financial need, and they all knew they considered it, anyway. "My concern, Annie, is that we have to improve our yield. When we accept early-decision applicants, they're legally bound to come to Cabot. If we defer this girl and then accept her in the spring, she may turn us down. That hurts our yield."

The almighty yield—the percentage of students who accepted Cabot College once Cabot College accepted them—was one of Dean Parisi's obsessions. A better yield gave the school a higher ranking on various top-colleges lists. Annie wanted Cabot to rank high on those lists, but not at the cost of accepting mediocre students. Not that Miranda Griffith was mediocre, but her parents did pay for her junket to Guatemala. And she did favor run-on sentences.

And then Annie's phone rang, and she saw the call was from her mother. "I'm sorry," she said to the group. "I have to take this call. I'll sign on to whatever you decide for Miranda Griffith." With that, she clicked off her camera and her audio.

It was too soon for Sarah to be out of surgery—unless something went drastically wrong in the operating room. Annie tapped her phone to connect the call. "Mom?"

"I'm going crazy here," her mother said. "They won't tell me anything."

"Who won't tell you anything?"

"The doctors! They wheeled her out of her room and down the hall, and I haven't heard anything since."

Annie let out a long breath, hoping to blow away the curses congealing on her tongue. "Mom. They're performing surgery on her. They aren't going to stop the operation in the middle of things and come out to talk to you."

"I'm her mother. I'm worried sick. I don't know how I'm supposed to just sit here and do nothing."

If they told anyone how Sarah's surgery was proceeding, they'd tell Gordon. He was Sarah's husband. Annie wondered where he was, and how he was surviving the morning with her mother. Lying on an operating table and getting your abdomen cut up was probably more fun than dealing with Gilda.

"Mom, I've got to get back to work."

"How can you be working? I thought you were at Sarah's house."

"I'm working from Sarah's house."

"And taking care of the kids?"

"They're in school."

"Oh." Her mother mulled that over for a minute. "I'm sorry, Annie. I'm going nuts. Someone should be keeping me informed."

"You know what?" Annie was desperate to get off the phone—and not only because she felt duty-bound to return to the meeting. "You said you found some support groups for parents of cancer patients.

Why don't you contact someone from one of those groups? They've been through what you're going through. Maybe they can hold your hand through this."

"What a good idea. Thank you, sweetheart. I have no idea where Gordon is, and I need someone to hold my hand. Your father should be here with me. I don't know why he went to work. I don't know why you're at work either. If the kids are in school, you could come and hold my hand."

"No, I can't. And I meant someone could hold your hand metaphorically. They could talk to you on the phone and let you vent, and reassure you."

"I don't know if I have anyone's phone number. I have *your* phone number—"

"And I can't come," Annie said firmly. "By the time I arrived at the hospital, I'd just have to turn around and drive back to Sarah's house so I could be here when Becky and Trevor get home from school."

Another pause. Annie imagined her mother was trying to process this information—not easy to do, since she was, by her own account, going nuts. "I'll call your father. He should leave work and come here."

"Good idea," Annie said. "Call Dad. I've got to go." Not waiting for her mother to come up with a counteroffer that would entail Annie's participation, she said goodbye and disconnected the call.

She set down her phone and clicked her laptop's camera and audio back on. Her colleagues all appeared in their little squares, engaged in an animated discussion about one Garth Hollinger, who claimed on his application that he played hockey and the bassoon, presumably not at the same time. "Did we make a decision on Miranda Griffith?" Annie asked.

"We're accepting her," Dean Parisi said.

It figured. But really, did it matter that much? Annie's sister had cancer, and she was in surgery. Annie's mother was going nuts. Gordon was apparently hiding from her—in the cafeteria, in another waiting room, underneath someone's bed. Would accepting Miranda Griffith, with her well-funded good deeds and run-on sentences, make any difference in Annie's life?

No, but it would help Cabot College's yield. Surely that counted for something.

chapter nine

Gordon phoned Annie around two o'clock to inform her that Sarah was out of surgery, that all had gone as expected, and that Sarah was being given powerful painkillers and was dazed, exhausted, and only vaguely coherent. He said that while she'd been under anesthesia and "opened up," as the surgeon put it, she'd had an abdominal port implanted.

Annie had no idea what a port was in the context of a person's abdomen, but if she asked, Gordon would think she was an idiot. She made a mental note to look it up after she got off the phone, and simply told Gordon she was glad Sarah was out of surgery.

"Would you do me a favor and stay with the kids until around eight thirty or nine?" Gordon asked her. "I'd like to be at the hospital with her as late as possible. I think they'll kick me out at eight."

Doing favors for the Adler family had apparently become Annie's new mission in life. "No problem," she assured him, her mind racing off in the direction of dinner preparations and bedtime routines for Trevor and Becky. Sarah hadn't written out any nighttime instructions. Annie would have to guess, or improvise...or prepare them cinnamon toast for supper. As long as she didn't serve the turkey from the farm in New Hampshire, Sarah couldn't object. "Is my mother still at the hospital?"

Gordon groaned. "I'm hoping she'll leave soon."

Annie considered his comment remarkably discreet. "I'm sorry you have to put up with her."

"She said she'd take over for the kids tomorrow, so you can go back to work," Gordon told Annie. "As long as she's at the house, she won't be at the hospital, so that works for me. And Becky and Trevor like her."

"She showers them with compliments," Annie explained. "She believes they're good kids because they have such a wonderful grandmother."

"They *are* good kids," Gordon said.

"Because they have a wonderful aunt," Annie joked. "Don't worry about the home front, Gordo. Go take care of Sarah. I'll make sure Trevor and Becky wash behind their ears before they go to bed."

She was sure they'd go to bed with clean ears, even without her intervention. Sarah had raised two better-than-good children. They came home from school, ate one piece of fruit each from the aesthetically arranged fruit-bowl centerpiece in the kitchen, and then went to their bedrooms to do their homework. At one point, Becky ventured into the dining room in search of Annie, requesting help with a problem on her math worksheet, and when she saw that Annie was still tied up in her Zoom call with the admissions office team, she stood silently in the doorway and waited until Annie could excuse herself from the meeting for a minute. The problem involved long division—were second graders already mastering that skill? Annie was pretty sure she herself hadn't tackled long division until at least third grade—and then Becky thanked her and departed, allowing Annie to return to the meeting.

Becky and Trevor deserved a magnificent dinner, something better than leftover lo mein and spring rolls. Annie found a bag of fresh elbow pasta in the refrigerator, a jar of tomato sauce, a can of stewed tomatoes, and a package of ground bison—no ordinary ground chuck for Sarah's family—and prepared a pot of what during her Cabot College student days the dining hall called American chop suey. She and her classmates had called it "train wreck," given its gruesome appearance: pale, shiny noodles that resembled entrails, blood-red sauce, and chunks of meat. Trevor and Becky laughed hysterically when she told them the dish was nicknamed "train wreck," so she felt she simply had to drive to the nearest Starbucks with them after dinner to buy them brownies for dessert. Sweets were hard to come by in Sarah's house.

"Is Mommy coming home tonight?" Becky asked as she and Trevor munched on their brownies at the kitchen table after returning home from Starbucks.

"No. She has to stay at the hospital for a couple of days. But Daddy will be home."

"Did you talk to him?" Trevor asked.

"Yes. He said your mom's surgery went well." She didn't add that Sarah had had a port inserted into her abdomen. She had Googled "abdominal port" during a break in her meeting—it was either research medical ports or go to the bathroom, and Annie had her priorities—and learned that a port was a device placed under the skin that would enable Sarah's oncologist to inject her chemo meds directly into her abdomen. It sounded awful, but it also sounded useful. According to what Annie had read, the direct application of the chemo to where a patient needed it was most effective, and this way Sarah wouldn't have to get poked in a vein in her arm each time she received an infusion of the medicine. Having the port installed at the same time she was having her womb uninstalled made a lot of sense.

Annie gazed across the table at Sarah's children, wondering how much they needed to know about their mother's condition. Trevor's expression remained wary as he nibbled on his brownie. He looked on the verge of speaking, but Becky cut him off before he could say anything. "Will you be here tomorrow?"

"No. Grandma will be, though."

Becky let out a cheer. "Grandma! Will she give us brownies too?"

"You'll have to discuss that with her." Annie turned back to Trevor, but his gaze was focused on his brownie. She tried to think of a way to coax his words out of him, but before she could come up with any ideas, her phone rang.

She glanced at the screen. Emmett. "Excuse me, guys," she said, swiping her phone and wandering out of the kitchen.

"Hey, where are you?" he asked.

"At my sister's."

"Still?"

"I'll be here a while longer," she told him.

"I was thinking I could come over tonight."

Not over to her sister's, she realized. Over to her condo. "Don't tell me you still haven't worked out the sleeping arrangements with Frank."

"Maybe I just want to see you," Emmett said.

Or maybe you still haven't worked out the sleeping arrangements with Frank. "Emmett, it's been a long, hard day." Not really true, at least not physically. Not so long and hard that she just wanted to drive home, trudge up the stairs, let herself into her condo, and collapse onto the bed. But long and hard emotionally. Sarah had lost her uterus and ovaries and gained a port. Her nephew looked as if he knew a huge, dark storm cloud was hanging over his mother's head, and therefore his own. Gilda had been needy and whiny. Miranda Griffith had been given an early-decision acceptance to Cabot College, despite her run-on sentences.

Annie didn't want to have to deal with Emmett. She didn't want to have to listen to him gripe about Frank. She didn't want to have to fake an orgasm. In fact, she didn't even want to have a real orgasm.

"Call me tomorrow," she said, because she couldn't bear to slam a figurative door in his face. He was a nice guy. He was eye candy—or, even better, an eye brownie. Or an eye ice cream cone, a little drippy, a little messy, but delicious. "I'll have a better idea what's going on then."

"Okay," he said reluctantly.

After saying goodbye, she returned to the kitchen. Trevor and Becky were rinsing off their brownie plates and stacking them in the dishwasher. Really, they were amazing children. Sarah would be so proud. So would Annie's mother, who would claim credit for their impeccable behavior.

The digital clock built into the microwave read 8:10. Gordon was probably on the road right now, driving home from the hospital. His day had undoubtedly been a lot longer and harder than Annie's. "How about some baths?" she suggested. The more she got done before Gordon arrived home, the less he would have to do.

"I don't take baths anymore," Trevor said. "I take showers."

"As long as you wash behind your ears," she said. He gave her a perplexed look, then followed Becky up the back stairs.

Annie filled the tub for Becky, adding an extra capful of bubble bath to the water. The surface of the water foamed like a slightly pink, floral-scented head on a glass of beer. Becky shrieked with delight when she saw it. "Mommy never puts that many bubbles into my bath!"

She seemed safe soaking herself in the tub, and she had two washcloths, a plastic tug boat, and a small menagerie of waterproof toy animals to play with. Annie left her and went to check on Trevor, marveling at how mothers—it was nearly always mothers—managed to oversee multiple children engaged in multiple activities simultaneously. It occurred to her that Becky could drown in the tub while Annie was making sure Trevor was all right—but Trevor could poke out his eye with a pencil while Annie was overseeing Becky. Terrible things could happen. Terrible things *did* happen. Motherhood, she reasoned, was the triumph of optimism over fear.

She found Trevor stretched out on his bed, reading a Marvel comic book. His bedroom's décor was as different from Becky's as a pickup truck was from a Barbie Dream Car. No cheerful cartoon Winnie-the-Pooh murals, no white carpet, no French-Provincial furniture. Instead, his room represented the ultimate in pre-teen machismo: brown carpeting, rustic maple furniture, a comforter featuring a green and brown plaid pattern, and posters of assorted professional athletes framed and hanging on the wall. When Annie had been growing up, she had taped a few posters to her bedroom walls—Jeff Bridges in *The Great Lebowski*, a life-size photo of Tupac Shakur and Snoop Dogg dressed in fancy suits—but her mother had made her remove them, and then bitched at her for weeks about the marks the tape had left on the wall paint. If only her mother had framed the posters and let Annie hang them with proper hardware, she wouldn't have had to resort to tape.

"You okay?" she asked Trevor.

He glanced up at her, then steered his gaze back to the comic book. "Yeah."

"Did you shower?" He was still dressed in the outfit he'd worn to school.

"I'll shower when I finish this." He lifted the comic book, then sent Annie a feeble smile. "And I'll wash behind my ears."

"Okay." She hovered in the open doorway, waiting to see if he had anything more to say. Sort of hoping he did, sort of hoping he didn't.

He did. Lifting his eyes once more, he said, "My mom is real sick, isn't she."

How much did he know? How much did Sarah want him to know? "She's sick," Annie said carefully, "but her doctors are going to do everything they can to make her better."

He digested her words, then shook his head. "Is she gonna die?"

"We're all going to die sooner or later," Annie said. Not exactly the sort of cheerful words anyone—let alone a ten-year-old boy whose mother was in the hospital—would want to hear right before bed. Because Annie didn't know what to say, she'd said something awful. Poor Trevor was probably going to suffer from nightmares for the rest of his life.

"Some of the guys in these comics don't die. They're mutants."

"Well, your mother isn't a mutant, but she's got super powers," Annie said. That prompted another, slightly firmer smile from Trevor.

She heard a noise coming from downstairs—footsteps, a door shutting. "I think your dad is home," she said. "Let me go get Becky out of the bath."

Gordon shouted a greeting up the stairs while Annie rushed down the hall to check on Becky. The air in the bathroom was thick with humidity and the flowery perfume of the bubble bath.

"Daddy's home," Annie told her. "Let's get you dried off."

Becky let out a joyful shout and climbed out of the tub, dripping sudsy water across the bathmat and onto the tiles. Annie caught her before she could race out of the bathroom naked, and wrapped her in a towel. "Go put on your PJs," she said, nudging Becky across the hall to her bedroom.

Exiting the bathroom, she spotted Gordon climbing the bridal stairs. He looked fatigued, his hair mussed, his jaw shadowed by a day's growth of beard. He flickered a smile at Annie and whispered, "Can you stick around for a few minutes?"

She nodded and stepped aside as he strode down the hall to Trevor's bedroom. Then she headed to the guest room to pack her things. It didn't take long. Her swimsuit had dried out, and she still had on the sweater she'd worn for the Zoom meeting. She unplugged her laptop and slid it into its case, then carried it and the duffel bag downstairs.

She heard voices drifting down from the second floor—Gordon's low and slow, Becky's shrill and babbling, and Trevor's somewhere in between. A few words jumped out, among them "brownies" and "train wreck." Annie wondered whether she would ever be welcome in Sarah's house again.

She waited in the kitchen, checking her email on her phone—nothing but ads and spam—while Gordon talked to his children. She was tired. She wanted to go home. She wanted to crawl into bed and fall asleep.

But she waited for Gordon, because he had asked her to. Because she was the official granter of favors, and waiting for him was a favor.

Finally—actually, only about ten minutes later, but it had felt like ten years—he descended the back stairs and arrived in the kitchen. As scruffy as he appeared, his shirt and jeans still looked starched. He rubbed a hand over his eyes, as if he could massage the weariness out of them, and smiled hesitantly. "You fed them something called 'train wreck'?"

"American chop suey," she explained. "Pasta, ground meat, tomato sauce. There are leftovers, if you're hungry."

"I am," he acknowledged, crossing to the refrigerator and locating the lidded plastic container that held what was left of the meal. He carried it to the microwave, punched the buttons to heat it, and turned back to Annie. "You want a drink?"

No. She wanted to go home.

She also wanted to hear how Sarah was doing, how she was feeling, when she would be discharged from the hospital, when her doctors would start pumping drugs into her abdominal port. "I have to drive," she reminded him.

He nodded and vanished into his office. When he returned, he was carrying a cut-crystal decanter containing something amber and no doubt well aged and expensive, and two highball glasses. He poured a half inch into one glass and two inches into the other, then pushed the smaller portion across the center island to her. "Cheers," he said, not sounding particularly cheery as he lifted his glass and took a swig.

The microwave beeped. He pulled out the plastic container, eased off the lid, plucked a fork from a drawer, and joined her at the center island. He proceeded to eat the American chop suey straight from the container. He didn't sit.

Annie couldn't imagine Sarah approving of such inappropriate behavior—eating from a plastic container while standing. For some reason, that Gordon would do such a thing endeared him to her.

She took a sip of the liquor. She was no connoisseur when it came to scotch and bourbon and all those other amber alcoholic beverages. She enjoyed wine, although she couldn't speak knowledgeably about it, couldn't pontificate about its nose and its bouquet and its finish of cloves. As for hard liquor, she wouldn't know the difference between Cointreau and moonshine. She would rather drink a chocolate malt than a single malt. Whatever Gordon had poured for her was undoubtedly expensive—this was the Adler house, after all—and its expense was utterly wasted on her.

Still, it didn't taste bad. She took another sip and felt the back of her throat go numb.

"So, Gordo, how did it go today?" she asked him.

"Shitty."

She had never heard him utter a vulgarity before. "Because of my mother?"

"Your mother was the whipped cream on top." He forked some of the noodle concoction into his mouth, chewed, swallowed, and said, "This is good." He sounded surprised. He was undoubtedly used to Sarah whipping up boeuf bourguignon or chicken marsala for dinner on a typical weeknight evening. He was probably also used to eating his gourmet meals in the dining room, or at least at the breakfast table by the bay window in the kitchen, not standing at the center island.

"It's easy to make." She hoped to boost his spirits with a joke. "You just park a car on the tracks, wait for a train to come along, and scoop up the mess."

He grimaced, then devoured another forkful. After swallowing, he said, "They found lesions on her bladder."

Lesions sounded bad. Lesions on her bladder, when this was just supposed to be about her ovaries, sounded very bad. "I wish I knew more about cancer," she said apologetically.

"No, you don't. The only people who know anything about cancer are the people who have to deal with it, because they have it or someone they love has it." He lowered his fork and—again, in a very not-Sarah-standard move—tore a square of paper towel from the roll attached to a decorative oak holder and wiped his mouth with it. "Her cancer has metastasized. They're going to blast her with chemo that's going to make her feel like hell, and then she's going to die."

"Don't be so negative," Annie argued. If he was going to be the un-Sarah by eating train wreck out of a plastic container at the center island and wiping his face with a paper towel, she was going to be the uber-Sarah, the positive thinker, forging ahead with the conviction that nothing bad would happen to Sarah. Nothing bad *could* happen to her, because she wouldn't stand for it.

Gordon sent her a skeptical look. "The doctors said the chemo may buy her a little time. It's not going to cure her. She's never going to get well."

"Did they tell her that?" Annie couldn't imagine Sarah lying passively in a hospital bed while a medical expert told her such a thing. She would retort that the expert was wrong, that she had no intention of dying, that the chemo would buy her fifty years, and that if her doctors couldn't figure out how that would happen, she would have to do it for them. Then she would come home and tell Gordon not to eat standing up out of a Tupperware dish.

"They'll talk to her tomorrow. She was too groggy from the surgery today." He sighed and drank some more of his fancy booze. "She deserves a restful night."

"They gave her good drugs?"

"The best."

Well, that was something.

"I shouldn't keep you," he said. "Thanks for taking care of the kids today." He paused, then added, "Even if you fed them Amtrak corpses."

"And brownies," she reminded him.

He shook his head, and a laugh, faint but real, escaped him. "That'll be our secret," he said. "Don't tell Sarah."

"I won't. But Becky probably will."

Another laugh. "Thanks again, Annie. Go home. I'll call you with an update tomorrow."

"Can I call Sarah myself?"

"She's got her phone with her, so you can try. If she's resting, she might not answer."

Annie nodded. She lifted her duffel bag and laptop case from the counter and hesitated. If she had a closer relationship with Gordon, she would have given him a hug, but they weren't on a hugging basis. Not even a kiss-on-the-cheek basis. Sarah was the bridge that spanned between them, connecting them. Without her, they were just two people, two in-laws.

But now they had one more thing to connect them: Annie had treated Trevor and Becky to brownies—and yesterday, Gordon had treated them to ice cream cones. Annie and Gordon were co-conspirators in the sweets-feeding of those two children.

Annie hoped Sarah would never forgive her for having slipped the kids some un-nutritious chocolate. If Sarah held a grudge against Annie for the next fifty years, that wouldn't be such a terrible thing.

chapter ten

THE DORM WAS ONE OF ANNIE'S FAVORITE HAUNTS. Its name was misleading; it wasn't a dorm. It wasn't even a part of Cabot College. It stood two blocks from the northernmost edge of the campus, close enough that she could leave her car parked in one of the staff lots and walk over, sparing herself the challenge of finding a parking space on charming and perpetually crowded Leverett Street, which was home to numerous bookstores, bodegas, and boutiques that catered to the Cabot students.

The Dorm didn't cater to the students, since it was primarily a drinking establishment, and most undergraduates were too young to buy booze legally. True, they could patronize the place to enjoy a burger or a platter of fried onion rings, and most of the college's seniors were old enough to order a drink more potent than club soda. And more than a few students had fake IDs. But the majority of the people occupying the tables and bar stools were Cabot staffers and townies. Annie occasionally visited the place after work with Jamal; they would order a round of beers and gossip about whatever Harold had bloviated about that day, or whether Dean Parisi and Professor Thurston were friends or *friends*. Annie had brought Emmett to the Dorm a couple of times, but he wasn't crazy about the place because it didn't have a wide-screen TV above the bar, broadcasting that evening's Red Sox or Patriots or Bruins game. The absence of a TV blasting professional sports was one of the things Annie liked best about the place.

She also liked that it wasn't fancy or pricy. The décor was barely a step above shabby, with paneled walls of knotty pine that had darkened to a gloomy brown over the years, and wooden booths into the surfaces of which a century's worth of graffitists had carved their initials. A faint perfume of hot oil hovered in the air. The lighting was dim and the wait staff called everyone "hon."

It was not the kind of place where you could order fancy aged liquor that would be poured from a cut-crystal decanter. You could order plenty of liquor, but it came out of bottles with screw-on caps, and the glasses it was served in didn't make a pinging sound if you tapped them.

Annie sat at one of the heavily carved tables, waiting for Chloe. At five forty on a weeknight, the pub wasn't crowded, and Annie didn't have to defend her table against hordes of customers standing and glaring impatiently at the patrons occupying the tables. Chloe was probably circling the block in her car, searching for a parking space. The elder residence where she worked in the business office, and where her mildly demented grandfather lived, was only a few miles away, but it was too far to walk after a long day at work.

While Annie waited, she checked her emails on her phone. Two were from Emmett, asking her where she was and whether he could crash at her condo. She felt kind of bitchy typing, *Not tonight, sorry*, but she really didn't want to see him. For one thing, she wanted to spend the evening catching up with Chloe. For another, she was tired of Emmett pretending he wanted to see her when, she suspected, he only wanted to avoid confronting his roommate. Emmett was a champion when it came to avoiding confrontations. That used to be one of the things Annie liked best about him. She and Emmett never argued. They never butted heads. They were both adept at yielding, accommodating, surrendering.

But lately, she was feeling pugnacious. She wanted to fight. Probably because she was so busy yielding, accommodating, and surrendering to Sarah.

Sarah was sick, though, and if Gordon was correct, she was going to die, sooner rather than later. How could Annie say no to her?

"I'm home," Sarah had informed her earlier that day when she'd phoned Annie at her office. "I feel like shit, but it's better to feel like shit at home than at the hospital."

"You felt like shit before the surgery," Annie had reminded her. "What a waste. This surgery was supposed to de-shittify your feelings."

Sarah had laughed weakly, then groaned. "I can't laugh. It hurts my belly. They told me to hold a pillow against my abdomen if I have to cough."

"So don't cough. Can you handle visitors yet?"

"Come by this weekend," Sarah had said. "Maybe I'll be feeling a little better then." She hesitated, then added, "I have a small favor to ask of you."

"What?" Annie had said cautiously.

"One of the oncology nurses told me I should cut my hair before I start chemo. She said it's going to fall out and clog the shower drain. If I cut it really short before it starts falling out, I'll have fewer problems with the plumbing. Will you cut it for me?"

"You don't want to go see—what's her name? Pixie, or Trixie, your stylist at the salon?"

"Lexie, and no. Why should I pay eighty dollars for a haircut when my hair's just going to fall out? I was hoping you'd be willing to do it for a glass of wine and a soak in the hot tub."

"I'm such a bargain," Annie had said. "How about Gordo? You don't want him to cut it?"

"I wouldn't let him within twenty feet of my hair with scissors," Sarah said. "And Mom. Oh my God, Mom. She's already offered three times to cut it for me. I never should have mentioned the nurse's advice."

"She used to cut our hair when we were kids," Annie reminded Sarah.

"I rest my case," Sarah shot back.

Annie stifled a groan at the memory of the haircuts Gilda used to give her and Sarah when they'd been in grade school. Sarah's hair had been thick and wavy enough to hide most of their mother's mistakes, but Annie's hair had been limp and straight, and every uneven strand, every lock cut too short or left too long, was visible, probably from satellites in outer space. By the time Sarah had reached middle school, she had insisted on having her hair cut professionally, and Gilda had conceded. But she'd continued to cut Annie's hair until Annie reached high school and decided to grow it long enough that she could trim the ends herself. Having waist-length hair which she could tie back in a ponytail or a braid was better than appearing in public blighted by one of her mother's ghastly haircuts.

Gilda, of course, believed she did a fabulous job as Annie's hair-dresser. She would hack away at Annie's drab brown mane, then set down her scissors and guide Annie to the bathroom mirror. In the glass, Annie would see her own hideous reflection and her mother's face behind her, beaming with unwarranted pride, as if the coiffure she'd created was a Michelangelo-caliber masterpiece.

Annie would not subject her dying sister to that. "Sure," she'd said. "I'll cut your hair. And I'll bring my bathing suit."

Now she sat in a booth at the Dorm, staring at her emails on her phone and trying to decide what to do about Emmett. It wasn't that she didn't want to see him ever, or even that she didn't want to see him soon. But she was tired of being exploited, even if her reward for her exploitation was satisfying sex or a soak in a hot tub. Did people like Sarah and Emmett believe they could use her because she was just Annie, an also-ran whose hair looked as dreary as the Dorm's décor, despite the fact that nowadays she patronized Tony's Clip Joint and paid real money to get her hair done rather than subjecting herself to her mother's wretched haircuts? Was it because she was convenient and not important enough to be too busy to help out? Was she emitting take-advantage-of-me vibes?

Seeing Chloe enter the pub, Annie stuffed her phone into her purse and her negative thoughts into a remote corner of her mind. From the doorway, Chloe surveyed the pub in search of Annie, who waved. Chloe spotted her and smiled, then elbowed her way past several people swarming alongside the bar to reach the table. Elbowing people out of her way was not a problem for Chloe. She was what Annie's father would call a Big Girl.

She settled herself on the bench opposite Annie and devoted her first few utterances to the sheer impossibility of finding a parking space in this neighborhood, and the idiot who swerved into an open parking space on Leverett Street just seconds ahead of Chloe, and did Annie want to help Chloe slash the idiot's tires. But her diatribe faded as soon as a waitress appeared at their table. "I'll have a Harpoon ale and an order of sweet potato fries," she requested, then flashed a grin at Annie. "You'll split the fries with me, okay?"

Annie wasn't terribly hungry, but if Chloe wanted to order fries and pretend she wasn't going to eat them all herself, Annie would play along. "I'll have a glass of Merlot," she told the waitress. Merlot was always a safe wine to order. No one expected you to pontificate about a Merlot's bouquet or its mouth or its finish.

"Be right back, hon," the waitress said. Annie wasn't sure which one of them was "hon"—Chloe or herself. Not that it mattered.

Annie had met Chloe when she was living in her first apartment after college, the basement unit within spitting distance of the commuter rail line's track. One evening, when she lugged her hamper across the hall to the laundry room that shared the basement level with her, two other apartments, and a bunch of storage cages, she found Chloe relaxing atop one of the molded-plastic chairs in the laundry room, watching her clothing through the glass porthole built into the door of the washing machine. In one hand Chloe held a paperback novel, and in the other a bottle of cheap wine.

At least Annie assumed it was cheap. Who drank a well-aged Bordeaux with a mouth and a bouquet and a finish while sitting in the basement of an eighty-year-old apartment building, in a laundry room that smelled of bleach and dryer sheets?

Annie dumped her laundry into one of the empty washers, added detergent, slid her credit card into the slot to start the machine, and retreated to the door, intending to head back across the hall to her apartment. Chloe stopped her, though. "Want some wine?" she asked, waving the bottle in Annie's direction. "This is too much for me to drink by myself."

As they sipped and chatted and listened to the sloshes and rumbles of the washing machines churning and spinning their laundry, they discovered they had a lot in common besides a tolerance for mediocre wine. They were both recent college graduates then, embarking on adult life with a mixture of excitement and dread. They were single. And, they discovered, they were both the inferior younger sisters of superior older siblings.

Chloe's brother, Justin, had been in medical school when Chloe and Annie had met. Now he was a full-fledged cardiologist at Mass General. Like Sarah, he was married, had two adorable children, and lived in a very large house. Like Sarah, he had a way of making his little sister feel like a failure. "He nags me about my weight all the time,"

Chloe often complained to Annie. "I found an article about a research-er who says people with higher body-mass indexes live longer than thin people. He said it was bullshit. He said extra weight strains the heart. But it's not like I'm obese or anything."

"Of course you're not obese," Annie would assure Chloe. It was true; she weighed maybe only about thirty pounds more than her ideal weight—or, perhaps, the weight at which she would wind up dying younger because she was too thin.

Chloe also griped that she had spent her whole life hearing teach-ers tell her how much smarter her brother was. She'd listened to peo-ple speak in reverent tones about the lives he was saving, the hearts he was healing, the medical miracles he was performing thanks to his knowledge and training. Meanwhile, Chloe helped to keep Medicare reimbursements flowing into the elder residence where she worked, so people thirty years older than her brother's average patients and miss-ing significant amounts of brainpower could still live comfortably and have their needs met. As far as Annie was concerned, Chloe was saving lives too.

"Now, tell me everything," Chloe said, shrugging out of her jacket and tossing it onto the bench beside her. "What's going on? How sick is your sister?"

"Very sick," Annie told her. Why didn't speaking those two words and acknowledging their truth fill her eyes with tears? Why wasn't she staggered with grief? What was wrong with her, that she could speak so clinically about Sarah's condition? "Her cancer has spread. Her prog-nosis sucks."

Their server chose that moment to deliver their drinks, a heaping plate of fragrant sweet potato fries, and a couple of cocktail napkins with "The Dorm" printed on them in bright red letters. With a few parting "hons," she waltzed off. Chloe poured her beer from its bottle into the cone-shaped glass the waitress had left for her, and raised it in a toast. "To you," she said.

Annie's wine glass had a line etched on it to show precisely how much wine the bartender ought to pour into it, and the bartender had scrupulously honored that line. She lifted it but frowned as she ab-sorbed Chloe's toast. "To Sarah," she said.

"No. To *you*. Sarah has plenty of other people drinking to her health. Besides, I've never even met her. Why should I drink a toast to someone I've never met?"

"Every year at Passover, my father drinks a toast to Moses," Annie noted. "They've never met."

Chloe laughed. "Your father is a hoot." They tasted their drinks, lowered their glasses, and Chloe plucked a fry from the plate. "How's the rest of the family coping?"

Annie sighed. "Sarah's husband is being macho and stoic. I think her son has a sense of what's going on, but her daughter is only eight. Sarah told me Becky asked if she could wear the hospital ID bracelet Sarah wore when she had her surgery."

"That paper thing they staple around your wrist?"

"Sarah told me she made the mistake of cutting it off with scissors. She had to tape it back together so Becky could wear it. Of course, it's too big for Becky. Every time she moves her arm, it falls off. But Sarah says she loves it."

"Nothing wrong with costume jewelry," Chloe observed. "It's more affordable than diamonds and gold. How are your parents holding up?"

Annie sighed again. "Sarah told me that when my father visited her in the hospital, he acted as if she was already dead. He kept weeping and clutching her hand and gazing at her with a tragic expression. My mother is in her element. She's loving every minute of this."

Chloe looked suitably horrified. "How could she love having her daughter so sick?"

"She's in the spotlight. People are showering her with sympathy. You know my mother. Well, you don't know her," Annie corrected herself. "But she loves attention. She loves having people fuss over her. And of course—I mean, her daughter has cancer. People are fussing over her. She's in her element."

"And you?" Chloe nudged the plate toward Annie, who thought for a moment that *and you* meant, *and you want a sweet potato fry?* Then she realized what Chloe was asking.

"I should be sad. I *am* sad," Annie said. "It doesn't exactly seem real to me. In time, it will. But right now..." Against her better judgment, she pulled a fry from the plate and bit into it. It tasted much too good, sweet and salty, crisp and hot. "I don't know. Sarah keeps asking me to do stuff for her. Then my mother phones and asks me to do stuff for Sarah—which always turns out to be doing stuff for my mother. Like, she called me last night and asked me to take a few of her books over to Sarah's house. She made it sound like she wanted to give Sarah these books so Sarah could read them, but she let slip that she wanted to get rid of them because they were taking up space on a shelf where she planned to display some photos of her and my dad from their vacation on Sanibel Island."

"She couldn't bring the books to Sarah herself?"

"Sarah must have told my mother not to come. My mother can drive Sarah crazy. Sarah doesn't need that right now." Annie took another fry, then pushed the plate back to Chloe's side of the table, as if those extra few inches between her fingers and the plate would keep her from grabbing any more fries. "So my mother's asking me to help her clear off her shelf, and I have to drive to her house to get the books, and then I have to drive to Sarah's house to deliver the books, and my mother will brag about how generous she was, giving Sarah a bunch of her books that she didn't want anyway."

Chloe nodded sympathetically. "It's because you're a spare."

"Huh?"

"A spare. You know, an heir and a spare?"

Annie's face must have registered her bewilderment.

"Remember when Princess Diana gave birth to two sons?" Chloe explained. "People said she'd produced an heir and a spare. The first-born, William, would be the heir to the throne, and Harry, the younger brother, was just in case something happened to William—like, he died and couldn't become the king. Of course, he didn't die, and he and his wife have now produced a bunch more children, so Prince Harry is way down in the order of succession. That's what happens to spares. They're there, just in case, and if just-in-case doesn't happen, they get passed over." She took a sip of beer and shrugged. "You and I are spares."

Annie had never thought about her position in the Baskin family that way. "My parents always told me they had me so Sarah wouldn't be an only child."

"There you go." Chloe waved an emphatic finger at Annie. "They didn't have you because they wanted you. They had you for Sarah's sake. My parents told me they had me because Justin asked them for a baby brother or sister. That's why we're here, Annie. We're the spares. We exist to fulfill some need of our older siblings."

Annie felt a cramp in her forehead as she scowled. "Do you really believe that?"

"I *know* it. Haven't you ever read any books about birth order and family roles?"

"Actually, no, I haven't," Annie said. Chloe had majored in psychology in college; she had undoubtedly read plenty of books about the psychological impact of being a second child. Annie had majored in English and read plenty of books by Eudora Welty, James Joyce, Jane Austen, and Herman Melville. Even trudging her way through Joseph Conrad's *Heart of Darkness* had to have been more interesting than reading a book that expounded on the worthlessness of kid sisters.

She had never felt worthless. Inferior, yes, but not without value. As it was, she was the one who took care of everything, because everyone else was too busy, too important. She was the one her mother called on to run errands, find a reliable plumber, or transport books from a shelf where she wanted to display vacation photos to a house where a patient might need something to occupy her while she healed from her surgery. Annie was the one who gave her sister free haircuts. She was the one who did the chores because Sarah always had more homework.

"Sarah's got the kids," Annie's mother always pointed out, rationalizing why she was asking Annie to give her a lift to and from the service station where her car was getting a brake job. "Sarah's got her library board meeting, and that damned thing is too heavy for me to lift," when she wanted Annie to get the propane tank refilled for her gas grill. Annie had learned that reminding her mother *she* had a job which placed at least as many demands on her as kids and volunteer activities placed on Sarah proved counterproductive. "I need you to help me figure out what all these house painter bids actually mean," her mother would say. "You work, you're a professional, you understand all this gobbledygook."

"Dad works too," Annie would remind her mother, not bothering to point out that evaluating college applications was a lot different from evaluating paint job proposals. "He can translate the gobbledygook as well as I can."

"He's useless when it comes to this stuff," her mother would argue.

"Sarah went to an Ivy League school. I'm sure she could figure it out," Annie would say.

"But she's so busy. Just come over here and read them. I won't be able to hire a painter until I know which bid is the best one. Bring Emmett. He does house painting, doesn't he?"

"He does construction."

"I bet he understands these bids. Bring him along with you."

"Gordon is a lawyer," Annie would argue. "If anyone understands gobbledygook, it's lawyers."

"He's too busy."

Evidently, being a spare meant never being too busy to pick up the pieces, clean up the messes, scrub the bathroom sink, translate the gobbledygook.

"I've never felt like a spare," she told Chloe. "I mean, I'm kind of essential. The family would fall apart without me. Who would take care of all the stupid little tasks? Who would they have to nag? Who would they have to feel superior to?"

"Okay, well, whatever. You really should read up on birth order, Annie. It's fascinating."

About as fascinating as measuring how much below the fill line on her glass her wine had dropped. Either she should sip more slowly or she should order another glass of wine. She had the feeling she would be choosing option two.

She already knew all the drawbacks of being the younger sister. She knew what it was like to fall short of her sister's magnificence. She knew what it was like to wear hand-me-down clothing while her sister got to wear brand-new clothing, and to use hand-me-down cosmetics when her sister decided she wanted a new look. And to have a living room filled with hand-me-down furniture. The only thing she had going for her, when compared to Sarah, was that she wasn't dying.

That was a terrible thought.

Being a younger sister, apparently, meant harboring terrible thoughts.

chapter eleven

NOT SURPRISINGLY, Sarah had official hair-cutting scissors, glistening silver and sharp, with a little finger rest curling off one of the loops like a diacritical mark. Of course Sarah would have just the right tool for the job. She didn't have a smock, but she had an old sheet which Annie could drape around her shoulders. The sheet had probably been on Becky's bed at one time, since it featured a pattern of Disney-version *Alice In Wonderland* characters. Alice, with her smooth blond hair held back by an elegant black ribbon, stared up at Annie from Sarah's left shoulder.

If Annie had been alone with just the sheet, she would have told Disney-Alice what to do with her pretty blond hair, her big blue eyes, and her tiny nose. Annie was not in a good mood. Before she'd arrived at Sarah's house, she had swung by her parents' house to pick up the books her mother wanted her to bring to Sarah. Annie had glanced at their spines and shaken her head. "I don't think Sarah will want to read these," she'd said.

"Of course she will," Gilda had argued.

"Mom. This one is about a little girl who gets kidnapped. This one—" she'd pointed to the second book in the pile "—is about a guy who tortures and murders people. And this one—" the third in the pile "—is about a woman with Alzheimer's."

"It got very good reviews," her mother had insisted. "I was going to read it, but then I dropped out of that book club. It wasn't a good group. They were always talking about things that didn't interest me."

"Like the books?" Annie had rolled her eyes.

Her father had ventured into the den, paused to smile at the framed photographs taken on Sanibel Island, now displayed on the shelf the books had once occupied, and then given Annie a quick hug. "Take the books," he'd murmured. "Just take them." He knew how to survive Gilda: do what she asked and don't argue.

Annie had taken the books.

By the time she'd arrived at Sarah's house, Gilda had phoned Sarah to assure her the books were on their way. Sarah had told Annie their mother had sworn Sarah would love them, and had gone on at length about how difficult it had been for her to part with them, but she wanted Sarah to have them even more than she wanted to keep them for herself. Sarah and Annie had both had a good laugh about that.

Now they were set up in the kitchen for Annie's transition from delivery person to barber, in part because the room had excellent lighting and in part because it would be easy to sweep the clippings off the white marble floor tiles, which, Sarah had once casually mentioned to Annie, had been imported from Italy. This was a factoid Annie found impossible to forget.

She was glad they were in the kitchen because there were no mirrors in that room, other than the shiny copper-bottomed pots hooked to a rack that dangled from the ceiling above the center island. Sarah couldn't see her reflection in those pots, so if Annie botched the haircut, Sarah wouldn't know about it until it was too late. She would not be able to assess the haircut while it was in progress and point out all the ways Annie was doing it incorrectly.

Not that it mattered. Sarah would be bald soon enough.

Becky sat facing her mother across the center island, both of them perched on stools. Gordon had taken Trevor golfing—it was an unseasonably mild day for October—but Becky had no interest in golf. "Only boys play it," she declared.

"That's not true," Annie said. "There are female golf champions."

"Name one," Becky challenged her.

Annie sifted through her memory bank and came up empty. What did she know about golf champions—male, female, or otherwise?

"Hairstyling is a more feminine pursuit," Sarah declared. She would know, much better than Annie, which activities were considered feminine pursuits. Femininity was one of her areas of expertise, incorporating fashion, home décor, and wifely and motherly duties, all of which Sarah excelled at. She had often lectured Annie on the feminine way to walk down the high school corridors ("Twist your arm so your wrist is visible") and the feminine way to look at boys ("Not directly; angle your head and look at them out the corner of your eyes, or else lower your head and glance at them from under your eyelashes.") When they were children, Sarah had instructed Annie at the playground that it was more feminine to sit on a swing than climb on the jungle gym. Why that should be, Annie had had no idea then and not much more of an idea now. On the swings, you just went back and forth and back and forth, never actually getting anywhere. On the jungle gym, you could climb and hang from your knees and jump. And break your neck, if you were reckless enough.

Recklessness must be a masculine activity, while swinging back and forth and going nowhere must be a feminine one.

"So, you want your hair very short?" she asked Sarah, running a brush through Sarah's lush, silky mane.

"Cut it all off," Sarah confirmed. "It's just going to fall out, anyway."

"Will you really be bald?" Becky asked. Evidently she'd been enlightened to some extent about the challenges her mother was facing.

"I really will."

"Why?"

"Because that's what happens when you take the medicine I have to take."

"I never want to take that medicine," Becky said solemnly.

"I hope you never have to. When are you going to start cutting, Annie?"

Sighing, Annie raised the scissors, curled her middle finger around the little metal hook, and snipped off a lock. Becky shrieked.

"Don't scream," Sarah scolded. "You'll scare Aunt Annie and she'll wind up cutting my ear off."

"I will not," Annie said. "I've got nerves of steel." That was a joke. She stared at the stubble behind Sarah's ear, where she'd cut off that first lock of hair, and wanted to scream herself.

Instead, she took another deep breath and cut off another lock. And Another. Becky's eyes grew rounder with each snip.

"Do you have some hats?" Annie asked. "Just in case I really blow it and you want to hide the damage."

"I'll be buying a wig," Sarah said.

"Oh, cool! When do you want to do that? I'm free tomorrow."

"I'm going with Diana," she said. "She's got better taste than you do."

Insulted, Annie contemplated cutting Sarah's ear on purpose—not all the way off, like Vincent van Gogh, just a nick that would bleed a lot. Diana Drucker had been Sarah's best friend in high school, and they were still close. Diana had always regarded Annie with a blend of amusement and contempt. "Oh, your little sister—she's so funny!" she would say when Annie did something not the least bit funny, like tripping on the sidewalk and scraping her knee, or complaining about having to do Sarah's chores.

Diana had been one of Sarah's bridesmaids, She had groused about the limited colors of nail enamel at the spa Annie had chosen for the bridesmaids' outing—only maybe one hundred different colors, rather than the hundred and fifty Diana would have preferred. As far as Annie was concerned, Diana was a bitch.

But Sarah believed her to have better taste than Annie. "Why didn't you ask her to cut your hair then?" Annie asked, wielding the scissors a bit more aggressively as she hacked away at her sister's hair.

"I did. She wasn't free this weekend. We'll go wig shopping on Monday."

"She doesn't have to work on Monday?"

"Her job is unpaid labor, like mine," Sarah said. "She's raising her kids, doing volunteer work. She's quite active in her town's garden club."

Annie hadn't known garden clubs still existed. She recalled her mother's brief participation in a garden club when Annie and Sarah were young. Gilda didn't last long in the club, once she'd realized that it was all about gardening.

"I guess if you know about worms and compost heaps, you're probably an expert when it comes to wigs," Annie muttered, sounding more bitter than she'd intended, and feeling an unwelcome surge of satisfaction as another lock of Sarah's hair fluttered to the floor.

"Worms are gross!" Becky made a face, then giggled. She definitely was her mother's daughter, too feminine to play golf. Annie had always liked worms as a child. After a drenching rain, they would wriggle up to the surface of the lawn, attracting hungry birds. They were weird and slimy and, Annie learned, useful at aerating the soil. Also useful at digesting compost and pooping it out, which for some reason made the compost nourishing to plants. One of Annie's former boyfriends had explained this to her in a monologue that had bored her into a stupor, which he'd found terribly insulting. Surely she ought to have relished his every word about the earthworm's digestive track.

"I don't think the garden club discusses worms," Sarah said. "It's mostly about pretty flowers. How's the haircut going? My neck feels cold."

"It's exposed," Annie reported, noticing the vertebrae at the nape of Sarah's neck, like large pebbles stuffed under skin so pale it looked translucent. "I'm almost done."

"You look so different," Becky said.

"Do I look good?" Sarah asked her daughter.

Becky bit her lip and shook her head. "You always say if I can't say something nice, I shouldn't say anything at all."

Interesting etiquette lesson, Annie thought as she guided the scissors around Sarah's other ear. Sarah had never hesitated to say not-nice things about Annie, touting the importance of honesty. For instance, that Annie didn't have as much taste as Diana when it came to evaluating wigs—as if any of them had ever had any expertise when it came to wigs.

Even though Annie allegedly had no taste, she did her best with the haircut, stretching hairs here and there to make sure she had cut them evenly, then fluffing her fingers through the short strands and creating a spiky effect across the crown of Sarah's head, which actually looked pretty good. At least it did to someone who had no taste.

"I think we're done," she said, eyeing Becky across the center island. "What do you think?"

"It looks better with the hairs sticking up on top," Becky said.

"I think so too," Annie said. *Solidarity forever*, she thought, the old union protest song spinning through her head. Younger sisters had to stick together and back each other up.

Clearly, Sarah remained unconvinced. She lowered herself from the stool, clapping a hand over her abdomen as if to hold back whatever post-op pain was still lurking there, and hobbled off to the bathroom to take a look. Before she returned, the mudroom door swung open and Gordon and Trevor bounded in. Trevor was as energetic as he'd been after his roller-skating outing last week. "I did real well," he boasted. "Where's Mom? Mom, I did real well. Hey, Aunt Annie! What's all over the floor?"

"Mommy's hair," Becky told him. "Aunt Annie cut it."

Gordon's gaze met Annie's. *Thank you,* he mouthed.

Sarah emerged from the bathroom, her expression pained—whether from the haircut or from her hysterectomy, Annie couldn't tell. "I look like a dyke," she said.

"You look cute," Gordon disputed her. "I like it. Maybe you should have cut your hair short years ago."

"Yeah, right." Sarah scowled.

Trevor gaped at his mother for a moment, then shrugged. "I golfed real well," he reported. "This guy at the country club said I have a natural swing."

"The golf pro," Gordon said. "Our membership fees pay his salary." Annie understood what he was actually saying: that the guy had to compliment Trevor's swing if he hoped to get a nice Christmas bonus from Gordon. She grinned.

"And we rode in a golf cart. Dad let me steer it."

"I want to ride in a golf cart," Becky said. "I don't want to golf, but I want to steer the cart."

"You're too young," Sarah told her.

Annie experienced a pang of sympathy for her niece. She recalled all the times Sarah got to do something fun and interesting when they were growing up, and she was told she was too young when she said she wanted to do that fun, interesting thing too.

"I should go," she said. She didn't like her resentment of Sarah's attitude, the sour mood draped over her like Becky's old bed sheet. She had come here to do Sarah a favor, and Sarah had insulted her. And now Sarah was pulling her older-sibling crap on Becky. Yes, Sarah was very sick. Annie had to cut her a few hundred yards of slack. But still... couldn't she *not* act like a big sister for once? Couldn't she not make Annie feel like...what was Chloe's word for it? A spare.

"Thanks for taking care of Sarah's hair," Gordon said aloud this time.

"Could you sweep the floor before you leave?" Sarah asked Annie. "I can't do that."

Of course Sarah can't do it. She has too much homework, Annie muttered under her breath. But before she could speak—whether to agree to sweep the floor or to tell Sarah to fuck off—Gordon said, "The kids and I can clean up the kitchen."

Annie almost returned his thank-you, then realized she had nothing to thank him for. Cleaning his own damned imported Italian floor tiles instead of demanding that she do it was only reasonable. She had already fulfilled her allotment of required favors for one day.

○ ○ ○

Emmett was sitting on the front steps of her condo when she arrived home. They had a plan for that evening, if ordering takeout and watching something on Netflix constituted a plan. But she had told him she would be out for much of the afternoon, and he had said something about putting in a few hours on a building site, even though today was Saturday. She had been pleasantly surprised by his unusual commitment to his job.

Obviously, he'd put in only a very few hours, if he was lounging on her building's porch at three thirty in the afternoon. For Emmett, commitment was a limited commodity. "Hey," he greeted her as she trudged up the front walk after parking her car. He pushed himself to his feet and gave her a hug which she lacked the energy to return. "Tough day?"

"I'm glad I'm not a hair stylist," she said. If that were her career, she would probably have to sweep the hair clippings off the floor along with everything else. At Tony's Clip Joint, she often saw the stylists pushing brooms around the floor—which was linoleum designed to resemble hardwood and definitely not imported from Italy.

"You did a nice thing for your sister," Emmett pointed out as Annie trudged up the front steps and pulled her key from the pocket of her cargo pants. "You deserve a gold star." He hoisted a ratty-looking backpack from the porch and slid one strap over his shoulder. She eyed the backpack suspiciously, wondering what he'd brought with him. Maybe some toiletries, so he could brush his teeth using his own toothpaste for a change. Maybe a discount coupon for one of the local take-out eateries. Maybe a gift for her.

No, probably not that. "Are you going to give me a gold star?" she asked.

His expression turned lewd. "I'm going to give you something even better."

Sex, she thought, wishing she felt a spark of enthusiasm at the prospect. It would be more fun than having her sister demand that she sweep the kitchen floor, at least.

They went upstairs to her condo. He gave her the gift he always gave her. It was okay. Marginally better than a gum-backed gold foil star, although not as good as a fourteen-karat-gold star on a necklace chain, or a star glittering in the night sky.

Something was seriously wrong with her, she thought as she lay naked in Emmett's arms atop her blanket. The bedroom was dimly lit—she'd closed the shades before getting undressed, as if anyone could possibly spy on them through the windows. Someone with a periscope, perhaps, or someone armed with binoculars in a neighboring building.

She felt sticky, a layer of sweat coating her body. The day was too warm for October, and her condo didn't have central air. The previous owner had left behind a window unit in the living room, but it hissed and clanked whenever Annie turned it on, and it took ages for the cooled air to make the journey down the hall to the bedroom. Besides, turning on the air conditioner in October seemed ecologically sinful.

Had the air conditioning been on in Sarah's house? Who knew? When she and Gordon had bought the place, Sarah had boasted to Annie about the five-zone atmosphere control, about how the temperature of each room could be fine-tuned. And of course, everything had been built with energy conservation in mind, unlike the building housing Annie's condo. The most efficient cooling of her rooms occurred in January, when frigid winter air seeped through cracks and gaps in the window frames.

"So, what are you thinking?" Emmett asked, lazily stroking her arm.

She doubted he would appreciate a truthful answer—what man wanted to learn that the woman he'd just made love to was contemplating the insufficient insulation in her condo? Instead, she lied and said, "Just wondering what you brought in your backpack."

"Nothing important," he said. "A couple of changes of underwear."

Clean underwear *was* important. A couple of changes went beyond important. It implied that he was planning to stay at her condo for longer than tonight. "What's going on with Frank?" she asked. "Is he still screwing around with that woman in your bedroom?"

"Yeah." Emmett sighed deeply, as if his roommate's selfish behavior was a tragedy.

"Why don't you tell him to cut it out?" Annie said. "You're paying rent. You deserve to sleep in your own bed."

"You don't want me to sleep in your bed?" Now he sounded not just tragic but gravely wounded.

She didn't want to hurt Emmett's feelings. He was a good guy. "I don't mind having you in my bed," she said, hoping he would hear the gentle humor in her voice. "I'm just saying, you pay half the rent. Frank needs to show you some respect."

"I'm sure the thing will burn itself out eventually," Emmett said. "In the meantime...here I am."

Here you are, Annie thought, nestling her head more snugly against his shoulder and wishing the glories of true love would blossom inside her. She wanted to love Emmett. But right now, she felt too bitter to think about love, let alone feel it. "My sister was mean to me today," she admitted. "She told me I have no taste and she didn't want me to help her pick out a wig."

"I don't know why you're so nice to her," Emmett said.

"She's going to go bald."

"Lots of people go bald. It's not the end of the world."

Easy for him to say, given the thick shock of hair covering his scalp. "When men go bald, it's no big deal. For women, it's a whole other thing. And besides, she's going to go bald and she's still going to die."

"Lots of people die too."

Lots of people didn't die before their fortieth birthdays, after first going bald due to medical treatments that would ultimately prove futile. Annie felt a pang of sympathy for Sarah so sharp she pressed her hand against her abdomen the way Sarah had when she'd risen from the stool in the kitchen.

And then she remembered Sarah's hair scattered across the floor, swirls and curls, like some sort of abstract art installation. And Sarah's demand that she sweep the floor—after first insulting Annie by telling her she didn't have enough taste to shop for wigs. Annie's sympathy evaporated like the sweat on her slowly cooling skin.

"I'm not nice," she said. Anyone who could resent her sister when her sister had only a forty-percent chance of surviving five years—probably less than forty percent, now that the doctors had found lesions on her other organs—was not a nice person. Annie might not have learned how to dress or walk in a feminine way or shop for wigs from her sister, but she'd learned how to be mean.

"I'm not nice at all," she said.

chapter twelve

"**I** NEED TO DO SOMETHING," Annie told Jamal.

They were seated at a booth in the Dorm. The table was so carved with graffiti, it was a miracle that the thing hadn't dissolved into sawdust ages ago. But somehow, gouges and scratches notwithstanding, it managed to hold Annie's and Jamal's glasses of beer and a platter of hummus and pita chips. The hummus wasn't gourmet quality, but Annie didn't care. She was hungry and thirsty, and she had to *do* something.

"Something as in something specific?" Jamal asked.

She gazed across the table at him. As usual, he was dressed more fashionably than she was, in a snug-fitting knit shirt and a black leather jacket which he'd opened but didn't remove, probably because he knew wearing it made him look extremely cool. His dark, curly hair was almost as short as Sarah's was after Annie had performed barber duty on Saturday, and his smile was easy and just a little perplexed.

"Something as in, if I have to listen to Dean Parisi lecture us about our yield one more time, I will scream."

"If we had a better yield, she'd stop lecturing us," Jamal said as he scooped some hummus onto a pita chip. He popped it into his mouth, chewed, and swallowed. "Today's meeting was seriously awful."

Annie nodded in agreement. "I love my job, but after a day like today I have fantasies about quitting. Just walking out of my office and slamming the door behind me. And I don't want to quit. I can't afford to quit. So I have to do something to make it better."

"Tomorrow might be better," Jamal said. "Maybe we won't have to listen to Evelyn drone on about college fairs anymore."

"Until the next college fair," Annie said, her forehead aching from her frown, or maybe from the iciness of her beer. "Listening to her go on and on about the college fairs she went to yesterday—I mean, did we really need to devote a whole freaking hour of the meeting to that?"

"She was on a roll," Jamal agreed. "I think sending her to those college fairs at high schools is a mistake. She exudes chilly vibes. If I were a high school kid at a college fair, I'd avoid her table just so I wouldn't get frostbite."

"Do high school kids even go to college fairs anymore?" Annie shook her head. "Kids get all their information on their phones, right? The last time I ran the Cabot College table at a college fair, the turnout sucked. Most of the kids were there because it was an excuse to get out of a class. A lot of them were probably thinking, if these colleges were all that wonderful, they wouldn't have someone sitting at a folding table in the gym and telling students how wonderful the colleges were."

"Yeah, probably."

"We should be reaching kids a different way. We need to meet them where they live."

"On their phones?"

"We should do a podcast," Annie said. She had been thinking about it ever since Evelyn and Dean Parisi had monopolized the meeting, Evelyn with her monologue about the college fairs she'd participated in yesterday and Dean Parisi with her standard lecture about boosting Cabot's yield. Not that Annie was especially creative or innovative, not that she had a reputation for proposing brilliant ideas, but really. A folding table covered with brochures, or a podcast? Most kids would choose the podcast.

Jamal's eyebrows shot up. "What did you have in mind?" He appeared intrigued by her idea. Maybe it wasn't as uncreative and un-innovative as she assumed. Maybe she had actually come up with something interesting and worthwhile.

"I don't know." She hadn't quite thought the idea through when it had occurred to her during the meeting. She thought it through now. "You and I could do it. We could invite Cabot students to talk about what they're doing on campus, what they love about the school. Someone from the chamber orchestra. Someone from the soccer team.

Someone doing independent research in chemistry. That kind of thing. And we could tell jokes about the slacker students playing Frisbee in the quad, or the food service offering a dish nicknamed 'train wreck.'"

Jamal chewed thoughtfully on a pita chip. "You're a goddamn genius," he said.

Annie tried not to beam. Had anyone ever called her a goddamn genius before? She didn't think so.

"We could use the studio at the media center," Jamal said. "Book it for a few hours, record a few podcasts, invite some student leaders—"

"And some student followers," Annie said. "Not everyone has to be a leader. I think kids get intimidated when they think everyone's, you know, a first-born."

"What do you mean, a first-born?"

"My friend Chloe told me about birth order," Annie said, not bothering to add that she'd Googled a few articles about birth order the previous morning when she was supposed to be reading essays about the Habitat for Humanity houses applicants to Cabot College had built, or the disabled children they'd tutored, or the inner-city kids they'd taught to swim at summer camp. She'd been curious about whether second-borns were more or less likely to be mean.

What she'd learned was that first-borns tended to be achievers and second-borns tended to be people-pleasers. First-borns had higher IQs, second-borns were less focused. First-borns were heirs, second-borns spares. None of the articles she read actually put it quite so bluntly, but the gist was that first-borns were leaders and second-borns followers.

She'd found nothing about a correlation between birth order and meanness.

"I'm a third-born," Jamal told her. "What does that make me, a leader or a follower?"

"A stray," Annie said. She hadn't read much about third-borns, but this sounded reasonable to her. "You go off in your own direction. You're not following anyone, and you don't care if anyone is following you."

"Bullshit." Jamal laughed. "I want the whole world to be following me." He took a swig of beer, then reached for another pita chip. "So, you're going to pitch this idea to Dean Parisi?"

"I guess. But only if you'll be a part of it. I'm not doing a podcast by myself."

"If you want to share the glory with me," he said, "I'm not going to argue."

○ ○ ○

She was still feeling pretty proud of herself—if not quite deserving of a "goddamn genius" designation—when she and Jamal left the Dorm twenty minutes later. They walked back to the staff parking lot on campus together, then parted ways to find their cars.

Thanks to the time she'd spent nursing her beer with Jamal, rush hour was already winding down. She had just reached the speed limit on Route 9 when her cell phone began humming "Pray For the Dead." Her gaze remaining on the road ahead, she groped in her bag, which sat next to her on the passenger seat, and pulled out the phone. As expected, the screen read *Gilda Baskin.*

Sighing, she swiped the screen. "Mom, can I call you back when I get home? I'm driving."

"You should be home by now. How long does it take you to get home from work?"

That she'd had a drink with a colleague before heading for home was none of her mother's business. "I can't talk while I'm driving."

"You should have one of those hands-free things, the computer in your dashboard. Sarah does."

Sarah had a much newer, much nicer car than Annie's ancient Honda. Reluctantly, she steered into the parking lot of a McDonald's and shifted her car into neutral. "All right," she said, not bothering to conceal her annoyance. "I'm not driving anymore."

"I need you to do a favor for me," her mother said. "Well, really, it's a favor for Sarah. She asked me to pick up some groceries for her while I was shopping for Dad and me, but I can't do it. My schedule is insane. Would you be a sweetheart and pick up these things for Sarah? She's not allowed to drive."

Annie wondered why her mother's schedule was insane. She wasn't in the garden club. She wasn't in the book club. She didn't have a job. "If you have to go shopping for you and Dad, why can't you pick up some things for Sarah too?"

"I would, but I haven't got the time. I figured you could pick these things up. You go shopping all the time."

"I don't go shopping all the time," Annie retorted. "I go shopping Saturday morning, with all the other people who work Monday through Friday and have to go to the supermarket on the weekend."

"That works out perfectly." Gilda sounded pleased. "You'll be at the supermarket on the weekend, so you can pick up a few things for Sarah too. It's not like you have to go out of your way."

"I *do* have to go out of my way. I have to drive the groceries to Sarah's house."

"Annie. Your sister is very sick." Her mother's voice cracked. "If you had children, you'd understand how hard it is for a mother to cope when her daughter is so sick. My heart is breaking. Everyone in my support group says yes, this is what happens. Your heart breaks."

"My heart is breaking too," Annie said.

"It's not the same. When you're a mother, when it's your own child..." Gilda's voice trailed off for a moment. Annie heard what sounded like a damp sigh. "The least you could do for your sister is buy her a quart of milk."

"That's what she wants? A quart of milk?"

"Well, three gallons of low-fat. The kids go through a lot of milk. And a few other items. Sarah sent me a list. I've got it here. Two pounds of antibiotic-free chicken breasts. Romaine lettuce—not iceberg, it's got no food value. It's like chewing on water."

"Mom, I can't write this down. I'm sitting in my car in a McDonald's parking lot."

"You shouldn't eat McDonald's. Their food has too much fat in it. All that fat, it can cause cancer."

Sarah always ate healthy foods, and she'd gotten cancer. Annie thought it best not to point that out to her mother. "I'm not eating here," she said. "I just pulled into the parking lot so I could talk to you."

"Okay." Another sigh, and a sniffle. "I'm glad you're not talking on the phone and driving at the same time. It isn't safe. I couldn't bear to lose you in a car accident when I'm already dealing with Sarah's cancer."

There might have been a compliment in Gilda's words. Then again, Annie's mother might have been saying that she *could* bear to lose Annie if Sarah wasn't battling cancer. Annie decided it was best not to analyze her mother's statement too deeply.

"So, you'll do a little shopping for your sister? She wants organic carrots, Brussels sprouts—also organic. I can't believe Trevor and Becky are eating Brussels sprouts. You never ate them when you were a child."

"You never made them. If you want me to buy this stuff, email me the list. I can't write it down."

"*I* don't want you to buy this stuff. It's for your sister. She'll be so grateful."

This time, the sigh was on Annie's end of the call. She repeated her request that her mother email her the list and said goodbye. Sure, Sarah would be grateful if Annie did her shopping for her. Their mother was the one who ought to be grateful, though. She was the one who was supposed to do Sarah's shopping. She was the one Annie was doing a favor for.

Annie supposed she was also doing a favor for Diana Drucker. Diana got to shop for wigs with Sarah, but not for low-fat milk and Brussels sprouts. Groceries weren't fun, but you didn't need any fashion sense to buy them.

The bottom line was, wig or no wig, fashion sense or no fashion sense, Annie's sister was ill. She couldn't drive. Someone had to buy her groceries for her. It might as well be Annie.

Her schedule wasn't insane, after all. She was just a spare.

chapter thirteen

THE WHEELS ON ANNIE'S SHOPPING CART WHINED as she pushed it out of the supermarket and across the asphalt to her car on Saturday. Annie wanted to whine too. The cart was heavy, one of the wheels kept swiveling sideways, and she was tired.

Emmett had spent the night—he'd spent every night at her condo that week—and she had asked him if he would accompany her to the store. An extra pair of hands would have helped, and his height would have enabled him to reach products on the upper shelves, where the unappetizing, nutritious items were displayed. All the truly tasty food was shelved at child's-eye level, and even though Annie was a grown woman of average height, her gaze always zeroed in on the chocolate chip cookies, the high-fat granola, the obscenely salty ramen noodles, the potato chips.

Of course, Sarah wouldn't want her children to eat those foods, so they didn't appear on the extensive shopping list Annie's mother had emailed her. Only nutritious foods, hard-to-reach foods, top-shelf-in-the-supermarket foods. Annie probably should have been grateful she didn't have to drive up to some farm in New Hampshire to buy the chicken.

Emmett, who seemed to have plenty of free time when it came to hanging out on the front porch of Annie's building, waiting for her to come home, didn't have time to shop with her on Saturday. "The foreman is busting our asses," he told Annie. "He wants the last three houses in the subdivision done before Christmas."

"That makes sense. You don't want to be building houses in a snow storm," Annie pointed out.

"We can do interiors in the winter. He's just being a bastard. I'd help you with the shopping if I could. I don't even know why you're doing this. Can't your sister do her own shopping?"

"She's not allowed to drive," Annie explained.

"She's got a husband."

"He's probably taking the kids bowling or something. He spends his weekends taking them places."

"He should take *you* bowling and make the kids go shopping," Emmett suggested.

Annie hadn't bothered to respond. She had simply kissed Emmett's cheek, pretended she hadn't heard him when he'd asked if he could have her spare key on the palm-tree key ring—in case he finished at work and returned to her condo before she got from her sister's house—and left for the supermarket.

Her own groceries barely filled a quarter of the cart. Sarah's shopping list, which Annie's mother had somehow found the time to type out and send to Annie despite her busy schedule, filled the rest of the cart. Annie managed to wedge all the bags into the trunk of her car, the bags filled with her own groceries at the front so she could access them easily and put them away before she drove on to Sarah's house.

Emmett was gone from the condo when Annie arrived home. She unloaded her bags from the trunk and lugged them up the stairs to her unit, grateful that she didn't have to shop for two growing children on a regular basis. She didn't have to shop for Emmett, either, but she had picked up a few items she knew he liked: a quart of half-and-half for his coffee, a bag of taco chips, a container of vanilla fudge ice cream which, if he didn't want it, she would simply have to eat by herself. Once she had taken care of all the foods that needed refrigeration, she raced back downstairs to her car to deliver Sarah's groceries before they melted or spoiled. Not that it was so hot today, but it was warm enough that a tub of ice cream could melt in a car's trunk—if ice cream had appeared on Sarah's shopping list. It hadn't, but the organic, antibiotic-free chicken might spoil if it spent too much time unrefrigerated.

Sarah answered when Annie rang the bell beside the beveled-glass sidelight of the Adlers' imposing front door. Sarah looked like shit—Annie was getting used to her beautiful older sister not looking so beautiful anymore—but today she looked like shit in a stylish wig. Its color was almost an exact match for her high-lighted and low-lighted auburn hair, and it was styled in a sassy bob that seemed reasonably chic to Annie's no-fashion-sense eyes. The face below the wig was pale and drawn, the lips chapped and the eyes rimmed with red. "You'll have to bring everything in," Sarah said by way of greeting. "Gordon and the kids are out, and I'm still not allowed to lift anything heavier than a teaspoon."

"I live to serve," Annie muttered, striding back down the front walk and pressing the trunk release button on her car key.

It took her four trips to haul all the groceries inside. At least she didn't have to lug them up a flight of stairs, as she would have had to at her condo. But the distance from the curb to Sarah's kitchen was fairly long, thanks to the size of the house and the length of the flagstone front walk, which was lined with leathery green rhododendron shrubs and littered with fallen leaves from nearby oak and maple trees.

"Do you want me to put everything away?" Annie asked, once all the bags were lined up like soldiers on the center island.

"If you wouldn't mind," Sarah said, lowering herself gingerly onto one of the chairs in the breakfast nook. "Sorry I can't help. That first round of chemo wrung me out. I was puking for days afterward."

"Didn't they give you something for the nausea?"

"Whatever they gave me didn't work. The Ezekiel bread goes in the freezer," she directed Annie. "We use it only a couple of slices at a time. The cans of garbanzo beans—you got the unsalted ones, right?—go in that cabinet. The milk goes in the fridge, of course. Can you put one six-pack of the energy drinks in the fridge too? That's the only stuff I can keep down. It tastes better cold."

Annie rummaged through the bags until she found the three six-packs of energy drinks, packaged as if they were something delicious, like beer.

As she carried one of the six-packs to the fridge, Sarah groaned. "Is that strawberry?"

Annie looked at the six-pack. "Yeah. I got one of each flavor—chocolate, vanilla, and strawberry."

"I only like the chocolate. The other flavors made me vomit."

Actually, it was the chemo that made her vomit. "Mom didn't specify what flavor to buy, so I bought one of each."

Sarah shook her head. Her neck looked thin to Annie, barely sturdy enough to hold up her stylishly bewigged skull. "I can't drink those other flavors. Just thinking about them makes me want to throw up."

Annie set the strawberry six-pack on the island and carried the chocolate six-pack to the refrigerator.

"I told Mom, just chocolate," Sarah insisted.

"She failed to pass along that information," Annie said.

Sarah sighed. "She's an idiot."

"She's very busy," Annie said, sarcasm layering her words. "She can't be bothered with details."

"I'll just skip her and send my shopping list directly to you next time," Sarah said.

You could send it to Diana Drucker, Annie thought. She had to concede that Diana had helped Sarah choose a nice wig, quite possibly a nicer one than Annie would have recommended. Diana would probably choose nicer chicken and eggs and Ezekiel bread, too, if Sarah asked her to buy the Adler family groceries. But then, Diana was Sarah's friend, not her kid sister. Not the family member designated to take care of everything no one else in the family wanted to take care of.

"Those other six-packs aren't opened," Sarah said. "You can take them back to the store and exchange them for chocolate. It's the only thing I can stomach these days. You'll do that for me, won't you?"

Of course Annie would do it. She was that designated family member. And Sarah was sixty-percent going to die.

Unfortunately, Annie hadn't done her shopping at the supermarket nearest Sarah's home. She had done it at the supermarket near her own home, which meant she had to drive all the way there and back. She was tempted to walk into Sarah's local supermarket and try to return the vanilla and strawberry drinks there, claiming she had lost the receipt, but what if they didn't sell that brand at Sarah's supermarket?

What the hell. Annie had nothing better to do than to drive back and forth with six-packs of energy drinks. If she finished this task early, she would just wind up going home, where she would eat the vanilla fudge ice cream straight out of the tub while writing down brilliant questions to ask the Cabot College students she and Jamal interviewed when they recorded their podcasts next week.

Dean Parisi had loved the podcast idea when Annie had presented it at the team's meeting yesterday. Harold had scoffed at it—scoffing was one of his major talents—and Evelyn had asked if she could do the podcast and have Annie do the college fairs at high schools instead. Dean Parisi claimed that since the podcast was Annie's idea, she should create it herself.

"How are you going to publicize it?" Evelyn had asked. "How are you going to get high school students to listen to it?"

"That can be your focus," Dean Parisi had told Evelyn. "Come up with some ideas for how we can get high school kids to listen to this thing."

"*I* don't listen to podcasts," Harold had groused.

"You're not a high school kid," Dean Parisi had said.

"Let's talk to Brittany," Annie had suggested. "She'll know how to get the word out."

Reliving that meeting in her mind cheered Annie up as she drove back to the supermarket, the rejected vanilla and strawberry six-packs occupying the passenger seat. She had come up with a good idea. Dean Parisi had thought it was a good idea. Brittany had actually clapped her hands and emitted a blissful chirp when Annie had asked for her assistance. "We should link it to the school website," she'd babbled, "and do an email blast to students and alums. And to high school guidance counselors. This is going to be fabulous!"

Annie would need to come up with cool topics to discuss on the podcast. She was hoping Jamal could help her there. He was so much cooler than she was.

Exchanging the energy drinks at the supermarket was a process just bureaucratic enough to dampen Annie's mood. There were no other chocolate six-packs on the shelves, and the woman at the customer service counter had to page someone named Stuart to check the stock that hadn't been shelved yet. After eight long minutes, two six-packs of chocolate were located, and Annie left the store feeling grouchy.

Her condo was only ten minutes away. A few therapeutic spoonfuls of ice cream might cheer her up.

She drove home, exhaled in relief that Emmett wasn't sitting on the front steps of the building, and realized she wasn't particularly hungry—for ice cream or any other food. Instead, she retrieved her swimsuit. If she was going to be Sarah's overworked, underappreciated gofer, she was damned well going to spend some time in the hot tub. She'd earned it.

She tossed the swimsuit, a comb, and her flip-flops into her duffel bag and hurried down the stairs and outside to her car. She wanted to be gone before Emmett showed up. Which wasn't a particularly romantic way to think about the guy who had spent the past week in her bed, but there it was. Emmett was Emmett. Easy on the eyes, good-natured, and terrific in bed, but... not a world-beater.

Right now, she didn't want to think about his sexual prowess or his passivity with his roommate. She didn't want to think about anything at all—not Emmett, not her sister's illness, not even her goddamn genius when it came to the podcast. She just wanted to splash her way into the hot tub and think about nothing.

When she rang the bell at her sister's house this time, Gordon answered the door. "I bought the wrong flavored energy drink," she explained. "Sarah asked me to exchange it for chocolate."

"You didn't have to do that," Gordon said.

"Yeah, I did. She said the other flavors made her throw up."

Gordon gestured toward her duffel bag. "Are you spending the night?" he asked.

"No, but I'd like some time in the hot tub." She felt strong and brave saying that. Maybe she should give Emmett some lessons in how to assert himself.

"Sure. Come on in."

Handing Gordon the bag containing the drinks, she followed him inside. She was on a roll, she thought happily—first coming up with an excellent idea at work and then demanding and receiving some hot-tub time at Sarah's.

"Go on upstairs and change," Gordon told her, angling his head toward the bridal staircase. "I'll turn on the hot tub."

She climbed the curving stairs, trying not to feel guilty that, at least right now, she loved her brother-in-law more than her sister. He could afford to be pleasant and accommodating, after all. He hadn't spent the past few days throwing up. He wasn't among the potentially doomed sixty percent. Nor had he gotten hit by a car while crossing the street.

In the guest room, she found the bathrobe—*her* bathrobe, she was beginning to think of it—hanging from the hook attached to the bathroom door. She carried it into the bedroom and saw Becky standing in the doorway. "Aunt Annie!" Becky shrieked.

Annie opened her arms and Becky catapulted herself at Annie for a hug.

"I didn't know you were here! We just got home. Daddy took us to this museum where they have lots of butterflies. It was so pretty. One of them landed on my nose. Daddy took a picture of it with his phone. And we had ice cream and I didn't drip any on myself. Are you going in the hot tub?"

"I am," Annie said. "I did a favor for your mother, and now I'm going to relax in the hot tub."

"Can I go in the hot tub with you?"

"Ask your dad." She wasn't sure whether Sarah would grant Becky permission to go in the tub, but Gordon seemed to be a soft touch when it came to his kids. "And then go get changed into a swimsuit. That's what I'm going to do."

By the time Annie descended the back stairs to the kitchen and stepped through the door to the patio, her flip-flops clapping against the decorative stones, Gordon had removed the hot tub's cover and turned on the motor. The water churned and foamed, but the air was warm enough that Annie didn't see any vapor rising from the surface.

She did see Becky, dressed in a cute pink two-piece that didn't have any words about female power stitched onto them. Becky's hair was tied back into a crooked ponytail, and she had a towel wrapped around her neck. She peered up at Gordon, who was instructing her on safety and proper behavior in the hot tub. "Remember," he said. "No swimming. No splashing. You sit and let the water bubble around you."

"I know," she said, nodding solemnly. "I'll be careful."

"Stick your toe in. Let me know if it's too hot."

She poked her toe into the water. "It's not too hot."

"Okay. You can go in. Carefully."

Becky draped her towel over a rack in the wall of the wooden hut that housed the hot tub's mechanics, and then settled gracefully into the water. She gave her father a big smile, but her eyes filled with tears.

Annie hurried over to the tub, dipped her toe into the water, and said, "It's too hot for me." She knew Becky was too proud to admit that the water was practically scalding. Annie would protect her niece's honor by pretending that Gordon had to adjust the temperature for her, not Becky.

He did, and Annie shed her robe and joined Becky in the tub. Becky looked relieved as the water cooled down a few degrees.

Satisfied that Becky was behaving decorously, Gordon wandered back into the house. Annie leaned back against the tiled wall of the tub and sighed. She would gladly exchange as many cases of energy drinks as Sarah asked her to if she could be guaranteed a half hour in the tub afterward. Well, maybe not gladly, but she'd do it for this soothing, relaxing soak.

She opened her eyes and found Becky gazing earnestly at her. "Tell me more about the butterflies," she said. Not quite a podcast question, but she could sense that Becky wanted to talk, if only Annie would do her the honor of asking her something.

Becky talked. About the butterflies, about the woman her dad had paid to let them in—"she had pink hair and these glittery fingernails, with little butterflies painted on them"—and how afterward her dad took her and Trevor to an ice cream stand that hadn't yet closed for the winter, and Becky got Moose Tracks ice cream, which was like ice cream with peanut butter cups stirred in. "I wish my mom came," she said. "But if she did, we wouldn't get ice cream. She would make us eat fruit. Like pineapples or something."

"Prunes, maybe," Annie suggested.

Becky wrinkled her little nose. "Eew. Yeah. Prunes."

A noise across the patio caught Annie's attention. The kitchen door flew open and Trevor hurled himself out and across the patio, bare-chested and clad in baggy swim trunks. "Look out, world!" he shrieked before doing a modified cannonball into the hot tub.

"No splashing!" Becky scolded. "Daddy said!"

Trevor surfaced, sputtering and laughing. "This is cold! We should turn up the temperature."

"It's hot enough," Annie said, feeling protective toward Becky. It wasn't fair that Trevor got to splash after his sister had been instructed not to. He wouldn't get to determine the water temperature as well.

"Hey, Aunt Annie," Trevor belatedly greeted her. "We went to a butterfly museum today."

"Becky was just telling me."

"And we had ice cream too."

"She told me."

Trevor glared at Becky. Evidently, he resented her having scooped him on all the headlines of the day's news.

Still, he did settle down on the bench, halfway between Annie and Becky. "I wish every day could be Saturday," he said. "Basketball starts next week."

The kitchen door opened again, and this time Gordon emerged, clad like Trevor in swim trunks. "Is there room for me?" he asked.

Annie shifted slightly on the bench, leaving a wide space for him. He eased himself in, settled on the bench, and sighed.

"How is Sarah?" Annie thought to ask.

"She's taking a nap. She's got a protein shake on the night table next to her."

Annie didn't ask any more questions. She didn't want to discuss Sarah with Gordon in front of the children, in case he had to inform her about things he didn't want them to know. As long as Sarah was all right by herself, resting, not vomiting, armed with an energy drink, all was well.

Annie slid lower into the water, letting it lap at her chin. Across the tub, Becky and Trevor engaged in a debate about which were prettier, the monarch butterflies or the luna butterflies. Next to her, Gordon sighed again, and then exchanged a smile with her.

As if this was his family. As if they were somehow whole, all together, enjoying the water's soothing massage.

As if Sarah wasn't dying.

chapter fourteen

FOR THEIR INAUGURAL PODCAST GUEST, Annie lined up Douglas Ryerson, a stocky, smiling young man who was the president of the Cabot College Student Government. On the simple studio set they'd arranged—Annie and Jamal seated left and right in front of a navy-blue curtain, both of them wearing Cabot College sweatshirts, with their guest perched on a third chair between them—Douglas seemed to fill the space like a multi-volume encyclopedia, with Annie and Jamal as his matching bookends. He talked as if he believed each of his words was a priceless treasure. He laughed at his own jokes. He spoke in a booming, robust voice, as if addressing a political rally in a football stadium.

But he said all the right things. "Cabot is the best school in the world," he declared. "And for a Division Three school, our teams are fantastic. Can I talk about the rugby team? Technically, it's a club sport, but man, our team is amazing. I'm on the boys' rugby team, by the way."

Jamal asked excellent questions. But Annie's questions were good too. "What made you choose Cabot?" she asked, and Douglas went on at length about the beautiful campus.

He also mentioned that he'd talked to some Cabot students while he was a high-schooler taking a campus tour, and they had all told him the party scene was awesome. "And also safe," he added prudently.

Jamal asked him about student governance, and he had plenty to say about that, as well, expounding on the improvements he'd shepherded through, none of which seemed particularly earth-shattering to Annie, although Douglas was clearly quite proud of them. "We negotiated with food service for a wider variety of breads in the dining halls.

Have you ever eaten Portuguese sweet bread? It's so good—and thanks to the student senate, we now have that available in all our dining halls. Monkey bread, too, although that's more like a dessert. You ever try that? It's Hawaiian. And we established a new policy about hanging things on the walls in the dorm rooms. We increased the number of student senators per dorm from two to three, so we'd have more voices and viewpoints in the senate. Student input is so important," Douglas said. "And I've got to say, participating in the student government is a great stepping stone for entering politics in real life."

He was obviously destined to become a politician, Annie concluded, then amended the thought. He already *was* a politician.

They taped a half-hour podcast with Douglas, then taped another half hour with Kalindra Sharma, who was the concertmaster of the school's orchestra. She talked a lot about music, and then noted that she was on Cabot's girls' rugby team, which she claimed was awesome.

"We're going to attract a lot of rugby players," Jamal murmured once Kalindra left the studio.

"Let them all apply," Annie responded. "It'll improve our yield."

They interviewed Martin Blitzberg, who was active in the theater program and burst into a passionate chorus of "Seasons of Love" from *Rent* in the middle of their discussion. He, apparently, did not play rugby, though he had an excellent voice. And when he was done belting out the hit show's theme song, even the technician who was recording the podcast applauded. Annie and Jamal also interviewed Mare Soppersmith, a religious studies major who talked about the many faith organizations on campus and her own experiences as a Bahá'í practitioner. She admitted to playing rugby her first two years at Cabot, but had to quit the team after she suffered a separated shoulder during a particularly grueling game against Vassar.

"Maybe we should edit that out," Jamal muttered after Mare had left the studio. "We don't want to scare off any rugby players."

"Or we can add a postscript about the superb health services available on campus," Annie said.

Jamal made a face and shook his head. He was right. The college infirmary, no matter how highly touted, was not going to attract applicants. "What is it with rugby?" he asked as they signed out of the studio. "When I was an undergrad here, I played ultimate Frisbee."

"I played Monopoly," Annie told him. "It was a great game. You could drink *while* you were playing it. You didn't have to wait until the end of the game before you popped open a beer." Actually, some of those late-night Monopoly games had been pretty cutthroat, with players accusing one another of being capitalistic assholes for overbuilding hotels on Boardwalk, or pinko commie dupes for creating joint ownership agreements for the railroads. Annie learned more about economics theory during those games than she did in her Econ-101 class.

"So, what happens now?" Jamal asked as they exited the media studies building and entered the quad. The late afternoon was chilly and overcast, but several students tossed a Frisbee back and forth across the expanses of dying grass and scattered leaves. Annie tried to recall if she'd ever seen Jamal playing Frisbee when she'd been a student. They had overlapped on campus, but she had hung out with the Monopoly kids, not the Frisbee kids. Besides, she probably would have been intimidated by his coolness then. She still was a little intimidated by it.

"I guess we'll listen to the podcasts and edit out that bit about Mare's shoulder injury. And then we'll broadcast them a week apart. Brittany said she'd figure that part out."

"And in the meantime, we'll make more podcasts?"

"Let's see how the first four are received. If they get some traction, sure."

"I think it's a brilliant idea," he said.

Annie laughed. "The word 'brilliant' has never been attached to anything I've done."

"Oh, come on." He must have thought she was being falsely modest.

"My sister is brilliant," she explained. "I live in her shadow."

"How's she doing?" he asked. Her colleagues knew about Sarah's cancer, but not about her odds of surviving.

Annie sighed. "Not good. The chemo is hard on her. She's got a gorgeous wig, though."

"I'm sorry you're going through this," Jamal said.

"I'm not going through anything," Annie argued. "Sarah is going through everything." She recalled Chloe's insistence on drinking a toast to her instead of Sarah. Why did people think Annie was the one who needed comforting? Unless she got hit by a car crossing the street, she was doing fine.

Except for all the errands she had to run. Except for her mother's frequent phone calls, during which she moaned about her breaking heart and her staggering grief. Except for her niggling worry about Becky, who didn't get to splash in the hot tub on Saturday, even though Trevor did.

Except for her boyfriend. She really did like Emmett, but when he'd returned to her condo Saturday evening after work, he had carried a few more of his personal items in a paper bag, as if he were a homeless person. And he hadn't showered before coming. Instead, he showered in her bathroom, using her soap and her shampoo and her towels. One of the items in his paper bag, she noted, was a beard trimmer.

How long was he planning to stay? When was Frank going to come up with a new arrangement for his trysts with his lady friend, who was alleged to be just a quick fling but was apparently still shagging Frank in the bedroom he was supposed to be sharing with Emmett?

Walking back to the admissions building, tuning out the Frisbee players, the students racing along the walkways to get to late-afternoon classes, and the students who weren't racing because they were dreaming or stoned or searching for the last few vibrantly colored leaves among all the brown foliage that marked the final stages of autumn, Annie shot a quick text to Chloe: *Dorm, 5:30?* In less than a minute, Chloe texted back: *Yes.*

Annie turned to Jamal. She didn't know much about his life outside of work, whether he was married and a father of three, whether he had a girlfriend—or a boyfriend—to go home to. She did know that he occasionally joined her for a post-work drink at the Dorm. "I'm meeting a friend at the Dorm at 5:30," Annie said. "Want to join us?"

To her great pleasure, Jamal said, "Sounds good."

They reached the quaint, gabled admissions building at the end of the quad and entered. "We are podcast stars!" Jamal bellowed, startling a couple of teenagers and their mothers who were sitting in the reception area, waiting for a tour.

Brittany grinned. Her smile made the already-well-lit room seem ten times brighter. "It went well?"

"We recorded four podcasts," Jamal said. "Did you know Annie Baskin is a freaking star?"

"I'm not a star," Annie said, feeling her cheeks grow hot. Blushing was not something she did very often; she briefly wondered if she was coming down with a fever. "It went well, but we might want to edit the podcasts a little before they go live."

"Very little," Jamal said. "Just that bull-hickey about a shoulder injury." He smiled at the prospective students who, not surprisingly, seemed to think Jamal was seriously cool, even though he was wearing a Cabot College sweatshirt. "I can't guarantee that if you attend Cabot—if you're lucky enough to be accepted to this fine institution of higher learning—you will never injure your shoulder," he told them. "But what's a shoulder injury when you've got the chance to spend four years on this magnificent campus, learning from the finest faculty in New England, if not the entire country?"

"Jamal Brockett and Annie Baskin are two of our admissions counselors," Brittany said sweetly. The mothers looked mildly alarmed, but their offspring appeared intrigued. "They're launching a podcast to spread the word about Cabot." Aiming her dazzling smile at the teenagers, she said, "You'd better get your applications in early. Once these podcasts go live, we're going to be inundated with applications."

"Let's take the tour first," one of the mothers said.

"And find out some more about the shoulder injuries," the other mother added.

Annie glared at Jamal, who grinned back at her. "The school has wonderful health care services," he told the mothers. They looked marginally less alarmed.

Jamal took Annie's arm and led her out of the reception area. "Come on," he said. "Let's go tell Wanda Parisi we rock."

Annie wasn't sure Dean Parisi would know what that meant. She might think Annie and Jamal had gone dancing or something.

But Annie liked hearing Jamal claim that she rocked. She had never thought of herself as rocking before. Or being a star. Or being brilliant.

Yeah. She liked it.

chapter fifteen

CHLOE JOINED ANNIE AND JAMAL AT THE DORM fifteen minutes after they'd claimed a booth near the back of the pub. The table's top was carved like a stone panel of ancient Egyptian hieroglyphics, and somewhere in the distance, beneath the din of voices fogging the air, Annie discerned music playing, those pleasant songs that were not quite rock 'n' roll and not quite country and western. She and Jamal had already ordered and received their drinks—bourbon for him, and Merlot for her, filled precisely to the line on the glass—but before they could take their first sips, Annie's phone pinged, announcing a text.

"Excuse me," she muttered, pulling it out of her purse. *Where R U?* Emmett messaged her.

Did she have to check in with him before going out for an after-work drink with her friends? Usually not, but right now he was probably pacing the front porch of her condo building, waiting for her to let him inside. If it were September, she wouldn't care. He would be warm on the porch. He'd probably order a pizza and sit on the front steps, eating it while he waited for her. But now it was early November, and the sun had set twenty minutes ago. The air was chilly and raw, and she hadn't given him her spare key on the palm-tree key chain. So he was probably cold.

Not that that would stop him from ordering a pizza and devouring it while he waited for her to come home.

He wouldn't be outside her building, with or without a pizza to keep him company, if he told his damned roommate to move his X-rated activities out of the bedroom the two men shared.

Work thing, she texted back to Emmett, then stuffed her phone into her bag. She wasn't going to get into a text debate with him. She wasn't going to justify her decision to go to the Dorm to celebrate Jamal's and her first day of recording podcasts. She was going to drink her wine with Jamal—and with Chloe, whom she saw working her way through the crowd that clogged the room between the front door and the bar, searching the tables until she spotted Annie. Emmett could freeze, or he could go to his own apartment and stake his claim on the bedroom. His choice.

Unwrapping the muffler from her neck, Chloe settled onto the bench next to Annie, across from Jamal. She unzipped her jacket, shrugged out of it, and launched into her familiar diatribe about the impossibility of finding a parking space on Leverett Street. "But you must have found one," Jamal argued gently, "because you're here. So it wasn't impossible. Hi, I'm Jamal Brockett."

"Jamal, Chloe. Chloe, Jamal," Annie introduced them, gesturing from one to the other with her hand. "Hurry up and order, Chloe. We have to drink a toast."

A server approached their table. Chloe requested a glass of Pinot Grigio and an order of what the Dorm called "Pretzel Fondue," which was a heaping bowl of mini pretzels accompanied by some sort of warm cheesy dip. "Coming right up, hon," the server said before waltzing away.

"I'm famished," Chloe said. "I didn't have lunch today. A stomach bug is making the rounds at the residence, so we're in lockdown." She proceeded to explain to Jamal what she did, where she worked, and why when one of the residents got sick, all the residents had to be confined in their own rooms until the threat of an epidemic passed. When everyone was confined, she told him, the entire staff—including Chloe and the other employees in the business office—needed to supplement the dining room staff, delivering meals to each resident and clearing the trays once they'd been emptied.

"Let's not talk about stomach bugs while we're pigging out on cheesy pretzels," Jamal suggested, giving Chloe a bright smile. "Did you know your friend Annie is a natural at podcasts?"

"There was nothing natural about the podcast," Annie protested.

Chloe dismissed Annie's comment with a sharp elbow to her side. "You smoked it, huh?"

"She did," Jamal said. "You want to be on our podcast?" He eyed Annie, then aimed his gaze back at Chloe. "Are you a Cabot alum? Maybe we can do a podcast with an alum. Have her talk about how valuable her Cabot degree is."

"Number one, I didn't graduate from Cabot College," Chloe told him. "Number two, I'm not sure how valuable my college degree is, if my job is all about serving old people their lunches during a stomach-bug lockdown."

She and Jamal continued bantering, engaging in the light, vague flirting that often occurred between people meeting for the first time. Annie wasn't sure Chloe was Jamal's type—in all honesty, she wasn't quite sure what Jamal's type was, although a few times last spring, a woman who looked a little like a young Michelle Obama had stopped by his office at the end of the day and left the admissions building with him. She might have been one of his sisters or his cousin or just a friend. But they'd made such a cute couple, Annie had figured there was something romantic going on between them. However, the Michelle Obama woman hadn't shown up at the office since the start of the new school term, so if there had been something romantic going on between them last spring, it didn't seem to be going on between them now.

Then again, for all Annie knew, Jamal might have someone who looked a little like a young Barack Obama waiting at home for him. He didn't emit gay vibes, but he really did know how to dress.

Sarah knew how to dress, too, and she wasn't gay. Lots of straight people knew how to dress. Just because Annie was apparel-challenged didn't mean anything about anyone's sexual inclinations.

While Jamal and Chloe argued playfully about various TV shows, movies, and musicians and munched on cheese-dipped pretzels, Annie ruminated about her well-dressed sister. Did Sarah ever go out for drinks with her friends after work? Well, of course not—she didn't work, at least not in the nine-to-five sense. But she and Diana Drucker, or Sarah's colleagues on the library board, or the mothers of Trevor's and Becky's soccer teammates... They probably went out sometimes. Not to a place like the Dorm, which was much too grungy for someone like Sarah and where pretzel fondue was one of the highlights on the menu, but to some elegant club where they could sit on curved, well upholstered leather banquettes and sip exotic cocktails in crystal glasses that didn't have fill lines etched onto them. Maybe they would talk about movies and TV shows, but more likely they would talk about their children and their husbands and which salon had the best selection of nail polish colors. Or they would talk about how funny Annie was, while Annie was off performing some favor for Sarah. Sarah would reminisce about how Annie had dragged her and her bridesmaids to an unfashionable spa salon to get their nails done, and she and her friends would all burst into snarky laughter, then take delicate sips of their cosmos and appletinis and nibble on tiny crab cakes and bite-size lobster quiches.

Sarah would never go slumming in a place like the Dorm. She was too classy. Too tasteful. Too perfect.

If Sarah use to indulge in girls' nights with her friends at snazzy, jazzy watering holes in the past, she would probably never get to do so in the future. With or without her wig, she would never get to hang out with her stylish pals, drinking expensive drinks and snacking on expensive hors d'oeuvres in a club with glass-topped tables and atmospheric lighting and ambient background music. For whatever time she had left, Sarah would be drinking chocolate energy drinks, because that was what you did when you were getting chemo to treat a lethal form of cancer.

The realization that Sarah would likely never go out clubbing with her friends again tore through Annie like a hot bullet, burning and biting her flesh at the same time. What kind of monster was she, to be thinking bitchy thoughts about her sister when her sister was dying?

A low sob escaped her, causing her diaphragm to spasm. Jamal and Chloe stopped chattering and stared at her. "Are you okay?" Chloe asked.

"No," Annie said as another sob engulfed her. She was a horrible person, resenting Sarah for being perfect, for being rich and chic and surrounding herself with rich, chic friends. For living in a fancy mansion and being married to a fancy lawyer and raising two fancy children. And Annie was a horrible person for leaving Emmett stranded on the front porch of her building, getting frostbite.

She was way beyond imperfect. She was petty and nasty, and her sister was going to die.

Annie cried. Chloe wrapped an arm around Annie's shoulders and rested Annie's head against her ample bosom. Jamal stared at her from the other side of the table, his expression that blend of alarm and anxiety that some men got when they were in the presence of a weeping woman. *Don't worry*, she wanted to tell him. *Women do this sometimes. Nobody's asking you to fix it.*

After a minute, she wound down. This was the first time she had cried since hearing Sarah's prognosis. She had been tough, she'd been stoic, she'd found fault with her sister. But she had never actually thought about how Sarah was dying, how she would depart from the world and never return. How Annie would no longer have a sister.

It would be just her alone, trying to figure out what to wear, how to behave, how to sit properly on a playground swing or walk properly down a high school corridor. How to deal with their mother. If their father ever went wacky, if one IRS Schedule C too many pushed him over the edge, Annie would have to deal with him alone too. But mostly she would have to deal with her mother, without any support from Sarah. She wouldn't be able to phone her sister and say, "You'll never guess what Mom did now!" and laugh with someone as familiar with Gilda Baskin as Annie was.

"I'm sorry," she finally managed to say as she mopped her tear-drenched face with a Dorm cocktail napkin.

Jamal attempted a joke. "I thought our podcasts went really well."

"They did." She sniffled, then forced a tepid smile. "It just hit me..." She released a tremulous sigh. Could she admit to these friends that she had finally, genuinely, acknowledged that her sister was dying and she herself was a bad person?

"Your sister, right?" Chloe said helpfully. "She's going to be okay."

"No, she's not."

"Well, look." Chloe used her own napkin to dab at a few tears that had skittered all the way down past Annie's chin. "You shouldn't grieve over her if she's not even gone. And anyway, you could get hit by a car crossing the street."

"There's a happy thought," Annie muttered. Why did people say that in these circumstances? Were you supposed to be cheered by the understanding that you could beat someone else in a race toward death?

Chloe turned to Jamal. "We're younger sisters of spectacular older siblings," she informed him. "We're spares. Also-rans. How about you?"

"I'm not anybody's sister," he said, his lips twitching into a mischievous grin.

Chloe smiled back. Annie was still too soggy to join their smile-fest. "Birth order, Jamal," Chloe clarified. "Are you the spectacular older brother or the also-ran younger brother?"

"I'm the third of five," he said, "and the only brother."

"You have four sisters?"

"The only boy out of five, and spoiled rotten," he said before dipping a pretzel into the cheese and popping it into his mouth.

"You are not spoiled rotten," Annie argued. She was feeling a little more human again.

"Neither are you," he told her. "We're just who we are, that's all. You aren't an also-ran. 'Spectacular' is a subjective judgment."

"Wow," Chloe murmured to Annie, loudly enough for Jamal to hear. "He sounds smart. He must be a Cabot College alumnus."

Jamal laughed. Annie managed another weak smile. Cabot, after all, wasn't Ivy League. It wasn't Brown, where her spectacular older sister had studied. Cabot's students were smart, but they weren't *smart*. They weren't Ivy Leaguers like Sarah.

Douglas Ryerson claimed Cabot was the best school in the world, which it wasn't. But it was what it was. Like her. She was who she was. Not someone's sometimes clumsy, sometimes ice-cream-stained, sometimes put-upon younger sister, not an also-ran, but herself.

Maybe Annie ought to stop resenting Sarah's spectacularness. Annie couldn't help being imperfect, and Sarah couldn't help being perfect. They were who they were.

But maybe Annie ought to be a better version of who she was. Maybe she ought to stop hating her sister before she lost her. Maybe she ought to try to be a little bit nicer.

chapter sixteen

EMMETT WAS, INDEED, SITTING ON THE FRONT PORCH when Annie steered up the driveway to her condo's parking area an hour later. An empty pizza box lay on the painted plank flooring beside him. He had on his fleece-lined denim jacket and a brown muffler that a former girlfriend had knitted for him a couple of Christmases ago. If Annie was a better person—and she honestly intended to become one—she would knit him a muffler this year for Christmas.

First, however, she would have to learn how to knit.

"I'm sorry," she said, because she was determined to be nice. If she couldn't be spectacular like Sarah, at least she could be considerate. "We had an after-work thing. It was kind of...mandatory." Sometimes a little dishonesty was nicer than the truth.

"It's okay," Emmett said, rising to his feet and folding the pizza box shut. "I ate."

"You must be freezing." She pulled her mail from the mailbox labeled #2 and unlocked the front door.

"The pizza kept me warm," he said as he followed her inside.

They climbed the stairs and entered her unit. Glimpsing the grease-stained pizza box, which featured on its lid a caricature of an Italian chef, complete with a curling mustache and a floppy chef's toque, Annie realized she was starving. Jamal and Chloe had scarfed down most of the pretzel fondue; after her meltdown, Annie hadn't had much appetite. She'd managed to finish her Merlot, and now she was sorely aware of her need for solid food.

She wasn't going to order another pizza. Instead, after shedding her jacket, she flipped through her mail—an invitation to join a fitness center, an ad from a chimney cleaning service, and a catalog from an absurdly pricy clothing company that Sarah had suggested she shop at—she swung open the refrigerator in search of something she could nibble on. She pulled out a half-consumed package of whole-wheat bread. No fancy Ezekiel bread for her. No Portuguese sweet bread or monkey bread either. But she had a jar of peanut butter somewhere, and a jar of honey. That would work.

Could she eat her sandwich in front of Emmett? Would that be rude? She was trying to be nice.

"Would you like a sandwich?" she asked him.

"Not now." He pulled her into his arms. "I need to warm up a little. Wanna thaw me out?"

Be nice, she reminded herself, letting him lead her out of the kitchen and down the hall to the bedroom. It wasn't as if she was going to waste away to a skeleton if she had sex with him before eating her sandwich. And since she wasn't going to give him her spare house key—she didn't intend to be *that* nice—the least she could do was thaw him out.

○ ○ ○

Afterward, her stomach growling impatiently as they lay in bed, she contemplated telling Emmett about the podcast. Would it be nice to share her work day with him? He hadn't asked her what she'd been do-ing all afternoon, or why she had been obliged to attend an after-work event. Was it nice to tell someone about her work day if he hadn't indi-cated any interest in hearing about it?

If she was going to be nice, she ought to inquire about his work day, instead. "So, how are things at the subdivision?" she asked. "Are you going to finish the houses by Christmas?"

"I think so," Emmett said. "God, your bed is comfortable."

So much for his work. Should she keep the conversation going by mentioning the podcast? Telling him her colleague thought she was a star?

No. Emmett had dropped out of UMass halfway through his first year there. He thought the fact that Annie worked at a reputable pri-vate college was a positive thing; it enabled her to earn enough money to afford a condo with a comfortable bed and without a roommate to quarrel with over the use of the bedroom. But he wasn't terribly impressed with academics or scholarship. He would be bored listening to her talk about Douglas Ryerson's political aspirations, Kalindra Sharma's violin virtuosity, Martin Blitzberg's show-biz pizzazz, and Mare Soppersmith's Bahá'í faith.

"Would you like a sandwich?" Annie asked, instead. "I'm going to make one for myself."

"Sure."

He remained in bed, relaxing, while she rose. She gathered her scattered clothing and tossed it onto a chair. Sarah would have taken the time to hang her blouse and slacks in the closet, but then, Sarah had organized closets and high-quality clothing.

Annie slid her arms through the sleeves of her bathrobe, tied the sash around her waist, and padded barefoot down the hall to the kitchen. As soon as she entered, she saw the message light flashing on her phone, which she had left on the counter next to her junk mail.

She tapped the message icon and listened to the message: "Annie, it's Mom. Call me."

Sighing, Annie obeyed. "Hi, Mom," she said, her belly grumbling again, pleading *Feed me!* in stomach language.

"Where were you?" her mother demanded. "I called you several times."

I was having sex with Emmett. "I was busy," she said, wondering if her new resolution to be nice had to extend to her interactions with her mother. Yes, it did. "I left my phone in the kitchen and didn't hear it ring. I'm sorry." Okay, that was nice enough.

"We have a situation. A good situation, I guess. Sarah told me she's hosting Thanksgiving this year."

Sarah always hosted Thanksgiving. She had the biggest dining room in the family. "She already bought her turkey," Annie said.

"Right. Up at that farm in Maine or whatever. She said Gordon's parents will be flying in from Chicago. The thing is, Sarah is in no shape to cook. I assured her that you and I would do all the cooking."

Oh, joy. Another favor. "What are you going to cook?" she asked her mother.

"I'll take care of the desserts. You can do the rest."

The rest meant the turkey, the stuffing, the cranberry sauce, the sweet potatoes, the green bean casserole, the dinner rolls, and the salad. Annie might as well host the party herself, except that she didn't have a dining room, let alone one large enough to seat everyone. And she didn't have an organic turkey—from New Hampshire, not Maine. "You're going to make pies?" she asked her mother. The Baskin Thanksgiving dinner always included apple pie and pumpkin pie for dessert.

"I can't make pies. I'm all thumbs when it comes to baking," her mother said. "I was figuring I'd pick up a couple of pies at the supermarket. Or maybe you could pick them up for me, since you'll be shopping for all the other food."

"We can't eat store-bought pies," Annie complained. "It's Thanksgiving."

"Store-bought pies are fine. If you don't want store-bought, you can make them yourself. I'm terrible at baking pies, Annie. My crusts come out dense and oily. Everyone will get heartburn."

Be nice. "Fine. I'll make the pies," Annie acquiesced, then said goodbye and ended the call.

She hadn't realized how difficult being nice could be. But being nice to Emmett wasn't quite as much of a challenge as being nice to her mother. Annie could make him a peanut butter and honey sandwich.

She slapped together two peanut butter and honey sandwiches and carried them, along with two bottles of beer, out of the kitchen. She had expected to find Emmett still sprawled out in her bed, but he had recuperated from his sexual performance enough to don his jeans and settle in the living room, the TV tuned to a Celtics game. "Who were you talking to?" he asked.

She took a moment to admire his naked chest, then set their sandwiches on the coffee table in front of the couch and rummaged in the drawer of one of the side tables for a couple of coasters for the beers. Ordinarily, she wouldn't have thought to protect the coffee table's surface from the damp beer bottles, but part of her effort to be nice entailed being nice to the table. It had once been Sarah's. It was probably used to having coasters protect it.

The coasters she found in the drawer were thick squares of cardboard with "Briny's" printed on them. Briny's was a bar she and Emmett had gone to during their long weekend on Martha's Vineyard. She wondered if Emmett remembered that, if he had nostalgic memories of their trip. That she herself remembered Briny's qualified as nice.

"I was talking to my mother," she answered him. "It seems I have to do all the cooking for Thanksgiving this year."

"Really?" He gazed around the living room. It wasn't tiny, but it wasn't big either. And it contained no dining table or chairs. "How are you going to do that?"

"We're having it at Sarah's house. But she can't do the cooking. My mother told Sarah she and I would do the cooking, but of course she won't do any of it, so I'll do all of it."

Emmett took a lusty bite of his sandwich while he mulled this over. "Your sister's so sick she can't cook?"

"I'll be amazed if she can even eat." Annie took a smaller bite of her own sandwich. It tasted like heaven, sweet and sticky. Her stomach rumbled its thanks.

"Well, that sucks," Emmett said. From him, such a comment counted as compassion—for Annie's ailing sister, and for Annie, who would have to do all the cooking. In his own limited way, he could be very nice.

So could she. Seized by a fresh spasm of niceness—no doubt due as much to the fact that she was finally eating as anything else—she said, "If you want to join us, you can."

That interrupted Emmett's communion with his sandwich. He twisted to look at her. "Your Thanksgiving dinner?"

"I assume your family will be having Thanksgiving, but if you want to come to our gathering, you can. We usually eat midafternoon. Maybe you could have a bite and then go on to your parents' Thanksgiving. Are they doing Thanksgiving?"

"They usually get a dinner reservation at a restaurant. I'll have to check with them. But yeah, I could come and eat a little with your family."

"Great," Annie said, wondering what her family would think when Emmett accompanied her to Sarah's house, and then telling herself she didn't care. Extending the invitation was her prerogative. If she was doing the cooking, she could damned well invite whomever she wanted.

No one had asked her if she wanted to cook for Gordon's parents, whom she found kind of scary. She had met them for the first time at Sarah and Gordon's wedding, and seen them a couple of times since then. They had come east for Trevor's *bris*, and she recalled them showing up to one of Sarah and Gordon's summer barbecues. Gordon's father did something in finance that earned him oceans of money, and Gordon's mother was the director of an art museum, which Annie found even more intimidating, despite her assumption that the job paid less than whatever it was that Gordon's father did. Both of Gordon's parents looked like escapees from one of those old Ralph Lauren ads in which all the models were gathered on a rustic but pricy family compound near a large body of water, and they were tall and thin and pouty.

If the senior Adlers were going to be sitting at Sarah's grand dining room table, eating the food Annie had prepared, she could sure as hell have Emmett seated at the table too. Gordon's mother could discuss some precious Renoir painting she'd just acquired for her museum, and Emmett could discuss the low-flow toilets being installed in the subdivision houses he was working on. It would make for an interesting Thanksgiving conversation.

"If you're doing all the cooking—" Emmett popped the last of his sandwich into his mouth and smiled "—sure, I'll come."

chapter seventeen

"Annie and Jamal's first podcast has been a big hit so far," Dean Parisi announced at the staff meeting a few days later. She tilted her head and patted her hands together in soundless applause. Evelyn and Harold chose not to join the ovation. "We've seen a bump in queries and submissions," Dean Parisi continued. "We'll definitely want you two to record more podcasts. Can you find some other students to interview?"

"Sure," Jamal said, then stared at Annie, silently urging her to speak.

She scrambled for a response. "It would be great if we could get one of the a cappella groups to sing on a podcast. I'm not sure we can do that, though. We were also thinking of a couple of pre-meds. They can talk about their research."

"They can talk about how they're barely passing organic chemistry," Evelyn said with a sniff. "How many of our pre-meds actually get into medical school?"

"Not everyone, of course," Dean Parisi said, "but a fair number do." She smiled at Annie. "You don't need to supply the numbers. Just record some more podcasts. I know finding the time will be hard, because we're running up to the deadline to finalize our E.D. applications. So far, we've got one hundred thirty-seven E.D. acceptances. I'd like to see that number at one hundred fifty." Annie had to remind herself that Dean Parisi used the abbreviation "E.D." to refer to "early decision." It had nothing to do with erectile dysfunction.

"What's so magical about one hundred fifty?" Jamal asked. "We've gone through the applications, and we've deferred about a hundred. If they were strong enough to admit, we would have given them a yes."

"I'm concerned with our yield," Dean Parisi said predictably. "And one hundred fifty is a nice, round number."

"I love round numbers," Harold said.

Annie couldn't tell if he was being sarcastic or kissing up to Dean Parisi. But if attaining a round number meant the team would have to go through all the deferred applications and contort themselves to accept thirteen more that they had not considered worthy of early acceptance a week ago, she didn't love round numbers.

"So," Dean Parisi said cheerfully, "I want you all to review the deferred applications over the next few days and see if you can find any that deserve a second look."

A fourth or fifth look at this point, since they'd all been looked at multiple times already. But Annie didn't say that. Instead, she said, "When do you want us to record the next few podcasts? We have to find students willing to participate."

"And an a cappella group," Jamal added, exchanging a glance with Annie, his faint smile signaling his agreement.

"It would probably be best if you record your podcasts in the evening," Dean Parisi suggested. "I can't justify your spending another afternoon out of the office before we've got the E.D.s finalized. More students may be available in the evening, anyway."

In the evening? After putting in a full day here in the admissions building? Annie had other things to do in the evening. She had to organize her shopping for Thanksgiving and then *do* that shopping, and be nice to Emmett, and eat and sleep.

Being nice to Emmett shouldn't pose a huge challenge, but it did. He was around all the time now. Every evening. Every night. It was almost as if they were living together, and she hadn't signed up for that.

She liked having her own space. If she had wanted to live with a guy, she would be married by now. She did want to get married someday, eventually. She wanted to get married and live in a house bigger than her condo—it didn't have to be as big as Sarah's house, but it might at least have a yard. And a den so the TV didn't have to be in the living room, and a dining room big enough that she could prepare the Thanksgiving meal and serve it under her own roof. She wouldn't object to a hot tub either.

But she didn't think Emmett was the man she wanted to host Thanksgiving and soak in a hot tub with, not for the rest of her life. He was a fun guy, he knew how to use his circumcised penis to great effect, but...

"Problem?" Dean Parisi asked Annie.

She hadn't realized she was frowning. She quickly rearranged her face into a smile. "No. We'll figure it out."

Jamal shot her another look, this one definitely not conveying agreement.

"So," Dean Parisi said with finality, "go back to your desks, review the E.D. deferrals, and let's see if we can scrape together another thirteen acceptances. Confer with each other if you need to. We want consensus."

"Consensus is everything," Harold said. Definitely kissing up.

Outside the conference room, Jamal grabbed Annie's elbow. "Come on," he whispered, pulling her down the hall.

"Come on where? We can't do the podcast now. We have to line up our guests, and we have to find thirteen—"

Jamal shook his head and continued with her down the hall to the office at the end, the one that overlooked the campus's arboretum. The foliage in that lush botanical acreage had peaked in color a couple of weeks ago, but even in early November, when nothing was pretty in New England, the arboretum was pretty. The trees, mostly bare now, still had beautiful shapes, their branches spreading and arching like the arms of ballerinas. Some of the trees and shrubs were evergreens, and although their color faded a bit in the winter, they still offered splashes and slashes of green. And the sky opened up above, often white or gray at this time of year, but occasionally a sweet, cloudless blue.

If Annie could choose her office, she would want the one at the end of the hall. But it would take a few miracles for that to happen. Dean Parisi would have to retire or die, and Annie would have to remain working in the admissions office until fate or choice had carried the dean off, and she would have to leapfrog over Harold and Evelyn and possibly Jamal, although she couldn't imagine Jamal sticking around long enough to move into the dean's office. Then again, she couldn't imagine herself sticking around that long either.

"What are we doing?" she asked.

Before Jamal could answer, Dean Parisi emerged from the restroom across the hall from her office and smiled at them. "Did you want to talk to me?"

"Yes," Jamal said, holding Annie back so that Dean Parisi could precede them through the door.

She entered her office, which was at least three times the size of Annie's, and settled behind her desk, a massive block of mahogany that might have carved from the same tree as the conference room table. If that table was suited to roistering medieval knights, Dean Parisi's desk might be where the queen sat when she had to write edicts and proclamations. The dean's office also featured staid, academic-looking paneling on the walls, a large framed photograph of the school's administration building, which loomed over the quad in stately red-brick grandeur, and a leather couch which, if it were in Annie's office, she would have used for afternoon naps—as if she had time for afternoon naps. Which she didn't.

Dean Parisi gestured toward the visitors' chairs facing her on the opposite side of the desk, and Annie and Jamal sat. Jamal looked confident. Annie had no idea how she looked, but she was as curious as Dean Parisi to hear what was on Jamal's mind.

"We need a raise," he said.

Annie clenched her jaw to keep it from flopping open. A raise? Well, sure, she would love a raise. But where had this idea come from?

"If you want us to work on the podcast after our regular hours," he explained, "you'll need to pay us. Putting together a podcast is a lot of work. Planning it takes time. Finding guests takes time. Recording it takes time. You want us doing it in the evening, because there's no time during the day. We should be compensated."

Annie wasn't sure why Jamal kept saying *we*. He hadn't conferred with her about this. He didn't know whether she agreed with him.

She did, of course. She wanted a raise. Everything he said was true—working nights, planning the podcast, scouring the student body for guests...well, yes. They should be compensated.

She met Dean Parisi's cool, steady gaze and nodded slightly. And wondered whether she and Jamal were going to get fired for being too demanding.

After a long moment, Dean Parisi turned to Jamal. "You know I'd love to pay you both more. But my budget is very tight."

"Our budgets are tight, too, Wanda," Jamal said, bravely using her first name. Annie wouldn't have gone that far—but then, Annie wouldn't have had the guts to ask for a raise. "You're asking us to put in a lot more time. We deserve to be compensated for that time."

"No question about that," Dean Parisi said. "But I can't get water from a stone."

"You're asking *us* to get water from a stone," Jamal said. "Am I right, Annie?"

She mustered her courage and said, "Yes." One single syllable, her voice rasping when she uttered it. But hearing herself speak emboldened her. "In addition to the—the E.D.s," she said, deliberately using Dean Parisi's term, "we've got the holidays coming up. It's a stressful time. And we're willing to do the podcasts, but the extra hours of work..." She trailed off. She wasn't used to asking for things. She wasn't even used to believing she merited more than she had. She was the loser Baskin sister, the klutzy one, the one with ice cream stains on her shirt.

"All right," Dean Parisi said. "I can't budget a raise for you. But I might be able to get a grant to cover your extra hours. I'm thinking the school's PR office might be able to justify spending on something like this. You *are* promoting the school."

Annie and Jamal exchanged another look. She wanted to slap him five, and then maybe leap onto the chair and shriek, "Woo-hoo!" But the grant wasn't a sure thing, and they might not get the raise.

"I would appreciate your not discussing this with Harold and Evelyn," Dean Parisi added. "Let me contact Marge Dominici in the public relations office and see what I can do."

"Thank you," Jamal said, his tone formal. No "Woo-hoo!" shriek from him. He was, as always, impressively cool.

Annie rose when he did, and echoed his thanks to Dean Parisi. She exited the office behind him, walking as calmly as he did. She strolled down the hall beside him, keeping her face passive in case Harold or Evelyn, or even Brittany, might glimpse them and wonder what they'd been up to, and followed Jamal into his own office. Like hers, it was tiny. It was a slight bit tidier than hers, though, and he'd hung a poster of a Black-Power fist, rendered artistically in red, green, and black, on one wall.

She closed the door behind herself and then turned on him. Suppressing the "Woo-hoo!" that tickled her lips, she took a deep breath and asked, "Why didn't you tell me you were going to do that?"

"I didn't know I was going to do it until the meeting broke up. And then I thought, damn, if she's going to ask us to put in more hours, we should be getting overtime. Except we're salaried, not hourly, so there's no such thing as overtime."

"You didn't just think it. You had the balls to ask for it."

"I do have the balls," he said with a boastful smile. "What was that stuff your friend was saying about birth order and all that? I grew up with a bunch of sisters. I learned pretty young that if I asked for things, odds were I'd get them."

Annie had not grown up asking for things. She didn't have balls. But she was infinitely grateful that she could tag along on Jamal's balls. "I think I'm even more excited about keeping this a secret from Harold and Evelyn than I am about getting a raise," she admitted.

"We haven't gotten anything yet," he pointed out. "Let's just keep our fingers crossed that she gets a grant."

"I can't use my computer keyboard with my fingers crossed," she joked, then flung her arms around him in a hug.

He hugged her back. "We deserve it, you know. You deserve it even more than me. The podcast was your idea."

The notion that she deserved something was alien to Annie, and as she released Jamal from her embrace, she considered it, mulling it over, tasting the word on her tongue. *Deserved.* What a concept.

If she could get used to being nice, she could get used to deserving things too.

She would be cooking Thanksgiving for Sarah—and baking pies for her mother—and she had invited Emmett to join their family feast. She was exerting herself, being generous, spreading good vibes into the world. Being nice.

She *deserved* things. Yes. She did.

Acknowledging that simple fact for the first time in her life filled her with joy.

chapter eighteen

"**Y**OU INVITED EMMETT TO OUR THANKSGIVING?" Gilda squawked. She was seated in the passenger seat of Annie's car. Annie had picked her up at the Toyota dealership, where she had dropped off her car to be serviced. The Toyota dealer was located only a couple of miles from the Cabot College campus, which, Gilda insisted, meant that this chore would take up hardly any of Annie's time, since she was already in the area. But as convenient as it was for Annie to drive over to the Toyota dealer during her lunch break, she then had to drive her mother home. And tomorrow she would have to pick her mother up at her house and drive her back to the Toyota dealership to retrieve her tuned-up Avalon. This chore would, in fact, take up a fair amount of Annie's time.

But what better way to spend your lunch hour than doing a favor for your mother?

At the moment, Annie was supposed to be spending her lunch hour reassessing early-decision applications in the hope of finding thirteen that might merit a promotion from deferred to accepted, because Dean Parisi liked round numbers. Annie hoped the dean would finagle grant money so she could compensate Annie and Jamal for all the extra work she was demanding of them with the podcast. If the roundness of the number on the grant check was due to a string of zeroes to the right of a digit—any digit, even a one would do—Annie would like round numbers too.

"Thanksgiving is a family holiday," her mother blathered. "Since when is Emmett part of our family?" Her eyes were hidden behind sunglasses, the frame cat's-eye-shaped and an odd pink hue. The lenses were nearly black. Somehow, Gilda's expression seemed more forbidding when Annie could see only the lower half of her face.

"Gordo's parents aren't my family, and they're going to be there," Annie said.

"His name is Gordon, not Gordo. And they're Sarah's family by marriage. We're making this Thanksgiving for Sarah."

We again. *We*, as if Annie's mother would be contributing anything to the feast. "*I'm* doing all the cooking," Annie said. "I'm fixing the whole damned meal. If I want Emmett there, I can invite him." Asserting herself that way filled her with a powerful heat, as if a vent had released high-pressure steam through her body. Claiming what she wanted and insisting on it made her feel like a warrior, even if she was currently creeping her car through traffic-clogged roads at her mother's behest. If Jamal could demand that Dean Parisi give him and Annie a raise, Annie could demand the right to bring Emmett to her family holiday, even if he wasn't part of the family.

"I'm in charge of the pies," her mother reminded her.

"Which you told me to buy, since I would be at the store anyway."

"Well, you *could* buy them. No one said you had to make them from scratch."

"We always have homemade pies for Thanksgiving. Sarah sometimes made them in the past, and I sometimes made them and brought them with me."

"We had plenty of Thanksgivings before you were old enough to make pies."

"Grandma Baskin made the pies from scratch back then," Annie reminded her mother. "She taught me how to make them. She let me help."

"Fine. So making pies is a fun thing for you. Stop kvetching."

"I'm not kvetching." Annie slowed to a halt at a red light and shot her mother an annoyed look. If Gilda noticed, Annie couldn't tell. With those ridiculously dark sunglasses on, Gilda could have been looking anywhere. "All I'm saying is that Emmett will be joining us. His family celebrates Thanksgiving at a restaurant, and that's…I don't know, cold. Not in the spirit of the holiday. I thought it would be nice to include him in our celebration."

Her mother chewed on that, then twisted in her seat, which led Annie to believe Gilda was actually looking at her. The light turned green and Annie's attention returned to the road, but she could sense her mother's movements peripherally. "You're right," her mother said. "I know restaurants serve very nice Thanksgiving dinners—you have to make a reservation months in advance. I'll tell you, if it wasn't for you and Sarah and the grandchildren, if it was just Dad and me, I'd go to a restaurant. But if you think Emmett belongs at our Thanksgiving, bring him." She paused for a moment, then said, "Maybe you should marry him."

"Marry Emmett?"

"Thanksgiving is a family holiday. If you want him at our Thanksgiving, maybe you want him in our family. That would mean marrying him, wouldn't it?"

"I don't think I can throw together a wedding in two weeks."

"You don't have to marry him before Thanksgiving," Gilda said, "but you should marry him soon. Sarah should be your matron of honor. She's your sister. If you don't get married soon..." She trailed off, then heaved a dramatic sigh.

Annie easily filled in the blanks. If she didn't get married soon, Sarah would die before she could be Annie's matron of honor. Which was not a very good reason to get married. "I'm not going to marry Emmett."

"Why not? Granted, he's no Gordon. And he's not Jewish. As if that mattered, all the time you spend in a synagogue these days."

Not that Annie's mother spent more time in a synagogue than Annie did. Maybe a little more time, on the High Holy Days. She liked to attend those so the other women in the sisterhood could see her lack of crow's feet and suffer pangs of envy.

"Maybe it's enough that your father thinks Emmett is Jewish. He's a good-looking boy. So marry him, already, and let your sister walk down the aisle with you before it's too late. You can always get a divorce later."

"I'm not going to marry him, Mom."

"You won't even do that for your sister, who's so sick?"

Annie took several deep, long breaths. Her mother's asking her to drive her back and forth to the Toyota dealer was a small—well, maybe a not-so-small—favor. Her mother's asking her to marry Emmett so Sarah could squeeze in a stint as her matron of honor before she lost her battle with cancer was a gigantic favor.

That marriage was not going to happen. She liked Emmett well enough. But she couldn't imagine spending the rest of her life with him, whiling away evening after evening seated beside him on her hand-me-down couch, drinking wine while he watched whatever sports event was in season on the TV.

Evidently, her silence was not an adequate answer for her mother. "Do you realize how sick Sarah is?" Gilda said.

"Yes."

Gilda continued as if Annie hadn't spoken. "She's bald. Even her eyelashes are gone. She had the most beautiful eyelashes in the world. It's a tragedy."

"She wore mascara, Mom."

"We all do."

"I don't."

"Which is probably why your eyelashes are so pale. A little mascara wouldn't kill you, Annie."

Fortunately, her parents' house was just a few blocks farther. Annie gritted her teeth and steered through the winding streets of their subdivision until she reached Red Robin Drive. After pulling into her parents' driveway, she stopped the car.

"What time will you pick me up tomorrow?" her mother asked. Not *Thank you.* Not *I appreciate you devoting your lunch break to chauffeuring me around.* Just a demand for another favor.

"Is there any way Dad can get you to the Toyota dealer tomorrow?" Annie asked.

"He's too busy. He works, Annie."

"I work too."

"Yes, but your campus is right near the dealer. If you can get here and pick me up around noon, the car should be ready by then. If it's not ready for some reason, I'll give you a call, and we'll pick it up later." With that, her mother exited the car.

Fuck you too, Annie thought as she backed out of the driveway.

She hadn't yet seen Sarah *sans* eyelashes. Did Sarah look like the cheap version of Mr. Potato Head, as she'd predicted she would? Did her eyes look like fried eggs?

Annie waited until she arrived back at her office before phoning Sarah. "How are you doing?" she asked.

"Blecch," Sarah replied. "Everything tastes funny these days. Even the chocolate energy drinks. But I'm losing too much weight. My oncologist says I have to keep drinking them. Can you imagine either of us would ever be in a situation where we *had* to gain weight?"

"The silver lining of cancer," Annie said. "I was wondering if I could come over this evening."

"You mean, just for a visit?"

"Unless you've got some favor you want me to do," Annie said, only half-joking. "Maybe we could discuss the logistics for Thanksgiving."

"What logistics? You and Mom can fix whatever you want. I'll probably just be drinking more energy drinks."

"I'm fixing dinner," Annie told her. "Mom isn't doing any of it, but you know she'll take full credit for it once everyone says how delicious all the food is. It'll be so delicious, you might not be able to resist eating some," she added, hoping to boost Sarah's spirits. "I've invited Emmett to join us at our Thanksgiving, by the way."

"The more the merrier," Sarah said, although she didn't sound at all merry. "Gordon's mother is going to chew him up and spit him out."

"No, she won't," Annie said hopefully. "She's going to be focusing on you. She'll probably tell you those energy drinks aren't healthy."

"Yeah. She'll mix up a nutritional smoothie full of kale and flaxseeds and make me drink it." Sarah laughed weakly.

"Hide the blender," Annie suggested. "Stick it in that carport in your kitchen."

"The appliance garage," Sarah corrected her. "Sure, come over for dinner tonight. Gordon was going to pick up some Mexican, but if you come, maybe you can help him fix some real food."

Great. Annie could go there for dinner, and then make the dinner. A preview of Thanksgiving.

But maybe after dinner, she could take a dip in the hot tub.

Back in her office, she shot Emmett a quick text: *I'm going to Sarah's for dinner 2nite. Tell Frank to free up the bedroom. CU tomorrow, maybe.*

She tapped her computer awake, waited for the screen to come into focus, and resumed reading Carlotta Crocci's application essay, which went into detail about the summer she'd spent living in her parents' second home on the Amalfi Coast. "You cannot believe the food," Carlotta had written. "Real Italian food is very different from what passes for Italian food here in America. It's just so awesome."

Yes, but how? Annie muttered. *Tell me how it looks and smells and tastes. Don't just tell me it's awesome.* Didn't they teach essay writing in high school anymore, those lessons about making a statement in each paragraph's title sentence and then elaborating on it? Annie wanted elaboration, especially since her lunch today was going to amount to RITZ Crackers and processed cheese from the vending machine near the restroom, eaten at her desk while she worked. She wanted to read Carlotta Crocci's description of the fresh seafood, the plum tomatoes and bell peppers simmered in olive oil, the garlic fumes spilling from every kitchen window. She wanted to live vicariously—or at least eat vicariously—through Carlotta Crocci.

But no, there were no descriptions. Just Carlotta's insistence that the food was awesome.

At least Carlotta wasn't a do-gooder like all those kids who had written essays about spending the summer in impoverished countries, building Habitat for Humanity houses, earning their angel wings—or at the very least, their admission to Cabot College. Carlotta traveled abroad to her parents' villa and ate awesome food. If her parents could afford a second home on the Amalfi Coast, Carlotta would probably not require financial aid. Another plus.

Still, her application didn't strike Annie as strong enough to merit automatic acceptance into Cabot. Of course it didn't. If it did, Annie would have recommended Carlotta for acceptance the first time she'd encountered the girl's application.

Her phone buzzed. She swiveled away from her computer and read the screen: *I'll meet U at UR condo after dinner.*

Oh, for God's sake. Why couldn't Emmett spend one freaking night back at his own apartment? What great power did Frank hold over him?

I may be sleeping at Sarah's, she texted back, only to force him to negotiate with his roommate. Now that she was learning to assert herself, she believed it was a skill Emmett should learn too. But as she considered it, she realized that spending the night at Sarah's might be an excellent idea. She could relax in the hot tub until midnight and not worry about drying off and driving home. She could drink a glass or two of some of that stuff Gordon kept in a cut-crystal decanter in his study and not have to worry about driving home. She could admire the closet in the guest bedroom, with its rods and shelves and modules. And the bathroom, with its broad marble counter. She could brush her teeth using that lovely sink, and not have to worry about driving home.

She could wake up with Trevor and Becky, sneak them a yummy breakfast, and send them off to school. Sarah could sleep in, and Gordon could leave for work whenever he wanted. Who knew? Maybe he would enjoy a yummy breakfast too.

A night in the grand, elegant Adler house might clear her mind a bit. She could think about the podcast—new guests to invite, new topics to discuss. She could imagine herself getting a raise and moving up a level or two, lifestyle-wise. Not that any raise Dean Parisi might scrape together for Annie and Jamal would enable her to afford a house like Sarah's, but she could pretend for a night.

And it wasn't just about her. By forcing Emmett to confront his selfish roommate, she would be doing him a favor—what a change of pace, doing a favor for someone who was not a member of her family! Annie spending the night at Sarah's so Emmett would not be able to spend the night at Annie's might actually be an act of kindness.

Assertive *and* nice. Annie could get the hang of this.

chapter nineteen

S OMEDAY, WHEN I GROW UP, I WANT A HOT TUB, Annie thought as she settled back against the smooth tiles rimming the edge of the hot tub in Sarah's backyard. Steamy water churned around her, a liquid massage, her reward for having cooked dinner for the Adlers that evening.

It hadn't been difficult. Sarah might not be able to do her own shopping, but her refrigerator and pantry were well stocked—thanks at least in part to Annie's having shopped for her. Evidently, Gordon had supplemented the supplies Annie had brought the last time she'd been here. Or maybe Diana Drucker had. If she could shop for wigs with Sarah, she could damned well shop for olive oil and garlic.

Those were two of the main ingredients in the meal Annie had prepared. She'd found a bag of shrimp in the freezer, cooked it in the olive oil and garlic, added some herbs and diced tomatoes and tossed it with spaghetti—fresh, of course; Sarah would never countenance the stiff dried pasta that came in long cardboard boxes. She had actually eaten a little of the scampi Annie had prepared, pronounced it tastier than her energy drinks, and managed to remain at the table with her husband and children and sister for the entire meal.

She looked lousy. She was, indeed, missing her eyelashes and eyebrows, which made her appear blank and somewhat startled. Instead of her stylish wig, she had tied a scarf around her head—a lovely silk scarf swirled with pastel splashes that resembled an abstract watercolor, *tres chic*. But the absence of eyelashes and eyebrows was more shocking to Annie than the hints of scalp visible along the edges of the scarf, where delicate tendrils of hair should have been peeking out. Without eyelashes and eyebrows, Sarah's eyes looked wearier than usual, circled in shadow, the lids droopy.

Trevor and Becky helped Annie clean the kitchen after dinner while Gordon went upstairs to get Sarah settled in bed. Trevor explained to Annie the importance of inserting each fork and knife into its own slot in the dishwasher's silverware compartment. "Mom taught us to do it this way," he told her. "They get cleaner if you separate them."

"I wouldn't have known that," Annie said, which made Trevor puff up a bit, taking pride in having enlightened a grown-up about something important. Actually, Annie did know that, although the aging, inexpensive dishwasher in her own kitchen didn't have individual slots for the silverware. Evidently, if you weren't willing to spend a king's ransom on a dishwasher, you didn't deserve to have impeccably clean forks and knives.

Becky had asked Gordon if she could join Annie in the hot tub after dinner, but he'd said no, it was a school night. Annie kept Becky company while she changed into her pajamas and arranged her school backpack for the next day—Sarah's kids were so organized—and read Becky a few chapters of *Winnie-the-Pooh*, using different voices for each character, which Becky claimed was almost as good as sitting in the hot tub with Annie.

Once Becky was settled, Annie changed into her swimsuit, wrapped herself in the plush robe in the guest bathroom, and took the back stairway down to the kitchen and out the glass slider from the kitchen to the patio. She dashed across the ornate stonework to the hot tub, her flip-flops whispering across the ornamental stones. The water felt blisteringly hot in contrast to the cold night air, but she got used to it in less than a minute.

She closed her eyes and listened to the rhythmic rumble of the motor that kept water pulsing out of the jets. The current swirled around her, easing her mind as it eased her muscles. She wondered if she could install a hot tub inside her condo. She couldn't install it in the backyard—she didn't have access to that. Or on the roof—not only did she not have access, but there was probably some structural reason that putting a huge vat filled with a lake's worth of water on the roof of an old building was not a wise idea. Maybe she should sell her condo and buy a house. She would need to get a raise to afford that, though. If Dean Parisi came through with a grant... a very large grant...

The sound of footsteps jolted her eyes awake. She saw Gordon stride across the patio in his swim trunks. The evening chill didn't seem to faze him at all. He carried a couple of towels in one hand. After draping them over the towel rack attached to the wooden fence, he lowered himself into the hot tub, settling onto the bench across from her, as far from her as he could be. White plumes of vapor rising into the air created a fog between them, making him appear blurry and mysterious.

Not that mysterious, actually. She had spent enough times in the hot tub with her brother-in-law recently to know the contours of his face, even in soft focus from the steam, and the shape of his shoulders. The rest of him remained submerged beneath the surface of the water.

"Is Sarah asleep?" Annie asked.

"She will be soon. The chemo really tires her out." He sighed. "This hot tub is my salvation."

"It's so relaxing." Annie regarded him through the clouds of hot tub mist. The drone of the motor and the rhythmic bubbling of the water created a hypnotic effect, lulling her into believing she and Gordon were actually friends. Before now, she had never cared enough about him to think of him as a friend. He had always seemed distant, too busy and successful and Type-A to need or expect friendship from his sister-in-law. But now they were in their swimsuits and wet, and they were allied in caring for Sarah, although Gordon was doing most of the caring.

Chloe and Jamal showed more interest in how Annie was coping with Sarah's illness than in how Sarah herself was coping. That was what friends were for—worrying more about their friends than about the people who needed to be worried about. The patient had the worst of it, obviously, but the people around the patient also suffered at times like this. Friends paid attention to things like that.

Now that Annie was Gordon's friend, she needed to be concerned for him. She had always assumed he was the sort of person who didn't need anyone to worry about him, but because of their growing friendship, she couldn't help but worry. "How are you holding up?" she asked him.

Even in the dark, she could see his eyebrows arch. Apparently her concern surprised him as much as it surprised her. "I'm hanging in there," he said. "Dinner was delicious, by the way. Thanks for making it."

"No problem. I enjoy cooking."

"As I understand it, you'll be making our Thanksgiving dinner?"

"That's the plan."

"You're very kind."

Annie wasn't kind—certainly not *very*—but she was trying to be. "My boyfriend Emmett is coming to our Thanksgiving too," she told him. "His parents celebrate Thanksgiving in a restaurant. That's just wrong."

Gordon smiled. "You can't let a guy spend Turkey Day in a restaurant. That would be cruel."

So Annie wasn't cruel. She wished she felt as kind as Gordon seemed to think she was. She wished *kind* was second nature to her. "I'm trying to be nicer," she admitted. That she should be confiding to Gordon about her psychological evolution struck her as odd—but maybe not. He and she were both auxiliaries in the Sarah drama, trying to find their own paths through the thicket. They were fellow travelers, both of them a little lost. "I'm also trying to be more assertive. That seems contradictory, doesn't it? Trying to be nice and assertive at the same time?"

He accepted her statement without blinking. "Assertiveness and niceness are not mutually exclusive. I'm assertive." He pondered for a minute, then chuckled. "I'm not nice, though. Maybe I should work on that."

"You seem nice enough to me, Gordo."

His chuckle swelled into a full-blown laugh. "How nice is nice enough? I suspect my adversaries in negotiations at work don't think I'm nice."

"But by being not-nice to your adversaries, you're being nice to your clients," Annie pointed out.

Gordon weighed that, then shrugged. "You're right. And it's *nice* of you to say so."

Annie knew he was joking—sort of—but his words still warmed her, almost as much as the steamy water did. Why was she comfortable talking to him about these things? Why was she sharing with him thoughts and feelings that she never had shared with Emmett, that she never *would* share with Emmett? Because she wasn't as close to Emmett, because his opinion of her didn't matter as much? Or because she and Gordon were both on Team Sarah, Gordon by choice and Annie by birth? Or maybe because they happened to be in the hot tub together?

"Does Sarah ever use the hot tub?" Annie asked. "It might make her feel better."

His smile vanished. "She says it wouldn't be safe. She thinks there's bacteria in the water, even though I use all the cleaning chemicals." He shook his head. "I think that's just an excuse. She's withdrawing, Annie. She's backing slowly out of the world."

"How bad is it?" Annie asked. "What are her doctors saying?"

"Her oncologist won't make any predictions until Sarah has completed this first round of chemo. But the chemo is draining her, and she feels awful all the time." He shrugged, his shoulders rising out of the water and sinking back into it. "She doesn't tell me much."

"You're her husband," Annie said indignantly. "She should share what she's going through with you. That's what marriage is all about." As if Annie was any kind of expert on the subject of marriage. "What do you and she talk about?"

"Not much, anymore."

That was blunt. "Why not?"

"She's withdrawn. Her oncologist says she's suffering from depression."

"Well, duh. She's got ovarian cancer."

"We've discussed anti-depressants, but she doesn't want to take them. She says it's her life, whatever is left of it, and she wants to live it without taking anything that might alter her mind or her emotions."

"Isn't depression one of those stages?" Annie struggled to recall the five stages of grief. Chloe would be able to rattle them off. Besides majoring in psychology in college, Chloe worked with old people who were all nearing the threshold of death. Many of them had dementia, which might be a useful way to avoid those five stages—how could you grieve the imminence of your death if you had no concept of what death even was? But some of them, or their loved ones, probably experienced those five stages. "Bargaining?" she tried to recall. "Anger?"

"Denial, bargaining, anger, depression, acceptance," Gordon recited them. He had probably studied up on them in the weeks since Sarah's diagnosis.

"She's already on stage four? That was fast."

"She skipped ahead," Gordon said. "I've been taking them in order. Denial—I think I went through that over the past year, when she had a bunch of symptoms that she kept insisting were nothing. I believed her. I guess we were both in denial then, although I don't know just how much she knew or suspected. Bargaining—she didn't waste time with that stage. I did. I thought if I put in fewer hours at the firm, spent more time with the kids, just downshifted a little, she would get better. I'm a good bargainer, but the other side has to be willing to compromise. Not this time. Cancer doesn't compromise. So... now I'm on anger."

"You don't seem very angry."

"I am," he said calmly. "Constantly."

"I wouldn't have guessed."

"You're lucky you don't see it." Still in that calm, level tone. "It's eating me up inside."

Annie had never given much thought to what was going on inside Gordon. He always seemed so competent and composed and on top of things. That anything—especially anger—could be eating him up inside boggled her mind.

"Sarah is somewhere between depression and acceptance," he said.

"But there's a forty-percent chance she's going to survive, right?"

"No." Annie must have looked stunned, because he elaborated. "It's metastasized. She's got lesions on her liver, her bladder, her pelvis. It's going to spread through her body and kill her. Probably pretty soon."

"None of us knows when we'll die," Annie argued. "I could get hit by a car tomorrow. Sarah said so."

A faint smile traced his lips. Not a happy smile. Annie could see that even from her distance on the opposite side of the hot tub. "I think you're capable enough to look both ways before you cross the street," he said. "There's no looking both ways before you cross cancer."

Silence settled over the patio. Above her, a cloud slid across the sky, an eerie, Halloween-gray scrim dimming the moon's light. Annie imagined herself looking both ways, checking to see if cancer was barreling down the street, a huge, noisy runaway truck with failing brakes. Could you see it from far enough away to avoid being struck down by it? Evidently not, if you were in denial.

When it came to Sarah, no one was in denial anymore. And Sarah had slid right past bargaining and anger. Depression wasn't much better, but maybe it was easier on the people around you. With depression, as Gordon said, you just withdrew. You backed out of life.

Yet his anger didn't seem so hard on the people around him either. He wasn't blowing up at the kids or, apparently, at Sarah. He accepted with equanimity the news about Emmett's joining the family for Thanksgiving.

Maybe he didn't seem angry because he was in the hot tub. His salvation, he called it.

Annie closed her eyes and acknowledged that it was difficult to feel angry when you were relaxing in a warm reservoir of swirling, throbbing water. The hot tub was her salvation too.

chapter twenty

BRITTANY MATERIALIZED IN THE OPEN DOOR OF ANNIE'S OFFICE. "Wanda wants to see you," she said.

Annie glanced up from her computer, the monitor aglow with the essay Cory Bellingham had submitted with their application. According to the essay, Cory was gender-fluid, which would make them an intriguing addition to the Cabot student body. But Cory had entered their senior year of high school with a 2.8 GPA, submitted no standardized test scores, listed the LBGTQ club as their only extra-curricular, and couldn't compose a grammatically stable sentence to save their life. "I really like who I am, I don't know who I am, but hey," Cory had written in their essay. "It's like, I'm really feel good about myself, once I figured out who I am. My pronouns are they/them."

I'm really glad you're really feel good about yourself, Annie thought. *I hope someday you'll earn enough money to be able to hire an editor to proofread your prose—if you ever figure out who you are, once you figured that out.*

Still, the school could use some more gender-fluid students. Maybe Cabot ought to accept Cory for diversity purposes.

That decision would have to wait. Dean Parisi wanted to see her. She tried to read Brittany's expression. Optimistic? Disappointed? Did Brittany know that Dean Parisi was trying to secure a raise for Annie and Jamal? Brittany generally knew everything about what was going on in the admissions office, but this was supposed to be a secret.

Annie bade Cory's application a temporary farewell and rose from her desk. Stepping out into the hall, she saw Jamal waiting. This was it, then. They were going to find out if they would be compensated for their podcast work. She should have dressed better for the occasion, made herself look more worthy of a raise. She was wearing only a plain long-sleeved T-shirt and stretchy, smoke-gray slacks. Jamal, as always, looked dashing in a V-neck sweater and the sort of jeans that shouldn't be called jeans because they obviously cost more than a hundred dollars. *He* looked like someone worthy of a raise.

They followed Brittany to the office at the end of the hall. Annie admired Brittany's height and posture, her lush blond waves, her confident stride in her clunky stack-heeled ankle boots. Maybe after Annie had mastered niceness and assertiveness, she should tackle learning how to walk like Brittany. And look like her. And wear uncomfortable-looking shoes without wincing.

Brittany waved them into Dean Parisi's office, then departed, closing the door behind her. Dean Parisi was seated at her desk, her posture rigid, her short gray hair molded to the contours of her skull, her expression neutral. Good news or bad? Annie couldn't tell.

"Have a seat," she said, gesturing to the visitors' chairs.

Bad news, Annie concluded. She and Jamal exchanged a glance. He looked slightly disappointed, but mostly indignant. Was he going to fight for the raise? Demand it? Threaten to go on strike if he and Annie weren't properly compensated for their time creating the podcast?

"I couldn't get the grant," Dean Parisi told them.

Disappointment swelled like a lump of ice in Annie's throat. She tried to swallow it back down.

"But here's what we're going to do," Dean Parisi continued. "We're going to put you two on the school's public relations payroll as consultants, and they will pay you separately for the podcast from their budget."

The lump in Annie's throat vanished. She grinned. Jamal continued to look combative. "Are we going to lose our salaries here?" he asked.

"No, of course not," Dean Parisi said. Jamal's expression finally relaxed into a tentative smile.

"The way we'll handle this is that, if it comes up, Harold and Evelyn can know that you're doing some work on the side for the public relations department. This way, they don't have to resent that you're being paid more here than they are. We *are* a team, after all. We want everyone on the team to feel like equals."

Annie might have pointed out that different players on a professional sports team received different salaries, based on their talent and their contributions to the team. Of course, the salaries she and Jamal received were significantly less than the income tax most professional athletes paid on their salaries. And she would bet some of her minuscule salary that Evelyn and Harold were earning more than she and Jamal were. They had worked here longer. They were older. George Orwell would claim that they were more equal.

But she and Jamal would be getting paid for their work on the podcast. Jamal had demanded money, and they were going to receive it. Assertiveness was a good thing.

"There will be some paperwork," Dean Parisi went on. "There's an admin in the public relations office who will assist you with that. The pay rate will be fifty dollars an hour. That's all they can afford, so don't ask for more." She accompanied that last statement with a sharp look in Jamal's direction.

Annie couldn't imagine demanding more. Fifty dollars an hour sounded pretty fricking generous to her. She had been paid a salary her entire adult life, so she wasn't sure what a reasonable hourly rate might be these days, but her memories of babysitting for three dollars an hour were still fresh in her mind.

"I think we're worth more," Jamal began.

Annie cut in. "But this is terrific. Thank you for arranging it."

Dean Parisi smiled brightly at Annie and dimly at Jamal. "I'll have Marge in the public relations office email you by the end of business today, explaining the paperwork. In the meantime, please get started recording some more podcasts."

Annie thanked her again. Jamal nodded. He preceded Annie out of the office and stalked down the hall, entering Annie's office instead of his own. Once she'd joined him inside, he closed the door.

She spun around to face him. "What the hell is wrong with you? We got the raise!"

"Technically, we didn't." But his face broke into a broad smile. "But shit, man, we did good."

"Then why are you acting so disappointed?"

"Good cop, bad cop. If we both looked too grateful, Parisi would have thought she was giving us too much and cut back our funding."

"It's not hers to cut back," Annie said. "It's coming from the PR department."

"At her request." His smile lifted his cheeks, causing his eyes to squint slightly. "She isn't going to renege, though. It's ours. 'We are the champions, my friend,'" he sang, then pumped his fist into the air. "We did it, Annie!"

"You did it," she said. "It wouldn't have even occurred to me to ask for the money."

"You're the idea person. I'm the money person. Talk about a team—we're *it*."

"Maybe we should come up with a name for the podcast, now that we're going to keep it going." She dropped onto her chair and closed her eyes, partly so she could concentrate on podcast names and partly so she wouldn't have to see Cory Bellingham's grammatically atrocious essay on her computer monitor. "The Cabot Chronicles," she suggested.

Jamal made a retching sound. "Cabot Mater," he said.

Annie frowned. "Huh?"

"Like the hymn, 'Stabat Mater.'"

"I don't know hymns. And we don't want kids to think this is a Catholic school. How about Cabot or Leave It?"

It was Jamal's turn to look perplexed. "You mean, like love it or leave it?" At Annie's nod, he shook his head. "Why would we want anyone to leave it? We're trying to get them to come here, not go away."

She conceded with a nod. "How about...Cabot College World?" Except that she didn't say Cabot College. She said "Cabbage."

"Cabbage World!" Jamal's exuberant grin brightened the atmosphere in her stuffy little office. Even her drooping geranium seemed to perk up. "I love it!"

"I *meant* Cabot College, not Cabbage."

"Freudian slip, Annie. You really meant Cabbage. The perfect mash-up. We are living in Cabbage World."

Not a Freudian slip. Not a mash-up. Just a stupid mistake. "No one will understand what that means."

"We'll make them understand. We'll explain it in every podcast. We'll turn the cabbage into a mascot for the school. It's funny, it's just the right amount of snark. They should give you a raise just for coming up with it." Jamal was on a roll. "We should get the bookstore to carry hoodies with the Cabot College Cabbage on the back. We should get the football players to put cabbages on their helmets." Annie must have looked supremely skeptical, because he settled down a little, lowering his voice, halting in his pacing—which wasn't too energetic given that if he took more than three steps in any direction, he would collide with a wall. "I'm serious, girl. Welcome to Cabbage World. It shows we're clever, we've got a sense of humor, students will have a good time here."

She couldn't argue with Jamal. For one thing, he seemed a hell of a lot savvier about such things than she was. For another... he was Jamal. He'd gotten them their raise. You don't argue with someone who gets you a raise. "All right. Cabbage World." Her gaze met his, and they smiled in unison. She could live with clever and funny. "We should celebrate," she said. "The Dorm after work today?"

He snorted. "Annie, we've got to celebrate big. The Dorm is a dive. Let's do dinner."

"Okay."

He pulled out his phone and tapped the screen, calling up his calendar. "Friday? I'll make a reservation."

Any restaurant that required a reservation dwelled a few stations above her usual eateries. You didn't need a reservation at most pizza joints and hamburger stands. "Okay," she said. Really, they did need to celebrate.

He was out of her office and she was seated at her desk, staring at Cory Bellingham's semi-literate essay, when the reality of Jamal's suggestion sank in. Dinner on a Friday night. At a restaurant that required reservations.

She remembered the woman who had visited Jamal at the office last spring. Utterly beautiful, utterly glamorous, utterly tall, a young Michelle Obama. Was Jamal still seeing her? If so, didn't he have to check with her before making a Friday-night dinner plan with another woman, even if that woman was nothing more than a colleague from work?

And what about Emmett? Annie usually saw him on Friday nights—although they'd never spent a Friday night dining at a restaurant that required reservations. Pizzerias and burger joints were pretty easy-breezy when it came to dining, even on Friday nights.

Which was irrelevant. What was relevant was that it hadn't even occurred to her to check with Emmett before agreeing to have dinner with Jamal.

Not that having dinner with Jamal meant anything. He was her colleague from work.

Still... Friday dinner was not the same as Wednesday or Thursday dinner.

If I were nice, she thought, *I'd tell Jamal I couldn't go because Emmett might not want me to. If I were assertive, I'd tell Emmett I was going out for dinner with Jamal and he'd just have to live with it.*

She couldn't decide which she was: assertive or nice. Gordon had said they weren't mutually exclusive, but as she analyzed it, they seemed like polar opposites.

She read Cory Bellingham's essay one more time, decided to defer the application again, and sent it out into the stream of applications she and the team were reevaluating. Then she wrote emails inviting a few of the younger professors to participate in the podcast. Maybe she was ageist, but she suspected older professors wouldn't be as amenable to the idea, especially if she and Jamal called the podcast "Cabbage World." Nor would older professors be as enticing to prospective students.

She also sent invitations to a first-year student majoring in studio art and a third-year pre-med. On a whim, she reached out to the head of the security department; some applicants might need to be reassured that Cabot College was a safe campus. And just for the hell of it, she emailed an invitation to the captain of the rugby team.

Then she texted Emmett: *Busy Friday evening. Maybe U can make plans with friends.* She read the text, mulled it over, and added, *It's a work thing,* her attempt to leaven her assertiveness with a little niceness. Was it nice enough? Should she be tormenting herself with angst over its niceness quotient?

The hell with nice, she told herself. This time she would be assertive.

She tapped the "send" icon.

○ ○ ○

Emmett was unhappy. Annie couldn't tell if he was unhappy because she had made a plan to celebrate her raise with Jamal on Friday or because he wouldn't be able to spend Friday evening at her house. In a slapdash attempt to be nice, she told him he could come over to her condo later in the evening. He pouted and said he'd think about it.

Emmett pouting was a remarkable thing. Unlike most people, he didn't look sulky and juvenile when he pouted. He actually looked sexy, like one of those surly models in the special fashion editions in the Sunday *New York Times*. In fact, he looked so sexy pouting that after preparing a dinner of roasted chicken with garlic and herbs, steamed broccoli, and a gigantic baked potato for him, she dragged him off to bed and, as he might put it, thawed him out. They both came rather dramatically, and as soon as he'd caught his breath, he sank into the pillows and resumed pouting.

Annie didn't pout. It had been a while since she'd come so spectacularly. A little niceness—a delicious home-cooked meal—could produce an excellent result.

But Emmett was still pouting.

She cuddled up next to him, resting her head on his shoulder, her hand on his taut, slightly hairy belly, and sighed. And tried to decipher exactly what existed between her and Emmett, where they were going, what she wanted from him. What he wanted from her.

Fabulous sex? She didn't think she was all that skilled. Sex had never fallen within five miles of fabulous with any of the other guys she'd dated. Emmett—the carpenter, the lanky, muscular guy, the lackadaisical, easygoing, generally uncomplicated man who usually seemed to be in her corner—could set her on fire. Not always, but more than fifty percent of the time.

Did she deserve more? Did she want more?

And what did he see in her? She wasn't that pretty. She wasn't svelte and graceful. Her hair was the color of pine bark, and she didn't have the money to get highlights and lowlights like Sarah—although after the school's PR department started paying her fifty dollars an hour, she might be able to afford that kind of pampering. Not that she would have that much time to spend at the hair salon, having Trixie or Lexie or whatever her name was turn her blah hair into a ravishing mane. She would be too busy recording Cabbage World podcasts.

Sarah would say that having gorgeous hair was more important than making podcasts—and also more important than paying the electric bill. But number one, Sarah was beautiful to begin with, so splurging on a fancy hair treatment was nothing like putting lipstick on a pig. And number two, Sarah didn't have to make podcasts to top off her piggy bank. She had Gordon, and a mansion, and a hot tub.

And she was dying. She didn't have hair at all. How could Annie possibly be envious of Sarah's beauty and affluence?

"Do you ever think about dying?" she asked the underside of Emmett's jaw.

He hesitated a respectful minute before replying. "No. Why?"

"My sister's dying."

"She's your sister. You don't like her," Emmett reminded Annie.

"But I love her. She's my sister."

He nudged her off his shoulder so he could look at her. For the moment, he wasn't pouting. "You told me she doesn't respect you. You told me she gave you shit all the time when you were growing up. You told me she's rich and spoiled—"

"Entitled," Annie corrected him. "I never said spoiled."

"Entitled is just another word for spoiled."

True enough. Annie reminded herself that Emmett did have a couple of months of college under his manly tool belt. She shouldn't be surprised that he could occasionally come up with a wise bit of insight. "Yes, but...she's still my sister. And she's given up on life. At least that's what her husband says. She's just kind of marking time, preparing to die. I can't begin to imagine what that's like."

"It's like living," Emmett said. "We're all gonna die."

"But not for a while. At least I hope not." She rested her head back on his shoulder. He let it remain there.

"We had a thing at work today," he said. "This guy Joe, he's always strutting, you know? Bragging about how fearless he is. So he was up on the roof of this house we're building, putting flashing around the chimney, and he slipped and fell."

"Oh my God!" Annie jerked back and sat up, the horror of the accident on Emmett's construction site alarming her—not only because she cared about his safety but because such a calamity seemed disturbingly close to getting hit by a car while crossing the street. Could a person look both ways before falling off a roof?

"The roof over the front porch broke his fall. He landed on the grass. Got a bruise on his ass. He said that proved he was indestructible. So he's just as fearless as he ever was. He figures if that fall didn't kill him, nothing will."

Annie contemplated that. Before Sarah's diagnosis, she had felt, if not fearless, indestructible to a certain degree. Annie hadn't wasted an ounce of gray matter on thoughts about cancer or prognoses or the looming perils of crossing the street. She had just gone about her life, assuming her life was going to go about her.

But now death seemed, if not imminent, at least possible. More than possible. As Emmett had said, they were all gonna die.

She closed her eyes and nestled closer to him. His body had cooled off some, but his skin still felt hotter than hers. She drew the blanket up over herself for warmth.

If she were going to die, not tomorrow but within the next year, as Sarah presumably would, what would she want what remained of her life to look like? Would Emmett be in it? Would she wish to spend more time with Jamal, recording podcasts? Would she knock herself out to make her hair prettier?

Would she take more walks through the arboretum on campus? Would she notice how beautiful the trees were, even though the vivid autumn foliage had given way to November's leaves, as dead a brown as Annie's hair? Would she grab every opportunity to sit in a hot tub? Would she hang out more with Trevor and Becky? If she didn't need her money to last more than one more year, would she dine out more often at restaurants that required reservations?

Would she dress better? Read more? Quit her job and devote herself to volunteer work? Tour museums? Drive to Nova Scotia and sleep under the stars, and maybe catch a glimpse of the aurora borealis?

Would she get married—in time for Sarah to be her matron of honor? Would she produce children of her own? Would she look for ways to give meaning to her life?

Or would she continue to do what she was already doing—going to work, coming home, having sex with someone she liked but couldn't imagine marrying and making babies with?

"If you go to this business dinner Friday night," Emmett said, and Annie entertained a crazy hope that he would provide an answer to all the life-and-death questions gnawing at her, "can I have your spare key so I can get into the condo?"

chapter twenty-one

THE FIRST INVITEE TO RESPOND TO ANNIE'S EMAILS WAS JEREMY KAUFMAN, the pre-med student. He arrived at the campus studio late Friday afternoon wearing a lab coat, evidently taking his performance seriously. He didn't quite know what to make of Annie's and Jamal's outfits—Jamal in a T-shirt with a large head of cabbage silkscreened on the front, Annie having pinned a fake flower that vaguely resembled a cabbage rose behind one ear. Not that it mattered what they wore. Although the student engineer recording their podcast was producing video as well as audio, Annie doubted anyone would ever view it. Most people would just listen to the podcast.

"This thing is really called Cabbage World?" Jeremy asked as he settled into the chair between her and Jamal.

"Annie's idea," Jamal said. Annie wondered if he was giving her credit or deflecting ridicule from himself. "Cabot College. Mash them up and you get cabbage."

"Yeah, I can see that," Jeremy said, then went on to answer their questions about the science curriculum at Cabot and the career support the school provided to pre-meds. Annie asked him if he played rugby, and he seemed a bit bewildered by the question. He admitted to playing chess and working out in the school's weight room—which gave Annie and Jamal an opening to describe Cabot's fitness center in glowing terms.

After they'd finished recording the podcast and thanked Jeremy, Annie and Jamal retired to an abandoned classroom and filled out forms documenting the eighty-four minutes they'd spent preparing and recording the podcast. Annie wasn't sure how the public relations department would calculate eighty-four minutes for reimbursement purposes. According to the calculator on her cell phone, eighty-four minutes paid at a fifty-dollar-per-sixty-minutes rate came to seventy dollars. That would cover the cost of a pricy meal, even at a restaurant that took reservations. Appetizer, entrée, dessert, and a glass or two of wine—she could splurge.

"Let's drive to the restaurant in my car," Jamal said. "I'll bring you back to the staff lot after."

That suited Annie well enough. She was relieved by his silly shirt; it implied that the establishment where he'd made a reservation wasn't too formal. But before they left the media center, he ducked into a bathroom carrying his stylish leather man-bag, and when he emerged he had on a crisp button-front shirt. A pair of expensive-looking jeans, too—this pair a faded black rather than the blue ones he wore he had on the day Dean Parisi had told them about their new job moonlighting as Public Relations department consultants—but still expensive-looking.

Did the fake cabbage rose blossoming above her right earlobe look sporty or tacky? Probably tacky. She tugged the hairpin that held it in place out of her hair, and stashed the flower in her tote. The rest of her outfit was her standard workday apparel—a beige tunic-length sweater to camouflage her butt, a pair of tapered black pants, and black slip-on flat-soled shoes. Both her mother and Sarah had often pointed out that her shoes were appallingly unfashionable, but Annie was a big fan of comfortable feet.

She felt a little weird walking with Jamal to the staff parking lot. She had walked there with him before, but never with the intention of eating dinner with him. They had always just been colleagues, allies, occasional collaborators. And that was what they were now, she reminded herself. This dinner was all about the podcast and the increase in their incomes. Nothing more.

She should have known his car would be newer, sharper, and shinier than her geriatric Honda, which had already been suffering the indignities of its advanced age when she'd bought it a few years ago. "What is this?" she asked as she lowered herself onto the seat of the sporty coupe.

"A BMW. You got a problem with that?"

"No, but it makes me wonder if you're earning a lot more than me."

"Of course I'm not," Jamal said with a modicum of indignation. "The admissions office staff is a team, remember?"

"Then explain how you can afford a late-model BMW." Did he have a wife who earned more than he did? That gorgeous woman who had visited him last spring—maybe she didn't just look like Michelle Obama. Maybe she was a lawyer like Michelle Obama too.

"I won the lottery," he said.

"Seriously?"

He laughed. "My grandmother owned a house—an ugly old thing in Roxbury. When she moved into senior living, she dumped the house on me. Told me to sell it. I fixed it up, cleaned it out, put on a new roof, and suddenly it was worth north of half a million dollars. She made so much money on it, she insisted on giving me a chunk of the profit. Well, she didn't give me the cash, because there's tax ramifications and all that. But she bought this car, which was a joke because she can't drive, and then she signed it over to me. So yeah, I did win the lottery."

"Didn't you still have to pay taxes on the car? A gift worth this much?"

Jamal shrugged, then revved the engine, which emitted an aggressive purr. "I gave all the information to my accountant and let him figure it out," he said as he backed out of his parking space.

Jamal had a BMW. He wore fancy jeans. He had an accountant.

He worked in the admissions office of Cabot College, so it wasn't as if he was a member of the elite. But he knew how to demand a raise, which might mean he *was* a member of the elite.

Which, in turn, might mean the restaurant they were going to was a lot more formal than she'd expected. The seventy dollars she'd just earned that afternoon might not go very far.

The restaurant turned out to be pretty formal. The tables were covered with linen tablecloths, and matching linen napkins were folded into pockets that held glittering sterling-silver flatware. The server who sat them presented them with a leather-bound wine list. She didn't call them "hon."

Annie read the menu from right to left. This was how her mother had taught her: "Read the price first. Never order the most expensive thing on the menu." This advice had applied to actual dates, where the guy was supposedly paying for everything. Annie had explained to her mother that guys generally didn't ask her out on dates, that people didn't date that way anymore, that everyone paid his or her own way. "Gordon always paid for your sister," her mother had pointed out, and of course he did. Sarah had lived an indulgent existence even before she'd met Gordon. She swanned through life, expecting people to do things for her—and they did.

The menu tired Annie's fingers with its weight. The prices tired her mind. Her seventy-dollar podcast gig that afternoon might not cover the entire cost of the meal, after all.

The server returned and asked if they wanted drinks. Annie realized that, with enough wine in her bloodstream, she might not mind the prices so much. She flipped quickly through the wine list, skimming the columns of ninety-dollar bottles and trying not to wince. Eventually, she reached the last page, which listed wines by the glass. The Merlot was the cheapest. Fortunately, she liked Merlots. "I'll have a glass of the Merlot," she said, hoping she sounded more sophisticated than she felt.

Jamal ordered a Glenlivet. Annie didn't even know what that was. Probably something you drank when you won the lottery and flipped your grandmother's house for a huge profit.

As soon as the server was gone, Annie resumed studying the menu. If she ordered one of the vegetarian meals, she would look like a cheapskate, and Jamal might presume she was a vegetarian, which she wasn't. The chicken dishes weren't too pricy, relatively speaking. She ordered one of them. It included wild rice and broccolini and some sort of sauce, the name of which sounded French. Jamal ordered a swordfish steak, which cost significantly more than the chicken.

He would think she was a cheapskate. But at least he wouldn't mistake her for a vegetarian.

"You seem nervous," he noted once the server had gathered their menus—their heft didn't seem to faze her—and departed. "You never seem nervous when we're doing the podcast, but you seem nervous now."

She decided she might as well be honest. "When I go out for dinner, it's usually to a pizza place. This is a little ritzy."

"We're celebrating," he reminded her. "When I celebrate, I go big."

"I need to learn how to go big," Annie said. Sarah probably dined at restaurants like this all the time, when she wasn't losing her hair and drinking energy shakes. She probably dined at restaurants like this even when she had nothing to celebrate. Sarah was confident and entitled. Annie needed to work on her sense of entitlement, which was currently about the size of a deer tick.

Jamal simply smiled at her, augmenting her nervousness, until the server returned with their drinks, along with a linen-lined basket filled with warm rolls in odd shapes—an effort to make them look hand-crafted, Annie figured. Before she could pluck one from the basket, Jamal lifted his glass in a toast. Annie lifted her wine glass. She noticed that it lacked a line to tell the bartender how much to pour. Without the line, he hadn't filled the glass terribly high, but it had a big bowl.

"To us," Jamal said. "To our success as podcasters and our bonus checks."

"Definitely," Annie agreed, tapping her glass against his. "To all those things." She sipped. This Merlot tasted a lot better than what she got at the Dorm.

Jamal settled back in his chair, still smiling, still looking as relaxed as an emperor lounging upon his custom-designed throne. "Tell me, Annie, how could we have gone to Cabot College at the same time and never met each other until we wound up working in admissions? It's not such a big school."

"You were a couple of years ahead of me," she pointed out.

"Big effin' deal. I knew people in your year. I bet you knew people in mine."

"What did you major in?" she asked.

"Philosophy."

She nearly dropped her glass. "Well, I sure didn't know any philosophy majors. Who majors in philosophy? Geniuses."

"And people who expect to win the lottery, because philosophy majors are unemployable." He laughed and took another sip of his drink. "You should have heard my parents howling when I declared my major. My mother's a nurse. My dad drives a bus for the city of Boston. Practical jobs, right? They wanted me to major in engineering."

"Thank God for your grandmother's house," she joked, which got him laughing again. "I majored in English. *So* much more practical than philosophy."

"The ability to write a lucid paragraph is a marketable skill. Look at some of the essays we have to slog through on those applications."

She flashed on a memory of the grammar nightmare that was Cory Bellingham's essay. "So why did you risk the wrath of your parents and major in philosophy?" she asked.

He remained silent while the server delivered their salads, china plates topped with exquisite-looking vegetables—Annie detected some pale yellow endive leaves lurking among the mixed greens, everything glistening with a delicate sheen of oil. Jamal waved away the foot-long pepper mill that the server aimed at his plate like a carved-wood cannon. Annie shook her head when the pepper mill was aimed her way, and the server wandered off. "I wanted to figure out the meaning of life," he told her.

"Did you?"

He guffawed. "I wish."

"How about the meaning of death?"

Mulling over the question, he lifted his fork and stabbed at the assorted leaves of his salad. "Basically death means nothing. I'm not saying it's meaningless, just that it's all about nothingness. If living is all about consciousness, death is the absence of that."

The very notion of Sarah being absent—not there, not *here*—unnerved Annie. A shudder passed through her.

Jamal must have noticed. "Your sister?" he guessed.

"She's not doing well. Her prognosis sucks. I promise I won't cry this time," Annie added, recalling her embarrassing sob-fest at the Dorm when she'd been there with Jamal and Chloe.

"You can cry as much as you like," he said graciously. "It doesn't bother me."

"Thanks." Annie managed a crooked grin and dug into her salad. It was delicious, the greens crisp, the oil mildly herbed.

"Philosophers probably think more about death than about life," Jamal told her. "It's the ultimate fear that motivates humans, or the ultimate curiosity, or...whatever. I mean, what *happens*? How can you just disappear? Do we have souls? Is there an afterlife?"

"What do philosophers have to say about all that?" Annie asked, genuinely curious. If Jamal could provide a concrete way of thinking about Sarah's fate, Annie might find it easier to be nice, or assertive—or more like Sarah. So far, Sarah's condition seemed abstract to Annie, even when she saw Sarah's lash-less eyes and hairless scalp. Was death like Sarah's eyebrows—simply disappeared, just not *here* anymore?

"Well, back in two-hundred-something B.C., this one dude, Zhuang Zhou, said death was the transformation of matter from one state to another," Jamal said, his pale brown eyes animated, his silverware glinting in the light from a wall sconce beside their table as he consumed his salad. "Socrates thought death would just be like an endless, dreamless sleep, although he did think there was an afterlife. Plato bought into pretty much the same idea. Sartre was all about consciousness or lack of it. Life is consciousness, death is the absence of consciousness. Wittgenstein said we live forever only if we live in the present. You're not really living if you live in the past or the future, but there's this eternal present that we're in, and that's what makes us alive." He chewed a forkful of salad and swallowed. "Then you've got the playwright Tom Stoppard, in his play *Rosencrantz and Guildenstern Are Dead*. Rosencrantz and Guildenstern get killed at the end—I hope that's not a spoiler, but you majored in English, so you probably know what happens to them from reading *Hamlet*. Anyway, at the end of the play, there's this spotlight on one of them, just his face. And he says, 'Now you see me, now you—' and just as he's about to say 'don't,' the spotlight goes dark and he vanishes. Maybe that's death. *Now you don't*."

Annie's first thought was, *Thank God I didn't major in philosophy*. It all sounded absurdly navel-gazing to her, words as light and insignificant as confetti, swirling in the air and landing on the ground and not actually meaning anything, not showing anything, not shaping any sort of pattern. But maybe that was just because death defied understanding. Now you were here, and now you weren't. You've got a light on you, and then, all of a sudden, the light gets switched off.

The idea of Sarah simply becoming a *wasn't* defied Annie's intellect. She'd known people who died: her father's parents, first his father and then his mother, and then her mother's father. They had been old. They'd been, if not senile, certainly befuddled and cranky. Her maternal grandmother was still alive, and whenever Annie visited her—she lived in an elder residence similar to the one where Chloe worked, although not in a memory care unit—Grandma scolded Annie for not being more like Sarah. "Still not married?" she'd caw, wagging an arthritic finger. "Look at your sister. She's married, she has children, what are you waiting for? You're getting old."

Not as old as you, Annie always wanted to retort.

But Sarah wasn't old. It didn't seem fair that her spotlight was about to get turned off and the world would no longer see her.

Fairness had nothing to do with it, of course. Fate was what it was. Annie could get hit by a car. Anything could happen. "Rosencrantz and Guildenstern didn't know they were going to die," she said, recalling the Shakespearean version of their story. "Hamlet swaps the letter instructing the King of England to kill him with a letter instructing the King of England to kill them instead. I mean, that would be like getting hit by a car you didn't see coming. My sister *knows* she's going to die."

"We all know we're all going to die," Jamal pointed out. "Your sister probably has a better idea than most of us of *how* she's going to die, and maybe *when*. But she doesn't know for certain either. She could get hit by a car. Or killed by the King of England, although that's probably less likely."

Annie smiled. Weird that she could smile while discussing her sister's imminent death. Which might not be imminent, she reminded herself. Sarah might still surprise them all and wind up among the forty percent.

"I'm sorry," Annie said. "We should talk about something cheerier. We're celebrating, right?"

"Philosophy always cheers me up, now that I don't have to take any exams in it," Jamal assured her, although he happily allowed the conversation to wander down a different path. As their entrees arrived, they gossiped about Harold's pomposity, Evelyn's tendency to be *far-bissener*, a Yiddish word Annie happened to know because it fit her sole surviving grandmother so perfectly—"It means kind of cold and bitter and forbidding," she explained—and whether it was appropriate to call Dean Parisi Wanda. "You called her Wanda when you were asking her for a raise," Annie reminded him.

"A negotiating tactic," he explained. "I wanted to demonstrate that I wasn't scared of her."

"Brittany must not be scared of her," Annie said. "She calls her Wanda all the time."

"Brittany wields all the power in the office," Jamal said. "Dean Parisi wouldn't survive without her."

"There were other administrative assistants before Brittany," Annie noted. "Dean Parisi survived."

"All right, so she might survive. She wouldn't thrive. Brittany is the lifeblood of our team. Her smile is like an energy source."

"You're mixing your metaphors," Annie scolded.

"Spoken like a true English major."

"This chicken is delicious, by the way."

They discussed the New England Patriots, which Jamal knew more about than Annie, despite her spending countless hours seated on the sofa next to Emmett while he watched football game after football game. They discussed the Boston Celtics, which Jamal knew more about than he knew about the Patriots. They discussed the importance of wearing comfortable shoes—Jamal had no trouble appreciating why Annie wore the shoes she did—and whether the density of the wool on last spring's woolly bear caterpillars accurately predicted how much snow would fall that winter. They discussed Thanksgiving. Jamal's oldest sister had inherited the holiday from his grandmother after he'd sold his grandmother's house and received his car, and with all his sisters' husbands and children, their dinner was always a chaotic mob scene. The meal had to be served buffet-style, because even though his oldest sister lived in a nice house in Milton, she didn't have a table big enough to seat everyone who showed up.

Sarah had a table big enough, and her mob would probably not be chaotic. The Adlers were too tidy and organized. Annie's mother might try to inject a little chaos, but she would be outnumbered.

The server arrived at their table to clear their plates. She asked if they would like dessert, but besides the fact that Annie wasn't sure her seventy-dollar bonus would stretch far enough to pay for some undoubtedly decadent and exorbitantly priced final course, her stomach was full. Ordinarily, she would have eaten only a little of her rice, but the wild rice with its slightly salty, slightly nutty flavor had been too tasty to leave behind. Annie had polished off every last black grain.

The server left and then returned with a single check, which was awkward. She must have assumed they were on an old-fashioned date. Annie would have just split it down the middle, but Jamal apologized and requested separate checks, and the server took care of providing corrected bills. Annie was relieved, given that her chicken had cost less than Jamal's swordfish steak. She was also impressed. Jamal hadn't seemed at all embarrassed about asking the server to redo their bill. Annie could learn some tips on assertiveness from him.

After paying—Annie added a large tip to cover the server's inconvenience with the checks—they left the restaurant. "That was delicious," Annie said. "I'll have to come back here again, after I make more money."

"It's a good place for special occasions," Jamal agreed, and Annie realized he viewed this dinner as a special occasion. Those rare meals when Annie dined at a pizzeria with Emmett were not special occasions. Maybe they had been when she and Emmett had first started seeing each other, but that had been five months ago, before they'd slid into the routine of eating take-out food or whatever Annie threw together at home. She had never eaten dinner at Emmett's apartment, but she had seen his and Frank's kitchen, and she would not feel comfortable eating any meal that was prepared there. The sink had been stained, the cabinets empty, the bananas on the counter black with age. She had spent the night at his place once, when Frank was out of town, and insisted that she and Emmett eat breakfast at Dunkin the next morning.

The drive back to campus in Jamal's sleek little BMW was a special occasion in itself. At night, the windows of the campus dormitories glowed golden, and the streetlamps lining the paths that cut through the quad and across the campus spilled overlapping circles of light onto the ground. As a student, Annie had often walked through the campus after dark, heading to the dining common or the library or a friend's dorm room. But as an employee, she didn't spend much time on campus once the sun set—just a quick jaunt from the admissions building to the staff lot when it was time to head for home.

As pretty as the campus was during the day, at night it seemed mysterious and magical. Like plants that did their growing overnight, in the dark, Annie imagined students growing and maturing during those late hours, in those rooms with their illuminated windows. Students were eating, drinking, studying. Getting high. Making love. Listening to music. Laughing or weeping. The most interesting aspects of being a college student were happening right now, as Jamal cruised slowly through the campus to the faculty lot.

The lot was nearly empty. Annie's car looked forlorn, parked all by itself at the end of one row. Jamal drove directly to it and pulled into the adjacent space. He left his engine idling as Annie unlatched her seatbelt. "This was fun," she said. "Thanks for taking me to that restaurant."

"Thanks for coming up with the idea of the podcast, and the name," he said. "Cabbages forever!" He reached across the console and gave her shoulder a squeeze.

She climbed out of his car, unlocked her own car, and settled behind the wheel, shivering in the nighttime chill. Savoring the evening—that delicious chicken, the tasty wine, the meaty discussion—warmed her from within. She and Jamal had always gotten along well, but now they were really friends. She started her engine, then waved to him. He returned her wave and drove away, his car gliding soundlessly across the lot to the gate and out.

Annie reached her condo a mere ten minutes later; driving home at that time spared her the challenges of rush-hour traffic. Steering down the narrow driveway to the rear of the building, she saw no silhouette on the porch. No Emmett. No empty pizza box. Relief swept over her, followed by guilt at feeling relieved by his absence.

She shoved the guilt away. She had told him he should make another plan for that evening because she would be busy—a work dinner, she'd insisted, and it had been that, sort of—and Emmett had apparently made another plan. She was glad he wasn't hanging out on her front porch, eating pizza and moping until she showed up and let him inside.

She truly liked him. He was good-looking and good-natured. She had included him in her family's Thanksgiving. But honestly, she didn't want to spend every minute she wasn't at work with him.

She walked from the parking area down the driveway to the front of the house. The sky was particularly dark, the moon a narrow crescent, like a smile tilted onto its side. Of course, there was much more moon in the sky, a full circle of it. But she couldn't see the circle. Only the sliver. Soon it would be a new moon, totally invisible.

But still there.

Now you see me, now you—

Was that what dying was like? A crescent moon? A sphere that existed but was no longer visible? A thing that was there but not there?

When Sarah was no longer there—assuming she didn't fall within the fortunate forty percent who survived for five years—would Annie still know Sarah was there, even if she could no longer see her?

chapter twenty-two

ANNIE WAS OBLIGATED TO WORK A FULL DAY THE WEDNESDAY BE-FORE THANKSGIVING. She recalled her public school days, when students were always dismissed at noon on that Wednesday—an extra half-day of vacation—and her time in college, when the campus generally emptied out for the entire week, even if classes were technically still in session. But in the admissions office, the day before Thanksgiving was the day the early-decision acceptances, deferrals, and rejections were sent. The team had managed to eke out a few more acceptances, bringing the total to one hundred forty-seven. Not exactly the round number Dean Parisi was dreaming of, but close enough. Cabot College's yield would be acceptable.

In addition to the push to compile the early-decision acceptances, Annie had spent the past couple of weeks recording Cabbage World podcasts with Jamal. They had interviewed a student from Nairobi whose dream of attending college in America had come true, thanks to Cabot. They'd interviewed a student double-majoring in modern dance and poetry; she had arrived at the studio in a leotard and recited a few obscure poems she'd written, and Annie contemplated whether her double major might make her even less employable than a philosophy major. They had interviewed a philosophy major who had engaged Jamal in a spirited discussion about phenomenology that was so arcane it made the double-major's poetry sound as concrete as a grocery shopping list. And they'd interviewed someone from campus security, who had rattled off statistics about how safe Cabot's campus was. Of the recent interviewees, both the philosophy major and the student from Kenya played rugby.

Current students seemed to love the podcast at least as much as applicants did. Annie received emails from several students asking if they could be interviewed on Cabbage World. She spotted several girls strolling through the quad with fake cabbage roses pinned to their hair. Also one boy sporting a cabbage rose in his hair, which was longer than Annie's. One anonymous fan dropped an actual head of cabbage off on Brittany's desk, along with a note reading, "Cabbage Rules!" The admissions office team elected Harold to receive custody of the cabbage. He protested modestly, but everyone else on the admissions office staff agreed that he was the most likely staff member to enjoy sauerkraut.

Now the early-decision acceptances were out, the campus was officially closed for the long holiday weekend, and Annie could spend Wednesday evening baking pies, which her mother would take credit for tomorrow at Sarah's Thanksgiving.

Emmett offered to help her make the pies, but he proved only marginally more useful than her mother. He peeled a few apples and then busied himself eating the peels. He also sliced the apples in Annie's food processor, which seemed to bring him great pleasure. The food processor was a noisy power tool, after all, and it contained a sharp blade. Once he'd sliced all the apples, he asked Annie if he could slice some carrots, just for fun. She said no, and he wandered off to the living room to watch whatever sporting event he could find on TV.

"Let me know if they're showing a rugby game," she called to him as she rolled her dough into flat circles for the pie crusts.

Emmett emerged from the living room to help again when he heard her using her hand-held electric egg beater to blend the canned pumpkin, eggs, spices and evaporated milk for her pumpkin pies. The electric egg beater was another noisy power tool, but it didn't cut anything into little pieces, so after watching her for a minute, he detoured to the refrigerator to help himself to a beer and then shuffled back to the living room.

He looked tired. He told her his foreman had worked his crew hard for the past few days to try to make their Christmas deadline. "It's pretty much all interior work from here on in," Emmett had told Annie over a quick supper of grilled cheese sandwiches. Annie lacked the time to prepare anything more elaborate than that, and when Emmett had suggested calling out for pizza, she'd told him she could add slices of tomato to their sandwiches, which would make them almost the same thing as pizza, only more nutritious. Their nutritional value didn't impress him, but he devoured three sandwiches.

Preparing an entire Thanksgiving dinner was a daunting task. It was even more daunting because she would have to do most of her cooking in Sarah's kitchen, not her own. How much prep should she do in advance? Should she assemble the stuffing here and then lug it over to Sarah's and cram it into Sarah's New-Hampshire-farm turkey, or should she drive to Sarah's house an hour earlier and assemble the stuffing there? Should she wash and trim the green beans here or there? The rolls she would heat up at Sarah's, and she could steam and mash the butternut squash while the turkey was roasting. But the turkey... Would Sarah have enough butter on hand? Did she have an adequate supply of paprika?

Sarah's kitchen was much larger and brighter than Annie's. And Trevor and Becky would probably provide more assistance than Emmett. But Gordon's parents would be at Sarah's, and Annie's parents too. How everyone would interact with everyone else was a question mark. She would be too busy to step in and resolve any conflicts that arose. That was usually her job—taking care of things, calming everyone down, doing what had to be done while the divas around her bitched and moaned. When no one else could scrub the bathroom or buy groceries because they were sick or they had homework or, like Annie's mother, they simply refused to do anything they didn't want to do, Annie took care of it.

She would take care of everything tomorrow too. She was making the pies now, and she would cook everything else in the morning. Sarah would be responsible for keeping the conversation going while Annie slaved away in the kitchen. Sarah would have to reinforce Gilda's sense of herself. She would have to assure their father that she wasn't about to die, and Gordon's parents that she was as classy as they were, and Emmett...

Sarah wouldn't assure Emmett of anything. That would be one more burden dumped on Annie.

Annie had been an idiot to invite him to the dinner in a spasm of niceness. But maybe it hadn't been just niceness that had inspired the invitation. Maybe it had been assertiveness too. Maybe she had realized that, if she was going to cook the damned meal, she ought to invite one of her friends to enjoy it.

And if Emmett was there, she wouldn't be the only person present who didn't measure up to everyone else's elite standards.

Once the pies were in the oven, she pulled out her list of foods that she would need to bring to Sarah's house tomorrow and reviewed it. Such organization wasn't typical for her, but the possibility of arriving at Sarah's and discovering she had forgotten to bring some essential ingredient—garlic, onions, celery for the stuffing, celery for the celery sticks—panicked her.

She could cut up the celery sticks while the pies baked. One less task for tomorrow.

Sarah would be impressed if she saw Annie's list. She would be astonished to realize that Annie had done some actual planning, some scheduling, some goal setting. She would be gobsmacked to see that Annie had thought to bring an apron with her to wear while she cooked. No doubt some food would find its way under the apron to stain her sweater, but at least she would *try* to keep her clothing spotless.

The pies were out of the oven by ten thirty, and Annie was more than ready for bed. She fell asleep while Emmett was still in the living room, communing with the Bruins.

She rose early Thanksgiving morning, took a quick shower, packed the pies and assorted other ingredients and her apron into her car, and drove to Sarah's house, powered on nothing but a travel mug filled with black coffee. Emmett remained in her bed, enjoying his slumber, his long-limbed body sprawled out to fill her half of the mattress once she'd arisen. Before she departed, she wrote Sarah's address on a sheet of paper and left it for him on the kitchen table, along with a reminder to arrive at Sarah's by one o'clock. "Make sure the door is locked when you leave," she wrote at the bottom of the note. "Just twist the button in the knob and slam it hard." He would not need the palm-tree spare key to lock up her condo.

The roads were surprisingly empty, given that Thanksgiving was supposed to be one of the most heavily traveled days of the year across the nation. Annie supposed that it became the most heavily traveled day after the sun rose; most people were too sensible to be cruising the streets before dawn in cars filled with loaves of bread for stuffing, bags of vegetables, jars of cranberry sauce, and pies wrapped in foil and carefully positioned so a rogue butternut squash wouldn't break free and roll on top of them, shattering their crusts.

To her relief, the Adlers were awake before dawn too. When Annie coasted up the driveway to their stately brick mansion, the front door swung open and two-child-size silhouettes, backlit by the light in the entry hall, filled the doorway, one half a head taller than the other. Annie smiled. Along with Emmett's sexual prowess, this was something Annie needed to give thanks for: her niece and nephew. She adored them, even if they were perfect. As far as Annie was concerned, the fact that Becky dripped ice cream on her clothes only made her more perfect, if such a thing was possible.

The children scampered outside into the raw, still-dark morning, shouting their welcomes and offering to carry things into the house. Annie got them organized, trusting Trevor with the apple pies and Becky with the pumpkin pies, which didn't have a top crust and were therefore slightly less likely to get damaged en route. She lugged the heavy bags with her uncooked ingredients for the feast into the house.

Gordon stood in the brightly lit kitchen, brewing coffee in an appliance that resembled something astronauts might use during a flight to Mars. Annie had never seen it before. "I'm making an Americano," Gordon told her as she settled her bags on the center island. "Do you want a cup?"

"If it has caffeine in it, yes." She noted that the children and Gordon were all dressed casually, in jeans and sweatshirts—although Gordon's sweatshirt was unnervingly crisp. She could make out faint creases in the fabric where the shirt had been folded inside a package. Evidently, it was brand new.

"Sarah's still asleep," Gordon told Annie, his gaze shuttling between his futuristic coffee maker and the piles of food Annie was unpacking. "She told me to tell you she defrosted the turkey."

"She also said if you run out of space in the refrigerator here, you can use the other refrigerator in the basement," Becky said. Annie hadn't known the Adlers had a second refrigerator, but the news didn't surprise her.

"I'll be leaving around ten to pick up my parents at the airport," Gordon continued, observing the coffee maker while it hissed and gurgled. After a minute, he produced a mug of steaming black coffee, placed it on the center island within Annie's reach, and returned to the machine to prepare another cup. "The kids should be in their nice clothes before we get back. Right, kids?" He sent them a stern look. They both rolled their eyes and nodded. "If you don't need any help from me," he added to Annie, "I'm going to see how Sarah's doing. She had a rough day yesterday."

"Everything's under control," Annie said, pleased that she sounded more confident than she felt. "But if I *do* need help, I've got two helpers right here." She beamed a smile at Trevor and Becky, who smiled back.

"Great, then." Gordon filled another cup with coffee and started toward the back stairs. Then he pivoted back and said, "Thanks, Annie. We really appreciate what you're doing."

She responded with a modest shrug, but the warmth inside her melted the chill she'd carried with her when she'd entered the house. She was used to doing favors for Sarah, but not used to being thanked for them. To be appreciated, even if only by her brother-in-law in his oddly stiff sweatshirt, shifted her mood, balanced it, elevated it. Gave her something more to be thankful for.

"We're going to set the table," Becky said once Gordon had vanished up the stairs. "Mommy told us which tablecloth to use."

"Becky wants to do something fancy with the napkins," Trevor said dubiously.

"I think that would be a great idea," Annie said as she removed her jacket and tossed it over the back of a chair in the breakfast nook. "It's a holiday, right? We don't want to have boring napkins."

"We're using cloth napkins that match the tablecloth," Becky elaborated. "That's better for the environment."

Annie wasn't sure whether running a load of laundry was necessarily better than throwing away paper napkins. The washing machine used electricity and gallons of water. But Sarah—or Annie, given that she was taking care of everything—would have to run a load whether or not cloth napkins were used. The tablecloth would have to be laundered—and quite possibly Becky's shirt too.

And maybe Annie's shirt, despite the apron she pulled out of one of the bags. She looped the bib's strap over her head and tied the strings around her waist. "Do I look like a chef now?" she asked as she resumed unpacking the bags she'd brought.

"You need one of those puffy white hats," Trevor said. He poked at the bags, peeking inside them, then peered at her. "Mom told us your boyfriend is coming."

"You've met him before," Annie reminded Trevor. "His name is Emmett."

"I remember him," Becky said cheerfully. "He came to our house once."

Annie wasn't surprised that he'd made an impression on Becky. He made an impression on most females. He and Annie had been seeing each other only about a month when she'd brought him with her to Sarah's Fourth of July barbecue, but Annie had been smitten, utterly captivated by his rugged good looks, his height, his sturdy shoulders, and his sexy, scruffy beard. Emmett hadn't said much that afternoon; he'd been shy around Annie's family, and her mother had dominated most of the conversations. Instead of asking him questions and drawing him out, Gilda had rattled on and on about the book club she'd just quit, the rudeness of other shoppers in the supermarket, and a painful blister on her foot. She had phoned Annie later that evening to complain that Emmett was too quiet, but she'd conceded that he was good-looking, although he could use a shave and a neater hair style. She'd asked if he was Jewish. "Your father wants to know," she said. "I could care less. Given your age, Annie, you really ought to be thinking about marriage."

Emmett had had the privilege of spending time with Annie's parents on a few other occasions since then, enough times to for them to decide they weren't crazy about him, and for him to decide that the feeling was mutual.

At least in theory, Annie's mother would be diluted by the Adlers today. Annie's father would probably be pleasant—a little teary, no doubt, but doing his best to be a good guest. He would ask Emmett how he could be Irish if his last name was Levy, and Emmett would look confused, and Annie would correct her father once again: *Dunleavy,* not Levy. Her father would propose multiple toasts, and each toast would be more sentimental than the last, and would make him more teary. He would do his best to be brave, and he would refuse to acknowledge how sick Sarah was, at least not out loud. Then he would go home with Annie's mother and cry his heart out, and lament that all he'd ever wanted was for his two beloved daughters to live long and healthy lives, and then he'd say, "So, how about Emmett Levy? A good husband for Annie, no?"

Why on Earth had she invited poor Emmett?

The turkey—which looked and smelled like every other turkey Annie had ever prepared, despite its auspicious origin at the organic farm in New Hampshire—was stuffed, seasoned, dabbed with butter, and hoisted into the oven by 9:00 a.m. The dining room table was set by nine fifteen, Becky and Trevor collaborating to spread the heavy linen cloth, arrange the napkins in odd, sausage-shaped rolls, and place a heavy bone-china dinner plate in front of each chair in the formal room. Who even bothered to entertain with bone-china dishware and sterling silver cutlery these days?

Sarah did, apparently. And when Sarah wasn't available to remove the elegant plates from the breakfront, where they were displayed when they weren't in use, she had trained her children to tackle that task. That they performed it without breaking a single dish was only more evidence of their brilliance.

"We need candle too," Becky said as she stood beside Annie and proudly surveyed the table. "Mommy keeps her silver candlesticks on the top shelf of the hutch. I can't reach them."

"I don't know about candles," Annie said. "We're going to have so much food on the table. The candles could get knocked over. And we'll be eating around two-ish, when it's still light outside."

"But candles are pretty," Becky explained.

"The table is already gorgeous. Come—we've got work to do in the kitchen."

Happily distracted, Becky followed Annie back to the kitchen, where yams and squash needed to be peeled and cut up, a salad needed to be prepared, and something had to be done with the plastic bag of celery sticks Annie had sliced last night and brought with her. She put Becky in charge of arranging the celery sticks on a plate and assigned

Trevor the job of opening the cardboard tubes that contained the un-baked rolls. She figured he would enjoy smacking the tubes against the edge of the counter until they popped open and revealed the circles of gooey dough inside.

At ten o'clock, Gordon reappeared in the kitchen, escorting Sarah. Gordon had changed into his official Thanksgiving apparel—crisp khakis and an oxford shirt. No necktie, thank goodness. Sarah had on her styl-ish wig and a demure knit dress that hung off her thin body like Spanish moss off a tree branch in the Deep South. She'd drawn eyebrows above her eyes with makeup and dusted some pink along her cheekbones. No doubt, fashionable Diana Drucker had given her tutorials in cosmetolo-gy if Sarah needed any instruction. She kissed Gordon's cheek and told him to drive carefully. "All the crazies are going to be on the road," she warned. "And half of them are probably driving to the airport."

"I'll be fine." He nodded at Annie and waved to Trevor and Becky. "Don't forget to put on your nice clothes," he reminded them.

"We won't," they chorused, slightly out of sync.

Becky grabbed Sarah's hand before she could sit. "Come see the table, Mommy. It's so pretty. Can we have candles?"

Annie heard Sarah echoing Annie's veto of the candles as they walked to the dining room together. Trevor watched them go, then met Annie's gaze for a flicker of a second before busying himself separating the cylinder of dough into biscuits on a cookie sheet.

"You okay?" Annie asked him quietly.

He shrugged. "Yeah." His voice cracked a little. He was too young to be entering puberty, so she assumed that vocal hitch was caused by emotion. "She's really sick," he murmured.

"I know." Annie lowered the knife she'd been using to hack the yams into chunks and gave him a quick squeeze. "But today is Thanks-giving, and we're going to make it a good one, right? For her sake as well as our own."

"She's lucky you're doing all the cooking," he said.

"She sure as hell is." Annie grinned to show she was joking. Trevor managed a fleeting smile too.

He was too old. Becky was still young enough to believe everything would be fine, her mother would have a happy-ever-after ending, and life would go on, the beautiful Adler family waltzing together into a future filled with sunshine, rainbows, and unicorns like the end of a Disney movie. Trevor knew better. He was trying to be stoic about it, but he could guess which stage of grief his mother had reached, though he himself hadn't reached that stage yet. Why weren't boys allowed to cry? Annie thought angrily. Trevor could use a good sob-fest.

Maybe arranging unbaked rolls for the oven was an adequate substitute. As the dough clung and then peeled away from his fingers, he smiled. "This is like slime," he said.

"Except it isn't green."

"We could use food coloring." He sent her a sly grin.

"We could, but that might give your grandparents heart attacks. And we don't want any heart attacks today."

"Oh, all right." He dramatized his deep disappointment. "We won't color them green."

Annie continued to work. The children came and went. Sarah came and went. At eleven o'clock, Annie sent Becky and Trevor upstairs to change into their official impress-the-grandparents attire.

Sarah made her way into the kitchen. It was warm, the air heavy with the fragrance of roasting turkey. Sarah crossed to the refrigerator and pulled out one of her chocolate energy shakes. "It smells delicious," she said.

"I'd tell you not to spoil your appetite with that drink," Annie teased, "but you need all the calories you can get."

"What I do need is to talk to you," Sarah said solemnly. "Later."

That sounded ominous. Annie reminded herself of what she had told Trevor: this was going to be a good Thanksgiving. Whatever dreadful thing Sarah had to discuss with her, Annie would not allow it to spoil the celebration.

Gordon arrived home a little before noon with his parents. Mr. and Mrs. Adler—Annie couldn't remember their first names—were a formidable couple. They were tall and slim like Gordon, and dressed in the sort of understated clothing that screamed *expensive*. Gordon's father had a rounder face than Gordon's, and his hair was a silver as shiny as the knives and forks tucked into the napkins on the dining room table. Gordon's mother wore her salt-and-pepper hair in a short style almost identical to Sarah's wig. "Hello, dear," she greeted Annie, which made Annie suspect that she couldn't remember Annie's name either. Before Annie could introduce herself, Mrs. Adler swept around the center island and gave Sarah a bracing hug. Annie hoped the woman didn't break any of Sarah's bones.

"Simon Adler," Gordon's father boomed, in case people three houses down the street needed to hear his name. He reached for Annie's hand, but she was holding a sharp knife, and he raised his arms as if to protect himself from attack. He issued a hearty laugh. "You're Sarah's little sister, aren't you."

"Annie," she reminded him. "And I'm not so little."

"Well. It's all about family." With that, he exited the kitchen, as if afraid he might be drafted to stir the gravy if he stuck around.

"Where are those magnificent grandchildren of mine?" Mrs. Adler asked, following her husband out of the kitchen.

Gordon trailed them out, then hollered up the bridal staircase: "Trevor? Becky? Your grandparents are here!"

Sarah made a face—half exasperation, half amusement—and joined the Adlers, abandoning Annie. That was fine. Annie didn't want to make small talk with Gordon's parents.

Or with her own, who arrived just a few minutes later. The doorbell rang, and then Annie heard her mother's voice: "Sarah, sweetheart, how are you feeling? Should you be sitting down? Here, Leo, take my jacket. I need to get Sarah to sit down."

Annie's father appeared in the kitchen doorway, holding her mother's jacket. "How are you, Annie?" he asked.

"Busy but good."

"Your mother asked me to take her coat." He looked at it, as if unsure how it had wound up in his hands. "I guess I should hang it up. God knows they've got more coat closets in this house than they know what to do with."

Annie shared a grin with her father.

"And that fellow you're dating—he's going to be joining us?"

"He'll get here around one," Annie confirmed, reaching for the baster and opening the oven. "Where is everyone settling? The living room? Go join them. I've got things covered here."

"You're a good girl," he said, which pleased her much more than it should have. "Your poor sister, she doesn't look so good."

"She's hanging in there," Annie assured him. Her father was desperate for reassurance, but that reassurance couldn't come from Annie. It had to come from someone who actually knew something, like Gordon or Sarah.

The chatter drifting in from the living room soothed Annie—especially because she didn't have to participate in it. Surrounded by her steamed squash and her yam casserole and the aroma of roasting turkey, she felt she was in good company. At one point, Trevor ventured into the kitchen and said, "Dad asked me to ask you if you wanted a glass of wine."

Annie thanked him and said she'd wait until they all sat down to eat.

She frequently glanced at the clock built into the microwave. She told herself she was monitoring the time so she would know when to take everything out of the oven, when to start carving the turkey, when to ask Becky and Trevor to help her carry the serving dishes to the dining room table. But she was also wondering when Emmett was going to show up.

He didn't show up at one o'clock. The turkey was out of the oven by then, sitting and solidifying while she scooped the stuffing from its cavities and tried not to think that those cavities had once held the turkey's heart, lungs, and digestive system. He didn't show up at one ten, when she pulled the yams out of the oven and transferred them to one of the exquisite serving bowls that matched Sarah's bone china. At one fifteen, she texted him: *Where are you?*

On my way, he texted back after a minute, which could either mean he hadn't been on his way until he'd seen her text, or else he was on the road and didn't want to text while he was driving. Either way, he would be here soon. Late, but soon.

At one thirty, after taking far longer to carve the turkey than she should have, she heard the doorbell ring. She let out a long breath.

"Hello, Emmett," she heard Sarah say, and then, "Oh, that's so nice. Why don't you bring that into the kitchen? Annie will take care of that."

That turned out to be a small bouquet of flowers, the sort usually for sale by the cash registers in the supermarket, where delinquent husbands could grab them on their way home to apologize to their wives for their transgressions. Mostly carnations, a few ferns, something that looked like an orange daisy, all stuffed into a cone of paper.

"Hi," Emmett said, showing her the flowers. "I stopped to buy these for your sister."

"That was very sweet of you," Annie said, meaning it. Sarah probably thought it was a tasteless bouquet, cheap and clichéd, but Annie appreciated Emmett's effort.

She didn't appreciate his outfit, a Henley shirt and jeans—nice ones, at least, not jeans he might have worn to a worksite. And moccasin-style shoes rather than his work boots. Then she thought, *screw it.* If he'd worn his work boots, that would have been fine too. He'd come. He'd brought flowers. He was only a half-hour late.

"Let me put these in some water," she said, taking the flowers and rummaging through the kitchen cabinets until she found a vase. She filled it at the sink, unwrapped the flowers, and balanced them inside the vase, which was too large for the skimpy array. But she didn't care. It was the thought that counted.

She realized, as she set the vase at the center of the island, that Emmett had never brought *her* flowers. But then, Annie wasn't the sort of girl who would get flowers. Sarah was.

Screw it, she thought again. She gave Emmett a big smile. "Let's eat," she said.

chapter twenty-three

THE FOOD WAS FINE. Delicious, even. The turkey had come out of the oven juicy and tender, the stuffing as moist and mushy at it needed to be, the yams piquant, both sweet and salty and nicely crisped. The green beans tasted like green beans, the celery like celery. The wine Gordon had opened, a California Chardonnay, was cold and dry but not too bland.

Other than the food, however, the meal sucked.

Gordon's mother pontificated at length about the museum where she was some high-and-mighty administrator. "Impressionism, impressionism! All anyone wants to see is impressionism! I curated an exhibit last summer on abstract expressionism and nobody wanted to see it. They all insisted on cramming into the impressionism wing and drooling over Monet. What do you think of Monet, Emmett?"

Emmett glanced nervously at Annie. "You mean, like, Janelle Monáe? The singer?"

"Monet the painter," Annie murmured out the side of her mouth.

Emmett shrugged. "I paint too."

"Really?" Gordon's mother gazed the length of her sharp, straight nose. "In what painting school do you fall?"

"I don't paint schools," Emmett shot back. "I paint houses. Interiors. Other people paint the exteriors."

That shut her up, although her left eyebrow arched nearly as high as her hairline. She stared dubiously at him for the rest of the meal.

Annie's mother was happy to steer the conversation in her own direction. "The bereavement support group I belong to has started bringing snacks to meetings. Home-baked things. It's like a competition to see who can make the best snack. They're crazy, those people."

"You enjoy their snacks, though," Sarah muttered as she picked at her food. She was doing pretty well, actually, consuming meat and stuffing and squash. Annie took personal pride in the fact that Sarah was eating the snacks Annie had made—if a slice of turkey with a few pearl-sized dabs of gravy on it, and a spoonful of stuffing, could be considered a snack. Real food had to be healthier for Sarah than chocolate energy shakes.

"I don't understand," Mrs. Adler said. "Are you bereaved?"

"Not at the moment," Gilda replied. "But I like to be prepared."

"Everything is delicious," Gordon broke in, refusing Gilda the opportunity to elaborate on what she was preparing herself for. "Thank you, Annie."

Before Annie could say, "You're welcome," her mother interjected, "Dessert was my responsibility. Save room for the pies, everyone."

Annie might have reminded Gilda that *she'd* made the pies. But Gilda hadn't exactly lied. She had taken responsibility for dessert, and then dumped that responsibility on Annie.

Annie didn't want to argue with her mother. She didn't want the spotlight, and her mother craved the spotlight. Let her have it. Annie was happy enough that Sarah was eating, and Gordon had thanked her, and Trevor and Becky were behaving well—better than their grandparents, really—and Emmett had silenced Mrs. Adler by claiming he painted interiors. That was enough to be thankful for.

The children helped Annie clear the table and carry in the pies. Even Sarah asked for a half-inch sliver of pumpkin pie. Emmett wolfed down a thick wedge of apple pie, then stood and excused himself. "I hate to have to leave," he said, towering over the table in his casual apparel, his hair mussed and a crumb of pie crust caught in his beard, "but I have to go eat a holiday dinner with my parents."

Gordon's father released a booming laugh. "Whoa, boy—one of these days all that food is going to catch up with you. I see these fellows at the golf course. They still eat the way they ate when they were teenagers, and oh, man. Talk about potbellies..."

"Beer bellies," his wife helpfully corrected him. "Pot has nothing to do with it."

Trevor and Becky exchanged a look and smothered their laughter behind their fancy linen napkins.

Annie rose as well. "I'll see Emmett out," she told everyone. To Gordon, she added, "When you get a chance, my wine glass could use a refill."

She escorted Emmett to the foyer and located his jacket in one of the coat closets. "Thanks," she whispered. "You did well. You held your own."

"The food was great," he said. "Worth all the bullshit." He planted a quick kiss on her mouth and stepped out into the blustery late afternoon.

Annie returned to the dining room. Half of her slice of apple pie remained on her dessert plate, but she was more interested in her goblet, which Gordon had topped off with wine, bless his heart. She settled into her chair and took a bracing sip.

"Talk about eating and running," her mother clucked. "Did he really have to leave?"

"He really did," Annie said.

"He just came for the food," her mother complained.

Which was better than the company, Annie thought. What she said was, "He brought Sarah some pretty flowers. They're in the kitchen."

"Ooh—I want to see the flowers!" Becky shoved back her chair and stood, then hesitated. "May I be excused?"

"Yes, you may," Sarah said, "but clear your place."

Becky and Trevor gathered their plates and dessert forks and scampered out of the dining room. Annie envied them, although unlike them, she had wine to see her through. From the kitchen, she heard Becky shout, "They're pretty!"

Gilda narrowed her gaze on Annie. "You and that boy ought to figure out where you're heading," she said. "Time's a-wasting. You're no spring chicken."

"We're not having this conversation," Annie shot back. Assertive. Her mother didn't deserve nice.

"So, it looks like the Bears are having a decent season," Gordon's father announced. The Adler men were now Annie's favorite people—one providing wine and the other providing a safe topic for conversation.

Relatively safe. "They haven't got a prayer," Annie's father said. "Now, the Patriots..."

The menfolk lost themselves in a thicket of football-speak. Annie consumed a generous gulp of wine, then stood. "I'm going to get started in the kitchen," she said, lifting her glass to bring with her. She would need the wine for fortification as she tackled the dishes, pots, and pans. "There's a lot of stuff to clean up."

Her mother gave her a sharp, almost condemning look, apparently believing Annie should remain at the table and listen to the men analyze passing arms and coaching strategies. But Gordon's mother joined the football talk and Sarah kept working on her pie, one tiny bite at a time. No one, other than possibly Gilda, would miss Annie if she escaped the dining room.

The kitchen was a mess. Annie knew that, since she'd created the mess herself. In the center of the island, the flowers Emmett had brought stood bravely in their oversized vase, surrounded by platters filled with leftovers and casserole dishes caked with dried sauce. Trevor was at the refrigerator, helping himself to a glass of milk. Becky perched on a stool by the island and was prying a leftover chunk of the yam casserole from the lip of its baking dish. Freeing it from the glass, she popped it into her mouth. "We can help you with the dishes if you want," she offered.

"You don't have to, but I'd enjoy the company," Annie said. "They're discussing football in the dining room."

That piqued Trevor's interest. "I can help with the dishes later," he said, slamming the refrigerator door and hurrying back to the dining room.

Annie smiled and ruffled his hair as he passed her. "Go talk football," she urged him. He vanished, his upper lip adorned with a faint milk mustache.

"I don't like football," Becky said. "It's a stupid game."

"Not like rugby," Annie agreed, surveying the array of dishes, silver, and cookware awaiting soap and hot water. The mere sight inspired her to take another fortifying sip of her wine. "Okay. Let's get some of these pots into the sink to soak, and then we can stack the dishwasher."

Voices drifted in from the dining room, occasionally raised, occasionally dissolved in laughter. Emmett would have enjoyed the sports talk, but he probably enjoyed leaving even more. Her mother undoubtedly hated the sports talk, but she would rather sit at the table and listen to it than come into the kitchen and help Annie scrub pans. Annie donned her apron, took one more sip of wine, and realized she would rather scrub pans.

"It was a great Thanksgiving," Becky said sweetly. "Mommy ate a lot. Did you see?"

"I sure did. I'm glad she enjoyed the meal."

"She eats hardly anything most of the time." Becky filled a glass with milk for herself, then added a discreet squirt of chocolate syrup. "Daddy said we can have chocolate milk sometimes. He said Mommy won't mind."

"Live it up," Annie said. She busied herself wrapping the leftover meat in aluminum foil, then transferring the other leftovers into the lidded plastic containers she found in one of the cabinets, sorted by size and color. "You guys will be enjoying Thanksgiving for the next three days," she noted as the leftovers began to pile up. "Your mom won't have to cook."

"She likes to show off for Daddy's parents," Becky said, "but she doesn't cook much these days."

"Well, they can enjoy the leftovers too. They're sticking around for a few days, right?"

Becky answered with a nod. She proved a diligent assistant, carefully rinsing and stacking the plates in the dishwasher, separating the silverware into their designated slots. *You are perfect*, Annie thought as she stood beside Becky, scrubbing the roaster pan that had held the turkey. *You don't have to be perfect, but you are.* She felt a wave of love for her niece so powerful it nearly staggered her. Funny how she never felt love like that for Emmett. But for Becky... Her love was fierce and angry and protective. She wanted to wrap her niece in her arms and shield her from all the bad things that were bound to happen to her in the future—in the near future, if Sarah didn't rebound. But if she grabbed Becky and hugged her now, she would startle the poor girl, and also splash warm, sudsy water all over her.

Gradually, the clutter filling the island and counters thinned out. From the dining room, Annie could hear the conversation thinning out too. Her parents entered the kitchen, her mother striding ahead of her father. "We're taking off," she said.

Annie turned from the sink and acknowledged them with a nod.

"Your sister looked so pretty today, didn't she?" Annie's mother declared before giving Annie a perfunctory kiss on the cheek. "Looks like you've got everything under control here. Leo?"

Annie's father circled around her mother and gave Annie a gentle squeeze. "I'm not saying you should get married," he murmured, "but he's a nice man. You could do worse."

"He isn't Jewish, Dad," Annie reminded him with a grin.

"I know. I remember. Strange, with a last name like Levy, but… Look, do what you want to do. As far as I'm concerned, you're still a spring chicken."

Annie smiled again and kissed her father's cheek. Over the food aromas that lingered in the brightly lit room, she caught a whiff of Old Spice, the same aftershave he'd been wearing since she was born. Her father never really changed, and that was all right. Her mother never changed, either, which was unfortunate.

Once her parents were gone, Gordon, his parents, and Trevor paraded into the kitchen. "Wow," Gordon said. "It looks as if the scullery maids deserve a raise!"

"Does that mean I get more allowance?" Becky asked, abandoning the dishwasher to give her father a hug.

"It means go put on a swimsuit. Grandma and Grandpa want to enjoy a soak in the hot tub."

"Okay!" Becky raced Trevor to the back stairs, although Trevor, being older and a boy, arrived at the stairway a fraction of a second ahead of her and edged her out of the way so he could climb the stairs first.

"You're welcome to join us," Gordon invited Annie, even though his parents looked less than thrilled by the prospect.

"Thanks, but I'll pass," she said, noting how Mrs. Adler's expression softened. "I'm just going to finish up here. Where's Sarah? Any chance she'll join you all in the hot tub?"

Gordon gave his head a slight shake, then ushered his parents out of the kitchen in the direction of the bridal staircase.

Much as she'd appreciated Becky's company, Annie also appreciated the peace of having the entire kitchen to herself. The ceiling spotlights reflected off the white cabinetry and the copper-bottomed pans dangling decoratively from the ceiling, illuminating every sticky spot and stain on every platter and casserole dish—and also a dot of brown gravy on her left sleeve. She rubbed a little dish soap into the sleeve, rinsed it out, and decided that having a soggy sweater sleeve wrapped around her arm was almost as good as sitting in the hot tub.

She finished scouring the serving dish from the squash, balanced it on the drying rack beside the sink, and wiped her hands and her wet sleeve on a dish towel. Turning to see what she might have missed, she noticed Sarah lurking in the doorway. "Good job," Sarah said, managing a smile. "I'll mail you your holiday bonus."

"Gee, Gordo promised me a raise," Annie joked. Her gaze drifted from her sister to her wine glass, still half full, standing on the island near the flowers Emmett had brought. She crossed to the island, grabbed her glass, and took a hefty sip.

"Can we talk?" Sarah asked.

Annie wondered if she would need her glass filled to the brim to get through this talk. But she would be driving home soon. Better not to overdo it with the wine.

She followed her sister out of the kitchen and into the living room. The last time Annie had been in this room, she had been searching for a decent backdrop for her video call with her colleagues at work, the morning Sarah underwent surgery. That seemed so long ago. Sarah had appeared so much healthier then, hopeful that the surgery would get rid of her cancer.

It hadn't, of course. Now the chemo was supposed to get rid of it. According to Gordon, that wasn't happening either.

Annie sat beside Sarah on the plush sofa—the sofa purchased to replace the sofa in Annie's living room. This one, Annie had to admit, was much more comfortable. The fabric looked fresh, not faded, and the upholstery was firm, not sagging. The glossy coffee table in front of her held a few sterling silver coasters, and Annie carefully set her glass down on one of them. She realized she still had on her apron, and her left sleeve was still damp—and still had a faint brown speck on it.

If Sarah noticed the stain, tough. If what she wanted to talk about was Annie's inability to cook and eat a meal without getting a little food on her sweater, so be it. At least Annie didn't have a pie-crust crumb on her face, as Emmett had.

"I need to ask a favor of you," Sarah said.

Wonderful. "I just cooked your whole Thanksgiving dinner," Annie said, hearing the weariness in her voice. "And cleaned your whole fucking kitchen. And refrained from strangling Mom. You really want to ask me to do something more?"

"This is...complicated," Sarah said.

Annie reached for her wine.

"It's about Gordon."

Annie glanced toward the rear of the house. If the weather had been mild, windows might have been open, and she might have heard Gordon, the children, and his parents laughing and splashing in the hot tub. But the windows were shut, and all she heard was a little click in her throat as she swallowed her wine.

"He's ready to blow," Sarah said.

"Blow?"

"Like a volcano. He's got all this anger building up inside him, and all this tension, and he's going to blow soon. It's because he hasn't had sex in over a year."

Thank God Annie hadn't taken another drink of wine. She would have choked on it, or spat it out. White wine wouldn't stain like gravy, and she still did have on the apron. But she would have hated to waste a mouthful of wine. If she'd heard Sarah correctly, she was going to need every last drop of the potent beverage in her glass to get through the conversation.

Evidently, Sarah interpreted Annie's stunned silence as an invitation to continue. "He's a very...*robust* man. He likes sex. A lot. And, well, we haven't—"

"I don't think I want to know this," Annie said.

She had never doubted that her sister and brother-in-law had a healthy sex life. They had produced two children, hadn't they? And Annie had seen Gordon in swim trunks. He looked normal. He looked male.

As for Sarah... Sex was simply something she and Annie didn't talk about. They certainly hadn't talked about it when they'd been young. Annie had learned about menstruation at the ripe old age of eight, by eavesdropping on her mother when she'd lectured eleven-year-old

Sarah on the subject. In Gilda's explanation, most women didn't find getting their periods much of an issue, but when Gilda had her period, she experienced abdominal pain, lower back pain, and headaches severe enough to prevent her from doing anything she didn't want to do.

After Annie had started menstruating—and gotten chewed out by Sarah for using what Sarah considered her own personal supply of tampons—Annie's mother had decided Annie needed to learn how not to get pregnant. "I gave Sarah a book all about it," Gilda had told Annie. "Tell her to give you the book."

In other words, hand-me-down sex education, just like the hand-me-down clothing Annie use to inherit from Sarah.

The book had been filled with explicit line drawings of male and female torsos. From these line drawings, Annie had learned the mechanics of sex. It was only years later, when she'd been in college and had her first, remarkably unsatisfactory sexual experience, that her roommate Jenna had informed her of what the hand-me-down book hadn't: "The most important sex organ is your brain." There had been no drawings of brains—or even heads—in that stupid book.

After Annie had read the book as a young teenager, she had asked Sarah to elaborate on a few of its teachings. Sarah had responded patronizingly, saying, "I think you're too young for me to explain that," or "You wouldn't understand."

Now, twenty years later, Sarah apparently no longer thought Annie was too young. That was unfortunate. Annie definitely wanted to be too young for this discussion. "Gordo's sex drive is none of my business," she said. "That's between you and him."

Sarah peered at Annie. Her eyes were too hard, too intense. "The trouble is, I'm his wife."

"Exactly. You're his wife."

"I've been sick a long time. I was sick before we knew I was sick. Sex hurt, so I just couldn't do it. I tried giving him blow jobs, but they made me vomit."

Too much information, Annie thought, wondering if clapping her hands over her ears might make Sarah shut up.

"And it's just...it's been so long, and I've talked to him about, like, going to a prostitute, or—I mean, just finding someone to have sex with.

For the release. But he won't listen to me. He says I'm his wife and I shouldn't be telling him these things."

"That sounds reasonable," Annie said carefully.

"I'm his wife and I can't have sex with him, and I want him to get his rocks off so he won't explode. I know there are online sites where you can find escorts. But even if I found them and sent him the links, he would ignore me. He won't even have this conversation with me."

I don't blame him, Annie thought, sipping her wine and wishing she could get drunk enough to pretend Sarah had never started the discussion.

"But you're younger than us, and you're—well, he thinks you're cool because you're single. You could check out these sites and find someone for him. You wouldn't have to pay for it or anything, just point him in that direction."

In this context, Annie didn't even want to think about the word *point*. And of course she wouldn't have to pay for a prostitute for her brother-in-law. Honestly. What Sarah was asking Annie to do was outrageous, even if Annie didn't have to foot the bill. "Sarah, this is crazy. If he won't listen to you, he sure as shit won't listen to me."

"He *will*, because you're not his wife and he thinks you're cool."

"I'm not cool. *You* know I'm not cool."

"Yes, but he thinks you are."

Leave it to Sarah to insult Annie even as she was begging for a favor. "So...what? I'm supposed to go online, find a hooker for him, and then what? Arrange a time and place? I mean, come on, Sarah."

"Just lead him to water. He'll drink if you lead him."

Great. Now Sarah was discussing her husband as if he were the horse in that old saying about how you could lead a horse to water but you couldn't make him drink. No matter how cool Gordon thought Annie was, she couldn't make him drink.

And she didn't want to. Sarah shouldn't be asking her to. Sarah had other people she could turn to. If she didn't think Annie was tasteful or intelligent or clever enough to help her pick out a wig, why did she think Annie was tasteful, intelligent, and clever enough to hire a prostitute for Gordon?

"Couldn't you ask Diana to do this?" Annie asked. "She's your best friend, right?"

Sarah scowled and shook her head. "She's my best friend, but she's always had a crush on Gordon. I remember the way she flirted with him at our wedding. And at the rehearsal dinner. Didn't you notice that? You were there."

No, Annie hadn't noticed. Although she was Sarah's maid of honor, she had remained isolated from the other bridesmaids, who had all been Sarah's friends and therefore Sarah's choice as attendants. Annie had been forced upon her, because when you had a sister, you had to make your sister your maid of honor.

That Diana had flirted with Gordon over the wedding weekend and Sarah still considered Diana her best friend boggled Annie's mind. But... "If Diana is your best friend, she ought to be willing to do this for you."

Sarah sniffed. "She'd volunteer to screw him herself."

"That would get the job done," Annie noted with some relief. Maybe this situation could be handled that easily: just get Diana Drucker to seduce Gordon.

"It has to be with someone he doesn't know," Sarah insisted. "Someone he has no emotional connection to. He's known Diana as long as he's known me. And I don't think he'd have sex with her, even if he had the opportunity."

It sounded as if he'd had the opportunity on several occasions. Annie thought it spoke well of him that he'd never acted on that opportunity.

"It has to be anonymous, basically," Sarah explained. "Someone he doesn't care about. No emotions involved. As long as there's no emotional involvement, it won't be like he cheated on me. It will be strictly a physical release."

Annie mulled over the idea, then shook her head. "I can't do this. Cooking Thanksgiving dinner—I made the pies from scratch, by the way—that was nothing. Asking Gordon to get it on with a call girl..."

"Please." Sarah's voice broke. "I'm dying, Annie. I need Gordon to be strong and healthy, to be able to deal with the children when I'm gone."

"Don't talk that way," Annie retorted. "Forty percent—"

"*Please.*" To Annie's surprise, Sarah reached over and grabbed Annie's free hand. Her other hand jerked, splashing a little wine.

Fortunately, the splatter landed on Annie's apron. "Gordon can put together mergers all day, he's a great lawyer—but when he comes home, he doesn't know what to do. His idea of being a dad is to take the kids skating or out for ice cream. He thinks giving them special treats is the way to be a father. And he thinks having a wife is the way to get sex on a regular basis. But it's been over a year, and he's freaking out."

"Has he ever heard of masturbation?" Annie asked dryly. Her gaze remained on Sarah's hand interlaced with hers. Sarah might think she was dying, but she'd managed to get a manicure at some point. Her nails were perfect opalescent-pink ovals. Annie's nails were clipped stubs. She lacked the patience to grow them long enough to do anything with them.

"It's not the same," Sarah said. "I've suggested that, but he says it's all about having a woman with him for the ride. He's very heterosexual."

Annie sighed. She wanted to slide her hand from Sarah's—but, she admitted, she also wanted to keep holding her sister's hand. When she'd been a child, trailing after her older sister, she had always tried to hold hands with Sarah, to feel in some way connected to whatever Sarah was doing, because whatever she was doing was always so much more interesting and accomplished and magnificent than anything Annie was doing. Annie wanted to be included in Sarah's glorious world.

Whenever Sarah had noticed Annie trailing along behind her, she would accelerate her pace, just to avoid Annie. Just to avoid holding Annie's hand.

But now they were holding hands—at Sarah's instigation, not Annie's. Did Sarah admire and envy Annie as much now as Annie had admired and envied Sarah then?

"Please," Sarah said again. "You like Gordon, don't you?"

"He's a good man," Annie allowed. A few months ago, she might not have said that. A few months ago, she hadn't known him well enough to say it.

"So do this for him. You don't have to do it for me. Do it for him."

Annie shuddered. She grimaced. But Sarah squeezed her hand, and she squeezed back. "I'll see," Annie said.

chapter twenty-four

IT WAS LATE WHEN ANNIE FINALLY ARRIVED BACK AT HER CONDO, her bags now light but bulky with empty food containers. After parking her car, she circled around to the front of the building and smiled when she saw the front porch empty. Not that she would have minded finding Emmett there—although if she'd found him there with an empty pizza box beside him, she might have worried a little about his developing a pot belly, or a beer belly. Or, in his case, a pizza belly. More immediately, she might have worried about his spending the night on his knees in front of the toilet, throwing up. Two Thanksgiving dinners was plenty enough for one man, even a large, physically active man like Emmett.

But he wasn't there. Maybe he was still dining with his parents. Maybe he had gone back to his own apartment to crash on the couch— or to force Frank and his sweetheart to crash on the couch so he could crash in his own bed. Wherever he crashed, Annie didn't want him in her bed tonight. As exhausted as she was, the only mattress activity she wanted to engage in was sleeping.

She let herself in the front door, trudged up the stairs, and slid her key into her unit's doorknob. It twisted, but the door didn't open. The dead bolt above the doorknob had been engaged.

It wasn't as if she was locked out. The same key opened both the knob and the dead bolt. But you couldn't lock the dead bolt without a key. If Emmett had locked it when he'd left her place earlier that afternoon...he must have a key.

Shit.

Suddenly, she didn't feel so exhausted. Anger washed over her like a stinging-cold ocean wave, jolting her back to life.

Had Emmett helped himself to her spare key?

She unlocked the dead bolt, shoved open the door, and stormed into the kitchen. After tossing her bags onto the counter, she yanked open the drawer where she kept her spare key on its palm-tree key ring. The drawer contained its usual clutter—pencil stubs, rubber bands, scissors, a roll of cellophane tape, a ruler, a set of old copper measuring spoons, a few stray grocery-store discount coupons, a cookie cutter in the shape of a penguin. No palm-tree key ring. No spare key.

Shit!

She was still staring at the contents of the drawer, as if she could conjure a vision of the tacky souvenir key ring simply by focusing her eyes on the space where it ought to have been, when her intercom buzzed, announcing a visitor downstairs on the front porch. She abandoned the drawer for the intercom speaker and pressed the button. "Who's there?"

"It's me," Emmett said. "Can you buzz me in?"

"You can let yourself in," she snapped. "You've got my fucking spare key."

A silence, and then he said, "Okay."

Did he know she was furious? Could he tell by the tone of her voice, by her dropping the f-bomb?

She wished she had more containers to put away, or to wash, or to bang around the kitchen. She didn't want her anger to dissipate in the time it would take Emmett to enter the building and climb to the second floor. She wanted to stay just as pissed off as she was right now.

A glance at the kitchen drawer where her spare key should have been fueled her, like a dry log tossed onto a fire. She could feel the flames blazing with renewed life.

The heat of her anger intensified when she heard the click of the key—*her* key—in the lock, first the dead bolt and then the doorknob. And then Emmett entered the condo.

Her condo.

He was dressed as he had been that afternoon, in his Henley shirt and jeans. He gave her a hopeful, somewhat sheepish smile and spread his arms wide, as if he expected her to leap into them.

She remained where she was, standing beside the counter in the kitchen, glaring at him.

"Hey," he said. Ordinarily, his adorable, dimpled smile would have thawed her anger. Tonight, however, she was too cold to thaw. She was subzero icy—which made no sense, since she'd just imagined her anger as an inferno of leaping, dancing hellfire flames.

"Your turkey was much better than the restaurant's turkey," he said. Was that his idea of making amends? Of course Annie's turkey was better than the restaurant's turkey. She had known it would be. That was why she'd asked Emmett to join her family for Thanksgiving dinner.

"You took my spare key."

Still grinning, he shrugged sheepishly, as if he were a child who had gotten caught reading under the blanket with a flashlight when he was supposed to be asleep. "I had to lock up when I left."

"You could have locked up without the key. I left you a note saying, just make sure the doorknob button was in the lock position."

"But then I couldn't lock the dead bolt."

"You didn't have to lock the dead bolt. The locked doorknob was enough."

"All right. Fine. I thought you'd want the dead bolt locked, for safety's sake."

How safe was locking the dead bolt supposed to make her feel? She hadn't been home. If a criminal had broken in, he wouldn't have been able to hurt her. And she didn't have much worth stealing. The television, maybe. Emmett did seem to love her television set. Maybe protecting the television was why he'd taken her spare key and double-locked the door.

She extended her hand, palm up, and glowered. Reluctantly, still with that juvenile *uh-oh* smile, he reached into a pocket of his jeans and pulled out the spare key on its Honolulu airport key ring. He dropped it into her palm. "Okay?"

No. Not okay. He avoided meeting her gaze, staring instead at the dishwasher, the microwave, the refrigerator, the counters cluttered with all the empty containers she'd brought home. Looking anywhere but at Annie.

Distrust slid a chill down her spine, as if an ice cube had been dropped under the neckline of her sweater in back. Forget about burning with anger. She was freezing with it. "You made a copy of my key," she guessed.

He still wouldn't make eye contact with her. A long, tense moment passed, and then he dug his hand back into his pocket and pulled out another key, this one unattached to a key ring.

Her anger switched from freezing to burning again. The nerve of him, making a copy of her key! Without her permission! If she hadn't guessed, he might never have told her, and then he could be coming and going whenever he wished, even if she wasn't home.

She would have figured out he had a key soon enough, if she arrived home after work and found him upstairs, sprawled out on her couch, munching on a slice of pizza while he viewed a Celtics or a Bruins game on her TV. *Her* TV. *Her* couch.

Her key.

"Get out," she said.

"Oh, come on." Maybe he hoped to soothe her, to make her laugh about this as if it were just some silly little thing she'd blown out of proportion. But his voice was edged in impatience. "I'm here all the time, anyway. It makes sense that I should have a key."

"It's *my* home," she retorted. "If I wanted you to have a key, I'd give you a key."

"You always make me feel welcome here. I just assumed—"

"It's one thing to make an assumption," she snapped. "It's another thing to take my key without my permission and make a copy of it. That's what thieves do."

"Come on, Annie! I'm not a thief."

No, but if he had kept his copy of the key, he would have stolen something: her privacy. Her ownership. Her right to decide who could enter her home, which she paid for, which she'd filled out a million mortgage application forms for, which she paid taxes on. Where she listened to her upstairs neighbor clomp around and pee. Where she received unsolicited address stickers from various charities she never donated to, but those address stickers had *her* name on them. Emmett had stolen the integrity of her home. And he'd shown up late for Sarah's

Thanksgiving dinner, probably because he had been driving around, searching for a hardware store that was open on the holiday so he could get a copy of the spare key made.

"Get your stuff and leave," she said.

"You're overreacting," he countered. "Come on, Annie. We're doing great. This isn't worth fighting over."

Maybe she was overreacting. Maybe her fatigue from baking and cooking and preparing a huge feast, compounded by having to deal with her mother's obnoxiousness, and Gordon's parents' superciliousness, and Sarah's illness and now her latest favor request, which was just so weird and ridiculous...

She was allowed to overreact.

"We're not doing great anymore," she said quietly. "You broke my trust."

He ventured a step closer to her. "It's late. I don't want to leave. I don't want to go back to my place and deal with Frank."

"Fine. Then you can spend the night on the couch. You can't sleep in my bed." *My* bed, she thought. Fuck being nice. He had stolen her key.

She marched into her bedroom and slammed the door so hard, she was sure both her upstairs and her downstairs neighbors would feel the building's walls trembling. Once inside the bedroom, she realized she had to use the bathroom. But she didn't want to see Emmett. She wanted to stew and seethe and wallow in her righteous anger.

She stripped off her clothes, set aside her sweater to toss into the laundry hamper, and rummaged through her dresser until she found a nightgown—a garment she hadn't worn since Emmett had started sleeping over. She wore it now, smoothing out its wrinkles so it would fall neatly to her ankles, and then added her bathrobe, tying the sash in a double knot. When she emerged from her bedroom, she found Emmett seated where he usually sat on the couch, his thumb tapping the remote control to turn on the television.

She shut herself inside the bathroom. The vanity counter held not just her toothbrush but Emmett's, along with his electric beard trimmer, his nail clipper, and a jar of some sort of manly moisturizer for, according to the label, hands that did hard work. She resisted the temptation to sweep his toiletries into the trash can and focused on brushing her teeth and washing her face. Staring at her reflection, she decided she looked different. A little less nice, perhaps. A little more outraged. A lot agitated.

She used the toilet, then left the bathroom. Emmett must have found a sports event to watch; she heard the din of fans cheering and shouting.

She returned to her bedroom, slammed the door again—because slamming it felt cathartic—and checked her reflection once more, this time in the mirror above her dresser.

This is what a woman who is breaking up with her boyfriend on Thanksgiving looks like, she thought. It wasn't what a woman who was supposed to pimp for her brother-in-law looked like. It wasn't what a woman who had come up with the name "Cabbage World" for the podcast she'd also come up with the idea for looked like. It wasn't what a woman whose mother was a narcissist and whose father was a nebbish and whose sister was dying looked like.

Or maybe it was.

chapter twenty-five

SHE FOUND EMMETT ASLEEP ON THE COUCH when she ventured out of her bedroom the next morning. She had been restless all night, her mind buzzing like a beehive with thoughts about her sister and brother-in-law and Emmett. But Emmett was deeply asleep when she found him, his breath emerging in a faint, steady snore. He had helped himself to a blanket and pillow from the linen closet—no pillowcase; his dark hair was splayed against the blue-and-white striped ticking of the pillow—and he might have been naked under the blanket. All she could see was his head, his thick shoulders, and one arm slung outside the blanket. His fingers were curled around the television's remote control.

The TV was on, although the sound was muted. A football game filled the screen, bulky men in uniforms scurrying around a field that was too green to be real grass. A chyron across the bottom of the screen announced that this was a rebroadcast of a game had been played on Thanksgiving. Annie left the TV on so she wouldn't inadvertently wake Emmett by prying the remote control from his somnolent grip.

She tiptoed to the bathroom, annoyed by her effort not to disturb him—she was so done with being nice. But then she acknowledged that she was trying to avoid waking him because she didn't want to deal with him, which wasn't particularly nice at all. She certainly wasn't nice enough to skip showering. The hiss of the water spilling full force from the shower head and bouncing against the tiles sounded raucous in the bathroom. If he could hear it through the wall, too bad.

After showering, she bundled herself back into her nightgown and robe; Emmett was no longer entitled to see her undressed. En route to her bedroom, she peeked at him and noted that he had shifted on the couch but was still snoring, still clutching the remote control. How he could sleep on that couch, Annie couldn't imagine. The couch Sarah had bought to replace it was infinitely more comfortable.

Annie donned yoga pants and an old sweatshirt, left her bedroom for the kitchen, and prepared a pot of coffee. While it brewed, she settled at the table with her laptop and Googled "prostitutes." A list of articles about prostitution appeared. Not what she was looking for.

"That coffee smells great," Emmett declared, startling her. Glancing up, she saw him filling the doorway, wearing just his jeans, displaying his physique, his honed muscles creating intriguing contours and shadows. She steered her gaze back to her laptop. She did *not* want Emmett and sex to occupy the same thought bubble in her brain.

"I'm supposed to be back at the worksite at..." He glanced at the digital clock in the microwave's control panel. "Five minutes ago. Oh, well. It's a holiday. I can show up late."

Not exactly a world-beater, Annie muttered to herself.

"Any chance I can convince you to scramble some eggs for me?"

No. But Annie realized she was also hungry. And maybe—all right, it wouldn't kill her to be slightly nice. Emmett had crossed a line last night, but he'd paid for his transgression by sleeping on the uncomfortable couch.

Besides, she wanted some eggs too.

She wasn't going to be nice enough to wish him a good morning, let alone kiss him. Closing her laptop, she shoved her chair back, stood, and got busy cracking eggs into a bowl.

"Your sister looked pretty bad yesterday," Emmett said.

She remembered that he had brought Sarah a bouquet of flowers yesterday. A thoughtful gesture, even if Annie and not Sarah had performed all the labor of hosting the meal. Emmett had never given Annie flowers. In fact, he had never given her anything, other than orgasms and an occasional slice of pizza.

"Your parents still don't like me," he said.

Which might be a good enough reason for Annie to give him her spare key. Just to spite them.

She said nothing. The eggs hissed when she poured them into a heated frying pan.

"Are you not going to talk to me?"

"I'm tired," she told him. "I didn't sleep well last night."

He laughed and moved behind her, wrapping his arms around her. "You needed a good fuck to relax you," he said.

She was tempted to smack him over the head with the pan. That might kill him, but it would also waste the eggs, so she refrained. Easing out of his embrace, she busied herself toasting a few slices of bread.

He pulled a mug from the cabinet above the sink, filled it with coffee, and took a cautious sip. She resented how easily he made himself at home in her condo, helping himself to blankets and pillows and coffee mugs. And her spare key, she reminded herself. Her spare key which he'd made a copy of. Had he figured he would slip the palm-tree key ring back into the drawer without her ever noticing that it had been missing? Would he have then used the copy he'd made to come and go at will? Or had he planned to tell her, eventually, that he had his own key to her place? What would have happened if he hadn't made the mistake of locking the deadbolt? She would never have searched for the spare key in the drawer.

By the time she had set their plates down on the table, she was no longer feeling even a scintilla of niceness toward him. They ate in silence, Emmett occasionally glancing at the microwave clock, as if calculating how much pay he was going to get docked by showing up late for work. Probably none at all. He would charm his foreman the way he charmed everyone. He was lazy, but...those shoulders. Those dimples. The bouquet that proved what a great guy he was.

Annie seethed.

"I hate to eat and run, but I've got to go," he said, not bothering to carry his empty dishes to the sink before he bounded out of the kitchen.

She remained at the table, picking at the yellow curds of egg that she no longer had an appetite for. She listened to him clomp and thump around the living room, getting dressed. "See you later," he shouted optimistically before swinging through the door and shutting it behind him.

She waited for a moment, half expecting him to lock the dead bolt. When he didn't, she took that as a sign that he hadn't made several copies of her spare key, holding onto one for himself.

Should she change her locks?

Oh, for God's sake. This was Emmett. The guy she slept with. The guy she had brought to her family's Thanksgiving. No need to get paranoid.

After she rinsed the dishes and stacked them in the dishwasher, she folded the blanket he'd left in a heap on the couch and turned off the damned TV. Then she returned to the kitchen, grabbed her phone, and called Chloe.

"Hey," Annie said, "I need to ask you about prostitutes."

"Oh, like I'm an expert?" Chloe laughed. "I haven't sold my body in years."

"Not *you*," Annie said. "You majored in psychology, though. You know about stuff. My sister thinks I need to find a prostitute for her husband so he can have sex."

"Wow." Chloe chewed on that for a minute. "Does he *want* to have sex?"

"My sister says that if he doesn't have sex soon, he's going to blow like Vesuvius. She's too sick to provide her services, and she doesn't want him to have sex with someone he knows, because then emotions might get involved."

"How about a sex surrogate?" Chloe said.

"What's that?"

"It's a person trained to give sex therapy to a patient. They usually work with people who have physical or psychological issues. Like, they're impotent, or they're paraplegics, or something like that. The surrogate will coach the patient so he can have some kind of sex life."

"That sounds kind of clinical," Annie said. "Besides, I don't think Gordo has any problems like that. He isn't paralyzed or anything. Sarah just thinks he needs to get his rocks off."

"With a prostitute?"

"It doesn't have to be a prostitute. It just has to be someone with no emotional involvement."

"In other words, a prostitute." Chloe sighed. "Craigslist, maybe? Or...how about someone from Cabot? They're college students. They're always broke. Maybe for the right price—"

"Are you kidding? No," Annie said emphatically. "They're *kids*."

"Actually, they're legal adults."

"And the power differential is ridiculous. They're broke, he's a hot-shot lawyer—"

"That's the same power differential that exists between hookers and their clients," Chloe pointed out.

"All right. Never mind. This is a stupid idea."

"I can't argue that." Chloe paused, then asked, "How was your Thanksgiving?"

"The food was good," Annie reported. "My sister looks awful. Gordo is painfully horny, according to her. His parents are snobs. My parents are idiots. The children behaved very well."

"Didn't you have Emmett at your Thanksgiving too?"

"Yeah. He behaved...not quite as well as the kids. He arrived late and left early."

"I left my family's Thanksgiving early too," Chloe said. "I told them I had to take Grandpa home, but it was really for me. My brother was a dick. He started yelling at me when I went for seconds on the stuffing, telling me I needed to lose weight or I would die of a heart attack. My sister-in-law told him I wasn't going to die of a heart attack, but then she lectured me on how no one was ever going to marry me unless I lost a few pounds. So I said, 'Grandpa, I think it's time to leave,' and Grandpa said, 'Okay.' He's so agreeable."

"I wish my parents had that kind of dementia," Annie said. "The pleasant kind."

"The handy-excuse kind," Chloe confirmed. "I've got to go. I'm at work right now. Some of us don't work for schools that give you the day after Thanksgiving off."

"Well, better to be at work instead of getting trampled by the mobs doing their Black Friday shopping," Annie said. "I'll do a little research into this surrogate thing. Thanks for the suggestion."

After ending the call, Annie refilled her coffee cup and opened her laptop again. But she didn't feel like researching sexual surrogates. Gordon didn't need therapy. He just needed sex. At least Sarah thought he did.

Annie was too tired to concentrate on Gordon. Too edgy. Too distracted by thoughts about Emmett. It didn't bother her that she wasn't a spring chicken, or even a summer or autumn chicken; she couldn't imagine herself marrying him. But he *had* brought flowers for Sarah. He had his moments.

Still...

He was awfully presumptuous, and maybe a touch dishonest.

She'd been seeing too much of him lately. Maybe if he returned to his own place every now and then, she would feel more kindly toward him.

Sighing, she decided to run a load of laundry. Sarah would be proud of her, exerting herself to clean the sweater she'd worn yesterday before the Thanksgiving stain became permanent. She would launder her apron, too, so it would look pristine the next time Sarah hired her to cater a dinner for her in-laws.

She entered the bathroom and tried not to scowl as her gaze took in the clutter of Emmett's grooming gear on the vanity counter. A door at the end of the small room opened onto an even smaller room—a utility closet, really—that held a stacked washer/dryer and her laundry hamper. Pulling the hamper out, she noticed that it held not just her sweater and assorted other articles of her clothing but also some boxer briefs. Emmett's boxer briefs.

He expected her to do his laundry too? He expected her to spend her electricity, her water, her detergent, and her labor on his undies?

Screw that.

Freshly incensed, she marched out of the bathroom and into the kitchen. She grabbed her keys, her purse, and her parka, and slammed out of the condo, pausing only to lock the dead bolt. She wanted her door locked. She wanted it super-double-locked. She wanted to keep Emmett out.

She jogged around the building to her car, settled behind the wheel, and revved the engine. It didn't purr like Jamal's BMW, but at least it didn't cough or wheeze. Cautioning herself not to break any laws—she was angry enough without augmenting her rage by getting a speeding ticket—she drove the eight miles to the building where Emmett shared an apartment with Frank.

The building was a dreary brick structure, six stories tall, its front façade displaying rows of narrow, rain-stained windows. One window was open, despite the chilly morning, and through the screen Annie heard a man and a woman yelling at each other. She couldn't tell whether their yells were happy or angry, but if she had to guess, she'd guess the people were snapping at each other because they were in the throes of massive hangovers. Their voices had that post-binge, whiny, wobbly quality.

She entered the vestibule and pressed the intercom button. "Yeah?" a man's voice crackled through the speaker. Not Emmett's voice. Annie had met Frank maybe three or four times, not often enough to identify his voice through a crappy intercom speaker. But what other man would be in Emmett's apartment?

"Frank?" she asked. "It's Annie Baskin. Emmett's girlfriend." She hated identifying herself like that. It sounded so high school—and so romantic. Not the sort of word that conjured images of unwelcome men's underwear in your laundry hamper.

"Oh, sure. Annie. Come on up," Frank said. A loud buzzer indicated that he'd released the lock on the inner door.

Annie pushed the door open. She had rarely visited Emmett's apartment, but she remembered that it was on the fourth floor, at the rear of the building. Lots of stairs to climb.

She didn't care. She was angry. Scaling all those steps might dilute her anger a little, tire her out so she wouldn't smack Frank across the face the moment she saw him.

She paused on the third floor to catch her breath, then continued to the fourth floor and down the hall. At the door she was pretty sure led to Frank and Emmett's apartment, she knocked.

Frank opened the door. He was a lanky man, his jeans drooping on his hips, his straw-colored hair tousled. He had a weaselly face—narrow and pointed, his eyes too close together. Annie gave him a faint smile.

"Hey, come on in," he said, gesturing her inside. "What's up?"

Annie stepped into the living room and shuddered. The living room reminded her of the seedy, beer-scented basements of Cabot's social houses, the residences that resembled fraternities in everything but name. Students could enter a lottery to live in one of the social houses. If they won the lottery, they would be responsible for hosting campus parties. Annie always thought "winning" was actually losing.

Who wanted to host a kegger every month and have your residence filled with loud, inebriated students hitting on one another while they pretended to dance?

Frank and Emmett were a good dozen years beyond college age, but they still lived like undergrads, their furniture tattered and faded, their walls nicked and dinged and adorned with movie posters. Frank gestured toward the sagging sofa and Annie decided she would rather stand, even though she had just trekked up all those stairs.

"So you got the day off too," Frank said pleasantly. "We're lucky, aren't we."

She supposed he was lucky he didn't have to be at work, given that he was unshaved—and he looked nowhere near as macho in a beard as Emmett did. He had on a long-sleeved T-shirt featuring Mickey Mouse and Donald Duck embracing in a vaguely homoerotic way across his thin chest. Definitely not apparel suitable for any job Annie could think of.

"Where's your lady friend?" Annie asked. "I want to talk to both of you."

Frank looked bewildered. "What lady friend?"

"The lady friend you've taken over the bedroom with, so Emmett can't sleep here."

"Huh?" Frank scratched his scalp and Annie fell back a step, just in case he unleashed a blizzard of dandruff. "I wish I had a lady friend to take over the bedroom with. You have any lady friends you could introduce me to?"

Annie felt her jaw tense and her brow tighten in a frown. She marched across the dingy room to the back hall and pushed open the bedroom door. Emmett's bed was more or less made, the blanket rumpled but spread across the mattress, the pillow at the correct end. Frank's bed was a mess, but there was no woman lounging in it. There were no signs of a woman having been in that room in the recent past. Or, for that matter, the not-so-recent past.

Annie took a deep breath. And another deep breath. When she was reasonably certain her lungs were functioning, she returned to the living room, where Frank was now slouched on his lumpy sofa, cradling a can. "You want a drink?" he asked, raising the can so she could see it. Cola, not beer.

Right now she wanted a beer. Or something stronger. A tall glass of that powerful elixir in the decanter in Gordon's study, on ice. It wasn't yet noon, but she was that angry.

She shook her head in response to Frank's question. "Emmett told me you had kicked him out of the bedroom because you were entertaining a woman there every night."

"In my dreams," Frank said, then frowned. "Why would he say something like that?"

"So I'd let him stay at my place," Annie answered, forcing the words out around a knot in her throat. Emmett had lied about Frank, he'd lied about the bedroom, he'd helped himself to her key and made a copy of it. How could she have trusted him?

"Yeah," Frank confirmed. "He really likes your condo. He says your TV is better than ours—but shit, any TV is better than ours. Much sharper picture. You subscribe to all those streaming services too. So your condo is really nice, huh?"

"Your TV would have a sharper picture if you cleaned it," she said, eyeing the dusty screen balanced on an ugly metal stand beneath a poster for *American Pie*, with all those supposed teenagers—actors no doubt well into their twenties—grinning salaciously around an apple pie. A few swipes with a dust rag would surely clarify the TV's picture. A few more swipes with a dust rag would improve the living room as a whole. A vacuum cleaner would transform the place.

Maybe Emmett just liked her condo because it was clean. She knew how to dust and vacuum; growing up, she always wound up doing those chores because Sarah had too much homework.

"So, just to be clear," she said, "no girlfriend."

"Not at the moment, but I'm open to suggestions."

Annie could think of a few suggestions, none of which included women. Faking a smile, she crossed to the door. She contemplated thanking Frank for his time, and for allowing her to see for herself that Emmett had been lying to her for weeks. But in truth, she didn't feel at all grateful for any of it.

Back at her condo, she pulled a plastic trash bag from the box beneath her kitchen sink. She carried the bag to the bathroom and dumped all of Emmett's toiletries into it—the toothbrush, the stick deodorant, the comb, the hand cream, the beard trimmer. From there, she moved to the laundry closet and picked through the hamper, pulling out not just several boxer briefs but also a few T-shirts that weren't hers. She added those to the trash bag. They were all trash, as far as she was concerned.

She wandered into her bedroom. Emmett's phone charger lay like an emaciated black snake on one of the night tables. She unplugged it and tossed it into the trash bag. In her closet, she found a sneaker big enough to take a bath in. Digging around on the floor, she found its mate. Also a pair of jeans long enough to reach her armpits if she put them on. When had Emmett moved so much of his shit into her condo? Why hadn't she noticed?

She noticed now. And it all went into the trash bag.

She wasn't going to throw his things into the dumpster behind the condo, even if that was the ultimate destination of most trash bags. She was still trying to be nice. Not that Emmett deserved niceness, but Annie wasn't about to scrap her be-nicer mission just because of him.

When she was sure she had collected all of Emmett's detritus, she closed the bag with a twist tie, lugged it down the stairs, and left it on the porch. Then she went back up to her condo and prepared to cry.

The tears wouldn't come.

Maybe she wasn't nice enough. Or maybe she was just too furious.

chapter twenty-six

EMMETT BUZZED HER THROUGH THE INTERCOM AT FOUR THIRTY. Either his foreman had sent everyone home early or Emmett had simply left early, after arriving late.

Annie listened as he identified himself. "I'm not going to let you up," she said into the intercom. "That's your shit in the bag on the porch."

A few seconds of silence. He was probably locating the bag, untwisting the tie, peeking inside. He pressed the intercom button again. "What the fuck?"

"Go away!" she hollered into the speaker on her end.

"Keep it down," the voice of her upstairs neighbor filtered through the ceiling. He had a nerve, telling her to be quiet when he clomped around all the time and peed loudly.

She wasn't going to let Emmett into her apartment. Instead, she pulled on her parka, grabbed her key—*her* key, not Emmett's—and went downstairs to talk to him on the porch.

He was clearly angry. She had never noticed how handsome he looked when he was angry, probably because she so rarely saw him angry, and never angry at her. Until now. He paced back and forth on the small porch, his work boots drumming against the wooden planks. Usually, when she saw him on the porch, he was seated and munching his way through a take-out pizza.

Usually, he was mellow. Not today.

"What the fuck is going on?" he asked, gesturing toward the garbage bag. "I gave you back your key."

"You lied about Frank's girlfriend!" Annie shouted. Her upstairs neighbor couldn't hear her on the porch unless he opened a window, and it was too cold for that. "He doesn't have a girlfriend."

"All right, so big fucking deal. What do you care if he has a girl-friend or not?"

Emmett, she noted, was not denying that he'd lied to her. Which was, of course, a big fucking deal. "If you wanted to stay at my place, why didn't you just say so? Why did you make up this bullshit about Frank having an orgy in your bedroom every night?"

"Because," Emmett retorted, then drew in a deep breath and scrubbed his hand through his hair. "Because," he said in a quieter voice, "what was I supposed to say? That I wanted to live here instead of my place? We weren't ready for that. We've only known each other, what, a couple of months?"

A little over five months, but Annie couldn't expect Emmett to re-member something as trivial as that. "So you wanted to live here, but you weren't ready to live with me," she translated.

"Yeah. I mean, come on. What would you have said if I told you I wanted to move in with you?"

"I don't know." Actually, Annie did know. She would have said, "Not yet. I'm not ready for you to live with me." What she said now was, "So it was just my condo you wanted? You were ready to live in my condo, but not ready to live with me?"

"It's a terrific condo," he rationalized. "Your bathroom is bigger than ours, and your kitchen—you've always got plenty of food. And everything is clean."

"I have plenty of food because I go to the store and buy it. Every-thing is clean because I clean it. What, you wanted to live here because I know how to use a toilet brush and I've got a generous supply of Chee-rios?"

"Well, yeah."

"All right. We're done." Annie yanked open the front door, entered the building, and slammed the door behind her. That slam felt good.

But by the time she reached her unit on the second floor, nothing felt good anymore. Emmett was an asshole. He had lied to her—repeatedly. He wanted to live with her because her condo was clean and well stocked.

True, she hadn't been ready for him to move in with her. But if that was even going to be a subject for discussion, he should have wanted to move in with her for *her*, not her condo.

But then, she was just a second-stringer. Not smart enough for the Ivy League, not pretty enough to have her pick of men, not fashionable enough to shop for wigs. Her primary contribution to the world was doing favors for others. Favors for her sister, favors for her mother, the favor of letting Emmett park his carcass in her condo because he was adept at lovemaking and good-looking, and the poor guy had practically been exiled from his own apartment. Or so he'd claimed.

She'd done him a favor by letting him stay.

It was at times like this, when her anger began to dissolve, melting into sorrow and self-pity, that a woman needed her sister. She dialed Sarah's number, but Sarah said she was too busy dealing with her in-laws to spend time on the phone. "Okay, fine," Annie said, hoping Sarah didn't hear the sob fringing her voice.

She disconnected and phoned Jenna. "The guy's a douche," Jenna said when Annie told her about her breakup with Emmett. "You're better off without him."

"I know that. I still feel awful, though."

"I wish I lived closer," Jenna's voice reached from two thousand miles away. "Oh, hush," she added, presumably to her baby, who'd let out a screech. "He's been fussing all day. Aren't you lucky you had the opportunity to kick Emmett to the curb? I can't do that with my baby, even when I want to. Don't tell anyone I said that," she added quickly.

They talked for another minute—that was all the baby would allow them before launching into a five-star scream-fest. With a sigh, Annie said goodbye to Jenna.

She phoned Chloe. "I can't talk," Chloe told her. "I volunteered to work this weekend so other people could take the holiday off. They're paying me double overtime, so it's worth it. But they dragged me away from my desk. I'm on the floor with the residents for the rest of the day. Hi, Mrs. Blansky," she said in a high, cheery voice, obviously to one of the residents.

"You're not a trained caregiver," Annie pointed out.

"Doesn't take much training to call bingo numbers or help someone with Parkinson's eat. I almost passed the bingo job along to my grandfather, but he kept cheating."

"How can you cheat at bingo?" Annie asked.

"He only called numbers that appeared on his own card. He cheats all the time. When he's losing at checkers, he'll bump the checkerboard with his knee and scatter all the checkers. He pretends it's an accident, but it only happens when he's losing, for some reason."

"He sounds too smart to be suffering from dementia," Annie said.

"Demented doesn't mean stupid. No one ever accused my grandfather of being stupid. We'll talk after the weekend, okay? I'm going to be working through Sunday. Love that double overtime."

"Okay."

"I love you," Chloe said, which made Annie's eyes brim with tears. "Forget about Emmett. He's a turd."

Annie got off the phone and allowed herself a few minutes of weeping. Yet crying emphasized in a painful way just exactly how alone she was. This was a situation when a person was supposed to be able to turn to her big sister for comfort and support, and Annie couldn't do that.

She went into the bathroom, tore off a strip of toilet paper, and blew her nose. A glimpse of her reflection in the mirror above the sink made her wince. Her cheeks were mottled, her eyes puffy. She looked like a woman who had just broken up with her boyfriend.

Her phone rang. She had left it in the kitchen, and with a deep breath that sounded just a bit too moist and tremulous, she abandoned the bathroom. She reached the kitchen by the phone's third dirge-like ring, and glanced at the screen. *Gilda Baskin.*

Grimacing, she connected the call. "Hi, Mom," she said, hoping her wavering voice wouldn't alert Gilda to the fact that Annie currently felt profoundly single and miserable, despite the fact that she was no spring chicken.

"I've just gotten home from my first Al-Anon meeting," her mother said. "I'm not sure how useful it's going to be."

Why a program for the families of alcoholics would be even remotely useful to her, Annie couldn't say. "Why did you go to an Al-Anon meeting?" she asked.

"Because your sister is a drug abuser."

"What are you talking about?"

"She's on OxyContin. Did you know that? It's an opiate. Her doctor is getting her hooked on an opiate."

Annie took a moment to digest this. If Sarah hadn't been taking OxyContin that long, she probably wasn't addicted. And if she *had* and she *was*, so what? It wasn't as if she would wind up on a street corner, buying pills from some sleazy drug dealer for ten dollars a pop. If she got addicted and was blessed with many more years of life, she could go into rehab and get weaned off the drug.

In any case, why did her mother have to attend an Al-Anon meeting? How was Sarah's prescription interfering with their mother's life?

She didn't have a chance to ask. "We sat in a circle and recited this prayer about wisdom and courage. And then everyone was supposed to—well, they call it sharing. Some of the sharing was kind of boring. This one's son was in jail on his third drunk driving charge. That one's husband lost his job due to drinking. Well, of course he'd lose his job, if he was drinking that much. What did he expect?"

"Mom—"

"These people think they have problems? When it was my turn to share, I told them what a *real* problem is. Your daughter taking OxyContin and going bald from cancer—*that's* a problem."

Annie couldn't argue. Sarah's cancer was a problem.

"A daughter with no eyebrows," her mother went on. "I told them my heart was breaking. Someone gave me a brownie."

"That was kind," Annie said.

"Not really. It was stale. God knows how long those brownies were sitting on a supermarket shelf before someone brought them to the meeting. But I'll go back. I need the support. Maybe these meetings will make my heart break a little less. Maybe these people can make me feel a little better."

Nothing would make Annie's mother feel better. Annie knew that, and maybe, deep in her broken heart, her mother knew that too. "The brownies might not be so stale next time," Annie said. "I wouldn't worry about Sarah becoming a drug addict, though."

"I worry about everything," Gilda said. "It's what mothers do."

"I know," Annie said, swallowing a tiny sob before it could escape. She couldn't let her mother hear how sad she was—about Sarah being in so much pain she needed to take a narcotic, about Annie's foolishness in not recognizing Emmett's dishonesty, about Gilda's heartbreak, about stale brownies. Gilda depended on Annie to take care of things. She had to be strong and steady, or Gilda wouldn't be able to cope—not that she coped all that well in any case. "I've got to run, Mom," she said. "I'm doing a load of laundry. I splashed some gravy on the sleeve of my sweater yesterday, and Sarah would kill me if I didn't take care of it right away."

"Sarah is right. You don't want that stain to set."

Of course Sarah was right. Sarah was always right, at least when it came to stains on garments. "If you think those Al-Anon meetings will help," Annie said, "keep going. And try not to worry."

"Ha. Fat chance." Gilda said goodbye, and Annie clicked off her phone.

She probably should run a load of laundry. But a glance at the digital clock in her microwave alerted her that it was nearly lunchtime—and she hadn't eaten much of her breakfast. She was hungry. In fact, her hunger trumped the urge to weep. Hunger could be a good thing.

She opened her well-stocked refrigerator, and her well-stocked pantry cabinet, and nothing appealed. She thought of all the delicious Thanksgiving leftovers at Sarah's house, and of the scrambled eggs she'd wound up throwing away that morning, and lifted her phone again.

She dialed, listened, and then heard Jamal's voice. "Annie? What's up?"

"I was wondering if you were free. I thought maybe we could have lunch."

"Can't do it today," he said, and she immediately pictured him with his gorgeous young-Michelle-Obama girlfriend stretched out on his couch, assuming he had a couch. Their legs were intertwined, his arm was around her shoulders, and— "Tomorrow looks good, though," he said. "What did you have in mind?"

"I just..." *I need a friend. I need a sister. I need someone to talk to.* "I thought maybe we could discuss what we want to do with the podcast, once we pass the deadline for general admissions applications to Cabot. I can throw something together here at my place."

"As long as it isn't leftover turkey. I don't even *like* turkey."

"I'll make something that isn't turkey," she promised. "Does noon work for you?"

"Noon works fine. I need your address, though."

She gave it to him, told him she would see him tomorrow, and hung up. And gazed around her. Would he be as impressed with her food inventory as Emmett was? As taken by her television? As wowed by her rudimentary cleanliness? It wasn't as if her condo would pass a white-glove test.

But with Chloe running bingo games at the senior residence all weekend, and Jenna halfway across the country with a screeching baby, and Sarah lacking eyebrows and possibly addicted to oxy and not really the most supportive sister, anyway, Annie would be delighted to spend a couple of hours with Jamal, talking about anything other than what a loser she was.

chapter twenty-seven

"**W**HAT IS THIS?" JAMAL ASKED. "AN OMELET?"

"A frittata," Annie told him. "It's kind of like a quiche, only without the pie crust. Because real men and all that." She smiled shyly. It was odd—at work, and lately in the tech studio where she and Jamal recorded their podcast, she felt totally at ease with him. But here in her condo—the first time he had ever visited her there—she felt awkward and insecure. She had cooked a very pretty-looking frittata, filled with diced bell peppers, zucchini, and basil, and she'd chilled a bottle of white wine and sliced a loaf of French bread into thick slabs. It was nothing fancy, nothing gourmet, nowhere near the amount of time she'd spent cooking Thanksgiving dinner. The thing about frittatas was that you could make one with whatever you had lying around inside your refrigerator, as long as one of the things you had lying around inside your refrigerator was a container of eggs.

As she well knew, she always had plenty of food lying inside her refrigerator. That was why Emmett had wanted to live with her, after all.

She shoved that thought away. Emmett might be hammering his fingernails into bruised pulps at a construction site, for all she cared. He was irrelevant to her life. He was history.

A big, unpleasant blob of history, sitting heavily on her abdomen, causing heartburn.

Jamal, she realized, was the un-Emmett, the anti-Emmett. Intellectual—a freaking philosophy major, for God's sake—and slender, and well dressed in casual gray slacks and a sweater that might be cashmere. Annie had to restrain herself from reaching out to stroke it, it looked so soft. Jamal was someone who would prefer a glass of Chardonnay to a beer, although he would probably prefer some of that nectar from Gordon's decanter to Annie's bargain Pinot Grigio. Jamal's hair was relatively neat and relatively short. No scruffy beard darkened his jaw.

This was exactly what she wanted. The company of someone who was not Emmett, so she wouldn't think about him—the way she was thinking about him right now.

Shoving thoughts of him into a remote corner of her mind, she sliced a hefty wedge of the frittata and levered it onto Jamal's plate, then took a narrower wedge for herself. They sat in her kitchen, which she had tidied for the occasion. She wished she had a dining room, so they wouldn't have to sit under a glaring light designed more for cooking than for ambiance. She wished they weren't surrounded by countertops and appliances. A dining room like Sarah's, long and formal and suitable for Zoom meetings, would have provided the right atmosphere. The anti-Emmett atmosphere.

Jamal didn't seem to mind the setting. "You have a great place here," he'd said after Annie had buzzed him in and let him into her unit. "So much space, all to yourself."

"Yeah, all to myself," she'd muttered as the Emmett thoughts she had banished to that dark corner stirred, reminding her that she had all this space to herself because she'd kicked him out.

Now, seated across from Jamal at the kitchen table, she took a sip of her cold, dry wine and wished she didn't feel so edgy. Jamal was her buddy, her friend, her colleague. She didn't have to impress him—and yet, for some reason, he seemed impressed.

"So, your Thanksgiving sucked?" he asked.

That eased her nerves. She laughed. "How could you tell?"

"First of all, no leftovers—which I'm really grateful for. Yesterday, we had turkey hash with fried eggs for breakfast, turkey and mayo sandwiches for lunch, and turkey with yams for dinner. All leftovers. I told my sister I was done staying at her house and going home so I could escape the turkey. She always makes two twenty-pounders for the holiday, and then she complains about all the leftovers and tries to get everyone to take care packages of turkey home with them."

"Well, as someone who cooked Thanksgiving dinner for my sister's family, I can tell you that a major advantage of having leftovers is you don't have to do so much cooking the next day."

"So where are your leftovers?"

"Still at my sister's, unless her crew has finished eating them by now. She's entertaining her in-laws from Chicago for the weekend."

"How's she doing?"

"Not good." Annie took a bite of her frittata. It was eggy, crunchy, slightly salty, and delicious. "She seems to be giving up the fight. She's taking painkillers and my mother thinks she's a drug addict. Her in-laws are pretentious twits; her kids know things are bad, but my brother-in-law distracts them by taking them to movies and roller-skating so they don't have time to get depressed. And he's a horny bastard."

"Really?" Jamal's eyebrows shot up.

"That's what my sister tells me. She wants me to fix him up so he can have sex with someone other than her."

"Wow." Jamal added a chunk of bread to his plate and then used the edge of his fork to break off a bite-size piece of his frittata. "Your family is a lot more out there than mine. I can't imagine my sisters ever asking me to procure a sex partner for their husbands."

"It wasn't something I could imagine, either, until my sister requested it." Annie sighed. "Maybe I should volunteer for the job. I just broke up with my boyfriend."

Jamal had been chewing, and he took a minute to swallow before speaking. "Okay, first of all, this crustless quiche stuff is amazing. Second, I'm sorry about your boyfriend."

"No need," Annie said flippantly. "I did the breaking up. I'm fine." *Yeah, right,* she thought.

"It's hard to break up with someone during a holiday." He sounded as if he was speaking from experience.

Annie tactfully opted not to question him. "Better to break up with him now than to wait until the new year. This way, I don't have to buy him a Christmas present."

"Or a Hanukkah present...?" Jamal sounded almost questioning.

"Nah. He was a Christmas sort of guy."

Jamal nodded, although he looked bemused. "Anyway, I thought you invited me over so we could discuss the podcast."

"We can talk about that," Annie said swiftly. Why had she thought Jamal would want her to confide in him about all the crazy, miserable stuff going on in her life? His life was so much saner than hers. Too much turkey, perhaps, but he hadn't had to cook it. No major breakups because, as he'd just said, breaking up during a holiday sucked. Jamal was so organized, he probably timed his breakups according to the calendar.

He surprised her by saying, "I don't want to talk about the podcast. Let's talk about your boyfriend. I didn't even know you had a boyfriend."

"Well, I don't anymore."

"Are you devastated?"

"Not really. Just a little...I don't know, sad, I guess. My friend Jenna told me the guy was a douche. Then again, she never met him."

"Was he a douche?"

"He was just...not completely honest," she conceded, then sighed. "He was the best-looking guy I was ever with. I'm not used to being with such good-looking guys."

"Why not?"

A deceptively simple question. Annie recalled the dinner she and Jamal had enjoyed at that fancy restaurant with the linen and silver and bone china, and the stratospheric prices. She recalled the Michelle Obama look-alike she'd seen him with last spring. His social life was clearly a lot more exalted than hers. But then, he was the pampered boy in a household full of sisters. And he was damned good-looking himself.

In Annie's world, the good-looking guys had always belonged to Sarah. She was the prestigious Baskin sister. The pretty one, the classy one, the smart one, the competent one. The one who knew what items of clothing matched, who knew the proper way to walk, who knew how to flirt.

Annie realized Jamal was waiting for an answer. "I guess love affairs aren't my strong suit," she said. "My sister was always popular. I was kind of an also-ran when it came to romance."

"Do you know what Aristotle says about love?" Jamal lowered his fork and leaned toward Annie. The table was not that large, and when he sat forward that way, his face loomed close enough for her to notice that his irises were not completely brown. They were edged with a ring of greenish-yellow. "Aristotle said that you can't experience any kind of love until you master self-love. You've got to love yourself in order to be capable of loving anyone else."

Annie snorted a laugh. "I guess my douche ex must be good at love, then, because he sure loved himself."

Jamal laughed too. "I'm just saying, anyone who claims love affairs aren't her strong suit is already starting off on the wrong foot. You've got to love yourself, Annie. And I'll tell you this." He speared another chunk of his frittata with his fork. "Anyone who can cook something this good ought to love herself. I'm in love with frittatas now."

"I guess you must love yourself, if you're capable of loving a fritta-ta," she joked. She needed to lighten the discussion. She didn't want Jamal to analyze her, with or without guidance from Aristotle. "Enough about Thanksgiving and frittatas. We need to discuss Cabbage World."

"It all comes down to food," Jamal said. "Cabbage. All right, what about Cabbage World?"

"The deadline for applications for regular admission to Cabot College is January fifteenth. Are we going to continue the podcast after that?"

"Hell, yeah," Jamal said. "We're famous. We're beloved."

"I don't know how famous we are. Or, for that matter, how beloved."

Jamal dragged Aristotle back into it. "Love yourself, Annie, and then you will be able to give and receive love. We can use the podcast to talk about campus happenings, college life in general, stuff going on in the world and how it impacts the school. I can think of plenty of things we can talk about."

"You think the public relations office will continue to support us?"

"Are you kidding? We're doing more for Cabot's public image than anyone in that office." He gave her a cocky grin. "We're rock stars. They love us."

"They must love themselves, if they're capable of loving us," Annie said.

His raised his wine glass in a toast to her. "There you go," he said. "You didn't have to study philosophy. You've already learned the most important lesson." His eyes were so bright, his smile so warm, Annie could almost believe him.

226

chapter twenty-eight

S HE ARRIVED AT THE ADMISSIONS BUILDING EARLY MONDAY MORNING. She had been eager to get back to work. Or, more accurately, to escape from her condo, her big, empty bed, and the lack of sports broadcasts on her television. She could have turned on any number of football games over the weekend, but she hadn't. No interest whatsoever. No hankering to see two mobs of men with profoundly padded shoulders slamming into each other or throwing a ball that wasn't ball-shaped. She hadn't even bothered to channel surf to see if she could locate a rugby game, where the players would be throwing around a non-ball-shaped ball but not wearing any padding.

Emmett's absence was like a phantom limb, something that throbbed even though it was gone. The silence of her bedroom without his muted snoring was like a noise itself.

She had no regrets about having sent him and his trash bag full of stuff away. She tugged open the drawer in her kitchen a neurotic number of times in order to gaze at the plastic palm tree with her spare key looped onto its ring. And the spare key's twin, which she needed to find another key ring for. Every time she saw those two keys lying safely in the drawer, she shuddered at the thought of Emmett's presumptuousness in stealing one and paying a hardware store employee to make the other. Not because he loved Annie. Because he loved her food supply and her TV.

Love yourself. Jamal's words echoed inside her head. Like most philosophy, the statement seemed rather vague, ethereal, devoid of substance. Of course Annie loved herself; would she have bought a half-gallon tub of premium butter pecan ice cream if she didn't?

Ice cream notwithstanding, she didn't love herself. She was Sarah's clumsy, inept kid sister. The one who wasn't pretty and didn't know how to dress. The one who never had enough homework to exempt her from chores. The one who never had gorgeous boyfriends, except for Emmett, who turned out to be an asshole. The one who did favors for everybody else, because if she didn't she would be even less lovable.

Fortunately, Jamal was not in the admissions building when she entered. If he'd been there, he would have noticed her gloominess right away.

Brittany was in the reception area, though, looking bouncy and perky and adorable as she straightened the brochures and catalogs on display along a wall of shelving. She must love herself, Annie thought, taking in the glossy, golden waves of Brittany's hair, her brightly colored sweater, her skinny trousers, and chunky leather boots. Women who bought expensive clothing for themselves probably had greater self-love than women who bought premium ice cream for themselves.

Not only did Brittany dress fabulously, but she smiled fabulously. She moved fabulously. She waltzed through life—or at least through the admissions office—with the confidence of someone who loved herself and didn't care if no one else did. Which undoubtedly meant that everyone else did. Annie certainly loved her.

"How was your holiday?" Annie asked as she unwound her scarf from around her neck and then unzipped her parka.

"Oh, it was great. I ate too much," Brittany said. She didn't look as if she'd eaten too much. Her tummy was flatter than a spatula. "How about you?"

"Eh." Annie shrugged. "I spent too much of it doing favors for my family."

"They must appreciate you," Brittany said. "What sort of favors?"

"Besides making the whole Thanksgiving dinner?" Annie sighed. She wished she could care as little about whether people loved her as Brittany seemed to. "My sister wants me to find a woman for her husband to have sex with," she said.

"What?" Brittany let out a hoot. "Why?"

"Because she's sick and can't have sex with him herself."

"Oh, wow! That's hilarious. Not that she's sick, but—I mean, don't you think that's bizarre?"

"Very bizarre." Not at all hilarious, but if Brittany thought it was... "What's your position on no-commitment sex, Brittany?"

Brittany leveled her gaze at Annie, which meant she actually had to look down. The heels on her boots added a good three inches to her height. "I think it's the best kind there is. I'm so not into commitment."

That view struck Annie as very Brittany-ish. Very insouciant and confident and self-loving. "Do you want to have sex with my brother-in-law?" she asked. "He's a good-looking guy."

"Would he want to have sex with me?" Brittany asked.

"Who wouldn't want to have sex with you?" Annie responded. "I'd have sex with you and I'm not even a lesbian."

That made Brittany laugh.

"My brother-in-law isn't a lesbian either," Annie said. "I'm sure he'd be thrilled to spend a night with you. Or even an afternoon." She pulled her phone from her bag and scrolled through the picture gallery, searching for a photo of Gordon. The only one she found was a formal wedding photo of him and Sarah, she in her lacy, fairy-tale wedding gown and he in his tux, a narrow bow tie underlining his chin and a white orchard pinned to his lapel. His arms circled Sarah as she leaned back into him. "Maybe this isn't the most appropriate picture to show you, but it's all I've got."

Brittany squinted at the photo. "Mmm, yeah. I mean, his *wedding* photo. He *is* good-looking, though."

"If I introduce you and he's interested, would you be willing to sleep with him? It would make my sister very happy."

"Your sister sounds pretty kinky," Brittany said. "But sure. I'm open to everything. It's the best way to be."

Perhaps it was. And perhaps if Brittany or Annie were dying of cancer, they'd be pretty kinky too. "I'll set something up," Annie said.

Inside her own office, she sank into her chair and closed her eyes. She felt uneasy. Unsettled. Introducing Gordon to Brittany wasn't kinky or even remotely hilarious. It was insane. Maybe it was also wrong, although neither Brittany nor Sarah seemed to think it was. Sarah had convinced Annie that she wanted Gordon to have sex with another woman because she loved him. Really? What if Sarah was just playing Annie, testing her to see how gullible she was and how far she'd let Sarah push her? What would Sarah have done if Annie had said no? Forced Diana Drucker to pimp for her?

Sarah was dying. *Dying.* How could Annie say no to her dying sister?

Be nice. Be assertive. Love yourself.

She tapped her phone awake and the wedding photo of Sarah and Gordon filled the screen. She hastily swiped it away, then tapped in Sarah's number. Sarah answered on the second ring. She sounded tired. "Annie?"

"Did I wake you?" Annie glanced at her watch. Eight thirty.

"No," Sarah said, then yawned. "I got up to send the kids to school and then I went back to bed. I didn't fall asleep, though. I feel like shit."

"I know." *Be nice.* "I'm sorry. I wish you could feel better."

"The oxy helps."

"Mom thinks you're going to get addicted."

Sarah laughed sourly. "Mom is an idiot."

"True." Annie managed a faint laugh herself. "Listen, Sarah, were you serious about wanting me to find a woman for Gordo to sleep with?"

"Of course I was serious. When am I not serious?"

True enough. Sarah was always serious. "I may have found someone. Are you sure you want me to introduce them?"

"I want him to get that release, Annie. He's making me crazy, holding everything in."

In the context of sex, the visual image those words conjured in Annie's mind were a bit disturbing. Trying not to grimace, she asked, "How am I supposed to set this up?"

"Who is she? Where is she?"

"It's someone I work with. She's young and pretty and into casual hookups."

"She sounds perfect," Sarah said. "She's at your office?"

"Yes."

"Fine. I'll tell him to swing by there."

"You're sure about this?" Annie asked one more time.

"Annie. Come on. Just do it. You'll be making us both happy. I mean me and Gordon."

Annie was not included in the *both* being made happy. This whole thing didn't make her happy at all. But Sarah was dying. And Gordon was about to explode. And Annie was determined to be nice. "I'll do my best," she promised Sarah before saying goodbye.

Voices in the reception area alerted her that her colleagues were arriving. Through her doorway, she heard Harold railing about how someone had parked in his favorite spot in the staff lot, and Jamal's retorting that if this was the only thing Harold could think of to complain about, he was pretty damned fortunate.

Annie's phone clicked with a text message: *Conference room, nine o'clock. Brittany will bring coffee.* Sighing, she trudged down the hall to the conference room and took her place at the far end of the table. Jamal sat across from her and sent her a smile that was just the slightest bit patronizing, as if he wanted to remind her of the wisdom he'd imparted over a frittata on Saturday. Evelyn and Harold entered together and took their seats—Harold next to Annie and Evelyn next to Jamal, as if they were at some fancy dinner party where the seating had to be boy-girl-boy-girl. Dean Parisi was the last to enter the conference room, sweeping in grandly, her short, silver hair fluttering and her neck concealed within a colorful, artfully twisted silk scarf.

Dean Parisi looked bright and chipper. So did Brittany as she entered, carrying a tray of coffee mugs embossed with the official Cabot College logo—a sharp-beaked, spread-winged falcon, not a head of cabbage.

"Well," Dean Parisi said brightly, settling into the armchair at the head of the medieval table, "we got all the early decisions out on time. Let's hear it for our yield!"

Harold shouted, "Hooray for our yield!" Evelyn clapped her hands.

"So today we'll start on the regular admissions."

"No rest for the weary," Jamal muttered.

"You've each got your files. Remember—new applicants first. We'll reassess the deferred applicants once we see what our new applicant pool looks like. Work efficiently, folks. We're going to be receiving more applications every day."

"Maybe Annie and Jamal should stop doing their podcast," Evelyn said, gesturing toward their end of the table. "It's attracting too many applicants."

"Nonsense," Dean Parisi said. "The more applications we receive, the smaller our percentage of acceptances. That's every bit as important as our yield."

Annie met Jamal's gaze. He grinned. If Dean Parisi wanted them to continue their podcast, it would continue—at least as long as the public relations department could compensate them for their time and labor.

She returned to her office and opened the first file she'd been sent. It contained a dozen applications. Some were stronger than others, but none of them dazzled her. Or else she was just plain un-dazzle-able at the moment. A thought kept nibbling at a corner of her brain: when she got home that evening, Emmett would not be seated on her building's front porch with a pizza box in his hand.

However, he also wouldn't be seated on her building's front porch if she hadn't broken up with him. He would be upstairs in her condo, lounging on her lumpy couch and munching on pizza while watching TV. He'd had a copy of her key. He would have let himself inside.

That understanding replaced her melancholia with anger. The nerve of him, having that much assertiveness, that strong a sense of entitlement. He must really love himself.

Well, good for him, because she sure as hell didn't love him.

Gordon didn't stop by Annie's office that day. She had no idea when, or even if, he would. He worked long hours at his law firm, and he was taking care of Sarah and the kids. And maybe he had no interest in meeting a pretty young woman who was willing to screw him, no strings attached.

He didn't visit Annie's office on Tuesday either. But Wednesday at around noon, just as Jamal swung through her door carrying an insulated lunch bag—"sliced turkey on rye, I'm almost done with the leftovers," he announced—Brittany peered around the doorjamb and said, "Annie? Your brother-in-law is here."

"Oh." Annie suppressed the urge to crawl under her desk and hide.

Jamal clearly recalled what she'd told him about Sarah's request over the weekend. His eyebrows darted upward and he said, "We can plan the podcast some other time."

She wanted to beg him to stay. She wanted to plan the podcast even more than she wanted to hide under her desk. She wanted Jamal to stand beside her, to give her enough support to enable her to explain to Gordon what Sarah wanted her to do. Or better yet, to have Brittany stand beside her, looking beautiful and happy and hot to trot.

But Gordon entered her office without Brittany, and Jamal raced off with his turkey sandwich. Annie had been about to pull out her own lunch—a cup of yogurt, a self-sealing bag of pretzels, and an apple that was slightly past its sell-by date and probably would lack crunch. Not that that mattered. She suddenly had no appetite.

Gordon looked slightly haggard, the jacket of his neatly tailored suit unbuttoned, his tie loosened, his initials monogrammed subtly, white thread against white fabric, on the cuff of his shirt sleeve. "Hi, Annie," he said before gazing around him. "This is your office?"

She realized he had never seen it before. Why would he have? Before Sarah had gotten sick, Annie and Gordon had had little to do with each other outside of family functions, which did not take place on Cabot College's campus.

"This is it," she said, forcing lightness into her tone and wishing she had watered her geranium, which looked dismal, its flowers shedding petals onto the window sill at an alarming rate.

"It's impressive," Gordon said, wandering around the office, which was too small to allow for much wandering.

"It's tiny," Annie argued. She had never seen Gordon's office, but she'd be willing to bet it was the size of a ballroom, or at the very least Dean Parisi's office.

"Tiny isn't bad," he said, dropping onto one of the visitor chairs—the chair where Jamal would have sat to eat his turkey sandwich if Gordon hadn't arrived. "The beauty of a small office is that people don't gather in it and waste your time when you need to be working. It's cozier too. Just you and your work. You can focus in a small office."

Annie shrugged and lowered herself into the chair behind her desk. She nudged her laptop out of the way so she could see Gordon. More than haggard, he looked sad. And maybe a little bitter. Maybe—who knew?—he was ready to explode.

"I'm glad Sarah told me to stop by," he said. "I need to talk to you."

"Oh?" Annie swallowed. "Did she tell you why she wanted you to stop by?"

"She said you had a surprise for me."

Annie didn't bother to conceal her grimace. "She's worried about you, Gordo." She hesitated, swallowed, wished she were hiding under her desk. *Just spit it out,* she ordered herself. "She thinks you need sex."

Gordon flinched. "What?"

"She wants me to find you someone to have sex with. Our admin out there—you must have met her when you came into the office. Brittany. She's interested."

"What?"

Annie gazed at Gordon. The width of her desk was not big enough to diffuse the waves of emotion emanating from him: confusion, incredulity, and perhaps a sprinkling of outrage.

But she had done what Sarah asked of her. She'd found someone for Gordon and presented the possibility to him. She couldn't pretend she hadn't, or Sarah hadn't. Or Brittany hadn't. She would have to see this discussion through. Quite possibly, Gordon's confusion, incredulity, and outrage were merely a cover. Perhaps he seriously *did* want sex.

She sucked in a deep breath and pushed onward. "Sarah thinks you need sex to relieve your stress and anger. She said she couldn't do this herself—it would be too icky or something—so she asked me to handle it for her. At first I thought she couldn't be serious, but she was. She insisted."

He shook his head. He closed his eyes. Maybe he was counting to ten before he spoke. He struck Annie as the sort of careful, methodical person who would.

Finally: "Yes, I'm stressed and angry. Of course I'm stressed and angry. My wife is dying of cancer. Am I supposed to be relaxed and happy?"

"Well, she thought sex might offer some relief. Kind of like therapy."

"Oh, for God's sake."

"I did some research on sex therapists," Annie told him, evidence of how diligently she'd approached her assignment. "They're really expensive, and they seem geared more toward people who are dealing with sexual dysfunction or something. Which I didn't think..." She trailed off, unsure how to complete the thought. Unsure of how she'd gotten even this far in the conversation. With Gordon, of all people.

Gordo, her brother-in-law, with whom the most intimate discussion she'd ever had before Sarah had gotten ill was about whether she'd wanted her burger rare or well done at one of their backyard barbecues.

"No," Gordon said quietly. "That isn't a problem."

"The problem is, you're angry."

"I'm crazy with anger," he said, his voice still low and taut. "You know that. I've told you that. I'm stuck on anger while Sarah has sailed straight through all the stages to acceptance." He sighed. "What does she think, I'm some teenage dickhead who would have sex with a stranger out of desperation? I need to know who I'm with. I need to care about her. Impersonal sex? Jesus Christ, I thought Sarah knew me better than that."

"She loves you," Annie defended her sister. "She cares about you."

"Not enough." He opened his eyes and they zeroed in on Annie, so intensely she could practically feel his stare, a relentless pressure in the center of her forehead. "The reason I'm not at work right now is that Sarah had an appointment with her oncologist this morning and Dr. Glassman asked that I come too." He sighed again, a shaky sigh this time. "They're discontinuing Sarah's chemo. It's not working. Her cancer has spread. It's..." He sighed. "It's everywhere. Dr. Glassman suggested that we switch to palliative care at this point. She's signed Sarah up for hospice."

The pressure moved lower, from Annie's skull to her sternum. "She's really dying?"

"Yes," Gordon said. "And it makes me angry. Fucking angry. Because Sarah just sat there, accepting this. She refuses to fight. She's never fought this. From the moment she was diagnosed, she just accepted it. And that infuriates me."

"That's just who Sarah is," Annie said, because it seemed so obvious to her. "She's never had to fight for anything. Everything's always come her way. She's smart, she's beautiful, she's popular, she *knows* things, all these things I could never figure out. She always had guys throwing themselves at her, and then she went to college and met you, and you were Mr. Wonderful, and she had you. And she had two children who are perfect. Really, I mean, Trevor and Becky are perfect. What has Sarah ever had to fight for? She tells them to make their beds and they make their beds. She doesn't even have to fight with them about that. How on earth would she know how to fight cancer?"

Gordon's gaze softened around the edges, taking on a gentle, pastel aura. "Holy shit," he murmured. "You're right."

Annie felt a bit *holy shit* herself. She had never before articulated the reality of Sarah so vividly. She had never before understood it. Maybe hanging out with Jamal had made her more philosophical. Maybe learning how to be assertive and nice had made her smarter.

But that was Sarah, through and through. She had never had to fight for anything. It had all been delivered to her, whatever she wanted, whatever she needed. Intelligence, grace, beauty, the comprehension that the world embraced her.

Meanwhile, Annie had always fought for everything. She had fought for her parents' attention, aware that a significant portion of it belonged to Sarah and would never be hers. She had fought to keep up with Sarah, to be able to do the things Sarah did with such ease. She'd fought to be her own person when so many people compared her to Sarah, when teachers actually called her Sarah by mistake, and then remarked, "No, you're not your sister." She'd fought hard, and she'd lost so many battles, and yet she just kept fighting.

"Annie." Gordon swallowed and leaned forward, his hands on his knees and his face downcast. He was no longer looking at her. "I need to ask a favor of you."

Of course. Why else would he be here?

"I have to tell the children—those two perfect children of mine— that their mother is dying. Will you help me tell them?"

"Shouldn't Sarah tell them that?"

"She'll tell them in her own way. But they won't hear it from her. They'll cry and beg and tell her it isn't true. If you help me tell them, maybe they'll understand."

How could Annie make them understand something that wasn't really understandable?

How could she say no to Gordon? In her eyes, Trevor and Becky were perfect because she adored them. If they needed her help to survive this awful, awful situation, she would help them.

"I live to serve," she said.

chapter twenty-nine

"**W**ILL YOU LIVE WITH US?" BECKY ASKED.

Annie sat on the couch in the Adler living room, Becky snuggled into the curve of her arm. Trevor sat on her other side, stiff and solemn, the inch of space between them as solid as a foot-thick wall. Gordon perched on the coffee table, facing them. Annie suspected Sarah would have gone ballistic if she'd seen him sitting on her gorgeous and undoubtedly expensive coffee table, its teak surface so polished it resembled a sheet of rich brown glass. But Sarah wasn't in the room. She was upstairs, avoiding this very difficult conversation.

Gordon had told the children, in as calm and even a tone as he could, that their mother was not going to get better, that the doctors had determined that the best thing to do was to make her comfortable and prevent her from feeling any pain.

"In other words, she's going to die," Trevor said curtly. He was his father's son. Anger simmered beneath his stoic surface, and it had nothing to do with pent-up sexual hunger. At least Annie hoped it didn't. The kid was only ten years old.

"I'll stay tonight," Annie assured Becky, "but I can't live here. This isn't my home."

"We have the guest bedroom. That could be your room," Becky said. "And you could help Mommy be comfortable."

"As I explained," Gordon broke in, his gaze briefly meeting Annie's before he focused on Becky, "Mommy will have nurses who come here to make her comfortable. Aunt Annie has to work. She has a job. She can't be here all the time."

"You work and you live here," Becky argued.

"Yes, but it's my house. It's our house. Aunt Annie has her own house."

"But she can be here sometimes, right?" Becky twisted to peer up at Annie. Becky's eyes were shiny with tears. "When we need you here?"

What could Annie say? It wasn't as if members of this family hadn't asked her for favors before. She was doing a favor for Gordon simply by sitting in his living room while he had this brutally painful conversation with his children. If Becky asked her for a favor, how could she say no?

Why would she say no? The couch in this living room was more comfortable than old one in Annie's living room. The kitchen here was bigger than hers. The en suite bathroom in the guest room was bigger than hers. There was a hot tub on the back patio.

And anyway, Annie couldn't bluntly deny Becky's plaintive request. Becky was a fellow younger sister. A fellow second-best. A fellow also-ran. An eight-year-old goddess, clad in a pullover sweatshirt embossed with the words "Girls Rock." Annie was reasonably sure the statement had nothing to do with geology or music.

If Trevor wanted Annie to live with the Adlers, he wasn't saying so. He sat rigidly, his arms folded across his chest, his chin thrust forward. "Why didn't Mom tell us?" he asked. "Where is she? Why isn't she here?"

"She's in bed," Gordon said quietly. "She isn't feeling well."

"She hasn't felt well since this whole thing began," Trevor retorted. "She should be here."

Gordon opened his mouth and then shut it. What could he say? Trevor had only spoken the truth.

Sarah didn't deserve to be defended, especially not by Annie. But they were sisters, so Annie defended her. "It's very hard, acknowledging that you aren't going to beat this terrible disease," she said. "I'm sure your mom will want to discuss this all with you eventually. But she's probably still trying to process it herself."

Trevor sized up Annie with a look, then shrugged and stood. "Fine. I'm going to go and process it myself too." With that, he stalked out of the living room. Becky seemed to view his departure as a reason to cuddle even closer to Annie. Her elbow jammed into Annie's ribs and her head felt like a boulder pressed into the soft flesh of Annie's armpit.

Annie gazed after Trevor, certain she'd blown it. What should she have said? How could she have made this sorrowful news easier for him to accept?

"It's okay," Gordon said, pushing himself to his feet. "Let's rustle up some dinner."

"Can I help?" Becky asked, unwedging herself from Annie's arm.

"Did you finish your homework?" Annie asked.

Becky pouted. "I have to write a stupid book report."

Annie gave her a quick hug. "No, you have to write a smart book report. What's the book?"

"I don't remember the title. It's about a horse. I didn't like it."

"Then say that in your report," Annie advised her. "But say it smartly."

Becky managed a smile before trudging up the bridal staircase.

Annie stood with Gordon at the bottom of the coiling stairway, watching until Becky vanished down the second-floor hall. "You don't need to write a book report, do you?" he said. "I could use some help fixing supper."

Annie nodded and accompanied him into the kitchen. "You're going to have to learn how to cook," she told him.

"Or you could live with us," he said.

Smiling, Annie shook her head. Gazing around at the spacious, brightly lit kitchen with its top-of-the-line equipment, its sleek countertops, and its cute little appliance garage, she acknowledged that there were worse fates in life than living in this house.

She located some individually wrapped salmon steaks in the freezer, removed a few, and thawed them in the microwave. Occasionally, she assigned Gordon a task: slicing tomatoes for a salad, or measuring rice and water into the rice cooker—of course Sarah would own a rice cooker, which she kept parked next to the food processor in the appliance garage. When Annie made rice at her condo, she made it the cheap, old-fashioned way: in a pot, on the stove. But that would be too pedestrian for Sarah. Here, in this superbly appointed kitchen, a rice cooker was *de rigueur*.

Once the salmon and rice were cooked, Gordon assembled plates for himself and Sarah and carried them upstairs to eat with her. Annie sat with the children at the kitchen table. She let them add chocolate syrup to their milk, which improved their spirits slightly. Trevor ate in silence; Becky complained at length about the stupid book for which she had to write a report. Annie made a mental note to remind Gordon that Trevor's and Becky's teachers needed to be informed of Sarah's status. That Annie knew this was necessary, even though she herself wasn't a mother, surprised her a little. It didn't seem like the sort of thing a single, childless aunt ought to be aware of.

After dinner, Trevor and Becky watched TV in the rec room downstairs while Annie cleaned the kitchen. *Imagine if this was my home,* she thought as she stacked the plates and silverware in the dishwasher, remembering to separate the forks and knives into their individual slots. Emmett would have never let her kick him out. He would have chained himself to the center island and sworn that he loved her, just to be able to hang out in this house instead of his scummy apartment.

Screw Emmett. If she phoned him and told him her sister was dying, he would probably remind her that her sister was mean to her. Which was true but irrelevant. Sarah was the only sister Annie had. Sometime in the not too distant future, Sarah would be gone. Annie would be the only sister, not the younger sister. All the birth-order research Chloe had explained to her would no longer apply.

Gordon arrived back in the kitchen as Annie was closing the door of the dishwasher. He carried his own empty plate and Sarah's nearly full one. "She wasn't hungry," he said apologetically. "It was delicious, though."

He didn't know where the aluminum foil was, so Annie showed him. He covered Sarah's plate and placed it in the refrigerator while Annie added his plate to the dishwasher. "I'd suggest a soak in the hot tub after we get the kids to bed," he said, "but it's snowing."

"Oh, no." Annie moved to the glass slider and flipped the switch to turn on the patio lights. Faint white flurries swirled through the air. "Maybe I should leave before the roads get messy."

"It's not going to stick," Gordon assured her. "The ground is too warm." He moved to the doorway to the stairs leading down to the rec room and called for Trevor and Becky to turn off the TV and get ready for bed. They clamored up the stairs, struggling to look disgruntled, and then Becky captured Annie's hand. "Will you read me a story?" she asked. "Not the stupid story about the horse."

"Go wash up and get into your PJs," Annie said, "and then I'll read you a not-stupid story."

She followed the children upstairs. While she waited for Becky to get ready, she poked her head into Trevor's bedroom. He was stretched out on his bed, an X-Men comic book spread across his knees. At Annie's entrance, he glanced up and glowered. "You okay?" Annie asked.

He snorted. "I knew she was going to die. I knew it and everyone said no, she'd get better."

"That was hope talking," Annie said. "We all thought that if we stayed optimistic, maybe our hopes would come true."

Her explanation seemed to thaw him a little. She ventured into the room, lowered herself to sit on his bed, and patted his knee. "You're allowed to feel whatever you feel, Trevor," she told him. "Anger. Resentment. Fear. Sadness. I hope in time you'll feel love and compassion too."

Another snort, but he didn't push her hand away. "She should have told us herself."

"She's doing the best she can," Annie said, wondering if that was true. "We're all doing the best we can."

He met Annie's gaze. His eyes were as shiny as Becky's had been earlier, as wet with tears. "Sometimes I hate her."

"You're allowed to feel what you feel," she repeated.

"I don't hate you," he admitted.

"And I love you very much." She leaned across his lap and gave him a hug. That he permitted her physical display of affection touched her. "I'm going to go read Becky a not stupid book," she said as she stood. "Don't stay up too late. You have school tomorrow."

The book Becky chose was moderately not stupid, about a rag doll that wanted nicer clothes. Not exactly the sort of story someone who wore shirts that said "Girls Rock"—and right now a nightgown with a pattern featuring Mulan from the Disney animated movie, brandishing her sword—ought to embrace. But at least Becky wasn't under any obligation to write a book report about it.

"You'll be here in the morning, right?" Becky asked as Annie closed the book and set it on Becky's tidy white night table.

"Yes. I'll see you then." Annie kissed Becky's forehead and turned off the bedside lamp. A night-light shaped like a scallop shell glowed from a socket near the door, filling the room with a soft, pink glow.

Annie descended the back stairs and found Gordon in the kitchen, staring out at the patio through the glass sliders. "You sure the snow isn't sticking?" she asked, joining him.

"Not only is it not sticking, but I'm wondering whether we should use the hot tub, after all."

"I'm not going out there," Annie said. "Especially not in a swimsuit. If it's snowing, it's much too cold."

He smiled faintly, then gestured for her to follow him. They left the kitchen, passed the dining room, and entered his study. He turned on the lamp, crossed to his desk, and pressed the button on a remote control sitting on the blotter. With a cheerful wheeze, a fire magically flared in the fireplace.

Annie hadn't realized it was one of those gas fireplaces—the best kind, as far as she was concerned. No need to stack wood or sweep ashes. Just press a button and create instant atmosphere.

He filled two glasses with whatever was in one of the decanters on the credenza, then motioned toward the armchairs. Annie sat and accepted a glass from him. He tapped his against hers, then sank into the other armchair.

Annie took a sip. "What is this?" she asked as the liquor heated a path down her throat.

"Courvoisier," he told her. "Cognac."

"Whatever it is, it's delicious. I guess I'm not driving home tonight."

"Good. Sarah said she'd like to talk to you tomorrow morning. She's not up to it tonight."

Annie nodded. No doubt Sarah had some more favors to ask of her. And Annie would do them. Of course she would.

"So, what's new with you?" Gordon asked.

His tone implied that he was eager to avoid any more discussion about Sarah—the massive black cloud hanging over the household—right now. Annie obliged by saying, "Emmett and I broke up."

He eyed her curiously, his brows arching, then raised his glass. "Cheers. That guy wasn't good enough for you."

"You're sweet," Annie said. "But I don't think it was a matter of anyone not being good enough."

"I'm not sweet," Gordon argued calmly.

"Actually, you are, much to my surprise." Annie sipped her cognac and smiled at him. "I didn't know that before. I'm sorry Sarah had to get sick for me to get to know you better, but for a cut-throat corporate lawyer, you're very sweet." Another sip, the proverbial liquid courage. "I should apologize for what happened at my office today. That whole thing about me fixing you up with Brittany. I checked with Sarah a few times, and she swore she was serious about finding someone for you to have sex with. But I should have known you were too sweet to do that with someone you didn't know."

"I'm not sweet," Gordon insisted. "And no need to apologize, unless that woman—your assistant, or whoever she was—was upset by what happened. Or didn't happen." He wasn't speaking like a cut-throat corporate lawyer right now. He was fumbling his words, addressing the fire to avoid looking at Annie. Maybe he was embarrassed about the whole thing. Or maybe the cognac was softening his brain the way it was softening hers. "The idea was Sarah's. If anyone should apologize, it's her," he said.

"She was doing what she thought was best for you," Annie defended her sister. "She had good intentions."

Gordon snorted a laugh.

They sat quietly for a while, gazing at the fire. Because the flames emerged from vents hidden within the fake logs, burning natural gas as it was pumped through the logs, the blaze never varied. It wasn't like a wood fire where the fuel snapped and hissed and dissolved into ash and the flames danced along the surfaces of bark, brighter here, then brighter there. Still, it was relaxing and hypnotic. Neat and easy and pretty.

Annie sipped her drink slowly, her tongue gradually growing numb. She tried to imagine what it must be like to know your death was imminent, to know that, in the foreseeable future, you would never again view a fire or drink liquor or...*be*. You would just stop *being*. How could anyone wait patiently for that?

Then again, Annie could get hit by a car tomorrow. Waiting and patience had nothing to do with it.

On the chance that she would be crushed beneath the tires of a carelessly driven vehicle in the near future, she tried to memorize the way the fire looked, the way the sturdy leather armchair felt against her back and her bottom, the way the glass curved against her lower lip when she raised it to drink. The way the cognac tasted—dark and warm and woodsy. The way Becky had felt pressed against her when they'd sat side by side on the living room couch, and Trevor had felt when she'd hugged him upstairs in his bedroom. The way Gordon felt now, even though he was in his own separate chair, several feet away from her. He was sipping the same drink as she was, staring at the same fire. They were connected somehow—by Sarah, by their joint efforts to keep the house functioning and the children moving forward. By the warmth of the fire spreading through the room, even if it wasn't quite real.

chapter thirty

ANNIE PREPARED OATMEAL WITH SLICED BANANAS AND BLUEBERRIES for Becky and Trevor the next morning. After letting them indulge in chocolate milk at dinner yesterday, she owed them something healthy to start their day, especially since this was going to be, as the cliché said, the first day of the rest of their lives. Unfortunately, the rest of their lives had been drastically altered. The rest of their lives was not going to be what they'd expected, what they'd signed up for. They would need solid nutrition to survive it.

Gordon helped himself to a small bowl of the cereal, too, although he skipped the fruit. He surprised Annie by kissing her cheek en route to the garage. It was a thank-you kiss, she knew—thank you for coming, thank you for staying, thank you for feeding the children a hearty breakfast and shooing them out the door in time to catch the school bus. Thank you for sticking around long enough to talk to Sarah.

Yet it felt ridiculously domestic, a scene from some 1950s television sitcom. The wifey sending hubby and the kiddies off at the start of the day, and remaining behind in the kitchen to scrub the oatmeal pot.

She scraped the last of the oatmeal into a bowl for Sarah, filled the pot with sudsy water, and wondered if Sarah's fancy dishwasher could clean a pot caked with gooey cereal. She wondered if you could make oatmeal in Sarah's rice cooker. Or, for that matter, if Sarah had an oatmeal cooker stashed somewhere in another appliance garage.

While the pot soaked, Annie sent Brittany a text message, saying she would be late arriving at the office. *Sister stuff*, she typed, not willing to go into detail in a text. Then she tucked her phone into her pocket and arranged the bowl of cereal, a spoon, and a bottle of chocolate energy drink on a tray and carried it up the stairs to the master bedroom.

Sarah was awake, sitting in bed. She hadn't bothered to don her wig, and Annie was momentarily startled to see Sarah's naked scalp, nearly as smooth as an incandescent light bulb. Drawing closer, Annie saw that a few hairs had sprouted and lay like gossamer cobwebs across her skull. She wore a gorgeous silk kimono with lush flowers embroidered on it. Her lash-less eyes were bright and focused, and she was propped up against her bed's headboard with a pile of pillows, the blanket draped over her legs and the rest of the king-size mattress. Across the room from her, a small flat-screen TV was on; the screen displayed a perky woman in a tight cocktail dress and spike heels, blathering about the cold front that had moved through the region last night. "Did you see those snowflakes?" she exclaimed, much too excited about the previous night's flurries.

"Who wears shoes like that at seven thirty in the morning?" Annie muttered as she set the tray on Sarah's French Provincial night table.

"Women with strong ankles," Sarah replied, aiming a remote control at the screen and clicking the television off.

"I brought you oatmeal and chocolate," Annie said, gesturing toward the tray.

"Thanks." Sarah shook the bottle to stir the drink, then twisted off the cap.

"How are you feeling?" Annie asked.

"Like shit," Sarah said, then shrugged and took a sip. "It'll get better. They'll give me good drugs."

Annie fidgeted for a moment, then lowered herself to sit on the bed. It was so big, she felt as if Sarah was miles away. In a sense, Sarah was. "Gordo told me you wanted to talk to me," she said.

Sarah slugged down her drink, her throat bobbing visibly as she swallowed. Her thirst slaked, she screwed the cap back onto the bottle and set it on the tray. "I don't know how much time I have left," she said. "I'm trying to get things organized."

As if she was strategizing a fund-raising campaign for the library, or formulating the logistics of a class trip. "Sarah..." Annie sighed. She was not going to cry. If Sarah could be so calm and reasonable, Annie couldn't fall apart. "Maybe you've still got years of life ahead of you. Maybe there's something the doctors haven't tried yet. Maybe you'll defy the odds and get written up in medical journals."

Sarah gave her a hard look. "I'm going to die. Soon. That's the reality, Annie."

"I don't know why you've just given up." Annie wondered if Gordon ever said those words to his wife, if he'd demanded to know why she'd skipped over all those stages of grief and nailed a perfect landing on acceptance. "I don't know why you aren't fighting this."

"Fighting what? It's a done deal." Sarah settled back against the pillows. "I'm not afraid to die. I believe in an afterlife, and I'll feel a lot better once I reach it. Because right now, I feel like shit." Her mantra. "This is going to happen. The world will keep spinning. It is what it is." She glanced at the tray, then apparently decided she wasn't in the mood for oatmeal. If Annie were dying, she wouldn't be in the mood for oatmeal either. She would want to consume her premium butter pecan ice cream for breakfast, and walnut-studded fudge for lunch. And Gordon's cognac for dinner.

"Obviously, I don't have to do anything about our finances. Gordon's in charge of that. But I have things. My clothing, for instance. I'm going to put Diana in charge of that. If there's any particular garment you want, you'll have to discuss it with her. But she's got a much better sense of fashion than you do. I kind of doubt you'd want any of my clothes, anyway." She slid her gaze over Annie's sweater and twill trousers, her usual work outfit. Nothing fashionable about it, for sure. "And my shoes—your feet are bigger than mine, so forget that. I have some nice pieces of jewelry too. I'll have Gordon hold onto them. Eventually, Trevor will get married and he'll want to give some of those pieces to his wife. Whatever is left, Becky can have."

Annie bit her lip to prevent herself from retorting that, number one, Trevor might not get married, or—who knew?—he might marry a man, or he might marry a woman who hated jewelry. And number two, why should Becky get the leftovers? Why should she get whatever Trevor's greedy, grasping wife decided she didn't want?

It didn't matter. Sarah's final wishes notwithstanding, Annie would look out for Becky.

"Everything else—my books, my tablet, my kitchen gadgets... Gordon can figure some of that out, but he might need your help. Not might—he *will* need your help. I know you love my kids. I want you to be there for them. Gordon will probably meet someone else and get remarried. He's not designed to stay single. But some stepmother—I don't know if she'll love my kids as much as you do. I want to know you'll keep an eye out for them."

Annie couldn't help it. Tears welled up in her eyes and spilled over her lashes. Who cared about Sarah's fashionable wardrobe and pricy bling? She was bequeathing to Annie the most important thing in her life: her children.

"Of course," Annie whispered.

"You'll protect them from Mom if she gets weird about things, okay? And Gordon's parents too. They can be a bit much."

"Of course." Annie swiped at her damp cheeks with her palms. "How can you do this, Sarah? How can you be so...so at peace with all this?"

"I plan," Sarah told her. "That's how I've had the life I had. I always plan things out. I figure out what I want, and then I make a plan. And then I stick to it. You never plan anything," she went on, her naked eyes laser-sharp as they narrowed on Annie. "You just drift along and try to avoid tripping on potholes. How did you end up with the job you had? You never said, 'Gee, when I grow up, I want to work as an admissions counselor at my alma mater.' You just graduated and didn't know what to do or where to go, so you took a job on the campus, and then another job, and now here you are. How did you wind up with Emmett? You didn't say, 'I'm going to snag a handsome carpenter who's about as deep as a rain puddle in the gutter.' He happened along, and so you figured, why not? Gordon told me Emmett broke up with you, by the way."

"*I* broke up with *him*," Annie said, her voice clearer now, more defensive. The genuine love she'd felt when Sarah had given her responsibility for Trevor and Becky seeped away, replaced by defensiveness as Sarah critiqued her.

"Well, good for you, then. I won't deny that he was hot, but honestly, who the hell was he? What, besides his sexy dimples, did he bring to the table? No education, no career, just those cute little dimples."

"They were really great dimples," Annie said. To her surprise, she laughed. Sarah did too.

"I've always planned everything," Sarah continued. "Every step. I wanted to attend a good college. I wanted to marry a handsome, high-earning husband. I wanted to live in a big house. I wanted two kids. If it was in my control, I controlled it. I wish my health was in my control, but..." She shrugged. "So I'm planning what I can. I don't want to leave a mess when I go."

"You need to talk to the kids," Annie said, her first job as Trevor's and Becky's *de facto* guardian. "They were upset that you weren't there when Gordo explained your prognosis yesterday. Especially Trevor."

"I'll talk to them when I'm ready. I've got it planned," Sarah said. "But I need you to tell Mom and Dad."

"No." The word slipped out so quickly, so easily, it startled Annie. If she was going to guide Becky and Trevor through the loss of their mother and whatever might come after, she was going to have to be assertive. Nice, but assertive. This was one favor she simply would not do. "You have to tell them. I'm not going to."

Sarah appeared startled. Then she smiled. "Fine. I'll tell them. Mom's probably already in a bereavement group, telling everyone her pain is worse than theirs."

"Dad will fall apart," Annie predicted.

"Then you'll have to put him back together," Sarah said.

Annie acknowledged the truth in that. She had always done more for her parents, because according to them, Sarah had too many other demands on her time. She had a husband, she had children, she had her volunteer obligations. She had too much homework. And once she was gone, Annie would be it. The single, solitary Baskin daughter. An only child.

"You're really going to abandon me?" she accused Sarah. "You're going to stick me with Mom and Dad, all by myself?"

"You can handle them if you make a plan," Sarah assured her.

○ ○ ○

By the time Annie and Jamal staggered into the Dorm at eight o'clock that evening, she was starving. After working their regular hours at the admissions office, they'd recorded another three hours of podcasts in the media center. Annie hadn't eaten anything all day, other than a box of raisins consumed at her desk while plowing through applications. She didn't even like raisins—they looked like rodent droppings to her—but she'd been ravenous, and Evelyn had had several single-serving boxes on her desk. "Leftovers from Halloween," she'd explained, which meant that they were old and stale and also that Evelyn was the kind of person who handed out raisins instead of candy to trick-or-treaters.

Throughout the day, Annie had tried to remain focused on the scores of applications filling her computer files. But Sarah's words that morning—her appearance, her hairless head, her criticisms of Annie, her eerie serenity in the face of death—it all buzzed inside Annie's brain like a mosquito, biting and biting, making Annie itch emotionally.

Everything Sarah had said about Annie was true. Well, maybe not everything. Annie might not be as knowledgeable as Sarah or Diana Drucker when it came to fashion, but she knew how to sort clothing and pack it up for Goodwill. Emmett might have been shallow, but he'd been friendly and easygoing and a dynamo in bed.

But Annie had drifted into that relationship, just as she'd drifted into her relationship with most guys. She'd drifted into her job. Hell, even the podcast—it had been her idea, but if Jamal hadn't pushed for it, it never would have been created, let alone earned them bonuses.

Annie needed to stop drifting. She needed to stop letting things happen to her: the podcast, Emmett, her job, everything. She needed to be more assertive.

"Hey, hon, what can I get you?" the server asked as she sidled up to the booth Annie and Jamal had taken.

"I'll have a quarter-pound burger," Annie said assertively. "With cheddar cheese. And..." she glanced at Jamal. "Want to split an order of sweet potato fries?"

"Sure." He ordered a burger as well—with Swiss, not cheddar—and two lagers for them to drink. Smart move. A burger and a beer—and sweet potato fries—would make Annie feel more assertive.

Once the server had departed with their order, Jamal leaned forward. "How are you doing, Annie? You've been wired all day."

"Too much coffee," she joked, although she knew that wasn't true.

Jamal easily guessed it wasn't true too. "Are you one of those people who get the holiday blues? You don't want to do that Yankee Swap shit that Brittany always organizes for Christmas?"

Annie shook her head. She didn't mind the Yankee Swap. Last year she'd wound up with a scented candle that she'd given to her mother, who said she would burn it in the bathroom when Annie's father went in there for his sit-down. The year before, Annie had gone home with a little book of Christmas poems burdened by forced rhymes that amused her. *All those lovely Christmas gifts/Give our spirits happy lifts.* Not quite on a par with what she'd studied in the twentieth-century British poetry seminar she'd taken as a senior at Cabot College, but good for a laugh.

"It's just been a rough day," she told Jamal, hearing her voice splinter around the edges. She had already cried in his presence once before, here at the Dorm. She didn't want to cry again.

"Your sister?" he guessed. He looked so earnest, so concerned.

She nodded. "They've stopped treatment. They're doing palliative care instead. And we talked this morning, and..." Annie sighed shakily. "She's dying."

"I'm so sorry." Jamal reached across the table and covered her hand with his. If she had told Emmett her sister was dying, he would have reminded her that she didn't love her sister anyway.

But she did love her sister. Sarah pissed her off, Sarah insulted her, Sarah made her feel inferior—but today, Sarah had entrusted her with the care of Trevor and Becky. Fuck the clothing, fuck the jewelry—Sarah had put Annie in charge of the two most important people in the world. And doing that had emboldened Annie enough to refuse to call Gilda with the latest bad news. Knowing Sarah wanted Annie to be a constant in her children's lives had given Annie strength.

"I'm trying to wrap my head around the idea of not having a sister," she said. "I've always had a sister. She's always been there—three steps ahead of me, three rungs above me. Shining like a star. When she's gone, what happens to me? I won't be Sarah's little sister anymore."

"I can give you one of my sisters," Jamal offered, smiling gently. "I've got plenty to spare."

He didn't release her hand when the server hustled over with their glasses of beer. "Food'll be right out," she promised before waltzing away.

Merely hearing the word *food* caused Annie's stomach to issue a happy groan. "My sister's dying, and all I can think about is that I'm starving."

"You're living in the present," he said. "That's good."

"In the present, I could eat a horse."

"I don't think the hamburgers here contain horse meat."

She shared his smile. And she discovered that, though the burger was big and sloppy, its thick slab of melted cheddar oozing out between the edges of the roll, she could manage to lift it to her mouth with just one hand. Because Jamal refused to let go of her other hand. He ate one-handed too—his hands were much larger than hers, so the task wasn't quite as challenging for him. But as they ate, they talked about sisters and families and whether you could plan for death, the way Sarah did, without losing your mind.

"You can't plan for everything," Jamal pointed out. "If you're planning for X, Y might happen and you'll miss the experience."

"Right. You could get hit by a car."

"Well, Y might turn out to be something wonderful. A miracle cure. A precious moment with someone you love. A gorgeous sunrise. If you've got your eyes on the ground to make sure you won't trip on your shoelaces, you might miss out on a rainbow."

"Is that what they teach you in philosophy classes?"

"Yep. It's all about rainbows. That's why so many people major in it."

Annie laughed at his joke, but his words put her into a contemplative mood. Rainbows didn't happen in New England in the winter. They rarely happened at all. Tripping on shoelaces occurred a lot more frequently.

"My sister told me she wanted me to keep an eye on her kids once she was gone—which was so...beautiful." Annie felt tears welling up in her eyes again, accumulating along her lower lids. "But she also told me she didn't trust me with her clothing."

To her surprise, Jamal guffawed. "And this matters to you because...?"

"Well, clothing is important. She was telling me she trusted me, and then telling me she didn't trust me. I was worthless. I'm an ignoramus when it comes to clothing."

"You dress fine," Jamal said, even though Annie knew Jamal dressed much better than she did. "Clothing is a commodity. Children are life itself. Your sister was giving you the greatest compliment she could. She was telling you that you're too good to be bothered with something as trivial as clothing."

"So why are you wearing a cashmere sweater?" Annie challenged him.

He shrugged sheepishly. "It's warm and soft," he said, then shrugged again. "All right, my sisters brainwashed me about fashion. They probably wouldn't trust me with their kids, though. They know I'd spoil them rotten."

"I'll probably spoil my niece and nephew too," Annie admitted.

They spent the rest of their meal discussing the podcast. They had interviewed three guests during their marathon recording session that evening: a computer science student who talked about robotics and claimed that ultimate Frisbee was a much better club sport than rugby; a student who worked in the dining center to supplement her financial aid package and boasted about the school's vegan menus—"I mean, really, you'd think you were eating meat, it's so good!" she'd insisted; and a first-year who had no idea what she wanted to major in, because there were so many cool things to study, but she really enjoyed playing rugby. "I guess I can't major in that, can I," she'd mused.

Jamal asked Annie what direction she thought they ought to take the podcast after the application deadline had passed, and she said she had no idea. "You've got plenty of ideas," he told her. "They're just buried under a blanket of sadness right now. We can figure that out later."

With food in her stomach, and the pleasantly bitter taste of beer lingering on her tongue, Annie felt better, the threat of tears receding. She and Jamal walked back to the campus together, his arm slung protectively around her shoulders. The previous night's flurries had left no trace of snow behind, but the grass was dead and frozen, crunching beneath their feet, and the air was December-cold.

"You will survive, Annie," he assured her. "You will grieve, but you will survive. You're braver than you know."

"I'm not that brave."

"You know that old saying about how God doesn't give you anything you can't handle?"

"I'm not on good terms with God right now," Annie muttered. "My sister's probably going to be dead before her fortieth birthday. What kind of God would allow that?"

"I think that's a pretty stupid saying myself," Jamal said. "God dumps all kinds of crap on people all the time. So screw having faith in God. Have faith in yourself."

"Is that the same thing as loving myself?" Annie asked. "Because I still haven't got that one down."

"It's different," Jamal said. "But you're smart. You'll learn. You're a Cabbage World alum. Maybe that's what we can do after the application deadline: discuss the school's graduates. What they're doing. Why they're doing it."

"Or we can talk about music. And beer."

"Right. Living in the present." Somehow he'd turned her joke into another philosophical notion. "That's your car?" He pointed to the rust-scabbed Honda sitting in its lonely spot in the middle of the staff lot, where earlier that day it had been surrounded by other cars. Jamal's sporty BMW was also isolated in its spot, several rows away.

"That's my present car," she said. "In the future, I'd like to have a car like yours. Am I allowed to project that far?"

"It's not that far in the future," he said. "We'll keep doing the podcast and earning all that extra money. And maybe you'll win the lottery."

"If I do," she conceded, "I might have to forgive God."

Grinning, Jamal gave her a hug, kissed her forehead, and cautioned her to drive safely. She watched him jog across the barren lot to his car then unlocked the Honda and slid onto the driver's seat, the vinyl upholstery icy beneath her butt. Twice that day a man had kissed her, neither kiss remotely erotic. Yet both kisses—Gordon's that morning, Jamal's that evening—made her feel better than any of Emmett's kisses ever had.

chapter thirty-one

SARAH DIED THE FIRST WEEK OF JANUARY.

"It's very common for people to die right after the new year begins," Chloe told Annie during the *shiva* reception at the Adler house after the funeral. "They'll hang on until they get past some major event. Their birthday, their anniversary, a holiday like Christmas or New Year's. And then, after the big day, they let go. We lose more residents in January than any other month."

Annie might have argued that the people who died at the elder residence where Chloe worked might be dying soon after New Year's Day because their aged bodies couldn't tolerate January's bitter-cold weather. She might have suggested that dying was not the same thing as letting go; it wasn't as if the old residents of the assisted living center— or, for that matter, Sarah—had been clinging to a window sill fifteen stories above the street and lost their grip.

But then, what did Annie know? Death might be exactly like that: hanging on to that sill until your fingers grew numb, until your palms grew slick with sweat and your hands slipped. Chloe had majored in psychology, after all, and she worked with frail, elderly people who were already standing at the open window when they moved into the complex—possibly even straddling the window sill, or leaning out, looking down, contemplating whether to jump.

The reception was a fine display of hospitality. At Gordon's request, Annie had hired the caterer, picked out the menu—finger sandwiches and salads and elegant hors d'oeuvres, and a side table filled with gourmet desserts. In the kitchen, an industrial-sized urn brewed coffee, and a simple bar set-up occupied one of the pristine granite counters, bottles of white and red wines flanked by inexpensive stemware glasses. Annie had never hosted a reception like this before. She'd never even talked to a caterer. Gordon had told her whom to employ. "We hire them for parties at the office," he'd said. "Sarah's hired them a few times too."

"What's your budget?" Annie had asked.

"Don't worry about it. Just use your judgment."

As if Annie had any judgment.

She had spent most of the final month of Sarah's life at the Adler house. She'd settled into the guest room, hanging a few garments in the elaborate closet, stuffing a couple of drawers with underwear and sweaters and a swimsuit, just in case she decided to brave the winter chill and enjoy the hot tub. She had left a spare comb and brush, deodorant, and a tub of moisturizing cream on the marble counter in the bathroom. She had pretty much taken over the kitchen—preparing meals, setting out snacks for Trevor and Becky when they got home from school, teaching Becky how to separate eggs and Trevor how to smash garlic cloves with the flat of a knife blade so the skin would slide off.

Every morning before she left for work, she checked on Sarah, who mostly remained in bed, hooked up to a morphine drip the hospice nurse had provided. She could control how much morphine she got, and she told Annie she didn't need too much. But their mother felt this was yet more proof that Sarah was now a drug addict, something she needed to share with her Al-Anon support group.

Annie tried to avoid her mother. Gilda usually stopped by to visit Sarah after Annie had departed for Cabot College. But Gilda insisted that Annie accompany her to one of her Al-Anon meetings. Annie had demurred, but Gilda promised Annie there would be homemade brownies and high-quality coffee at the meeting.

The coffee had not been high-quality, and the brownies had not been homemade. Annie had taken one bite of the latter and one sip of the former, and then deposited both her cup and her brownie in the nearest trash bin. The attendees had sat on folding chairs in a circle in a basement room provided by the local Methodist church. The chairs were occupied by a group of pleasant people representing a wide variety of ages, races, and other demographic markers. But Gilda had dominated the meeting. When it was her turn to share, she'd said, "I can't believe my daughter Sarah is dying—and spending her final days in a drug-induced haze. Sarah was such a perfect daughter. So beautiful—you wouldn't know it to see her now, but she was ravishing. And brilliant, an Ivy League graduate. She did everything right. She married well, bought a mansion with her husband, produced two spectacular grandchildren, and you should have seen her when she fixed herself up for an event. But she got cancer, and now all she wants is her morphine. I don't know if she's still taking the OxyContin, but she's definitely mainlining morphine. This—" she'd clapped her hand against Annie's shoulder hard enough to cause Annie's eyes to tear up "—is my other daughter. Annie, say hello to these wonderful people."

"Hello," Annie had managed, rubbing her shoulder where her mother had smacked it.

"Annie is my other daughter," Gilda had repeated. "As far as I know, she's not on drugs. But she causes me pain, too, in her own way. Children always cause their mothers pain. I don't know why that is, but they do. I can't begin to describe the pain I'm in..." And then Gilda had spent the next seven minutes describing the pain she was in, until a man who looked vaguely like Santa Claus, with a snow-white beard and flowing white hair, said, "Your time is up."

Annie didn't want to listen to her mother rant about how much agony she was in. Fortunately, she had the excuse of her job, which enabled her to escape the house when Gilda chose to visit Sarah. Their father's visits, in the evening after work, were equally difficult, but not because he flaunted his ego the way Gilda did. He just gazed at Sarah and wept. Usually, after a few minutes of silent weeping, Gordon would basically utter his own version of "Your time is up" and send his father-in-law on his way.

Despite it all—the disruption of her life, the dislocation, the grief, the chronic pressure Annie felt to take care of everything that needed taking care of, spending some time chatting with Sarah in the evenings, making sure Trevor and Becky got to bed at a reasonable hour and out to the school bus on time in the morning—Annie managed to fulfill her professional obligations. She treasured her time in her office, which somehow didn't seem quite so cramped to her now that Gordon had seen it and pointed out the advantages of having a small work space.

She read the applications in her files with a sharper eye and a softer heart. Who knew what lay ahead for these teenagers who were vying for a slot at Cabot College? Who knew if they would go on to win a Nobel Prize, or wind up with a fatal cancer? Or get hit by a car while crossing the street?

Annie wanted to make them happy. She couldn't accept them all—and a significant percentage didn't deserve to be accepted—but she loved them. She wanted to make them feel good about themselves. She wanted them to have fulfilling lives, however long those lives might last.

Sarah seemed to believe she'd had a fulfilling life. She was often muddled, thanks to her pain meds. She would drift, doze off in mid-sentence, and then wake up ten minutes later and complete the sentence she'd begun before zoning out. But she'd told Annie more than once, "It's been a good life. I can't ask for more."

Which sounded more like Annie than like Sarah. Annie was the one who had always felt she couldn't ask for more. She'd felt she wasn't worthy. She was just the schlubby kid sister, trailing after Sarah, wishing she could *be* Sarah.

The *shiva* reception indicated that, while she hadn't turned into Sarah, she had at least learned how to organize a classy, well-attended gathering. The Adler house was mobbed with people who had driven there from the cemetery after the burial: Sarah's wide circle of friends from town, from Trevor and Becky's school, from the library. Friends dating back to Sarah's undergraduate days at Brown, and further back to her high school days. Most of those high school friends were still kind of snooty, even if they no longer had a right to be. They were no longer the queens of the locker-lined high school corridors. They no longer reigned supreme in their ecosystem. Some had gained weight, some had gotten frumpy, but they all behaved as if they were still the most popular girls around.

A large sampling of Gordon's colleagues from the law firm were also in attendance, dressed nearly uniformly in dark suits, white shirts, and dark ties. Annie occasionally overheard them talking shop, which struck her as inappropriate, but it wasn't her job to police their conversations. If they wanted to remember Gordon's lovely wife by analyzing recent rulings by the SEC, let them.

A smattering of Baskin relatives showed up, along with Gordon's parents, who had flown in from Chicago and told everyone they had to return home that night, due to the demands of their oh-so-essential jobs. Annie bit her lip to keep from haranguing them. Their son had just lost his wife. Their grandchildren had just lost their mother. But Gordon's mother evidently believed that arranging proper lighting for the Mark Rothko painting her museum had just acquired was more important, as was Gordon's father's racquetball tournament. A man had to stay fit in the winter if he hoped to golf all summer, he told Annie before asking where her carpenter boyfriend was.

"He couldn't make it," she retorted, not wanting to give him the satisfaction of knowing she and Emmett were no longer a couple.

Her team from the admissions office had attended the funeral. Harold had kissed her cheek when he saw her at the funeral home, and that had been kind of icky. Dean Parisi had clasped Annie's hands and said, "Take as much time as you need." Evelyn had mentioned a good therapist, if Annie required one.

Only Brittany and Jamal came back to the Adler house for the reception. They loitered with Chloe near the dining room table, helping themselves to food and chatting. At one point, Brittany approached Annie and asked if she was still supposed to have sex with Gordon. "He's very good-looking," she noted.

Brittany couldn't have gotten close to him, though, let alone seduced him. Diana Drucker kept buzzing around him like a gnat, and Gordon was polite enough not to swat at her.

At least twenty children—friends and classmates of Trevor and Becky—showed up at the house. Once they had vanquished the dessert table like locusts devouring a wheat field, Annie led them all downstairs to the rec room and loaded *The Princess Bride* onto the wide-screen television for them to watch, something both ten-year-old boys and eight-year-old girls would enjoy.

At the top of the stairs, she bumped into her mother, who steered her into the kitchen and glared at the row of wine bottles. "Why are there no mixed drinks?" she demanded to know.

"We would have had to hire a bartender," Annie said. "I didn't want to do that."

"Oh, for God's sake. We're all adults. We can mix our own drinks. I know how to make a martini." Scowling with distaste, she filled a glass with white wine and studied Annie. "Where did you get that dress?"

"It's Sarah's," Annie said. She had realized she owned nothing appropriate to wear to her sister's funeral. The only dresses she owned were her extremely ugly maid-of-honor gown from Sarah's wedding, a slightly less ugly cocktail-length bridesmaid's dress from her friend Jenna's wedding, and a couple of sleeveless cotton summer dresses with bright floral patterns which she'd bought at a discount department store and wore, bare-legged and shod in sandals, when she and Chloe went barhopping in the summer. They were cute dresses. She had been wearing one when she'd met Emmett during a pub crawl last July.

But they were not suitable for a funeral, especially not in January. She had a brown skirt and a sweater-set that sort of matched the skirt, but she looked like a secretary from the 1950s when she wore that outfit. She also had a decent pants suit, although the jacket's lapel had a mysterious stain on it. And a woman shouldn't wear trousers to her sister's funeral. "Wear something of Sarah's," Gordon had suggested.

She had ventured nervously into Sarah's walk-in closet, a space bigger than her kitchen at the condo, and rifled through Sarah's extensive wardrobe. Sarah had apparel for every occasion—outfits suitable for library board meetings, for class trips, for proper dinners with Gordon's clients in downtown Boston, for glittery parties of the sort she might have attended on New Year's Eve if she hadn't spent that festive night lying in bed, declining food, and nudging the speed of her morphine drip upward. Most of Sarah's clothing probably wouldn't fit Annie well, since she was thicker around the waist and smaller at the bust and hips than Sarah had been. But she found a knit charcoal-gray sweater dress shapeless enough to accommodate her figure. The fabric was a cashmere blend, so soft it felt like goose down against her skin. It had a high neck, long sleeves, and a hem that fell just below Annie's knees. As funeral attire, it came closer to perfection than any garment Annie had ever owned.

"You borrowed something of Sarah's?" Annie's mother assessed Annie, her gaze shuttling up and down the length of the dress.

Oh, for God's sake, Annie almost blurted out. But all she said, rather dryly, was, "At this point, I don't think she'd mind."

"Well, it looks wonderful on you. Neiman-Marcus, I bet," Gilda said, nudging Annie's shoulder so she had to pivot, allowing Gilda to view the dress from the back. "It would probably look even better if you wore heels with it."

Annie had chosen to wear flats. Sarah's funeral was tragic enough without enduring sore feet.

"Who chose what the kids wore?"

"They did. I had final approval," Annie said. Gordon had been busy discussing arrangements with the funeral home, the rabbi affiliated with it, and the cemetery. He'd told Annie to make sure Becky didn't attend her mother's funeral in a sweatshirt that said "Warrior Goddess" or some such thing. In fact, Becky had chosen a demure dress of navy blue knit, and Trevor had worn his one pair of dress slacks, his one blazer, and his one dress shirt. He'd borrowed a tie from Gordon. He could almost pass as a pint-size version of the attorneys schmoozing with Gordon in the living room.

Annie wandered back to the living room, her mother trailing her, clutching her glass of white Bordeaux. Someone Annie vaguely recognized—one of the Adlers' neighbors—approached Gilda, carrying a plate holding several finger sandwiches. "Such a sad occasion, but this is truly a lovely reception."

Gilda smiled. "Thank you. We went with a caterer Sarah used to hire for all her affairs. They were such a pleasure to work with. They do such a good job."

Not that Gilda had any idea who they were, or how much of a pleasure they were to work with. She had contributed exactly nothing to the reception, although she was happy to take credit for it. Annoyed, Annie strode over to the couch and settled into the cushions next to her father, who was munching on a slice of marble pound cake while tears ran in rivulets from his eyes to his jaw. "It's okay," Annie murmured, kissing his cheek.

Across the room, she saw Gordon surrounded by a small circle of lawyer types. He looked weary but handsome in his impeccably tailored suit. One of the men he was talking to had his arm around Gordon's shoulders, although Gordon didn't appear to be in need of comforting. Over the past month, his anger had eroded, replaced by an almost eerie calm. He had reached that final stage of grief, Annie realized: acceptance.

She had reached it too. She wasn't sure she'd gone through the other four stages, however. She had never bargained, never really gotten depressed. Sad, yes. Frustrated. Exasperated that Sarah had surrendered to her illness so easily. Irritated that she was constantly being called on to do favors for the family—and irritated with herself that she nearly always said yes.

"Nothing will be the same without Sarah," her father said in a quavering voice. "But at least we still have you."

At least, Annie thought bitterly. One stage she hadn't skipped was anger.

Some of that anger, she acknowledged, was directed at Sarah. How could she leave Annie all by herself to deal with their parents? Who would Annie turn to to bitch about them when they diminished Annie's value or took credit for the things Annie did? If she couldn't call Sarah and whine to her—or laugh with her—whom could she call?

"I'm not an *at least*," she said, deciding to jettison nice and opt for assertive. "I'm your other daughter. That's all." She pushed away from the couch's comfortable upholstery and headed toward the dining room. Anger made her hungry.

As she entered the dining room, Jamal saw her and waved her over. Her own people, she thought with a sigh of relief as she joined him, Brittany, and Chloe in their corner. En route, she snagged a finger sandwich from one of the platters and devoured it in three bites. She had always thought the term "finger sandwiches" alluded to the fact that you could easily hold such a sandwich with your fingers. But maybe it meant the sandwich was not much larger than your thumb.

Jamal gave her a crushing hug. "How are you holding up?" he asked.

"I'm okay," she said. "I'm wearing comfortable shoes."

"That can make all the difference in the world," Chloe said.

Brittany glanced down at her spike-heeled black leather boots and shrugged. "These are comfortable."

"When you're twenty-five, everything is comfortable," Annie said.

"Excuse me," a harsh female voice penetrated their little circle. Annie spun around to find Diana Drucker bearing down on her. "A word?" Diana bleated.

"What?"

Diana glanced at Annie's friends and apparently realized that Annie wasn't going to leave them to listen privately to Diana's word. She sighed, then said, "Sarah put me in charge of her clothing. This dress you're wearing—your mother just told me it's Sarah's. From Neiman-Marcus, right?"

"I have no idea where she bought it," Annie said.

Diana shook her head. "You'll have to dry-clean it before you return it to Sarah's closet."

Assertive, Annie told herself. "I'm not returning it," she said. "It's mine now."

"It's part of Sarah's estate. Did she bequeath it to you?"

Assertive but nice, Annie mentally amended. "Look, Diana. I know you're upset. You've lost your best friend. I'm upset too. I've lost my sister—even if you and she use to laugh about me behind my back. Gordo told me to wear this dress, and I'm wearing it. Now, if you want to go hit on Gordo, be my guest. Just make sure your husband isn't in the same room." Okay, that wasn't very nice at all. Annie didn't care. She felt empowered. She felt strong. She felt as if she loved herself.

Diana stormed off in a huff. "What was that about?" Jamal asked.

"Nothing. My sister's best friend from high school."

"What a bitch," Chloe muttered. Even without a degree in psychology, Annie could have reached the same conclusion.

"My sister didn't have the best taste in friends," Annie admitted.

"She had great taste in clothes, though," Brittany said. "That dress looks fabulous on you."

Annie decided she loved Brittany. She loved Chloe. She loved Jamal. They were her family. She wasn't a younger sister to any of them. She wasn't a clumsy oaf with stains on her sleeves, a clueless dweeb who didn't know the proper way to walk, the other Baskin girl. She wasn't a loser.

True, she'd lost her sister. But she had these people. Her friends. Her team.

Her family.

chapter thirty-two

BY SIX-THIRTY, THE HOUSE WAS EMPTY OF GUESTS. The caterers wrapped the leftovers in plastic and left them in several tidy piles on the kitchen island. Annie wedged most of the sandwiches, salads, and hors d'oeuvres into the kitchen's refrigerator, then carried the rest downstairs to store inside the spare fridge.

Considering that the basement rec room had been the staging area for a group of unsupervised youngsters, Annie was relieved to see the place had not been torn apart. A few bolster pillows on the sofa had been displaced, and a generous smattering of cake and cookie crumbs had been ground into the carpeting. Sarah would throw a fit when she saw the carpet.

Except that she wouldn't see it. Or if she saw it from the afterlife she was certain existed, she would not be able to whip out a vacuum cleaner and revert her floor to its usual pristine state.

Annie would vacuum it tomorrow, or maybe ask Trevor and Becky to vacuum it. Everyone was too tired to flip the switch on the vacuum cleaner right now. It had been a long day: the service at the chapel, the caravan to the gravesite, more prayers, the lowering of Sarah's plain pine casket into the ground, the ritual shoveling. As Sarah's sister, Annie heaved several shovels full of dirt into the grave, worrying all the while that she might soil the fancy dress she had borrowed from Sarah's closet. When they were growing up, Sarah had never let Annie borrow any of her clothing, because when Annie returned the borrowed garment, it was inevitably marked with a splotch of something that didn't belong on it.

Fortunately, her coat had acted as an apron, covering and protecting the dress. She did get a little dirt on the coat's hem, but she was able to dust it off.

After the cemetery, the family had endured the drive home, the reception, the crowds, the din of yammering voices. But now, at last, the house was still and quiet. No hospice nurses. No in-laws. Just the surviving Adlers and Annie.

Trevor was hungry. No surprise; he was always hungry these days. A boy on the cusp of puberty had a lot of growing to do, and he needed constant refueling. Annie heated some soup for him, and Becky decided she wanted some too. Annie pulled a few rolls from the leftover stash to supplement the soup, and set the kids up on stools at the center island. "We're staying home tomorrow, right?" Trevor asked as Annie ladled the soup into bowls.

"I was thinking we could go someplace," Gordon told them. "The Museum of Science, maybe. We could check out the show at the theater there, have lunch in the cafeteria, astronaut ice cream for dessert." He eyed them expectantly.

"So we don't have to sit around the house?" Trevor asked.

"No."

"Will you come too?" Becky asked Annie.

Annie shook her head. "I've got to put in a little time at work." She had missed plenty of days this month, and Dean Parisi had been generous about that. But the school's application deadline for general admission was bearing down on Annie's colleagues, and they had received nearly twice as many applications as last year. Jamal had attributed this to the podcast, a theory Evelyn reluctantly agreed with and Harold dismissed, but one the dean endorsed. Even though the avalanche of applications meant more work for the team, Dean Parisi was thrilled. The more applications, the smaller the ratio of acceptances, which would boost Cabot College's ranking in national surveys.

Becky pouted, her cute lower lip protruding. "Will you be here when we come home?"

Annie circled the island to give her a hug. "We'll see. If not tomorrow, I'll come by over the weekend."

"I wish you could stay here forever," Becky told Annie, her voice tremulous. Trevor didn't second that suggestion, but he gave Annie a hopeful look before scooping more soup into his mouth.

"I have my own home," Annie reminded them. She had spent so little time at the condo lately, she couldn't blame Becky and Trevor if they'd forgotten that fact. And she had to admit she hadn't missed the condo that much, even though the mornings and evenings she'd spent at the Adler house had been both hectic and sad. In the mornings, she'd fed the children and sent them off to catch their school bus. In the evenings, she'd helped them with their homework and prepared dinner, or else sat in the quiet, dimly lit master bedroom and watched Sarah gradually shut down, her attention drifting with the morphine infusions, her appetite dwindling until, a few days before she died, she stopped eating altogether. Annie had sat beside the bed, watching as Sarah's breath grew heavier, more uneven, her words sporadic. Annie would talk to Sarah, but she had no idea if Sarah could hear her. She would inform Sarah that it was snowing, or that Becky had gotten an A on her math test, or that Trevor had scored eight points in his most recent basketball game. Sarah would sometimes nod, sometimes sigh, sometimes do nothing at all.

On her last day, Gordon had brought the children into the master bedroom to say goodbye to their mother. Annie hoped Sarah had heard them, but she would never know for sure. She had spent the rest of the day with them downstairs in the rec room, reading, watching raucous cartoons, attempting a game of pool—both Trevor and Becky had astounded her with their superior play, even though Becky still used a shorter child-size cue stick—and keeping them occupied and distracted while, two floors above them, with Gordon and one of the hospice nurses in attendance, Sarah had let go.

The funeral was organized quickly—not quite within twenty-four hours, as the Jewish tradition demanded, but within forty-eight. Annie hadn't gone to work or to her condo in all that time. She couldn't blame Becky for thinking she might as well live here forever.

The idea tempted her. This house was so spacious, so lovely, so shiny. The appliances were all so much newer than hers, and so much more reliable. The furniture had been purchased, not inherited, and the décor came together in a unified way, the drapes matching the upholstery, which matched the rugs. The shower in the guest bathroom was so big, Annie could shave her legs without getting water in her eyes, and the spray came out of one of those disk-shaped showerheads designed to simulate rain. The dryer in the laundry room didn't make syncopated clunking noises the way Annie's did. The wine was always the perfect temperature, because Gordon stored several bottles at a time in a special wine cooler installed under one of the kitchen counters. The guest bedroom bed, with its hybrid memory-foam mattress, was so comfortable, Annie gave it as much credit as the absence of Emmett's snoring for her restful sleep of late. And of course there was the hot tub, and the push-button fireplace in Gordon's study.

Annie was the Baskin sister no one would ever imagine living in a house like this. She was the Baskin sister she herself would never imagine living in a house like this.

Yet for the past month—the past few months, really—she had eased into this world, one task at a time. One favor at a time.

And she wasn't anyone's awkward kid sister anymore.

That thought left her ambivalent. She hadn't changed her identity. She was still awkward, even if she had managed to spend all day in a chic Neiman-Marcus dress without getting a single spot on it. She was still someone who drifted along, who had wound up in this gorgeous house because it had been Sarah's home and Sarah had needed her, not because Annie had planned to wind up here. She was still her parents' *other* daughter.

But Sarah was gone. Like a massive oak tree cut down on a sunny day, she no longer cast a shadow over Annie.

Or maybe she did. Maybe she always would. She might be dead, but she was still alive in Annie's head, reminding Annie that she lacked the competence to take care of Sarah's wardrobe after Sarah was gone.

Soup, rolls, and leftover butter cookies from the reception devoured, Becky and Trevor clambered up the back stairs. Their mood seemed ambivalent, devastated by the loss of their mother but cheerful about skipping school tomorrow and going to the science museum. Watching a movie in the museum's huge domed theater would be more fun than reviewing math and English assignments.

Gordon gazed at Annie from across the room, leaning against the counter near the appliance garage. He looked tousled. She couldn't remember ever seeing him with his tie loosened before, and the collar of his shirt undone. Even when dressed casually, he always looked starched and stuffy.

Maybe starched-and-stuffy wasn't who he was. Maybe he had always looked impeccable because Sarah had wanted him to look that way, and now that the oak tree had been chopped down, he was going to start looking more slovenly, like Annie. Not likely, but who knew?

"Once the kids are in bed," he said, "let's soak in the hot tub."

"Are you kidding? It's two degrees out."

"Close to thirty. The water will be hot, and I'll hang our robes on the towel heater so they'll be warm when we get out."

He was crazy. But his wife had just been buried and he and Annie were both wrung out. "Okay," she said. Maybe she was crazy too.

She saw Trevor and Becky through their evening rituals. Once Becky was washed and in her pajamas, Annie crawled into bed beside her to read her a couple of chapters from *Alice's Adventures in Wonderland*, which Becky had already read but wanted Annie to read to her, making the characters speak with exaggerated British accents. Once Alice had eaten the cake that said "Eat Me," Annie set aside the book and gave Becky a big hug. "I want you to stay here forever," Becky whispered into the hollow of Annie's neck. Annie could feel dampness there, Becky's tears.

"I will always be in your life," Annie promised her. "I will always be your Aunt Annie and you will always be able to find me."

After turning off Becky's lamp and making sure the shell-shaped night-light was glowing, Annie walked down the hall to Trevor's room. He was reading in bed—a real book, not a comic book—and she crossed the room to give him a good-night kiss. Nothing as intense as what Becky preferred, just a light brush of her lips against the crown of his head. To her surprise, he lowered the book and wrapped his arms around her. "Thank you," he said.

She didn't ask what he was thanking her for. The soup and cookies, perhaps. Her labor keeping the household functioning during Sarah's illness. Her managing to organize the reception.

Or simply being there. Maybe he wanted her to stay forever too.

After reminding him to shut off his light by nine o'clock, she left his bedroom and strolled down the hall to her own room. She had spent so much time there lately, she no longer thought of it as the guest room. She thought of it as hers.

She moved to the window, parted the curtains, and gazed down. The patio lights were on, as were the underwater lights in the hot tub. She could see the water churning, clouds of vapor rising from the surface into the wintry air. Clearly, Gordon had turned everything on. Freezing January air notwithstanding, he was determined to relax in the hot tub.

All right, then. She would pin up her hair and don her swimsuit, bathrobe, and flip-flops. She would bravely walk across that blustery patio in the ice-cold January night and submerge herself in the steaming, bubbling water.

Gordon was waiting for her by the kitchen door out to the patio, an elegant decanter of some no doubt potent liquor in one hand and two glasses in the other. "Can you get the door?" he asked.

She slid it open and they raced through the frigid air to the hot tub. Gordon set the glasses and decanter on the edge of the tub, then took her robe. She jumped into the water, stifling a scream at its searing heat. "Shit," she muttered. "I'm going to wind up with third-degree burns."

"It only feels too hot because of the cold air," he assured her as he draped her robe and his own over one of the towel racks. Then he eased into the tub, settling onto the bench next to her rather than across the way.

She didn't mind. She felt spiritually close to Gordon tonight. They had been through so much together over the last few weeks, the last few days. She might as well be physically close to him too.

He poured their drinks, handed her one of the glasses, and tapped his glass to hers. "Here's to the next phase in our lives, whatever it may be," he said.

She sipped. As always, the beverage numbed her tongue and bathed her throat in a heat quite different from the steamy water churning around her.

Gordon looped an arm around her shoulders and drew her close to him. "God, what a day," he said.

"How are you, Gordo? I mean, seriously."

"I'm okay." He sighed. "I've been preparing myself mentally for weeks. Months, probably. I knew from the start that Sarah wasn't going to be able to beat this. She isn't a fighter. *Wasn't*," he corrected himself, then shook his head. "Wasn't a fighter. Not like you."

"I'm not a fighter," Annie said. "Sarah said I just drift along. She was right. I never plan. I never think ahead. Someone asks me to do something, and I do it. She always had a plan."

"Cancer wasn't part of her plan." He drank, his gaze softening as he stared across the tub. Annie wondered what he saw there. All she saw was the rear façade of the house, the kitchen windows brightly lit, the bay window in the dining room arching out from the brick, the slate and brick of the patio creating a decorative mosaic. She rolled her head back, resting against Gordon's shoulder, and stared up at the sky. Through the mist surrounding the hot tub, she could see stars scattered across the black expanse, tiny flecks of light, jeweled tacks holding up the sky.

"What are you feeding me?" Annie asked, holding out her glass. "Is this that cognac stuff?"

"This is a very fine bourbon," he told her. "If you don't know the difference between a bourbon and a cognac, I need to educate you."

"I'm obviously an ignoramus," Annie joked. "Not one of those Ivy Leaguers, like you."

She took a drink, decided she liked very fine bourbon, and nestled closer to Gordon. For the first time in days—in weeks, in the months since Sarah had phoned her at work to say that she had ovarian can-cer—Annie felt relaxed. Plenty of tasks awaited her, both at work and here, taking care of Trevor and Becky and, she supposed, Gordon. But right now, lounging in the hot tub with the silent winter air above her and the steamy water gurgling around her, warming her skin the way the bourbon warmed her throat, she would take care of nothing and no one. She would close her eyes and appreciate the strength of Gordon's arm around her, and not perform any favors for anyone.

It all felt so natural, so inevitable. Annie had run Sarah's house. She had worn Sarah's dress. She had fed Sarah's children and tucked them into bed. She had become so deeply embedded into the Adler family that she felt like one of them. Not an aunt. Not a sister-in-law. An Adler. Someone who could live here forever.

Someone who could cement her place here with a kiss.

It felt so easy to kiss Gordon. So right.

Sarah's widower, this man who was allegedly filled to bursting with anger and sexual frustration, didn't feel angry right now. His kiss wasn't angry. It was quiet, gentle, flavored with very fine bourbon.

They climbed out of the hot tub and wrapped themselves in their robes. Annie darted inside, then watched through the glass slider as Gordon shut off the hot tub's motor and arranged the cover over the tub. The cold air didn't seem to faze him. He worked slowly, methodically, making sure the cover was centered properly before he strode across the patio and joined Annie inside.

Annie hit the light switch by the back stairs, throwing the kitchen into darkness. They climbed the back stairs, walked directly to the guest room, shut the door, and shed their wet swimsuits, tossing them into the bathroom sink. Then they tumbled into bed.

No, not anger. Not desperation. Not a frantic hunger, a crazed need for release. They kissed. They touched. They made love slowly, with resignation as much as passion. Gordon lacked Emmett's free-wheeling style of sex; he was precise, almost intellectual about it, as if he'd done his research, prepared thoroughly, entered into the process as the alpha attorney in the room, determined to win.

Afterward, he gave her a final kiss and then sank into a deep sleep.

Annie lay awake for a long while. *This is it,* she thought, staring into the room's shadows. *This is Sarah's life. This is what it feels like to be perfect.* Annie was no longer the messy kid sister. She was no longer the second-born, the child added to the family for her sister's benefit. She was no longer anyone's *other* daughter. In some strange, indefinable sense, she had become Sarah.

Was this really what perfection felt like? Shouldn't she feel more... triumphant? More like an alpha attorney who'd won? Shouldn't she feel beautiful and competent and poised, tasteful and feminine, wise in the secret powers of women to get what they wanted, to make a plan and then bring it to fruition? Shouldn't she feel like someone who would wear a shirt with "Princess Power" emblazoned across it in silver and never drip ice cream on it?

Was she a princess now? Or a queen? A goddess or a warrior?

Or just someone's younger sister, still struggling to keep up?

chapter thirty-three

THEY AWAKENED IN THE DARK, before six a.m. A good thing, since it would be awkward, at the very least, for Trevor or Becky to see Gordon emerging from Annie's room wearing nothing but a soggy swimsuit. He appeared mildly surprised to find Annie next to him, but not disappointed. "It's an old Jewish tradition," he murmured, "that when a woman is widowed, she's supposed to marry her husband's brother. Maybe this is a feminist twist on that."

"I'm not marrying you," Annie murmured back, herself surprised that the mere notion of marrying Gordon didn't shock her.

"No, of course not." He pushed himself to sit, shoved his hair out of his face—his hair wasn't particularly long and didn't require much shoving—and rubbed the sleep from his eyes. "I'm just saying, maybe Becky wasn't so far from the mark when she asked you to stay here forever."

Before Annie could respond, he swung out of bed. She admired his naked body as he strode to the bathroom to retrieve his swimsuit. Pretty buff for a lawyer who maintained his muscle tone by working out on exercise machines. He wasn't Emmett. But then, Emmett wasn't Gordon either.

He peeked out into the hall. Evidently, the children's bedroom doors were still closed, and he hurried out of the room, his bare feet noiseless as he padded down the hall. Annie fell back against the pillows and sighed. God, this bed was comfortable.

She wasn't sure if she'd drifted back to sleep, but the sound of Becky and Trevor storming down the stairs forced her fully awake. She showered, washing the hot tub's water out of her hair and Gordon off her skin, and dressed in a pair of jeans and an old wool sweater, the knit ribbing of which was stretched out of shape. She didn't care. It was comfortable.

"We're not going to school today," Becky reminded her as she descended the back stairs to the kitchen, where Trevor was foraging through the cabinets in search of breakfast food.

"That's right," Annie said. "You're going to the Museum of Science with your dad."

"Mommy would want us to do that," Becky said uncertainly. Trevor glanced over his shoulder, a box of Cheerios clutched in his hand. He looked dubious.

Annie chased away his skepticism and Becky's concern. "Your mother definitely would want you to do that. She'd want you to have a peaceful day, to learn some interesting things and spend time with your dad and still be a family. Put the Cheerios away, Trevor. I'll make French toast."

She let Trevor crack the eggs and Becky fetch the cinnamon and nutmeg from Sarah's impeccably organized spice drawer. By the time she had several slices of bread saturated in batter and sizzling in a pan, Gordon arrived in the kitchen, dressed as crisply as usual, in jeans that appeared to have been ironed, an oxford shirt featuring a tidy plaid pattern and over it a V-neck sweater. He could have passed for a frat boy from fifty years ago. In her baggy, saggy sweater and faded jeans, Annie could have passed for the woman the fraternity hired to scrub the toilets.

Gordon sent her a shy smile, then helped himself to a cup of coffee. "Smells good," he said, nodding toward the French toast.

"Tell Aunt Annie we want her to come to the museum with us," Becky said.

His brows rose in a question. "You're welcome to join us," he said rather formally.

Whether he genuinely meant the invitation or was simply being polite didn't matter. "I can't," she said. "I've got too much stuff to do."

Not until after Gordon and the children had devoured the French toast and departed for the museum did Annie pause to reflect exactly what stuff she had to do. At the top of her list: launder the guest room sheets where she and Gordon had made love. After cleaning the pan and stacking the plates and silverware in the dishwasher, she climbed the stairs to the guest bedroom. She felt no pangs of guilt as she gazed at the rumpled sheets and the two pillows with head indentations in them. No regrets. Last night had been last night. Tonight could be tonight, if she wanted. Gordon had asked her to stay forever. She had been thinking of this room as hers for the past month. It could continue to be hers for as long as she wished.

She stripped the linens off the bed. Not enough for a full load. She might as well launder the kids' sheets too. And while she was at it, the sheets in the master bedroom.

Would Gordon object to that? she wondered as she entered the bedroom he had shared with Sarah for twelve years. Would he be sentimental about Sarah's lingering scent on the pillowcase?

No. Annie had gotten to know him well enough to realize that he'd prefer clean sheets. The only scent lingering in the room was a faint, stale smell: urine, medicine, death. Annie folded down the blanket and removed the sheets. She unzipped the protective waterproof mattress cover the hospice nurses had advised Gordon to use to protect the mattress "in case of a bedpan mishap," they'd explained. Gordon didn't need that protection on his bed anymore.

She carried all the linens downstairs to the laundry room off the kitchen, then continued to the basement rec room, where she vacuumed the crumbs and dirt from the carpet and straightened the furniture. It was a wonderful room, even if it lacked windows. The stained-glass lamp hanging over the pool table filled the air with tinted light—amber, scarlet, pine green. The cushions on the sofa had a tweedy surface that echoed the texture of the carpeting. All the toys were stored neatly inside the built-ins lining the wall. If Trevor and Becky didn't appreciate this room now, they would appreciate it when they were teenagers and wanted to hang out with their friends, out of Gordon's sight but safely under his roof.

Satisfied by the room's appearance, Annie returned to the laundry room to transfer the linens to the dryer. Then she wandered through the main floor of the house, appreciating everything about it. The exquisite furniture. The generous proportions of the rooms. The beauty and comfort of the living room couch, the elegance of the dining room, the cozy charm of Gordon's study, a room that used to intimidate her but that she had grown to love—and not just because of the array of decanters on the credenza, filled with pricy booze.

And of course the kitchen, with its spaciousness, its state-of-the-art appliances, its appliance garage and its spice drawer and those shimmering copper-bottom pots and pans dangling from the ceiling. What amazing feasts Annie could prepare in a room like this. What amazing feasts she *had* prepared. The French toast she'd made that morning had tasted better than any French toast she made in her condo, because Sarah had a griddle pan that heated evenly on her chef-grade gas stove.

This could all be Annie's, for as long as she wished. She could live in this magnificent house and cook in this magnificent kitchen, and clean loads of dirty clothes in the quiet, energy-efficient washer and dryer occupying the laundry room. All she had to do was say, "Yes, I'll stay."

Would Sarah approve of her staying? Probably not. She wouldn't want Annie living in her beautiful home, her ineptitude making it a little less beautiful, a little less Sarah's. A flame of resentment flared inside Annie, doused by a bucket of remorse.

Sarah was gone. She was *gone*. This wasn't her house anymore, and Annie's resentment of her perfect sister melted into a pool of grief.

The dryer buzzed. Shaking her head clear, Annie gathered the linens and carried them back up the stairs. She made Trevor's and Becky's beds first, smoothing their blankets over the fresh, clean sheets. Then she made the guest room bed up, and finally the master bedroom.

King-size beds, she realized, were more difficult to make. They were too damned big. All that walking from one side to another, adjusting the sheet over one corner and then another and then hiking back to the other side. Why would anyone want to sleep in a bed that big, anyway? If you liked the person you were sharing the bed with, you wouldn't need an acre of mattress between you and your bedmate. And if you didn't like the person you were sharing the bed with, you shouldn't be sharing the bed—and you wouldn't need such a humongous mattress if you were sleeping alone.

But Sarah had wanted a king-size bed because...she was Sarah. Because she always wanted the biggest, the best. Because she felt she deserved the biggest and the best, for no other reason than that she was Sarah.

Annie wandered to Sarah's closet and stepped inside. Racks filled both sides and drawers were built into the far wall, with shelving above them to display Sarah's impressive collection of shoes. As Sarah herself had pointed out, none of those shoes would fit Annie, whose feet were bigger than Sarah's. Not that she would have wanted to wear any of them, anyway. They were too stylish. Too expensive. Scuff the toe of one, and you'd feel compelled to kill yourself.

The clothing too, Annie realized. It was just as well that Diana Drucker would be taking care of all these garments—the dresses for every occasion, the eleven different pairs of black trousers hung neatly on trouser hangers, the array of blazers, the skirts, the sweaters, the blouses, enough clothing to stock a boutique. All of it beautiful. All of it expensive.

None of it right for Annie.

She abandoned the closet and strolled down the hall to the guest room, where she had hung the cashmere knit dress she'd worn yesterday. It had been appropriate for a funeral, and it had looked good on her, if the compliments she'd heard at the reception were honest. But it wasn't her style. It wasn't *her*.

She draped the dress over her arm and marched back down the hall to the master bedroom. She wasn't going to dry-clean the dress to satisfy Diana. She had survived the entire day without getting any dirt on it. If that wasn't good enough for Diana, the bitch could dry-clean the dress herself.

Annie hung it in the closet, then crossed to the drawers, curious about what Sarah might have stored there. One drawer was filled with scarfs—dozens of them, and all of them felt like silk. Another drawer held leather gloves in six different colors. Really? Who needed orange leather gloves?

A third drawer contained Sarah's jewelry. She hadn't been a big fan of garish or gaudy ornaments, but what she owned was classy. No costume jewelry for her. No big glass beads or chunky brass earrings. Each item was stored in its own velvet-lined box: diamond earrings, a diamond pendant, a necklace strung with pearls as big as grapes.

And the gold filigreed watch their great-grandfather had smuggled out of Romania, nested in its own cushioned box. The watch Sarah had been given because she was the first-born.

Sarah had told Annie that Gordon would be in charge of distributing her jewelry, setting aside pieces for Trevor's wife, if he should marry, and for Becky. No doubt the pocket watch would be passed on to Trevor, because he was the first-born.

Which wasn't fair.

Annie closed the box containing the pocket watch and pulled it out of the drawer. The watch would not go to Trevor. It would go to Becky. Annie would make sure of it.

She returned to the guest room. With the newly laundered linens on the bed, the room smelled of fresh detergent and lemony dryer sheets. It didn't smell like the room Annie had been living in for the past month, the room she'd shared with Gordon last night.

She packed her clothes, zipped her laptop into its carrying case, and tucked the pocket watch into her purse. She would give it to Becky in a couple of years, when Becky was ready for it. When she no longer got scolded for dripping ice cream on her shirt. When she could roller-blade as well as Trevor. When she understood that being a second-born was not a curse, that it didn't mean you were an also-ran, that she wasn't Gordon's *other* child. When she was tough enough to make sure everyone in her life, everyone who mattered to her, understood that too.

◌ ◌ ◌

Annie paused to collect her mail before climbing the stairs to her condo. Three days' worth, since she hadn't stopped by to empty her mailbox since Sarah had died. Everything cramming the tiny mailbox was junk. She tossed it into the recycling pile and gazed around her kitchen.

It was small. It was dark. It was in dire need of updating.

It was home.

She unpacked, tossed most of her clothing from her duffel bag into the laundry hamper, plugged in her laptop to recharge the battery, and then roamed from room to room. Unlike Sarah's house, a stroll through her condo took all of three minutes. But... when she was here, she was home.

It wasn't that she could never have lived Sarah's life, with Sarah's family, in Sarah's house. It was that she didn't want to.

She glanced at the clock in her microwave: a little past three. Gordon and the kids might have had their fill of the museum's offerings by now, and be on their way back to the house. Annie sent Gordon a quick text: *Needed to go home. I'll be in touch. Love you all. PS: Plenty of leftovers in the fridge.*

She opened her own refrigerator. She had shopped last weekend, and although she hadn't bought much, since she'd known she would be spending most of her time at the Adler house, what she had bought still looked edible. She had plenty of eggs, a tub of mushrooms, a crown of broccoli.

This is where I belong, she told herself. *This is who I am. And it's all right.*

Better than all right. She might no longer have an older sister, but she was still herself.

She closed the refrigerator door, lifted her phone, and tapped a contact. It rang twice.

"Annie?" Jamal said. "Hey, girl. How are you?"

"I'm good," she told him.

"Yesterday was...well, intense. But really, you were a champ through the whole thing. You were a star."

Annie could have argued. She could have deflected his praise. But he was right. She'd been a champ and a star. "Are you free after work?" she asked him.

"For you, sure. Want to meet at the Dorm?"

"I was thinking—" she opened her refrigerator again, glanced inside, and swung the door shut "—you could come to my place for dinner."

"You want to do that?"

"I do. I want to cook for you, Jamal. I want to cook for both of us."

"Oh." He hesitated, then said, "That sounds nice."

"Yes, because I'm a nice person," Annie joked.

"You are." He didn't sound as if he was joking at all. "Would you make that quiche-y thing that real men are allowed to eat?"

"A frittata. You bet."

"I'll be there." She could almost hear his smile in his voice. "I'll bring wine."

"Great."

After saying goodbye to Jamal, Annie wandered into her living room. There was the lumpy sofa Sarah had given her. Every time she sat on it she would think of her sister, think of the cast-offs Sarah had passed along to her. She would think of how condescending Sarah could be, how judgmental, and how generous. She would think about how Sarah criticized her, possibly because she cared about her. She had only been trying to improve Annie, to make her cleaner and cooler and more competent—more like Sarah herself.

But Annie wasn't like Sarah, and never would be. And thanks to Jamal, she knew that was okay. She was learning to love herself.

She crossed to the window and gazed out at the street. A fringe of gray slush had frozen along the curbs, left over from a snowstorm just before New Year's Eve. Patches of ice glazed the indentations in the sidewalk, creating tiny skating rinks. Trees that had lost their leaves two months ago stood stark and bare. A car drove down the road, its tires making hissing sounds against the damp pavement where the snow had melted.

Above the street, above the roofs of the buildings, above the naked branches of the trees, the sky was a vivid, cloudless blue. It was the most brilliant, most glorious blue Annie had ever seen.

acknowledgements

One of the luckiest moments in my professional life was the evening when, over a couple of glasses of wine at a writers' conference, Lou Aronica and I realized we wanted to work together. I am immeasurably grateful to him for his willingness to edit and publish my novels, and for his unflagging guidance, support, and enthusiasm. And yes, the karaoke duets.

I am also grateful for the behind-the-scenes labor of the rest of the Story Plant team, in particular Elizabeth Long and Allison Maretti. Thanks, as well, to Kimberly Huther for catching my errors.

The greatest blessings in my life are my two sons. Although they emerged from the same gene pool and grew up in the same environment, they are wildly different in their strengths, weaknesses, and temperaments (although they are both phenomenal guitarists.) Watching them grow up has taught me more about the dynamics of sibling relationships than my own relationship with my sister ever did. I am enormously proud of the men they have become, and the closeness of their loving bond fills me with joy. If not for them, I could not have written this book.

And if not for their father, my sons would not exist. So my husband deserves a big thank-you too.

about the author

Judith Arnold is the bestselling, award-winning author of more than one hundred novels and several plays. A New York native, she lives with her husband near Boston in a house with four guitars, three pianos, a violin, a kazoo, a balalaika, and a set of bongo drums. She treasures good books, good music, good chocolate, and good wine—although she will settle for mediocre wine if good wine isn't available.